The Fiery Pi

IMMORTAL SOULS
VOL. 3

The Fiery Pillars of War

Jane Hawking

ALMA BOOKS

ALMA CLASSICS
an imprint of

ALMA BOOKS LTD
60 High Street
Wimbledon Village
London SW19 5EE
United Kingdom
www.almaclassics.com

Represented by:
Authorised Rep Compliance Ltd
Ground Floor
71 Lower Baggot Street
Dublin, D02 P593
Ireland
www.arccompliance.com

First published by Alma Books Ltd in 2025

© Jane Hawking, 2025

Cover design: Jem Butcher

Jane Hawking asserts her moral right to be identified as the author of this work in accordance with the Copyright, Designs and Patents Act 1988

Printed in Great Britain by CPI Group (UK) Ltd, Croydon CR0 4YY

ISBN: 978-1-84688-473-3

TO MY ELDEST SON, ROBERT,
WITH MY HEARTFELT THANKS FOR HIS HELP
IN SO MANY WAYS OVER SO MANY YEARS.

I

Twenty-year-old Shirley Marlow was infuriated when her mother, Jacqueline, dressed in a smart suit and bedecked with pearls, sauntered in unannounced from America, to ask her father, Reggie, quite casually, for a divorce. That request brought on an acute recurrence of shell shock, the result of Reggie's terrifying experiences in the Great War. He stayed in bed for days, scarcely able to move further than his room and the bathroom, while she, Shirley, kept him supplied with tea and toast. That her French mother had decided to administer this particular blow at such a critical time, September 1940, when all around the frightening reality of war for the second time in twenty-six years was coming ever closer to London, seemed incredibly callous to her. Searching through a drawer in the sideboard, she found a handful of tablets for easing her father's symptoms: these were from an old prescription, dating back to the days when he suffered frequently from shell shock, and when his work as an engineer on the railways had become too stressful for him.

For fear of adding to his anxieties Shirley decided that this was not an opportune moment to tell her father that she was expecting a baby. Anyhow there was no need to tell him since as yet, there was no visible sign of the pregnancy. In due course, when her father had recovered sufficiently, she was sure he would be delighted that Alan, her beloved fighter pilot, would live on in her child. For the time being she would have to share her excitement only with Eileen, Cousin Archie's wife, and ask her to keep the matter secret.

Until the pills fully took effect, she was yet again obliged to take over Reggie's duties in the newsagent's downstairs, as well as running the household both for him and herself, and for her brother Ted, when he was at home. As far as anyone knew, since he had seen General De Gaulle when the latter took refuge in London, Ted was mostly out with the Free French, working in their London Office under the direction of General De Gaulle, and only came home once or twice a week to sleep and eat. The slight consolation, amid so much uncertainty, was that Shirley had her brother Ted's ration books at her disposal and used them without any compunction, as though he were regularly in residence.

One morning, two weeks later, as Reggie was beginning to regain his equanimity thanks to the pills and his daughter's care, he was astounded by a letter that he found lying on the dining table after one of Ted's visits. It read:

My dear Pa,

Plans are moving fast for the Free French to go into action. I am going undercover with some of the volunteers and am probably flying out tonight. I did not tell you sooner as I did not want to upset you. I am taking my haversack with me so will not have to come home to collect it. I hope to be able to send you messages from time to time. Could you let the office know that I shall not be working on patrol? Don't worry about me. Please destroy this note as soon as you have read it, and don't tell anyone what I am doing.

Your loving son,

Ted

Reggie's hand shook as he replaced the letter onto the table, where Shirley saw it: thus, already Ted's injunction not to share the news with anyone was broken. She read its contents and if anything, she was more shocked than her father: her first reaction was that Ted's behaviour was as cruel as their mother's. She sighed ruefully: Ted was a hot head if ever there was one.

"I've no idea at all where he's going," her father replied, ignoring a comment she had just made about the WAAF, the Women's Auxiliary Air Force. "Maybe he's gone to a training camp somewhere, or perhaps he's parachuting into France. Who knows where? No doubt it all has to be kept secret. I bet he's concocted some madcap scheme to join the Resistance and set booby traps for the Germans. Let's hope he doesn't blow himself up."

He took a few moments to ruminate on his son's situation. "But when you think about it, France might be the best place for him," he announced, adding, "maybe that's why he hasn't been called up here yet. He is, after all, nineteen now and call-up for eighteen-year-olds began last year. I really feared he was going to be called up then. So long as he has his French passport and is working for De Gaulle, perhaps he's exempt."

Considering how scared Reggie had been only a couple of weeks earlier, the shock of Ted's note passed surprisingly quickly, much sooner than Shirley expected. Perhaps the tablets had numbed his reactions, or perhaps in his heart of hearts he was proud that his son was taking part in active service, wherever that might be, especially if his French nationality had protected him from the call-up in Britain.

"If you don't mind, Shirl, I'll turn the War Report on tonight," he said.

"Of course not; I know the worst and the best, so it doesn't much matter to me, except of course where Ted's concerned," she replied, "and don't worry, I'll do his ARP duties. I'm not afraid of Bert."

"Oh, Bert!" her father exclaimed, smacking himself on the forehead. "There's something I forgot to tell you!"

Bert, who, like Reggie, was also a railwayman, had won his encouragement when he had first shown an interest in Shirley, despite her detestation of him, but when he had attacked her as she went out on the night-time Air Raid Precaution duties which she, Ted and their father had signed up for before the War, Reggie promptly went to talk to the authorities, many of whom were friends of his.

"I've been meaning to tell you," he went on, "Bert has left the ARP and has been moved away to some railway posting north of Crewe, so he won't be bothering you any more."

Shirley suspected that her father had had something to do with ugly Bert's removal from the scene, but rather than dwell on that, she heaved a sigh and said, "Well, Pa, thank goodness Alan came to the rescue!" Then, bowing her head, she bit her lip hard. "You remember, that was the last time I saw Alan!" she whispered. "And I never want to see Bert again!" she added fiercely, before running out to sit down quaking at the top of the stairs that led down to the shop.

That evening she and her father listened, as they usually did, to the News, expecting to hear the sonorous, unforgettable voice of their Prime Minister, Winston Churchill. They had already listened to the speeches he had made since his first address to Parliament on 13th May, during the Battle of France. Then he had warned the nation, saying, "I have nothing to offer but blood, toil, tears and sweat." Announcing British Action against the captured French fleet in his second address to the nation on June 4th, he had declared, "We shall go on to the end, we shall fight in France" – which like Holland and Norway had fallen to the enemy – "we shall fight on the seas and oceans... we shall fight on the beaches, we shall fight on the landing grounds, we shall fight in the fields and in the streets, we shall fight in the hills; we shall never surrender."

Churchill's third speech on 20th August had brought Shirley to tears; she could hardly bear to listen to it, but felt that out of duty to her lost fiancé, Alan, she had to. "Never," said the Prime Minister, in reference to the RAF and other Allied air forces, fighting in the Battle of Britain, "never in the field of human conflict was so much owed by so many to so few." Shirley had run from the room to her bedroom where she sobbed all through the night. Her father brought her cups of tea and slices of toast, but she did not drink or eat them. He sat silently by her bedside for hours on end, but she kept her face turned towards the wall. When finally at the break of day, as the light streamed through the curtains, she sat up, her face swollen and tear-stained. "What time is it, Pa?" she croaked. It's ten o'clock, Poppet," he replied, handing her his handkerchief. "I must get going," she said, jumping out of bed and heading for the bathroom.

As the September nights began to lengthen and the days to shorten, there was no let-up in the News reports, indeed they were even more disturbing, warning all listeners that air raids prior to a possible German invasion were imminent, and they should start to make preparations by storing up buckets of water, stocking up on tinned food and searching out old camping stoves. A thousand people had already been killed in sporadic attacks, which were now occurring by day as well as by night. After a period of training, Shirley went into counter-attack by carrying out her ARP patrols with a vehemence and an application inspired by Alan's example, by her burning desire for revenge and by her determination to give her baby the promise of a world at peace with itself.

Whenever she saw a light, she would rap loudly on the door of the offending property and shout out to the inhabitants that she would report their infringement of the regulations. Often, she gave the habitual offenders no warning. In her opinion they had had long enough to learn what to do without a second chance. Putting a light out or closing the curtains was so easy by comparison with the ultimate sacrifice that Alan had made to protect those careless people and others like them.

There was an autumnal glow in the western sky as she marched purposefully along the streets of South Cross, recently promoted to a borough rather than simply an area of London, and checked the houses, especially those occupied by people known to her, to make sure that all was well with them. Tilly's mother's house, Cousin Archie's, Madame Belinskaya's ballet school – everywhere was quiet apart from the rumble of trains as they passed through the station then turned to the south or south-west, clattering over the points where the lines divided.

It was going to be a clear night, with stars already twinkling high in the sky. She wondered if the Earth could be seen from space, from the stars or from the moon, and if so whether the bombing would be visible from so far away. Anyone living up there and witnessing the horror and the chaos caused by the human race would know better than to visit this particular planet.

Out of doors under the stars, she was at peace and free to commune with Alan, whom she imagined to be at her side, as he was for the very last time that night when he had come to her rescue and warded off Bert's unwelcome advances. In the darkness, as she often did when out alone on patrol, she retraced the course of their relationship, beginning with that stormy Channel crossing on the return from France at the end of the summer of 1937, when in a chance meeting lasting no time at all, their eyes met and a spark, leaping from the depths of their souls, passed between them, uniting them in an unbreakable bond. Her memory skipped the painful years in between, when they had hopelessly searched for each other, until their glorious, unforeseen encounter in Sadler's Wells Theatre in July. That encounter unleashed a passion which she would not forget to her dying day, and which could never be repeated.

She recalled every moment of their drives out to the country in his yellow sports car, of their walks and picnics on the North Downs, of their long embraces, and of their plans for their future together when they would marry, have children and live to a ripe old age in a half-timbered cottage with roses round the door. That future no longer existed, except in her memory: it was in the past.

The most painful recollection of those few short days was the look of foreboding on Alan's face as he grew to realize how rash he had been when, despairing of ever seeing her again, he had signed up to be a fighter pilot. By the time they met in July 1940, it was far too late for him to change his commitment to the RAF, nor would she bring shame down on his head by trying to persuade him to do so. They both had an intimation of what was going to befall, in the dreadful knowledge that they were powerless to prevent it.

Now, alone and in the dead of night, she communed with Alan's unseen presence, confiding for the hundredth time her despair at his loss, and the deep, indelible pain of the hopeless longing she felt for him. How would she ever recover from that? She herself was aware that over the past weeks her personality had undergone a monumental sea-change: normally so bright, lively, determined and enthusiastic, she was ageing into a lethargic, elderly spinster with little to live for. She repeated to herself that she certainly would never marry again. Yet there was that tiny flame of hope, flaring, growing inside her as once more she reminded herself and the ghost of her lost love, of the miraculous news that he would live on, because she was going to bear his precious child! The baby, who was bound to be a boy, would be born the next spring, by which time she hoped with all her might that this terrible War would be over.

She hummed a tune from one of the practice pieces they used in the ballet school. Then, enlarging on a thought she had already contemplated, she for the first time since Alan's disappearance, almost subconsciously started to make plans for a new ballet in which the inhabitants of the earth would be involved in a catastrophe, like the War, though even worse. Without warning the planet would be visited by some creatures from outer space, who, undeterred by what they saw and descending from the stars, would in a sudden single stroke obliterate the human race, and establish their own just and harmonious society worldwide. She was not sure how the ballet would end, but thinking about it reminded her that the school would be opening again after the summer holidays and so she ought to call on Madame Belinskaya, her teacher and mentor. She vowed to visit her the following day.

Delighted to see Shirley, early though it was the next morning, Madame was amused by her plans for a new ballet. As always, they conversed in French because Madame's command of English was still erratic, and Shirley, on account of her mother's nationality, was fluent in French, which was Madame's second language after Russian.

"Your idea would certainly give the boys plenty of fun. Perhaps it's time they had their turn," Madame said, gesturing towards a chair. "I'm so glad to see you, *ma chérie*, come, sit down and tell me about your summer. You were so unhappy when you last came in here. I do not like to pry, but you do seem a little better now."

Shirley embarked with some hesitation on an incoherent account of the events in her life since July. She glossed over the more intimate details, but related in fits and starts the story of her encounter with Alan at Sadler's Wells and their whirlwind romance. With the greatest reluctance she forced herself to tell of his disappearance in that dogfight over the Channel on 14th July.

"Let me fetch you a drink," Madame said, hurrying off to the tiny space that served as her kitchen. Meanwhile, Shirley wiped the moisture from her eyes. Outlining the story of her love for Alan to Madame Belinskaya had reawakened for the hundredth time the unbearable grief, which was always so close to the surface, and always would be.

Madame returned bearing a tray of drinks and a pile of clean handkerchiefs; her eyes were red too. She handed Shirley a glass of lemonade and pushed a couple of the handkerchiefs in her direction.

"Don't worry about me," Shirley said, steeling herself, "I'm going to have a baby, so I think I shall be fine."

"Ah, that's wonderful!" Madame replied wholeheartedly without any show of surprise. "But I have to say that what happened to you reminds me so much of what happened to me – not simply the story I have already told you of having my ankles broken when I was a young hopeful dancer, but later, during the Great War. I loved a man passionately, just like you, but he was killed at the Battle of Tannenberg, early in that War, on the frontier with Prussia. It was the worst defeat we Russians had ever known." Here she too mopped her eyes. "My story is even more like yours because I was expecting his child. My baby was born in 1915 and grew into a beautiful little boy, my Sergei."

Madame fought to hold back the tears. "But my darling child died when we had to flee Russia in the winter of 1917. He was only two years old. We were dragged from our carriage by the Red Guard. I never saw my boy again. I don't know what happened to him." She held her head in her hands and unleashed a flow of tears which must have been held back for nigh on a quarter of a century.

"I am so sorry, Madame," Shirley whispered, leaning over to touch her teacher lightly on the arm.

She, too, was doubly upset, and wondered whether to stay or to leave Madame with her sorrow. At last she decided to slip away, because she knew that Madame would not welcome sympathy, nor would she like to be seen in such a vulnerable state. Madame Belinskaya's story had disturbed her deeply because, although they were from different times and from very different backgrounds, Madame's losses were so similar to her own, or at least to what they might become in circumstances she did not dare contemplate. Thrown headlong again into her own grieving for Alan, from which the news of the baby had brought some relief, the tale she had just heard made her very anxious for the well-being of the child. If he were to die in this War, then, like Madame, she would have nothing left.

In a state of agitated confusion, she crossed over and, almost unaware of what she was doing, allowed her steps to stray into the churchyard which stood well back from the main road, its lich-gate into the church-yard being nearly opposite the shop.

Shirley had never felt inclined to go inside the church. Since her mother's departure, church, any church, had held little appeal for her. At the forefront of her mind was the image of her *maman* setting out for church on a Sunday morning. Yet for all her visits to the confessional and her regular attendance at mass, her conscience had not prevented her from abandoning her family and going off with that Monsieur Levasseur to work in the French Embassy in Washington. At this, Shirley's waver-ing scepticism about the power of religion had promptly resolved itself into indifference.

She had no idea what sort of church this one was, whether it was Anglican or Catholic or Non-conformist, although she had been into the church hall for the weekly ARP training sessions. She had also recently been shown where the nearest siren was located. It was installed on the top of the church tower, and the wiring for it was attached to the wall of the porch, its switch protected from the elements by a small metal box, for which she kept the key pinned to her ARP uniform.

On entering the porch, she looked to see if the box was still there, and was reassured to find that it was securely in its place and had not been vandalized. She promised herself that she would return with the key, all the while thinking that if only this church were the church where Alan's father was the vicar, an introduction to his family would be a possibility. The romance and its sorry end had happened so quickly there had not even been time for Alan to buy her an engagement ring, which made visiting his parents in their vicarage only a few miles away out of the question. Since she had never met them, she could hardly turn up, knock on the door and announce, "Hello! I'm Shirley, your son's fiancée!"

Nevertheless, the temptation kept recurring, and she had to steel herself against the very idea of going across to Camberwell for fear that if a visit there went wrong, it only would increase her own unhappiness and maybe that of Alan's parents. Indeed, were she to go over there, her steps would inevitably venture into that church, and if she were recognized for some unknown reason, she might well be given the cold shoulder. The memories of her mother's suffering at English hostility, together with her own imponderable grief, were enough to deter her from exposing herself to the same sort of disapproving rejection. In any case, visiting his family was not going to bring Alan back.

She crept silently into the stillness of the empty church and sat down. Lost in memories of Alan, missing him, longing for him, she felt as if part of her own being had been wrenched away, and, despite the promise of the baby, the pain was so deep, she expected her heart to shatter like a crystal vase which gleamed and glistened in the sunlight, but which when broken was useless, empty, devoid of all purpose or value. In the depths of her misery, one single thought seemed to hover above her head and then float down into her brain like thistledown. For all its lightness and delicacy, it brought a strong, simple message that she had not considered before – or, if she had thought of it in passing, she had dismissed it as impossible. A voice seemed to be saying to her, "Supposing Alan is not dead?"

He was officially declared missing but was only "presumed" dead. Suppose he had been rescued after that notice was sent out? In that case, he could still be alive. But reason intervened, crushing the thistledown and insisting that had he been found and were he still alive, his newly married sister, Elizabeth Robinson, would definitely not have sent that letter announcing his disappearance, "presumed dead". Alternatively, if Alan had been found after she had sent the letter, his sister would, on his instruction, almost certainly have sent another one contradicting the first. After all, weeks had passed not only since 14th July but also since the arrival of the bad news: if Alan had not been found in that time, it was highly unlikely that he could still be alive. The best that could be hoped for was that his body would eventually be recovered from the Channel. She shuddered at the horrible vision of his beautiful, firm, muscular body lying blue and cold, disintegrating at the bottom of the sea. She stood up and left the church to make her way home.

2

The next day, 7th September 1940, dawned bright and clear, although over to the east, the bright innocence of the blue morning sky grew misty and dim, not with rainclouds but with criss-crossing aeroplane trails. People stood out in the streets, craning their necks to look upwards and shaking their heads in disbelief.

"The battle's coming closer," said Cousin Archie, the former owner of the shop who, reluctant to face retirement, had come back to work for his cousin, Reggie, "and I don't like the look of it. Those are our pilots up there, giving their lives to keep the Nazis at bay." There was nothing facile or flippant about Archie's observations. For once he was speaking in deadly earnest; his face was unusually grim.

Later, at about five o'clock in the afternoon, distant detonations rumbled on the clear air, which soon clouded over with an acrid smoke. "Sounds as if some of them have got through," Archie announced. That night Archie's worst fears were fulfilled.

Having shaken off, at least for the time being, the lingering traces of shell shock, though suffering from the onset of a heavy cold, Reggie shivered at the reality of modern warfare and the reports of civilian casualties. The trenches had been bad enough, but to imagine such devastation being inflicted on the civilian population was appalling. Who were these monsters? He was tempted to think that they certainly weren't human beings, but then, the ones he had fought in the trenches were mere boys who had been directed to fight by Kaiser Bill, so probably the pilots blitzing London from those aircraft, were only following their instructions, however evil those commands were. Like the boys in the trenches, many of them would certainly lose their lives in the process.

If he dared but think it, probably the ones who had directed the Allied side of the Great War from London were no better than the Kaiser. After all, on each side, they had been content to use thousands of young men as cannon fodder. From both sides everyone seemed hell-bent on destroying civilization in the course of the twentieth century. In all likelihood if they, whoever they were, didn't manage to do so this time, then another crowd of madmen, or some other man-made disaster, would finish the job off later.

That evening his bad cold – which had been brewing for a couple of days, during which time the customers had left a swarm of autumn germs in the shop – grew worse; he was a sorry sight, sitting huddled by the wireless listening to the reports of that first major air raid on London. Wave upon wave of German bombers, protected by hundreds of fighters, came up the Thames to bomb the East End, the Docklands and the City. That first raid went on until 8 p.m.

"I'll do your rounds for you, Pa," his daughter offered, "if you'll stay here manning the listening post and sound the siren if you receive the call. You have your key to the box and mine is always with me." A sudden awareness that she had been lacking in her duties hit her. "Oh! I forgot to try to open that little box in the church porch where we have to turn the siren on! I must dash out straight away and see if I can manage it!"

She ran across to the church, only to find that the door to the box on the wall of the porch was jammed, so she had to sprint home to collect her father's tools and a tin of oil, which she applied to the lock and the surrounds of the door. Then she tugged and tugged with all her might until at last the lock yielded, sending her flying backwards across the porch to the other side, where she hit her head on the stone wall. Stunned, she sank to the floor and sat there for a minute until she was able to pull herself together and see to the matter in hand, that is to say, checking the working of the siren. Relieved to find that it worked and was whirring itself into action, she hastily turned it off, before it could send its blood-curdling wail out into the night sky, and went home to return the tools and the oil to her father.

He protested that he could not allow her to go out again on such an evening, but she insisted that the bombers must have done their worst for that day, so marched out regardless on her rounds. She was relieved to find that her area was intact, untouched by the enemy attack, though the sky over the City of London was alight with flames. She stood watching, horrified, scared and fascinated. Finally, as there were no bombers overhead or even audible in the distance, she went home and took some aspirin. Nonetheless, her sleep was fitful, her dreams disturbed by the visions of the hell over London she had witnessed.

Overnight Reggie's cold turned into 'flu, confining him to bed all day, although in the evening he was well enough to sit on the sofa. He told his daughter to call him if he were needed, so yet again Shirley set out on her rounds alone and found a group of wardens, all men, waiting for her on the corner.

"Ah, Miss Marlow!" She was greeted by Commander Bristow, the elderly navy veteran leader of the platoon who usually conducted the weekly Air Raid Patrol meetings in the church hall, the lines in his forehead creasing as he enquired, "Isn't your father coming this evening? We shall need him tonight!"

She shook her head and explained that her father was not at all well. "Right, in that case, I think you had better come with me, Miss Marlow. We have been instructed to work in pairs tonight, and we are definitely going to have work to do!"

He looked her up and down with a sceptical stare. "Can you run, Miss Marlow?" he asked.

"Yes, of course I can!" she retorted defiantly.

"I trust you know where the siren is then?"

"Yes, of course I do!" she said with an exasperated sigh, but glad that she had oiled the door and the keyhole of the box. "It's on the church tower. I have a key to the box here in my pocket and I have oiled and eased the lock, which was jammed!" Indignant and defiant, she added, "My father will man the listening post."

"Good! Quick march, everyone! Let's get going, then!" the Commander exclaimed with relish. He talked as they walked, confiding jovially, even gleefully, in his young companion, "It was bad enough yesterday, wasn't it? And it looks as if there will be much heavier action tonight, so we must be on our toes!"

Shirley grinned at the image of the portly old sailor on his toes, wondering what use he would be in an attack. In truth the Commander's gait was much less brisk than his manner, and it was also much less brisk than Shirley's usual pace. At first, she was irritated at having this old sea dog for company. She had imagined an evening walking alone beside Alan's shadow and talking to him. However, when the old man began to recount his experiences in the Great War, she listened more carefully and unwittingly became quite engrossed in his story of the Battle of Jutland, where misinformation had led the British fleet in the wrong direction.

He was enjoying the rare chance to engage young ears in this recital when Shirley detected sounds other than his voice.

"Listen!" she yelled, interrupting his flow. "I can hear a droning in the sky over there in the south!"

The Commander was too deaf to hear anything. "Oh, I expect it's a train," he said, shrugging off her warning.

She wanted to shake him and shout that it was not a train, and that, whatever it was, it was coming nearer by the second. Why, she wondered, had the siren not sounded? Pa should have been manning the post and already run over to sound the siren. "It's an air raid!" she bellowed in his ear and without waiting for his reply, dashed off to the church.

Shining her pocket torch onto the box, she put her key in the hole and turned it. The lock gave way eventually, so she was able to switch the siren on. From above there came the whirring of the motor and then the clanking of the pump as the mechanism lazily started to awake from its slumbers, like a dragon that has been disturbed in its lair and is gathering its breath for an almighty roar. Holding her own breath, she slumped for a couple of seconds against the cold, stone wall, and heaved a thankful sigh when the machine ponderously came to life, sending its threatening, oscillating warning out over the district. Momentarily she congratulated herself for having put the door to rights, but that moment was extremely brief, for the warplanes were coming closer and closer. They were deafeningly loud, suggesting that there must have been hundreds of them. She would have words about the siren box with the Commander later, she promised herself, because presumably he was in charge of maintaining the siren and the access to it.

She ran back to her route to check that all the inhabitants were making for cover, only to find the Commander busy ticking off names on a chart by torchlight. "There's no time for that!" she screamed, taking charge and hurriedly sending off the sleepy residents to their shelters. She ran down the road, shining her torch right and left, until she was satisfied that the houses were emptying fast. The ballet school was in darkness; the front door was firmly closed and there was no sign of Madame. Shirley hoped and trusted that she had taken shelter in the Anderson shelter that she had so much hated when it was installed, but it was impossible to tell where she was, since the back gate into the garden was locked, and no amount of banging on the front door succeeded in rousing her.

Only then did she remember her father, who had had probably taken some aspirin and fallen asleep, despite the thunderous noise of the planes, which were coming precisely in their direction and would be overhead in no time at all: there were hundreds of them arriving from the south and heading for London. Desperately trying to ignore them, she ran home to the shop where, once inside, she yelled up the stairs but met no reply. Two by two she ascended the steep flight and burst into the living room on the first floor, where Reggie, dressed in his uniform and wearing his boots, had fallen asleep on the sofa. She shook him by the shoulder, calling, "Wake up, Pa! There's an air raid! Hundreds of them and they're overhead now!"

He sat up, rubbed his eyes, grabbed his helmet, stood up and, without a word, but coughing and spluttering, followed her down the stairs and out into the street. "I'm so sorry; I'm so sorry," he gasped.

Together they hastened to Archie's house, through the front garden, along the passage and into the back garden where a dim light showed through the keyhole from the Anderson shelter.

"Thank goodness you've come, Shirley dear, and you too, Reggie!" Eileen exclaimed. "Now Archie, you can close the door!"

"No, let me out first – I'm on duty tonight and I have to keep watch! Pa, you stay there!" Shirley shouted, pushing her way past Archie to get out into the open.

Then, remembering Mrs Fothergill, she ran back to check whether she was safe. She banged on her door, to be met, after an age, by a sleepy, ghost-like figure who appeared on the threshold, brushing her long grey hair out of her eyes. "What do you want?" the figure demanded sharply.

"It's me, Shirley, Mrs Fothergill," she answered. "Come quickly, there's an air raid – I've come to take you to the shelter." If Shirley was expecting some reluctance on Mrs Fothergill's part, she was pleasantly surprised when the elderly neighbour offered none. Instead, clutching her dressing gown round her, she followed her meekly to Cousin Archie's, where Eileen busily rearranged the cramped seating to make room for the newcomer.

Squadrons of enemy planes were passing overhead in a terrifying roar of engines, undeterred by the searchlights seeking them out, or by the few distant ack-ack guns firing from somewhere miles away in futile attempts to bring them down. Out of doors, Shirley crouched in Archie's porch with her head between her knees, expecting that at any moment the bombs would begin to fall, but to her amazement the roar gradually faded as the planes disappeared, heading northwards. The sky cleared and silence reigned, leaving the neighbourhood so far intact and free from damage. There was no sign of the Commander or any of the other wardens.

Shirley blinked, wondering what to do next. She appeared to be on her own, solely responsible for the fate of the neighbourhood. Should she sound the all-clear? Should she send people back into the comfort of their beds to resume their sleep? Or should she leave them in their shelters? She was about to sit down on the damp grass of the front lawn to consider what to do next, when from the general direction of the City and the docks, distant flashes lit up the darkness and explosions resounded off buildings. Orange flares shot into the sky, which once again was soon red with flames. It was like a gigantic firework display magnified a million times, utterly beyond all human attempts to control it.

She had already made up her mind to leave her charges in their bunkers when, on the night air, her ears detected the same murderous sound she had heard earlier, at first faintly, then louder. The planes were coming back the way they had gone! For a split second, she was petrified; then she pulled herself together and sprinted down the road for the umpteenth time that night.

At the end of the street, she was startled to find a tall, thin figure in a white nightgown visible in the malevolent glow across the sky, dancing in the middle of the road. It was Madame Belinskaya.

"Quickly, Madame! Get into your shelter!" she shouted, with enough presence of mind to frame her orders in French. "*Nyet! Nyet!* I will not go in there alone!" Madame screamed. "The Red Guard will find me there!" Shirley grabbed her by the arm and dragged her all the way up the street to Cousin Archie's shelter. "Please take her in!" she called to Eileen, shoving Madame through the door. "I must go back on patrol!"

The planes were approaching again – not only were they heralded by the roar of their engines, but this time also by booming shell bursts, shattering crashes and dazzling flares, while from the ground the too-remote and rather useless ack-ack guns went into action again. Bombs began to fall on the neighbourhood. With an almighty thunderclap one landed on the railway line behind the houses. The whirlwind from the massive blast blew tiles off the roofs and windows into the street; beams cracked as walls gave way and came crashing to the ground. Perhaps, she thought, those poor souls one saw out in the street wearing placards which proclaimed "The End of the World is Nigh!" were not as crazy as they seemed.

Abandoning her attempt to patrol the streets in the certainty that all the inhabitants were safe, whatever happened to their houses, Shirley took shelter for the second time that night in Archie's porch, where she sat quivering, rounded into a ball with her head between her knees. There was nothing more that she could do. It was time to protect herself and her baby. How she hoped and prayed that he would survive! Until now she had not given him any thought because she had been far too occupied with the safety of others.

A rumbling sound not very far away attracted her attention. She stood up and watched in horrified disbelief as a house on the bend in the road – from her vantage point clearly visible in the evil light from the sky – began to crumble. The ground floor collapsed, and the top floor fell to a resting place at a sloping angle to the ground. The sky was so bright with fire that it was easy to see a bed sliding out of the bedroom and coming to rest in the front garden.

A figure sat up in the bed screaming. "Albert! Albert! Where is my baby, Albert?"

It was Tilly. Shirley was appalled. How could she have forgotten Tilly and her family? She ran to her and, scrambling over glass, wood, bricks and all sorts of other debris, pulled her out of the wreckage. "Where is Albert?" she demanded.

Tilly was prostrate, only able to murmur, "He's in the back bedroom. And so is Mother." She then sank to the ground in a faint. Other wardens, including the geriatric Commander, stumbled out of the corners where they had been sheltering, to take charge of Tilly, call the fire service and ambulances and do what they could to aid the rescue.

Shirley picked her way over the wreckage strewn about the garden, and then clambered up over the planks, the broken glass and the bricks, tearing at the obstacles in her way: the seats of chairs, curtain rails, wardrobe doors, table legs, everything tipped out onto the lawn in a great heap of destruction. She climbed over the bed, still warm where Tilly had been sleeping, and reached the leaning floor of the bedroom. Easing herself gradually up onto it, she was relieved that it held firm. Illuminated only by the pall of light-reflecting crimson smoke that hung in the air outside, she clawed her way up the tilting bedroom floor and came into darkness at the top end of it. She hit her head on jutting beams, while exposed but invisible nails tore at her hair and skin. The torch was all but useless, its tiny light shining weakly on only a small ring of the devastation.

She heard a faint cry and listened again. It was coming from somewhere beyond the fallen bedroom. She searched for an opening between the slanting floor and the collapsed ceiling and there found a gap, glowing red, like the entrance to hell in that horrible opera she had so much disliked, though at that instant she could not remember what it was called. The gap was just large enough for her to squeeze through into another bedroom which was tipping the other way, down towards the back garden, which gave out onto the section of railway line where the bomb had landed minutes earlier.

The cry was closer, in the same room.

"Hello! Who is there?" she shouted out.

"It's me – please help me!" she heard the voice of Tilly's mother calling weakly from the far corner. "I think my bed is going to slide down into the garden!"

"Keep very still. The fire engines are on their way!" Shirley shouted, hoping that this was in fact the case. More calmly she asked where Albert was.

"He's in his cot, somewhere in here," came the muffled answer.

Her way lit by the hot, red glare of the flames from the railway line, Shirley crawled across the rubble spread over the room, afraid of catching herself on a live cable, or causing the floor to collapse. She banged her helmet on a solid frame, which proved to be the base of Albert's cot, standing undamaged among the chaos. Bits of plaster fell about her shoulders, but she scarcely felt them in her determination to reach the child and whisk him out of harm's way.

In the feeble light of the torch, she saw him sleeping angelically, unperturbed by the commotion. Gingerly she struggled to her feet and picked him up gently; then, shuffling on her knees to avoid the broken beams above her head and with the child grasped tightly under one arm, she made her way back to the sloping front bedroom. Thankful that in his deep sleep he was not aware of the drama, she pushed him through the gap, while still maintaining her grip on him. Crawling, she eased her own body through the hole. Clutching Albert and perching on the slender ridge between the front and the back of the house, she shouted to anyone who could hear to come and help.

A comforting cheer went up when a fire engine arrived. Seconds later, with her heart in her mouth, she listened breathlessly to the sound of a ladder being extended up over the perilous floor of the front bedroom. In no time the dark shape of a fireman appeared, silhouetted against the ominous orange background. He relieved her of the weight of the sleeping baby before carefully lowering him into the arms of helpers on the ground. He then picked Shirley up and carried her to safety.

Tilly was hugging Albert close to her chest, weeping profusely. "Oh, Shirley, you are a heroine!" she cried.

The firemen then moved their equipment to the rear of the house to rescue Tilly's mother, whom they brought out on a stretcher: she was trembling, and bleeding from cuts on her head. The traumatized family was ushered quickly into a waiting ambulance, which left at full speed. Shirley, meanwhile, mopped her cuts with a handkerchief and continued with her duties.

As was to be expected, the road was full of broken bricks, planks, tiles, timber and glass, which glimmered with an evil glow: it did not diminish the further along the street she went. If battered from the blasts, most of the other houses seemed to be still standing, probably even habitable except for broken windows and missing tiles, but when she came to the last house, the ballet school, all that remained was the front wall with gaping hollows in place of the windows, through which an inferno burned. The body of the house had disappeared altogether. She stood aghast, staring at the ruin outlined against the angry clouds of crimson smoke.

Footsteps approached and a hand took her by the arm. Fleetingly she thought it might be Alan, until she heard her father's voice.

"Come on, Shirl, I'm taking you home. You've done quite enough for one night," he declared.

Dissolving into sobs, she allowed herself to be led away, but then remembered that the "all clear" had to be sounded, so broke free from her father's grasp and rushed off, broken glass crunching under her feet, to the church, where she flicked the switch to propel the motor into action; as she did so, an explosion rent the air from over by the railway line and once again, flames filled the sky.

"Tilly's house," she thought, closing her eyes and leaning against the cold stone of the porch wall, where only the previous day she had banged her head. Even the monotonous drone of the all-clear siren sounded weary as it sent out its chilling cry to greet the cheerless dawn.

3

Eileen was waiting in the middle of the road for Reggie and Shirley after the ambulances, their bells clanging, had driven away.

"They should have taken you in the ambulance too, Shirley," she declared, "but I'm going to dress those wounds. There's no water or electricity in our house so we can't go in there. Let's hope there's some in your flat. I know about first aid, so don't worry, I know what to do."

"Really, I'm fine – just a few scratches, that's all," Shirley protested, struggling to conceal the exhaustion that was overwhelming her, despite the strange exhilaration she felt at her rescue of Tilly's family: at last, she was making a valid contribution to the war effort, a contribution of which Alan would have been proud. "Look, there are all these people who need help more than I do. What's more, Pa is really not at all well," she maintained.

In fact, a procession, consisting of Archie, Mrs Fothergill, and Mme Belinskaya, who had not yet been told what had happened to her house, plus a collection of dazed neighbours, excluded from their damaged homes, followed father, daughter and Eileen home. Streaming from the nose, Reggie was annoyed.

"Archie," he whispered to his cousin, "we don't want all these people with us just at the moment. Anyhow, we don't know if our house is safe."

"Don't worry, I'll deal with them," Archie promised. After picking their way through the burning rubble to the row of shops, which were more or less unscathed, apart from losing all their windows, and reasonably safe to enter, Archie turned to Mrs Fothergill and said gently but firmly, "Now, my dear, you'll need some company tonight, so you let Madame here come and stay with you."

Mrs Fothergill acquiesced readily, but Madame stopped in her tracks, standing stock still. "*Nyet! Nyet!* I am going home to my own house!" she insisted, suddenly reasserting herself.

"No, Madame, you can't do that – the road is closed for the rest of the night. It's too dangerous to go down there," Archie affirmed, assuming the authority of a self-appointed ARP warden. With that he shepherded Madame into the door that Mrs Fothergill had opened, wishing them a firm "Goodnight, ladies!" Then he directed the other homeless people to the church hall, where the ladies of the Women's Royal Voluntary Service – the WRVS – were preparing tea on a camping stove and laying out palliasses for the homeless to sleep on.

There was no electricity anywhere, so only the little blackout torches that everyone carried in their pockets, or candles, lit the perilous way; nor was there any water, excepting that collected in buckets for emergencies such as this. Workers were already cutting off the gas to all the houses and digging up the road to check and, if necessary, begin repairing the gas main. Eileen, who under Shirley's strict instructions had not so much as mentioned the pregnancy to anyone, least of all Reggie, was as good as her word. Undeterred by Shirley's protests, she expertly dressed the cuts on her face, hands, arms and legs, bandaged them and, having swept up the broken glass in her bedroom, put her to bed, limiting herself to saying gently, "I do think, dear, that you should see a doctor in the morning."

Although too weak to utter another word, Shirley did not fall asleep immediately. Her body was exhausted, but the raw cuts on her face and limbs burned and her head buzzed with the night's drama, which had been challenging yet weirdly energizing.

Eileen's advice about going to the doctor's proved to be easier said than done, on account of the turmoil and the debris which met all eyes that Monday morning. Out in the road many-hued shards of glass glistened and sparkled with malicious intent in the foggy, grey light of day, while a small army of local people, armed with brooms were doing their best to sweep them away, their efforts impeded by the bricks, tiles, charred timbers, shrapnel, broken windows and the scattered household effects that littered the streets. The gas men were still at work, digging up more of the road in their efforts to check the main, as a result of which all the residents were then deprived of every one of the utilities they usually took for granted, gas as well as water and electricity. The Belisha beacons marking the crossing which had just been installed on the main road, but which did not function because of the blackout, lay in the road, their orange globes smashed to smithereens.

"Don't you think you should have those cuts attended to by a doctor, Shirl?" Reggie asked. "Although I'm not sure how we are going to manage that. I can see those wounds must be painful, but how are you in yourself?"

"Not to worry, Pa," Shirley replied absent-mindedly, reflecting, as she gazed out onto the chaos, that after all it was not her heart that had shattered into tiny fragments of glass, but the livelihoods, if not the lives, of many people. She was both shocked and mystified by that weird sense of exhilaration she had experienced the night before, and the remnants of which were still with her. It reminded her of her reaction on crossing the Channel when she and her brother had escaped from France at the time of the Nazi invasion. That strange exhilaration had helped her to understand how Alan had felt about going into battle. For those few hours the previous night, she, like him, had risen to the challenge of warfare and had found the courage to face extreme danger. She was proud that she had not let him down.

Out of the blue, it crossed her mind that, had she and her baby died in the attack, they would have been united with her fiancé in death and there they would have stayed with him for eternity. Only two months ago, she had expected to live with him for the rest of her life, but since that hope was denied her, how much better it would be to join him in death. Only a fine line divided life from death. He had crossed that line: last night she had come close to doing so as well. She vowed that she would fulfil her duties as warden every night, everywhere that she was needed, until eventually her time would come.

With her decision came a fearlessness she did not know she possessed but which found its origins in her proven ability to survive disaster, as if she somehow enjoyed special protection. If she really were protected for reasons unknown, there was no question but that her baby would be safe as well, for as long as she was carrying him. She had survived the escape from France before his conception and last night, some nine or ten weeks into her pregnancy, she had done so again. Despite all the hazards she had encountered, the broken glass, the fallen beams and the nails, not to mention the contortions into which she had had to twist her body to squeeze through tiny gaps, she had, as if by a miracle, experienced no pain internally. Her baby had survived. If only his father had survived too!

She awoke from her reverie to find her father standing at her elbow by the window; he was peering through the holes in the cardboard and sticky tape with which he had sealed over the glass, while waiting for an answer to his question.

"I'm fine, Pa. Obviously, we can't go over to Dr Forbes today. The roads are all closed," she said. An appointment with Dr Forbes no longer held the added attraction of a visit to the Salvatores, that kind couple who had taught her all she knew about running a newsagent's; they had sold up and gone to live in Italy before the War began. "Anyhow," she went on, "I feel all right. I haven't done myself any damage apart from these few cuts and bruises. They really are smarting, but Eileen did a good job on them last night. She said she would come round to dress them today."

She turned to face him and was shocked by his wan, worried appearance. "But if you ask me, *you're* the one who should be in bed, Pa. You were so poorly yesterday, yet you came out on patrol. Were you hurt?" she asked.

"No, I wasn't hurt, and yes, indeed, Eileen was and is a great help," he replied, disregarding his daughter's concern. "You know, don't you, that she trained as an auxiliary nurse after they lost their son in the Great War?"

"No, I didn't know that!" was Shirley's astounded reply on discovering Eileen's hidden depths, which she was too modest and too shy to advertise. Suddenly she realized that all the women around her – Eileen, Mrs Fothergill and Madame Belinskaya – all had lost the people they cherished most in wartime. Their fortitude was an inspiration to her.

That reflection brought her back to the present. "Goodness! I must go and see Mrs Fothergill and Madame!" she exclaimed. "When Madame finds out about her house, she will be distraught."

Her father observed drily with a not altogether sympathetic sigh, "That woman" – he meant Madame – "will take some calming down."

"Wait a moment though, Pa!" Shirley cried out, "You remember the church hall where we have the ARP meetings?" Her father frowned. "Yes, what about it?"

"There was a *barre* in there, round the walls, I'm sure. The one thing that will matter most to Madame is losing the ballet school, but if she knows there is an alternative, maybe she won't be so upset."

Her father shrugged. "I don't know anything about that – I can't say I care, but one thing I do know is that *you* should rest today. That woman will have to look after herself! I'm going to lie down for a bit, then I expect I'll be back on duty tonight. There's no point in opening the shop; I doubt that the paper deliveries will get through, and anyhow

Archie and I, we'll have to put more tape and cardboard over the windows. And there's still a lot of sweeping up to do." With that he limped off to his bedroom.

Spurred on by her good intention, regardless of her father's concern, Shirley put on a stout pair of shoes, since her ARP boots were torn and full of holes after the night's escapade, and went downstairs, where Cousin Archie had already taken it upon himself to open the shop and was already at work while talking to a customer. "Hm, so much for that League of Nations agreement two years ago," Archie was saying. "That was supposed to be unanimous, wasn't it?"

"You're right there, Archie," said his customer. "A lot of good that was! It was supposed to protect civilians like us from bombing in the event of all-out war. Just as well our government had the sense to invest in all those shelters in case the Nazis did try it on."

Archie noticed Shirley out of the corner of his eye and, at the sight of her face and hands covered in sticking plasters, exclaimed, "Oh! Our heroine! You wear your battle scars well, Shirley!"

She ignored this remark, well-intentioned though it was supposed to be, and instead coolly asked how the business was going. There were no newspapers yet, he said, but he was expecting that they would arrive, despite everything, and in the mean time he was doing an excellent trade in cigarettes and magazines, while Tilly was preparing glasses of lemonade on a small table by the door for the hastily assembled members of the workforce who were doing their best to clear a way down the middle of the street.

"Tilly! What are you doing here? I thought you were in hospital! I'm so sorry I didn't wake you and your mother when I did my rounds. I feel so guilty about that!" Shirley exclaimed when she saw Tilly standing by her table.

She, covered like Shirley in sticking plasters and bandages, did not answer, but burst into tears, leading a horrified Shirley to believe that either her mother or little Albert, or both, had died in the night.

"Oh, Shirley! You were wonderful! Thank you so much!" Tilly cried out, embracing her in a gentle bear-hug. "If it hadn't been for you, Mother and Albert would both be dead by now." She wiped her eyes before recovering her usual stoicism, and sniffed. "As it is, they are fine – they're living over there in the church hall. I'll go and see them at lunchtime." She gestured across the road.

"Ah, really?" Shirley said, breathing a sigh of huge relief. "I'm just going out, so I'll call on them."

Before leaving, she thanked her father's cousin for all his help the previous night.

"Eileen's coming round here with some dinner for us all in a while – you'll see her then," he said. "It'll only be cold, whatever she can find in the larder – luckily that wasn't damaged – but cold food's better than nothing."

Satisfied that she had the perfect excuse for going into the church hall, and therefore checking the existence of a *barre*, Shirley grabbed a couple of bars of chocolate for Albert and Tilly's mother from a shelf and made for the door.

"Mind how you go!" Archie called after her.

A dirty fog and the bitter smell of crushed, burning brick and molten metal assaulted her when she opened the door. Wisps of smoke, smelling of tar and curling upwards from the street of the two demolished houses, wafted over on the slight breeze, which also carried thick dust from the railway line and from the burnt trees in the gardens near the blast. The noise from the workmen with their tools in the street was as loud as the thunderous crashes, deafening thuds and bangs, signalling destruction, from the previous night. She stood in the doorway for a moment debating whether it was wise to go out after all.

However, the reception that greeted her left her no choice: a cheer went up from the workforce, consisting of neighbours as well as professionals, out in the street. "Our heroine!" they shouted, massing around her, jostling to shake her hand or kiss her on whatever patch of cheek was visible between the plasters. "If it hadn't been for you, Shirley Marlow, we'd all be dead by now," they chorused. To her surprise, she was treated like royalty, even by those householders who had hurled abuse at her when she had yelled at them to put their lights out or close their curtains. "You deserve a medal, Shirley Marlow!" someone shouted, while someone else called out, "You should be the leader of the patrol, not that old Commander. Where did he disappear to last night?"

She attempted to smile, but that hurt too much, so, holding her head high, she simply said, "I'm glad no one was killed round here." They cleared a way through the treacherous debris for her to cross the road. As she tiptoed over splinters of glass, voices called after her, offering help to redecorate, mend broken doors or windows, or even provide a taxi service, whenever she or her father needed it, once the glass had been cleared away.

With a faint swell of pride, she was about to make her way round to the hall at the back of the church, but first thought she ought to check the siren because she suspected that Commander Bristow had forgotten it, his powers of memory being unreliable. The box containing the switch was firmly closed, undamaged from the night's attack but undoubtedly in need of easing again; she tried the key in the lock only to find that it was as stiff as it had been two evenings before. From outside, the tower seemed to be all in one piece, but it had to be checked for safety, so before going into the church hall, she retraced her steps to ask some of the workforce out in the road to ease the box and oil its lock, then climb up to the top of the medieval tower to test the mechanism and examine the structure for flaws. In all its hundreds of years of history it could never have witnessed anything as horrendous as last night's blitz.

Food and drinks were spread out on trestle tables in the hall. Pausing on the threshold, Shirley cast her eye round the sides of the room and, as she expected, discovered that attached to the walls there were *barres* for ballet practice, albeit rather ancient ones. Madame would be able to resume her classes here once the normal formalities, which effectively only involved seeking the vicar's blessing, had been completed. She did not anticipate any problems. In fact, the vicar and his wife were standing behind one of the tables, so she waved to them but first went to talk to Tilly's mother. Little Albert was toddling round the hall playing with other small children, while his grandmother sat on a chair chatting with other elderly ladies. They were all delighted to see and shake hands with the heroine of the hour.

"You saved my life, and my little grandson's!" exclaimed Tilly's mother with tears in her eyes. Shirley was embarrassed. She had saved Albert's, but it was her negligence that had put him and his grandmother in peril in the first place.

"I didn't do anything special – it was the firemen who saved you," she muttered, "and I'm glad to see you are safe and well now. Can I get you a cup of tea?"

"Yes, please, dear, that would be lovely, and please one for my friend here." Tilly's mother gestured to the person sitting next to her."

Shirley grasped the excuse to escape from more undeserved, fulsome praise, and took the opportunity to have a word with the vicar.

"Oh, Miss Marlow! We've heard all about your bravery last night! A real act of courage," he exclaimed, while his wife, holding a teapot in one hand, stood beaming at her. "We heard all about you from the hordes of people who came in here last night. But you were wounded! You're covered in plasters! They are your medals for bravery! Now, come and have a cup of tea. We heated the water from the water butt on our camping gas stove out in the churchyard!"

Shirley smiled at the vicar and his wife limply in return. If only these people knew where the source and the inspiration of her courage lay: it was Alan, not she, who should be receiving their adulation. "Thank you," she said, "I won't have tea, but could I have two cups for the elderly ladies over there, on the other side of the floor, please."

Keen to distract attention from herself, she broached the main subject of her visit. "I see that you have a *barre* for ballet, and I was wondering if Madame Belinskaya, the Russian ballet teacher, could give her classes and lessons here, because her house has been flattened, and she has nowhere to go? I think it would help her tremendously to know that there's a chance for her to continue with her teaching."

The vicar nodded. "Mm, yes, I don't see why not," he replied. "There are the usual groups and clubs – Scouts, Guides, Young Wives and so on – that meet here in the evenings, but the Mothers' Union is the only one that meets during the day. Then, of course, there are the bazaars and parties, but, on the whole, the hall is empty. Of course, our hall is a shelter at present, and we will have to wait for all these poor people to be rehoused, but ask Madame Be… Belisky to come and see me, would you?"

"Yes, I will do that," Shirley agreed, not letting on that apparently all the homeless in the hall were going to be moved out to the air-raid shelter. She was turning away to take the tea over to Tilly's mother when the vicar called her back.

"Oh, by the way," he said, "it would be most inspiring if you could come and talk to our groups one of these days. You could tell them what it's like to be an ARP warden. I am sure they would be extremely interested in that."

Shirley said nothing except a polite "Maybe, one day". The last thing she wanted at that moment was to find herself giving talks and lectures on the life of an ARP warden.

4

From the church, she ambled slowly back to the main road, where the workers had cleared a wide enough passage for ambulances and such-like vehicles to pass through, and had also revealed a few of the studs of the pedestrian crossing which had disappeared under the mass of wreckage. Crossing the road, she wondered whether she had done the right thing in finding out so soon about the availability of the church hall for Madame, who most likely would be in a hysterical state and by no means yet recovered from the shock of losing her house and her ballet school. The news of that disaster must certainly have reached her by now. Because there was only one way of finding out, she knocked on the door of the one-time sweetshop in trepidation, and was taken aback when without delay, it was opened by Mrs Fothergill.

"Come in, my dear, come in!" the old lady cried out, as if Shirley were a long-awaited and welcome guest. "Come in! Anastasia and I were just making a cup of coffee. Won't you have one with us? She will be so pleased to see you!" Speechless in amazement, Shirley tiptoed over the glass-strewn, dusty shop and followed an uncharacteristically genial Mrs Fothergill upstairs.

Madame was in the kitchen wrestling the top off a tin and boiling a kettle, filled from a bucket, over an ancient camping stove. "Ah, *ma chérie*!" she said. "'Ow are you today? You were so braf een ze nyt! You save so manee lifz; wisout you, I would not be 'ere now!" The words all came tumbling out in broken English, delivered with an incredible passion and speed.

"But, but…" Shirley stammered, lost for words.

"Zees may be wartime," Madame went on, "I may 'ave lost my 'ouse, but I 'ave found a friend. I aven't 'ad a friend for az long az I remember; a friend is zo much more important zan a 'ouse." She pointed to Mrs Fothergill, who stood quietly by with a broad smile on her face. "Emilee and I 'ave so much een common. We talk oll nyt and she invite me to leeve 'ere for zee present, and togezer we will start 'er beezeeness again!"

"Oh, good – but I thought you might want to keep your ballet classes going, so I went to talk to the vicar about using the church hall. It's survived the bombing and all the homeless people in there have cleared up the broken glass and plaster," said Shirley.

"There's a practice *barre* all around the room, and a wooden floor and a piano. And there's a tall mirror at one end, and I'll lend you my gramophone and records," Shirley blurted out all in one breath.

"Yes, yes, we can do all zat az well," Madame remarked impatiently, in what Shirley considered to be a rather discourteous, dismissive reaction to all her careful planning. The matter was then settled in the brusque manner that Shirley knew so well. "You can 'elp me wiz zee teaching while Emilee runs 'er beezeeness," Madame said, bringing the question to a close.

Wavering between amusement and irritation at the unpredictable change both in Madame and in Mrs Fothergill, Shirley sipped her coffee, which was remarkably delicious; it certainly was not the Camp coffee that she was used to. She herself would be glad to be able to dance in the church hall, but as for taking up teaching again, of that she was not certain. It might be that she had other plans.

Ideas had begun to formulate in her mind: after the experiences of the previous night, she had already decided that there was no way she could simply go back to being a shop-girl and a part-time ballet teacher. If there really was no hope of her ever being able to perform on the stage, whether at Sadler's Wells, which had closed its Islington theatre and moved to central London, or anywhere else, then when so many were losing their lives to fight for freedom from Nazi oppression, she must find something more positive to do to help the war effort. As yet she did not know what that would be, but since her baby had not suffered in the air raid, she was confident that he would survive whatever she chose to do, not that she was going to choose any occupation that would jeopardize his safety.

Instead of going home, she wandered the mile and a half down to the council offices, to the employment exchange, which was undamaged apart from three broken windows, already boarded over, and blackened, though not burnt, walls. The exchange was open for business as usual, as if nothing very untoward had happened overnight, except for the upturned filing cabinets and papers all over the floor. A young clerk, somewhat dishevelled and bleary-eyed, was trying to tidy up a sheaf of papers and rearrange them on a table, despite his bandaged hands and arms. Shirley's facial wounds hurt when she smiled at him and asked if he too had had a rough night in his area. Yes, he said, he certainly had – broken glass had torn his fingers and thumbs, so it was very difficult for him to do any useful work at all. He had run home from the pub as the planes were flying over and had managed to wake his parents and bundle them out to the shelter just in time. He in turn asked what had happened to Shirley.

She, grateful to be able to use her hands, glossed over her injuries and turned to thumb through the leaflets he was clumsily laying out on a table. Most of them were advertising the Land Army, exhorting women and girls to leave the city for the safety and the fresh air of the country, where they would till the land and gather in the crops. The Land Army did not appeal to her at all. She loved the countryside in France, but that was only because her grandfather Pépé's farm was where her French roots lay. Unlike Ted, she did not relish the outdoor life, the dirt, the mud, the unpredictability of the weather and the primitive sanitary arrangements. The Land Army would be perfect for Ted, but he had found a special mission for himself, and in any case, he would never be allowed to join the Land Army. A fit and healthy young man like him would be called up and sent off on active service. As for herself, she was determined to find some other way of supporting the war effort.

In among the leaflets with their photos of smiling Land Girls driving tractors, heaving bales of straw and feeding pigs, someone had slipped in a newspaper cutting which caught her eye and grabbed her attention, sending a shiver of excitement down her spine. It was about the aviator, Amy Johnson, who about ten years earlier had flown solo to Australia. According to the scrap of newspaper, Amy Johnson was now spearheading the ATA – the Air Transport Auxiliary – an offshoot of the RAF, which was enrolling women flyers to ferry all sorts of aeroplanes, including Spitfires, from the factory to the airbases where they were needed.

Shirley was thrilled by what she read. Flying had been her original plan before she had found out about the baby, and later she was excluded from joining up by the doctor, who had told her she was pregnant. Presented with it again, she did not have to think twice: it was exactly what she wanted to do. To fly a Spitfire, the plane that Alan had loved almost as much as he loved her, suddenly became an overpowering ambition that she desperately had to fulfil. The work would be dangerous, but that did not matter. So much the better if she too died while flying a Spitfire. She closed her eyes and imagined herself sitting in the cockpit, wearing a helmet and goggles, ready to start up the engine and taxi down the runway. Who knows, she thought, she might find herself having to go into battle if she encountered enemy aircraft on her journeys.

This flight of fancy gave way to more practical considerations. The article did not contain much information. It was not even publicity for the ATA, nothing more than a newspaper cutting, and gave no telephone number or address, other than the name of the headquarters of the ATA at White Waltham near Maidenhead. She recalled that Alan had learnt to fly when he was up at Oxford and had become an associate member of a London flying club, from where many of his posh friends who possessed their own aeroplanes, flew. They took him up for a spin now and then, even allowing him to take the controls, so that when he enrolled for lessons he already knew the basics. Training in the RAF had come naturally to him, and he quickly clocked up the necessary flying hours. He had once promised her that after the War he would teach her to fly. If only he had begun to teach her sooner! She pocketed the newspaper cutting, determined to find out more and not let her ignorance of aeronautics stand in her way.

The recruiting office, just round the corner, was the obvious port of call; like the employment exchange the office was in a mess with filing cabinets and boxes upturned. There was one clerk on duty, painstakingly trying to sweep up glass and assemble and sort out torn papers at a desk behind the counter. She stared at the visitor, covered in plasters, and evidently decided that this person was clearly not in her right mind after the night's events, and feigned ignorance about the ATA.

"I can't tell you, miss; we have so many of these initials, and anyhow at the moment my job is to sort out this mess," she replied caustically to Shirley's enquiry, but she stood her ground.

"Would you look it up, please?" she persisted. "It must have something to do with flying."

Yet another member of staff who overheard the conversation joined in, taking a break from the mess on *her* desk. "I think it's something to do with teaching women to fly," she interrupted helpfully.

"Yes, that's right! So they can ferry new planes to airbases," Shirley informed her in exasperation. "I simply want to find out more."

"Oh, well then, you'd best call the War Ministry; as you can see, with all this chaos, we are too busy," the first counter clerk retorted sharply, indicating the piles of papers still lying on the floor and anxious to be rid of this demanding young woman.

"Certainly I will, if you'll kindly give me the number," Shirley retorted, in no mood to be further delayed by such incompetence. She would call the Ministry of War as soon as she could lay hands on a telephone.

Although she was impatient to phone the War Office, duty called, so she went on a depressing tour of the streets on her round after that visit to the recruitment office. Her feet crunched over more debris and broken glass from the air raid, as she carefully skirted further trenches being dug in the road for repairs to the water and gas mains. Her thoughts were focused on her abortive attempt to join the Air Force several weeks earlier. Despite her condition, nothing would deter her now from applying to the ATA, the Air Transport Auxiliary, come what may and the sooner the better. The more she reflected, the more she was convinced that the chaos inflicted by the air raids might well, with luck, have wrought havoc on the bureaucratic processes which otherwise would have resulted in some clerk or other trawling through her medical notes and discovering her pregnancy. If her notes had been lost – as well they might, judging by the mess in the recruiting office – she would be able to keep her secret for as long as she could keep her slim figure.

She was surprised to find Eileen minding the shop with no sign of her father, Archie or Tilly, but without stopping to enquire where they were, she bounded up the stairs, hoping to use the telephone, which, unlike the gas and water supplies, was still operational, or had rather become so again because of the importance of the property as an Air Raid Warden's post. She intended to call the War Ministry with her request, but a meeting was in progress in the living room.

"Ah, Shirl, here you are," her father announced as she entered the crowded room. "Because the church hall is being used as a refuge, we are having an emergency meeting of the ARP here to discuss a strategy for tonight. We have been warned to expect more air raids."

Shirley glanced round the room and nodded in recognition of many of the faces of those present. They were the regular attendees at ARP meetings and came not simply from the neighbouring streets but from the whole district. Cousin Archie, despite his age, appeared to have been informally recruited to join them, although Commander Bristow was conspicuously absent.

Her father read her thoughts. "The old Commander doesn't think he's up to it," he explained, "so Archie has volunteered to make up our numbers. Sit down and let's plan how to proceed." Pa's chill was better, and he had taken control.

"As I was saying," he resumed, "we have been warned to expect more raids tonight. The raids of the past two nights were not the end of it by any means. The Germans are amassing their aircraft on airfields on the other side of the Channel, ready to take off in a desperate attempt to bring us to our knees, and, believe it or not, Goering is there to cheer them on! We may have to expect raids by day as well as by night, and the bombing is targeted: they are trying to disable our society by destroying our supply routes and our transport networks, that is to say, all our main roads and railway lines. In so doing, though, they don't care what harm they inflict on the civilian population. The problem is that we don't have any barrage balloons hereabouts to divert the enemy planes away from us."

Shirley was astounded: she had never considered her father capable of such a Churchillian speech. She wondered with a surge of pride whether his information might have come from her brother Ted, if he were in northern France, although that seemed improbable since she had no idea how he could have transmitted the information.

Like the rest of the audience, she sat waiting respectfully while Reggie blew his nose and drew breath before continuing: "It means that we shall be fully stretched for as long as Jerry rains his bombs down on us, but I know we are equal to the task. I suggest we tour our neighbourhoods this afternoon, warning our inhabitants to be prepared for another night of bombing and making sure that they all have food, and water – from the tanker that's just appeared on the corner. They must be ready to run for their shelters as soon as the siren goes off." He paused for his audience to digest his information and instructions, before picking up his thread again.

"Despite all she suffered last night," he continued, "Tilly, whom you normally see working in the shop, is our valiant new recruit. She will man the phone and will run across to the church to set off the alarm. When this meeting is over, I am going to give her a key and take her over there to show her how the siren works. Well, that is, I hope it is still working."

Here there was a slight pause peppered with cries of "Well done, Tilly! Brave girl for coming on patrol so soon!"

Tilly suppressed a yawn and gave a pale smile, profoundly glad and grateful that she, her baby and her mother had been taken in by Archie and Eileen after their discharge from hospital and would not have to bed down in the church hall.

Shirley took the opportunity to speak up. "There's no need to worry about the alarm. I checked the box again this morning: it was still not easy to open but the workmen clearing up out in the road and mending the mains, promised to repair it; they will go up the tower and check the siren."

"I should add," her father said, reasserting his authority, "the German strategy seems to consist of setting off incendiary bombs for guidance in future raids. As you will have seen, the fires are still burning on the railway line at the back here and in the ruin of those houses, our Tilly's and Madame's houses, further down the road, so the enemy will probably use them tonight to light the way. We must tell our neighbours that if they live near the line, they must not hide in their cellars, because if a bomb goes off and their houses collapse, we might not be able to get them out. The good news is that we shall have our very own ack-ack gun parked in the road outside here."

As the meeting drew to a close, someone was heard to proclaim, "I reckon your Shirley was the bravest of the lot, Reg! She deserves a medal!" There was a round of applause, which Shirley acknowledged graciously. Her father, irritated by yet another interruption, persevered with the urgent matter in hand: "There are many families who will need shelter, because we will probably not use the church hall any more. In fact we should go and clear it now. The church is too conspicuous, and it seems these Nazi pilots have no respect for religion or anything else. However, we can use the public shelter in the bunker on the recreation ground behind the primary school, so a lot of people can be sent over there. But for our immediate neighbourhood, can I have a show of hands of people with space in their shelters?"

"Pa, you were wonderful!" Shirley exclaimed when the company had silently and soberly dispersed to their own homes to eat as well as they could, probably with only one saucepan, and a kettle full of cold water for heating on their camping stoves in the absence of gas and electricity. Then they were to rest and prepare for whatever the remaining hours of the day and the night might bring.

"How did you find all that out?" she asked. Her father did not reply, and when she pressed him for an answer, he simply said, "Let's say while you were out this morning, a little bird called and gave me some classified information, shall we? But don't say a word about it, because we don't want to get our little bird into trouble. So, I took it upon myself to summon a meeting here."

She wrinkled her nose in impatience but asked no further questions, sure now that a secret message might have come, even indirectly, from Ted, in which case her pa certainly would not reveal his source even to her.

As promised, Eileen came armed with a substantial lunch of cold meats, eggs and salad. While they ate their meal, the menfolk discussed the situation. Once again Archie brought up the subject of the League of Nations agreement banning the bombing of civilians.

"That's as may be," remarked Reggie, "but don't forget we've just bombed Berlin, so Hitler felt himself to be justified in bombing us."

Archie spluttered. "Come on, Reg, they bombed our airfields in August, remember? And a few of their bombs landed in the suburbs, so they deserved to be taught a short, sharp lesson. And they bombed Norhambury on 9th July!"

"Yes, I know, and that was a dreadful warning," Reggie countered, "but it was bound to happen sometime, because he and Goering are planning to invade us willy-nilly, and bombing from the air is the only way they can gain control, because we have the naval strength."

The newspapers had arrived, so then they turned to the news of the bombing so far. "Did you know," asked Archie, "they came twice on 7th September, once in the afternoon and then again, as we know, at night? Four hundred people were killed that first night of the bombing in the Docklands."

"Yes, I've heard that," Reggie replied, shifting uneasily in his seat, aware that Archie's news was upsetting the ladies, especially Shirley, as the talk was getting too close to that fateful day in July when Alan had been brought down by enemy fire.

Archie was unstoppable. "And they say sixteen hundred were badly injured, and that's not counting the cost of their damaged houses."

Eileen and Shirley sat silently through this conversation wishing that they could turn it to another topic, but there was no topic that was not in some way connected with the War.

After lunch Shirley set out intending to join the long queues of women anxious to stock up with as many candles, as much bread and whatever fresh food was available to tide them and their families over for as long as possible. Supplies were scant and strictly rationed, leading her to hope that Eileen might soon be receiving a consignment from her brother's farm, although she could not bring herself to ask Eileen outright about that possibility.

5

On returning to the shop with a handful of paltry provisions, Shirley was astounded to find a large lorry laden with a huge gun, parked in the middle of the road, in between the potholes and trenches dug by the workmen who were mending the mains.

"It's an anti-aircraft gun, an ack-ack gun," Archie explained helpfully. "It'll most likely blow your windows out, but it's just what we need, because, as your pa has warned us, there'll be activity again round here tonight. I suppose they're at least trying to do something for us with that ack-ack gun as we don't have any barrage balloons in our area."

"Maybe – who knows?" Shirley said with a weary shrug of the shoulders. "I must put these things away and stoke up the fire to heat up a tin of something for supper, maybe pilchards. Then I must do a quick tour to check that everyone is all right and ready for tonight."

At least, she said to herself, her father had, in anticipation of what was to come, risen to the engineering challenge of building a trivet large enough to hold a saucepan or a kettle above the coals in the grate. Additionally, he had filled every possible receptacle with water, lining up all the full buckets, jugs and spare pans in the bathroom to avoid having to draw water from the tanker in the street. He had also assembled a collection of candle holders.

His words to the meeting proved to be prophetic. That night was even worse than the one before, although the population and the wardens were better prepared. Still overcome with gratitude for Archie's offer of accommodation for her family – though unbeknown to her the offer really came from Eileen, who had persuaded Archie that it was the right thing to do – Tilly had insisted yet again on staying late at work. As soon as she had eaten a very basic supper of boiled carrots, onions and potato with Reggie and Shirley, she took a candle and went back downstairs to add up the day's takings, which were considerably larger than usual given the circumstances, thus leaving Reggie and Shirley free to go out on patrol.

Therefore, Tilly was in the shop when the phone call came through. Without further ado, she ran over to the church porch to set the siren going.

As its moan echoed through the darkening sky, families ran for safety, either to their own shelters or to the long bunker on the recreation ground behind the church hall, while the wardens supervised the orderly relocation of so many people. The church hall had already been cleared of its occupants, all of whom had been directed to the bunker. Shirley toured her streets again, checking the shelters: to her relief, she found that every inhabitant was accounted for.

When the planes, the sound of their engines immediately recognizable as enemy bombers, came closer, the anti-aircraft gun went into action right outside the shop, shaking the building and sending loud crackling reports into the still air. The formations thundered overhead, dropping some of their load on their way into London and the Docklands. If the noise was deafening for the civilians breathing in toxic fumes from lamps in the airless safety of their stuffy, damp shelters, for the wardens outside it was terrifying. Engines roared, gunfire resonated, bombs exploded, buildings crashed to the ground and timbers cracked. The population sitting in comparative safety underground were spared the horrific spectacle that the wardens witnessed as great tongues of flame shot into the darkness and flares fell to earth.

"This really is the end of the world and everything in it," Shirley said to herself as she crouched in Archie's porch. She reached out to her father, who was leaning against the door, resting one leg on an upturned flowerpot. He put a hand on her shoulder. "London's burning, Pa! Look at all those pillars of fire! They are red-hot!" she exclaimed, the sobs audible in her voice.

"Yes, my poppet, you're right. London's burning, and those pillars of fire are the price of the War," he calmly replied, and then fell silent. Contrary to expectation, he displayed an admirable calmness and composure, with no trace of shell shock; this comforted her and gave her much-needed strength, for if this inferno continued much longer, she and her child would be going to join Alan quite soon.

Thanks to Reggie's organizational powers, the neighbours were safe that night in their shelters, and also those squeezed into the bunker on the recreation ground. More bombs fell on the railway line, but these were further away, and their repercussions were felt in other districts.

Possibly because of the presence of the anti-aircraft gun, the bombers did not return by the same route, so eventually Tilly received word that she should sound the all clear.

On emerging from their underground shelters to go to work, the tired, sleepy, red-eyed population found that more damage than expected, some of it catastrophic, had been inflicted on their properties, if not themselves, which only hardened their resolve and their hatred of the enemy. Some were allowed to go to their homes, others had to make do with the church for shelter, once it had been cleared of the medieval glass that had been blown out of the windows, leaving the building, at the best of times, chilly, even colder than usual.

Far worse was the damage to the church hall, which had been blown to bits, spelling the end of its use as a refuge, or indeed as a possible alternative ballet school. Not a pane of glass in the shop fronts, the houses or the flats remained intact, although everyone had carefully applied sticky tape to all their windows, around the edges and across the middle of each pane, only the day before. The row of shops, however, still stood tall and proudly erect, defying the Nazi bombers to do their worst.

Madame was philosophical at the sudden end to any burgeoning hopes she may have held for a new ballet school in the church hall. "I am not ready for it yet," she said to Shirley, resorting to French. "Maybe I will start again when my house is rebuilt. For now, Emily Fothergill and I are glad to be alive."

Reggie was tacking sheets of packaging cardboard, of which there was a plentiful amount stacked in the cellar, over his windows when word came that there had been many casualties who had not been able to get to their shelters in time, or who had been travelling when the sirens sounded. Most of them were the residents of areas other than those patrolled by himself and his daughter. Nearer to home, however, on the other side of the road, near the church hall, Commander Bristow had been leading his wife down steps in their garden, heading for their shelter, when he tripped over and fell heavily. Evidently she had tried to help him stand up, but he was a large man and had not been able to struggle to his feet. They were both caught in the blast that demolished the hall.

Reggie received the news in silence. "Poor old boy," he remarked finally. "A valiant combatant who had given his best for his country, even if he was really too old to be leading the patrol these days. What a life he had led! Nothing but war!"

Those words of sympathy for Commander Bristow were in fact a heartfelt lament for the fate of his own generation. He subsided again into silence, though it was an angry silence, conveying a burning desire for vengeance on the inhumanity and the butchery which, from the same source for the second time in his life, rained down slaughter for no good reason, if ever there were a good reason for such behaviour. This time the furious attacks were even worse because they were directed onto innocent civilians instead of troops on the field of battle. He was certain that, in spite of the optimistic predictions that this War would not last long – which, of course, was what people had said about the Great War – it would drag on for years, in all likelihood even longer than that still-recent war, with an even higher toll in terms of human life and suffering.

Reggie was not afraid for himself, but he was scared for his son and his daughter. Although he credited them with no shortage of common sense, he was worried by their steely determination to be involved in the war effort. Ted had slipped away and without a shadow of a doubt had gone to France, not only to fight for that country but also, it would appear, to glean whatever information he could to warn of German attacks on England. He suspected that the anonymous telephone call warning of the air raids had indirectly come from Ted, who had doubtless persuaded a returning colleague to get in touch with him. It must have all been unofficial and contrary to orders, but it had been a life-saving message for the immediate community. He regretted that there was no way that he could pass a message to Ted to tell him how helpful that information had been.

To add to Reggie's frustration at the lack of contact with his son, there had been little information about the Resistance of late. The news bulletins and the papers had been dominated by the Battle of Britain, and then by the London Blitz. Some said that although the Luftwaffe were believed to have reported back to base that London was 'an ocean of flames', it would still take ten years to raze the capital to the ground if the raids were to continue at their current rate of three hundred bombers per night coming over to drop their loads. By all accounts, Goering had promised Hitler that he would bring Britain to its knees, telling him that he would destroy the RAF to prepare for an invasion, which he had failed to do so far. His attacks on shipping in the Channel had not achieved his objective – except, as Reggie ruefully realized, they had brought about the death of his prospective son-in-law. Next Goering tried bombing airfields in Britain, which provoked the British reaction of the bombing of Berlin. At last Goering himself went to the front line in northern France, where he said, "This is the historic hour when our air force for the first time delivers its blows right into the enemy's heart." To judge by the reports, doubtless with great satisfaction, he watched wave upon wave of Luftwaffe planes leaving for England.

As for the reporting of the state of affairs in France, Reggie had gleaned that in June the Fascist Vichy government under Marshal Pétain, a hero of the Great War, had replaced the patriotic cry of *"Liberté, égalité, fraternité"* with a new slogan, *"Travail, famille, patrie"* (work, family, homeland), which appalled all patriotic French citizens. Then in August, four former prime ministers, prominent opponents of the Vichy regime, had been rounded up, accused of "causing the defeat of France" and shot. De Gaulle, now a Brigadier General, escaped the death penalty because he was in London, from where he was directing Resistance operations. Ted, of course, had been working closely with the General, after signing up in response to his July clarion call speech to arms, addressed to Frenchmen living in Britain.

Ted's commitment to the Free French had taken him away from his job in De Gaulle's London office, leading Reggie to believe that he had been flown into the area he knew so well, the Pas-de-Calais in northern France. There, before the War had become a dangerous reality, he had been peacefully fulfilling his dream of working on his grandfather's farm. It was rumoured in pub talk that various French patriots were leaving London to pursue clandestine operations in France. For some, like Ted, Reggie reckoned, their prime objective was to collect information about enemy movements and send it back to London. Some were going to recruit sympathizers to De Gaulle's mission to free France from the enemy, others to set up networks between the different groups of agents, while many more went to join the Free French navy. Doubtless, Reggie thought, sabotage would be one of the most effective ways of disrupting the enemy's progress, and that would certainly appeal to Ted.

As for Shirley, Reggie was extremely concerned for her. There was no point in mentioning this to her, for it was useless to try to persuade his strong-willed daughter to take more care of herself and avoid acting the part of the heroine. He had certainly been proud of her quick thinking and energy when he had been taken ill at the onset of the Blitz, without even mentioning her courageous rescue of little Albert, but for a girl as slight and small as she was, clambering over rubble and climbing up into collapsing buildings with fire breaking out all around was foolhardy.

At least, he reassured himself, she was not pregnant. Had she been so, surely she would have told him by now, and it was all of three months since her fiancé had been one of the first casualties of the Battle of Britain. Surely by now there would have been some indication of a baby on the way. What a fine young man he was, that Alan! Reggie longed to take her away, out of this hellish situation, but means of escape there was none. Anyhow, she would be certain to say that she preferred to stay put. As for himself, he would have to remain strong and not let the terrors of that earlier nightmare affect his ability to take the lead in this present conflict.

The Blitz was to last not simply for weeks but for months, bringing the war-weary but defiant population to the edge of exhaustion. Hitler might have thought himself very close to fulfilling his aim of reducing the country to surrender, but he underestimated the resilience and the determination of the British people to resist and survive all challenges, particularly under the leadership of that great orator, their Prime Minister. Constantly inspired by Mr Churchill's speech in tribute to the Battle of Britain pilots in August when he had said, "Never in the field of human conflict was so much owed by so many to so few." Shirley was no exception.

Winston Churchill's speech had struck her to the heart. Proud in the certain knowledge that it was addressed to Alan and his courage, she ran into other areas to help rescue their stricken inhabitants when her own neighbourhood was left unharmed by the raids. Nights spent on duty in the open, in over-crowded Anderson shelters, bunkers or in the depths of Tube stations, were naturally not conducive to restful sleep for anyone, but she survived, growing ever more adventurous and daring.

By day, the Germans too became even more adventurous, and by using the telltale signs of smoke or fire from their earlier attacks, they benefited from a visible, ready-planned route to their targets. When eventually the anti-aircraft guns became more effective and raids over south London eased off, another threat materialized in the shape of enemy planes that could fly low over city and suburban streets: from these, pilots could machine-gun individuals as they went about their daily business.

6

A very physical threat hung over Shirley's head one morning when she was out searching for alternative premises for Madame who, despite her pleasure and gratitude at finding a friend in Emily Fothergill and living in her flat, was becoming apologetically restive. She did not lament the loss of her material goods – her house or its fittings, the small studios upstairs, the wardrobe containing a huge range of dusty costumes in the basement or even the record player and the collection of records – because they could all be replaced with some effort and even more money, but what she did regret was losing her large dance studio, her pupils, and consequently having to stand idly by.

"If I don't open my school again soon, my pupils will go somewhere else, and all my ideas will be wasted! I must do something to help the war effort since you have saved my life, Shirley! But what can an old woman like me do?" she lamented, in French, her preferred means of communication, insisting that by bringing entertainment to the population she would ease their troubles and unite the community.

In admiration for Madame's resolve, though not at all sure that it could be satisfied, Shirley, anxiously searching for a hall appropriate for ballet classes, picked her way through the rubble which still clogged the streets, and skirted the hazardous trenches in the road where workmen were constantly mending broken pipes and cables. Her search brought her into contact with the clergy of several local churches of various denominations. Naturally enough, the vicar over the road was unable to help, since he had lost his church hall, though he did give her an introduction to one of his colleagues a mile or so away. The colleague was old and deaf; his church and church hall were both badly in need of repair from the damage, caused not so much by Nazi bombs, but by that old enemy, Time. Shirley took one look at the hall, which was as decrepit as the poor old vicar, and decided that it could not easily or quickly be made suitable, given how busy the local builders were with repairing badly blitzed properties.

Nor was the Catholic church hall a viable possibility, even though it was in good repair, on account of the stone floor which would cause untold harm to the dancers' feet, toes and legs. In any case it was a condition of using that hall that a member of the dance school had to be a Catholic, which of course Shirley was, but when the priest asked if that was a problem, she mumbled something about not being sure and quickly took her leave of him. In the appalling circumstances of the War, her faith in a benevolent God would have died altogether, had it not been for the miraculous conception of her baby, and his survival.

Half a mile further on she encountered another church, red-brick and more modern than the others. It was not on her list, and did not seem at all appealing from the outside. Nevertheless, when she knocked on the door of the house standing next to it, she was given a friendly welcome by a young woman with a babe in arms who summoned her husband, the Methodist minister, and then went to make tea for him and the visitor. The minister invited Shirley into his study, where he listened to her request sympathetically.

"I think that's quite possible; we would be happy to help if the hours you require can fit in with our other activities," he said thoughtfully. "The only proviso is that, if there are more air raids and we need to use the hall to accommodate the homeless, the classes would have to stop. But come and see for yourself."

The hall was warm and comfortable with a clean wooden floor. Although there was no *barre*, Shirley was sure that, with the minister's permission, Madame would be happy to have one installed at her own expense.

She thanked him and had scarcely set off for home when the droning of a single aircraft put her teeth on edge: she recognized the sound of the engines. This was not a squadron of bombers but a single Focke-Wulf, the type of plane that customers in the shop had been talking about. They had said it was a single-seater, equipped with a gun that the pilot could train on any individual walking along the street, and shoot him or her down in cold blood.

All other passers-by rapidly dashed for cover, hiding under trees or bushes, sheltering in doorways, or disappearing into gardens. Shirley was furious. Blitzing London was one thing, but how dare they direct their fire indiscriminately at helpless individuals who just happened to be out of doors, shopping or going about their daily tasks? This was too much: she would not be cowed. She straightened her back and walked purposefully along the street. The plane came closer, so close and loud that it seemed to be just above her head, almost scraping the tops of the few wizened trees and such dilapidated buildings as had survived the War so far.

Then she did precisely what she and everyone else had always been told never to do: she looked up and stared the pilot in the eye, defying him to pepper her with bullets. After what seemed like an age, he smiled, waved and flew off. Her heart beating fast, she tried to run for home, but to her horror, her left leg would not run, only limp, and she had to drag it along behind her. Home seemed a very long way off, but once there and inside the door, she slumped against the wall, panting heavily, before collapsing onto the bottom step of the staircase, unnerved and angry that the Infantile Paralysis which she had suffered three years earlier, was still able to make its presence felt when she needed all her strength. Thank goodness it had not slowed her down during the recent attacks in the Blitz! The more she reflected, though, the more she realized that the present weakness in her leg was more likely to be the combined effects of all the extremely distressful circumstances, and the grief and anxiety she had had to bear since July, as well as the fright of that German plane. That was undoubtedly how Sister Kenny, the Australian nurse who had brought her leg back to life after the illness, would have viewed it.

No one in the shop, from which came a general hum of lively conversation, had noticed her return, so, once she had recovered her breath, she slowly and silently crept upstairs, determined not to tell her father about her recent experience. As she climbed to the first floor, she thought she saw a shadow flitting across the wall of the landing. She was certain that she had heard her father's voice talking to his cousin Archie when she came in through the private entrance, yet this was not the day when Eileen, Archie's wife, helped out, so she stopped halfway up the stairs, wondering who could be there. She called out "Hello, who's there?" – but was met with silence.

Her imagination began to run riot, as once again her heart started to beat fast, and her left leg dragged behind her. Trembling with fright, she feared that the enemy had invaded in ones and twos, stealthily and unnoticed. Perhaps that pilot in the Focke-Wulf had dropped a parachutist somewhere close-by, and he and others had started to occupy the area! Perhaps the flat had been taken over already! Shivering with fright, she made it to the top of the stairs. Hardly daring to peer into the living room, she sidled into the kitchen. Footsteps followed her into the tiny space, and she leant on the sink to prevent herself from collapsing onto the floor.

A well-known voice spoke quietly. "Hello, Shirl!" it said. "Are you all right?"

She spun round on her right leg, about to exclaim "Ted!", but the figure who stood before her was bearded, dirty and drooping with tiredness. He might well have been a tramp who had come in off the street! Then the smile he gave her as he put his finger to his mouth was instantly familiar, so she flung herself into his arms.

"Tell me," he asked, pulling away from her, "are you and Pa all right? I've never seen anything like the chaos outside. The Blitz has really hit here, hasn't it? I'm surprised the shops are still standing and you are still alive. There must have been an awful lot of casualties."

"Go and sit down and I'll make you some coffee. It'll be Camp coffee, remember? It's not French coffee. Then I'll tell you all about it," his sister said, leaning against the draining board and slowly recovering her breath.

She was still trembling when, moments later, she sat down to talk with her brother over cups of the sweet, dark brew. Although he turned his nose up at it, he drank it in one gulp. With furrowed brow, he then enquired why she was so pale and trembling. It was a comfort for Shirley to be able to tell her brother the truth about her encounter with the enemy, and she swore him to secrecy. Above all he must not tell their father what had happened. He was shocked to hear about the Focke-Wulf episode, but after confiding in him, she began to feel better and plied *him* with questions: for instance, why had he come? Where had he been? Why was he in disguise, looking like a tramp? Did their pa know he was home?

To this interrogation Ted simply replied, "Look, Shirl, I've come home to check that all is well here. I've been very concerned for you and Pa, because I know the Blitz so far must have been dreadful. I'm surprised the shop and the rest of the building are still standing. I've seen the devastation. You must understand, though, I have to be very careful. No one else must know I am here. I've come home for a good night's sleep, and then I must get going again."

Certainly he looked as though he hadn't slept in days, and he also looked as if he needed a good meal and a good wash.

Since her questions unsurprisingly had evoked no satisfactory response, she allowed him to shower her with his questions, although after she had told him everything she had seen and experienced over the past days, touching only briefly on her rescue of Tilly's family, these turned to matters of a purely practical nature.

"Is there anything to eat here?" he asked in desperation. "Oh, and I would like a good wash. Is there any hot water?"

To these Shirley was able to reply that Eileen had brought them eggs and bacon from her brother's farm, so yes, there was something to eat, and she would cook it for lunch. As for a bath, the water was back on, and it was hot from the back boiler in the fireplace. Generously, she said he could have her total allowance of five inches of water in which to relax and scrub himself clean: she and their father would make do with a quick splash for the rest of the week. "Oh, thank goodness for that!" he sighed as his head lolled onto the table.

Shirley left him sleeping while she attended to the usual challenge of rustling up what might pass for a meal. Today was easier than most because of the extra provisions from the farm, which she eked out, improving upon the fare afforded by the ration books, meagre even with Ted's rations. Nevertheless the shortage of hot water after he had run his bath, and the incursions made into the once-monthly packet of Oxydol washing powder by his muddy, oily, smelly clothes, which, she suspected, were also flea-ridden, were going to stretch her powers of improvisation to the limit.

In a flash of inspiration she hit on a solution and wondered why she hadn't used it earlier. She shouted through the bathroom door, "Don't run the water out, Ted, I'll need it for washing your clothes!" However, if he were intending to leave again sometime soon – today, tonight, tomorrow – she had no idea how she would manage to dry out his washing in time. Moreover if this was to be a regular occurrence – Ted turning up tired, dirty and hungry after a sortie to goodness knows where, and expecting food to be on the table, hot water in the bath and clean clothes to be provided at no notice – then her own way of life would become severely restricted, despite Eileen's willing help. Her conscience stung by such an irritable conclusion, she told herself severely that Ted was now fully committed to active service, about which she had no right to complain. Maybe indeed, the information he was gathering was protecting them all as far as possible.

By the time their father came upstairs for lunch, Ted had had his bath, put on clean clothes and dried in front of the fire. At first glance, Reggie thought that a mysterious stranger had come into their midst.

"Hello, there! Who are you?" he enquired, baffled.

Ted laughed quietly and closed the living-room door. "Well, shush Pa – but if you don't recognize me, my disguise must be working!"

"Oh, is it you, Ted, with that beard? I'd never have thought it! Is it real?"

At this, for the first time in days and weeks, general merriment reigned, caused by Ted's return and the success of his disguise. Contrary to her intentions, Shirley then gave a vivid account of her hair-raising experience earlier that day, and that succeeded in drawing their father's attention away from Ted's situation. So horrified was he by the episode of the Focke-Wulf that he tactfully refrained from asking Ted more questions until after lunch.

While Shirley cleared the table, he cleared his throat and remarked pointedly that his son owed them a quick update about his movements. "You see," he said, "some very useful messages have come our way which have helped us prepare the population for the attacks."

Ted was not to be drawn in by his father's attempts to fish for information.

"Sorry, Pa. I can't tell you anything. Careless talk costs lives, you know. You'll just have to use your imagination," came the non-committal answer.

"That was what I was afraid of," said his father. "That means you've been in enemy territory, and it's my guess you've been sending back messages to protect us."

Ted had changed drastically from the carefree farmer's boy who had been brought to safety from his grandfather's small farm in France by his sister on the advance of the Germans to the Channel ports. He had become a serious, committed combatant working for the Resistance.

"*Don't* ask me!" he insisted. "My lips are sealed. And above all, please *don't* tell anyone that I've been here!"

The commanding tone, verging on anger, in which he issued this plea, silenced his father. A hush descended on the family before Ted spoke again. "You must keep Archie occupied downstairs, while I'm here. For Heaven's sake, *don't* even mention me. I'll be in trouble if anyone finds out I've come home. Of course, if I'm seen by spies then all my good work will be undone – and worse," he added sombrely.

Chastened and alarmed, both Reggie and Shirley muttered that they understood and would make sure that Ted's identity would be kept safe.

Turning to his daughter, their father warned her in no uncertain terms, "Don't you ever do that again, Shirl, will you? If you hear one of those Focke-Wulf 190s coming down the road, make sure you hide. Promise me you'll do that!"

"Yes, Pa," Shirley agreed meekly: she had no wish to repeat that experience ever again.

That evening after the News, Ted declared that he needed a walk before bed, so would accompany Shirley on her patrol. He reasoned that if he wore his father's helmet in the pitch-black outside, no one would recognize him with his beard.

Reggie started to protest. "But you've only just come home, and you need to rest!"

"No, no, I'm fine. My sleep on the dinner table before lunch recharged my batteries."

"Well, why don't I come with you, and Shirley can have an early night? She must need it after that scare she had this morning."

Ted glanced at Shirley with a look that seemed to say, "No, please persuade Pa to go to bed; I want to talk to *you*!"

She rose to the challenge. "It's time I went out on patrol, and anyhow I could do with a longish walk," she said. "I need to walk off that scare this morning and get my leg moving again, so you go to bed, Pa, and I'll go out with Ted."

"But what about the siren, if I'm asleep?" their father argued, not taking the hint.

"It'll be fine," Ted assured him. "Those Germans probably took too many hits when they came this way last time, so I expect they'll leave you in peace for a while." He spoke like someone who definitely had insider knowledge.

"Did you really mean what you said to Pa about the Luftwaffe leaving us in peace?" Shirley whispered to her brother when they were out in the street.

Ted shrugged. "It's common sense. They're not likely to waste more bombs on somewhere they've already bombed to pieces, or risk their aircraft when they know there's an ack-ack gun waiting for them outside our front door! My guess is that they will come back to bomb the station, so that's what you should look out for, but perhaps that will be in their next round."

"Ah," was all Shirley could say; she was not at all sure how to protect the station.

"Anyhow, I wanted to have a word with you," Ted went on, speaking in a low voice but opening up much more than he had in the flat, "because I have some news that you *will* be glad to hear."

A light, visible through the curtains of a house they were passing, reminded Shirley that she was in fact out on patrol, not simply out for a night-time walk. She ran up to the front door, banged loudly and shouted at the top of her voice, "Put that light out and close your curtains! If you don't, I shall report you straight away to the authorities!" The light went out at once.

"What's your news, then?" she whispered to her brother as they resumed their walk through the darkened streets.

"I think you will be glad to hear that Grandfather Pépé and our step-granny Céline are alive and well!" he murmured.

She gasped. "How do you know that?"

"I told you not to ask questions!" Ted replied brusquely. "If you do, I won't tell you anything at all!" He clammed up and walked on ahead in angry silence.

"I'm sorry," she stuttered. "I was so happy and excited to hear about Grandfather Pépé and dear Céline that I quite forgot."

"Try to be more careful," he said sharply, like a headmaster talking to a naughty schoolchild.

"Yes, I will, but if you can tell me more, I should be so happy and relieved! I often think about them," she replied meekly.

"Silly us," she exclaimed under her breath, "Why don't we talk in French?"

Ted continued his account in that language. "All I can say is that the farm is carrying on as usual, so they have plenty to eat, but Pépé is struggling to keep going on his own. I wish I could be there with them," he said with a catch in his voice.

"I'm sure that whatever it is you're doing at present is more important," she said encouragingly, "but please bring me news of them whenever you can. I won't tell anyone else, and Pa's not likely to ask."

The round of the local streets was, as Ted had predicted, uneventful, even though, in the distance to the north, the throb of hundreds of enemy aeroplane engines, the constant bursts of gunfire from ack-ack guns, the endless bombs exploding and the crashing buildings falling to the ground filled the night air with deafening blasts, while the sky was lit up in the glow from the many fires, and white in the beam of the searchlights. Ted put his arm round his sister protectively as they stood gazing at the horrendous spectacle.

"Think of all those poor people!" Shirley cried.

"It's unbelievably awful," Ted agreed, "but this is what we are fighting against. And we have to win!"

Although it was late by the time they went to bed, there was no sign of Ted the following morning; he had left before the shop opened and before anyone was up and about. The only indication that he had been at home at all, was a note on the table: "*À bientôt!*" it said. He did not sign his name. Reggie read the note and turned it over to see if there was anything on the other side. He was so despondent that Shirley took pity on him.

"Try not to worry, Pa," she said, putting her arm round his substantial girth. "I'm sure Ted knows what he's doing, and he *is* very disciplined, so he won't take unnecessary chances.

Her father merely sighed, "Yes, I expect you're right, but I can't help worrying about him."

His daughter sensed that this was a good moment to break the news that she had been keeping under wraps since that day of her mother's visit, just after she had seen the military doctor. "Well, Pa, I have some news for you – which, I hope, will cheer you up." Reggie regarded her with a dubious expression, as much as if to say that in the present circumstances, nothing could cheer him up.

Undeterred, Shirley took a deep breath before announcing, "I'm going to have a baby, Pa – Alan's baby!"

After a moment of hesitation, a smile spread across Reggie's prematurely worn features. "That's wonderful news, Shirl! I am so glad! I'll have to protect you, won't I?" he exclaimed, and gave her a hug.

7

Reggie had cheered up at Shirley's announcement, particularly since it came as a complete surprise, quite the contrary to what he had assumed.

"I really feel," he declared with unaccustomed jollity, "that your news has given me a new lease of life, Shirl!" He patted her on the back, saying, "I know you won't like it if I fuss over you, because you've got a stubborn head on your shoulders, but you must let me know if you need anything or if you're tired, or…"

At this he ran out of ideas so limited himself to saying, "Well, you know what I mean, and you mustn't work too hard, what with the ARP duties and your work in the shop. What a little ray of sunshine this baby will bring to our lives!" Then a hint of doubt in his manner suggested that he was about to ask her a question, but evidently thought better of it. She, however, had already read his mind.

"It's all right, Pa; it's no secret. It's Alan's baby and I am very happy, and I hope you will be too. Alan had asked me to marry him, you know. He didn't have time to buy me a ring, but I do consider myself to be his fiancée and always will." Her father nodded, "Don't you worry; I won't let anyone blame you or criticize you."

A couple of days later, after he had fully digested the news that he was going to be a grandfather, Reggie's attitude hardened, not towards his daughter personally, but towards her propensity for endangering herself, which would now also pose a threat to her precious unborn child. He decided that especially after those escapades when she had climbed up through a collapsing house to rescue little Albert, and had taunted the pilot of a Focke-Wulf, it was time to speak out to bring her to her senses. Summoning the determination to speak very firmly, he counted on the fact that his leadership role in the ARP would invest him with more authority than he possessed as a mere father.

"Look, Shirl," he said, "I've been thinking – you have been very brave and saved lives, but now it's time to take care of yourself and your baby." He sensed her mounting indignation and anticipated her response:

she would of course, as usual, say that she was fine so, quickly and undaunted, he continued,

"If your medical notes had been passed to the ARP, you probably wouldn't be *allowed* to go out on patrol, running all over the place, climbing ladders, rescuing many people, young and old, and not getting any sleep – and if that's not enough, rushing off by day to search out church halls for that Madame what's-her-name. As the leader of the patrol and your father, I cannot allow it!"

This definitive outcry was so unlike him that, surprised at his own eloquence, he had to pause to draw breath, which gave Shirley the opportunity to intervene.

"I must carry on, Pa!" she cried, not in anger but with deep conviction. "You don't understand, Pa! It's only when I'm out on patrol and actively doing something to help all these poor people and fighting against those dreadful Nazis that I feel I'm being true to Alan. Then I know that he's there with me and our baby and he's protecting us!" Tears rolled down her cheeks as she spoke.

At this her father's heart melted. "There, there, Shirl," he said gently, "I don't want to upset you, though I have to say I'm sure that Alan would not have wanted you to put yourself or his baby at risk."

Gradually the sobbing subsided. "Perhaps you're right," she conceded.

"So," he went on, "I'm going to arrange to put you on fire-watching duties for a bit, and I'm going to request a weekend off for us so we can get away from all this turmoil."

Relatively submissive, Shirley obeyed.

"You need a rest from the ARP duties," he said, "and fire-watching on only three nights a week, sitting in the comfort of an upstairs room, is just the job. There's that house up the road belonging to an elderly couple, and they put it at the disposal of the fire-watching teams; it would be just right for you."

Shirley knew the house; it stood atop rising ground not far from home, and the duties were said not to be very demanding, for at that stage in the War, fire-watching was an activity that was answerable to no official body, but to her it sounded unutterably boring. She vowed to give it a try for a week, certain that one week would be enough.

Having come to a satisfactory understanding with his daughter, and hot under the collar from his close involvement in such an intimate conversation, Reggie was on the point of leaving the room when the telephone rang. He was closest to it, standing in the doorway near the sideboard on which it stood, so he picked it up. Shirley watched his face sag as he listened to a long harangue from the other end. She guessed straight away who the caller was. She rushed over to stand right in front of her father to warn him to be guarded in any talk of Ted and his activities, and above all, not to mention her pregnancy: she rapped him on the shoulder and pointed both to a photo of Ted on the sideboard and to her tummy, shaking her head and wagging her index finger vigorously at him. He nodded.

After a good five minutes of being harangued on the phone, he was at last given the opportunity to speak. "Yes, yes, well, hello, Mother! I have been meaning to ring you, but we've been very busy here because as you will have heard, the enemy planes keep coming over and bombing anything and everything."

There was a lengthy interruption from the caller before he had another chance to speak. "Yes, Mother, of course, I've kept a close watch on the news – we see the papers here every day of course – and I know that Birmingham has been badly bombed, but I expected you'd be safe because you're such a long way out of the city. No, no, we've been lucky so far: our building hasn't been bombed, but there's been a lot of damage round here and we are having to patrol the streets, take people to safety and rescue those who've been trapped, so there hasn't been time to phone you."

The caller must then have asked about Ted, because Reggie said, "Well, Ted's not here at present, but maybe you'd like a word with Shirley?"

She raised her eyes to heaven and, with a grimace, snatched the phone from her father's hand before he could so much as mention the baby. "Hello, Granny," she said, with a theatrical display of tedium in her voice, which predictably was lost on her grandmother.

"Shirley, dear," she whined, "As I was saying to your father, why haven't I heard from you lately?"

"I think Pa has already told you how busy we are," Shirley replied tersely, "and of course there's the shop to run as well as taking care of our area – I'm an ARP warden, you know – so this is not the time to waste on chats over the phone." She emphasized "waste on chats", at which her grandparent bridled.

"I wouldn't say that ringing me to find out how I am is 'a waste of time', especially considering how badly Birmingham has been bombed," she complained, "and I do think you and your father should come and pay me a visit soon! Anyhow, I wanted to ask how my lovely boy is and what is he doing?"

"Oh, Ted's fine, thank you, Granny. Because he's bilingual, he's working for the government delivering messages to and from General De Gaulle and the Prime Minister when the phone lines are down."

This seemed to be a sufficiently plausible if inaccurate summary of Ted's part in the War; it was sufficient for their grandmother's ears. Shirley counted on the fact that Granny Marlow wouldn't know what 'bilingual' meant and that she would then spread the word around Birmingham about her grandson's very important job in Whitehall.

"Ooh, is that so? That's nice, that sounds very important!" said Granny, duly impressed. "I am glad to know that dear!"

Before her granny could ask anything else, Shirley exclaimed, "Oh, Granny, I must go! I've just seen a Focke-Wulf flying past the window!" With that she put the phone down, relieved that her father had not mentioned the baby.

Reggie had taken evasive action – from his mother, not from the imaginary Focke-Wulf – and had gone down to the shop, so it was not until after closing time that Shirley was able to tell him about her conversation with her granny. He shook his head and chuckled. "Oh, Shirl, you are naughty! But you know I think a little trip to Birmingham might do us good. They've been badly bombed there too, but not out on the edge of the country where Mother and Winnie and Horace are. And if you don't want to come and stay with your granny and Winnie, you could stay with your Cousin Edith, and I could go on to Birmingham and keep poor Harold company." Horace, his brother-in-law, with the patience of a saint, coped day in and day out with Winnie, his demanding wife, Reggie's sister, and with Granny Marlow, his mother-in-law.

"Maybe I forgot to tell you?" Reggie continued, "Edith and Jim and their little boy have moved to Coventry, because Jim's working in one of the factories making spare parts for the RAF, so you should be safe there and I could drop you off on the way to Birmingham. They reckon the Germans won't bomb Coventry because it lies in a dip and is always covered in fog, so those Nazi pilots wouldn't have a clue where they are. There's plenty of petrol in the car and I haven't used the rations, so I'll see what I can do to arrange something, shall I?"

CHAPTER 7

Shirley welcomed his suggestion: she had grown to like her cousin Edith over the years, and looked forward to seeing her again, although she hoped that Edith's little boy would not ruin her clothes as he had the last time, when he sat on her knee with a leaking, dirty nappy. What's more, a weekend away at Edith's might be precisely the break she needed, and afterwards she would resume her ARP duties refreshed, with no more thoughts of fire-watching.

Nonetheless, suspecting that her father would indulge in a bout of repressive amnesia to help him forget his mother's demands, she did not mention the proposed trip again. She dutifully tried fire-watching for just one week and then announced she couldn't stand it any longer. It was very tedious – it put her to sleep, which was no good if you had to be awake all the time, so, having tried that, she would be putting her ARP uniform on again. Reggie gave a sigh, acknowledging defeat. As it turned out, he was not indulging in repressive amnesia, because whilst he was hugely relieved that his mother was no longer living in South London, the more he thought about it, the more guilty he felt at leaving his poor, benighted brother-in-law to shoulder the burden of having to listen to the constant whinging complaints of those two women all day and every day.

"Poor chap," Reggie said to himself, and later expressed those thoughts to Shirley. "The least I can do is to go and cheer poor Horace up for a day or two. That would give him someone else to talk to and to listen to, even if that someone is only me. It's a pity for him that Edith moved away. She used to be so good at dealing with her mother, though perhaps she's moved to get away from her grandmother." Shirley was amused at her father's perceptive grasp of family politics.

Reggie put his plan into effect with moderate enthusiasm and told Shirley what he had done.

"The car's in good shape," he said, his rather splendid Lanchester naturally being his priority, "and we haven't used our travel allowance or the petrol rations, because the car's been in Archie's garage all this time, so there's no problem about that. I've also been in touch with Horace, who would be delighted to see us both, but he's not surprised that you might prefer to go to Edith's in Coventry. He's checked with her and that's fine – 'Anytime for Shirley. I'd love to see her!' Edith said – so I suggest we go as soon as I've had time to reorganize the patrol. We are certainly owed a break."

He smiled with satisfaction at his own efficiency. "Oh, and by the way, I told them down at the ARP office that you will be coming back on patrol, since you gave up the fire-watching, but that you *are* expecting. I hope you're not offended at that. They're pleased to have you back and agreed to my request for a weekend away. They asked, though, if we could postpone it for a while because they're very short-staffed at present and they need me, and you, too, for the time being. I insisted I wouldn't let you go clambering about in the rubble after an air raid again, only monitoring the population. They said of course you should only do light duties, and they are valuable too."

"I don't see any problem with that," said Shirley, who in fact was rather glad that the trip was not imminent, because Madame Belinskaya had taken up her suggestion of running her classes in the Methodist church hall, and together they were organizing a grand opening. "It's fine by me, whenever we go," Shirley went on; she was certainly not offended with her father for using her pregnancy as the excuse for going away. In any case, eventually her secret would have to come out. She didn't really care when they went so long as she could look forward to a brief change of scene.

Time was rolling by and not much that was positive happened these days, apart from discussions with Eileen about knitting patterns for baby clothes and making plans with a very enthusiastic Madame Belinskaya for inaugurating her new venue. It was not as if she could apply to a company to dance principal roles – or even in the *corps de ballet* – in her condition. As for her ambitious plans to apply to the Air Transport Auxiliary, those were still very much on her mind but shelved for the present, because she was having doubts about them now that the faint stirrings of the new life inside her were becoming stronger with each day. This baby, previously only an idea, was revealing himself to be a real human being with tiny feet that kicked gently, and as such her sense of responsibility towards the child grew. He, after all, was the most positive aspect of her existence.

If there was not much else that was positive in life these days, in Shirley's life, apart from her pregnancy – or anyone else's for that matter, there was plenty that was negative, with the threat each night of more air raids hanging over the population of London, of whom some seven thousand people had already been killed. Although she had to admit that the tension and tiredness were beginning to take their toll, she was hugely glad that she had not given up her regular rounds in the Air Raid Precautions patrol of an area which she now considered her own. There she was recognized and respected, even by those inhabitants who initially had been so dismissive of the ARP and reluctant to pay attention to her instructions. One week of fire-watching, which had seemed marginally a good alternative, had, as she suspected, proved to be too tedious for words by comparison with the ARP. Fortunately her father respected her decision to remain on duty, so long as she agreed to minimize her part by agreeing simply to verify the safety of households and their inhabitants, and not act the heroine by climbing into ruined, smoking buildings.

"So when do you expect we shall be able to go to the Midlands?" she asked one day, wondering whether her present wardrobe would still fit her, or whether she would have to look out for some material, even some of the old curtains up in the loft from their former home, out of which Eileen might be able to make her a couple of maternity dresses.

"I imagine we might be able to leave sometime in early November," he answered, stroking his chin in meditation.

However, after Madame's grand opening ceremony in the Methodist church hall one Saturday afternoon in late October, the weather turned so bad that they were both of one mind that it would be better to postpone the trip for a week or two, a decision which produced an inordinate amount of grumbling from Granny Marlow over the phone late one afternoon, when the sky was darkening outside. "Well, dear," she complained, "I was just *thinking* of baking a lovely cake for your father for his tea. You'll miss that, of course, because I gather you're not coming to Birmingham at all, and he's not coming here for another two weeks!"

In exasperation, Shirley, who had relieved her father by taking the phone out of his hand, answered through gritted teeth, "I'm sure, Granny, your cake will taste just as good if you begin to *think* of making it in a fortnight's time, or even earlier!"

Steps on the staircase announced a visitor. They were evidently not her father's, for his lumbering gait always announced his return from the very bottom of the staircase; these were the deliberately light footsteps of someone trying to evade detection.

"Sorry, Granny, I must go; I hear someone coming up the stairs!" said Shirley and slammed the phone down. She turned round quickly and found Ted standing before her on the landing.

She uttered a slight indication of pleasure, but, recalling in time his strict warnings on his previous visit, stopped herself from crying out in glee at the sight of him. She also stopped herself from crying out in horror when she saw the bruises on his face and the pockmarks on his hands. His drooping eyelids were enough to tell her that he was worn out, so she ushered him into the living room and sat him down in their father's chair before going out to make some tea.

"*Est-ce que Papa est ici?*" he asked as soon as she returned.

"*Mais oui!* He's down in the shop," she replied.

"Ah, well," he said, still speaking French, as though he had lost his command of English, "I want to talk to you before he closes the shop and comes upstairs."

"Oh, what's that about?" she enquired tentatively, hoping not to appear tactless and thereby invite a scolding.

"You and Pa must go away from here on the 14th. They" – he gestured vaguely in the direction of the South or South-East – "they are planning a massive attack on London and are lining up about seven hundred bombers!"

There was no doubt whom he meant by "they", but Shirley was baffled. "They've bombed us to smithereens already, so what more do they want?" she asked.

"Oh, don't ask me: I can't read their minds. I'm only telling you what I know," he replied.

"As it happens," Shirley replied, "we are thinking of going away that weekend. Pa's going to Birmingham to keep Uncle Horace company and I'm going to stay with Edith, who lives in Coventry now, so we should be all right. But come on, let me clean you up. You do look a mess, and Pa will be so upset if he sees you looking like that."

Fortunately there was water, and hot water at that, in the pipes. Ted allowed himself to be led into the bathroom like a three-year-old. After he'd had a bath, Shirley raided the medicine cupboard for ointments with which she dressed his wounds and his bruises without asking how he had come by them. All she said was, "Eileen would do this so much better than me, but I suppose you don't want me to fetch her, do you?"

"*Ah, mais non!*" Ted replied emphatically, as if that was a question that Shirley should not have bothered to ask.

Shirley's makeshift nursing skills and the hot bath in a minimal amount of water rendered Ted more or less presentable when their father came upstairs at the end of the day. After supper Ted went to bed and slept for twenty-four hours, waking the following evening a few minutes before Reggie reappeared after his day's work.

He took advantage of those few minutes' privacy to tell his sister news of their grandfather. "Pépé and Céline are in a difficult situation," he said. "I haven't seen them for some time, because the Germans come every day to the farm for eggs and milk. Pépé even had to slaughter a pig for them." He scowled.

Shirley kept quiet; this much information alone confirmed that Ted's secret operations were still being carried out in northern France near to the family farm. In addition, it was obvious that up to now Ted had still been visiting their grandfather and Céline, his housekeeper, as he had let slip the last time he was home. To judge by his wounds, Ted must have narrowly escaped a German attack, or something similar, but she refrained from asking questions. It was much better to wait to be told.

Ted did willingly proffer more information, but not the sort of information that Shirley was glad to hear. He said that there was a chance he might be meeting up with Hélène, who, he gathered, had also joined the Resistance, but as yet he did not know where or when their reunion might be. Although she bit her lip to avoid showing her dismay, Shirley was well aware that Ted would risk life and limb for his girlfriend, Hélène.

Reggie, having caught up with French news by experimenting with the controls on his wireless and turning them through different and distant frequencies, recited what he had heard from outside France. He surprised his son by being so well-informed.

"I've heard quite a lot about France," he innocently announced over supper. "I gather that in October there was a meeting between Hitler and Pétain in some remote corner of France. Would you believe it, that old idiot, Pétain, thought that by shaking Hitler's hand and sealing a pact of collaboration, France would become Germany's ally instead of an occupied nation!

He might have believed that this pact might make life easier for the French, and prisoners of war would be better treated, and so on, but my goodness, he discovered his mistake pretty quickly, didn't he? There and then, Hitler reminded him that he held France to be his enemy, responsible for the War and France would have to pay the price unless it mobilized all its energies against England. I was astounded!"

"You weren't the only one, Pa," Ted observed quietly. "Now everyone knows what we're fighting against..." With that he wished his father and sister "*bonne nuit*" and went off to bed.

By the next morning he was gone. Over breakfast, without even hinting at Ted's information, Shirley suggested to her father that the following weekend, or failing that, the one after, would be a good time for their trip to the Midlands: it would suit her well, considering that she would soon have more commitments in the ballet studio.

Granny Marlow was less than enthusiastic when Shirley later rang to tell her. "Oh!" she exclaimed indignantly. "You haven't given me much time to bake a cake for your father, have you, dear?"

"Granny," Shirley retorted, "you've had weeks to *think* about baking a cake; I'd have expected you would have made it and iced it by now!" Granny was not at all amused, although Shirley was.

8

One Thursday in mid-November 1940, Reggie and Shirley set out for Birmingham via Coventry in Reggie's stately vehicle, his Lanchester, which, stored away in Archie's garage, had so far survived all attempts by the Luftwaffe to destroy it. The day dawned dull with a tendency to drizzle, but, by the time they stopped for lunch, the skies were clearing.

"Looks as if we might have nice weather," Reggie remarked.

"Mm, I'm not too worried about the weather," Shirley replied. "It's good to be out of London, and I'm looking forward to catching up with Edith."

The cousins had discovered that they had more in common than a casual observer of the two of them – large, loud Edith and dainty, quick-witted Shirley – might have supposed: they shared a grandmother whose selfishness appalled them both, but whose turns of phrase and mannerisms made them laugh out loud, especially when Shirley mimicked her, as she often did when talking to Edith over the phone.

Of late an added dimension to their relationship had emerged, because they were both missing their siblings: Ted was away, goodness knows where and certainly in dangerous circumstances, and Edith's younger sister, Thelma, had died of Infantile Paralysis in 1937. In the autumn of that year, at the time of Edith's wedding, Shirley had caught the disease from Thelma, and that had put an end to her hopes of becoming a prima ballerina.

In her eagerness to see inside Edith's house, a sizeable Victorian property in a leafy suburb, Shirley waved goodbye to her father only perfunctorily as he set out from Coventry for Birmingham.

"Ooh, Shirley, come and see our lovely house!" Edith declared as soon as she had given her cousin a hug. "We're so much better off here in Coventry than in Birmingham! Jim doesn't have to take the bus any more: he can even walk to work, can you believe it? And the bus takes me right into the middle of town, and it goes out into the country in the other direction! If the weather's nice, we could go out into the country at the weekend!"

Edith's keenness to show her cousin over the house was overwhelming, but by that stage, after a long journey, Shirley would have preferred a drink. However, she meekly followed Edith on her tour, all the time trying to summon up the appropriate expressions of enthusiasm.

"What a beautiful, big sitting room!" she exclaimed, after duly patting Sam, the erstwhile baby, now a toddler sitting in a playpen, on the top of his head.

"Ooh, I know, it's marvellous, isn't it?" Edith replied, basking in her cousin's admiration. "And how do you like my gold curtains, and the carpet and the covers?" she asked. "I made the curtains myself!"

"Very nice – you are clever, Edith, I couldn't do that!" Shirley replied, already reflecting on how different this was from the bare, colourless flat above a shop in bombed-out South Cross, the run-down area of London where she lived.

Edith then took her upstairs and into the main bedroom, where pink was the dominant colour – pink curtains, pink carpet, pink bedspread, pink everything. Shirley was beginning to feel a little sick.

"And how do you like this? Pink's my favourite, you see?" Edith enquired, expecting only one answer. "Father paid for it all and Mother helped me choose the fittings. We didn't take Granny out with us when we bought it all, because she wouldn't have liked the colour and she would have said so. We'd never have heard the end of it. But it's my house and I can do what I like!" "Of course!" Shirley agreed, but was thinking that for once their granny was undoubtedly right.

The tour continued through two of the other bedrooms – little Sam's bedroom, all in blue, and the guest room, which was more soberly decorated.

"If you don't mind, I would like to use the bathroom," Shirley ventured.

"Ooh, I'm so sorry! I should have thought of that before!" Edith apologized. "Then, when you've unpacked in your room here, I'll show you round the garden. Come down when you're ready."

Tired and thirsty, Shirley lingered long in the bathroom, cupping her hands to collect water from the tap above the basin to quench her thirst. In the guest bedroom she did not unpack; instead, she lay down on the bed and closed her eyes, doubting that, after all, this break was going to be the restful weekend she had longed for.

She dozed until she heard Edith's voice calling up the stairs, "Shirley, Jim's home! Would you like to see the garden before we go out?"

"Yes, I'll be down in a minute!" Shirley answered sleepily. She stood up, yawned and went down to where her cousin and Jim, her husband, were waiting for her. Edith already had her coat on.

"I do want you to see our garden, Shirley; it's still so pretty, or it was until Jim stuck that great big Anderson shelter right in the middle of it, and it will be dark by the time we come home," she said laughingly. Jim, a man of few words, was roused.

"Now, Edie, that's not fair! I know we haven't had to use the shelter yet, but you never know when we might have to with these madmen about, dropping bombs everywhere," he protested.

"Oh well, if you say so, but it hasn't happened yet," Edith replied casually. "Anyhow, Shirl. Come on, I'll show you the garden and you can ignore the shelter."

Jim was not to be so easily dismissed. "Hold on!" he complained. "Have you forgotten we've had the Jerry bombers over already, and we were lucky they didn't hit us – but I tell you, one day we're going to need our shelter in a hurry, and it's the last word in size and luxury!"

Edith harrumphed, but smiled in acknowledgement of her husband's skills. "I will say this: Jim's a dab hand at gardening. He knows the names of all the plants, don't you, Jim? And he's going to look after Sam this afternoon, so we can go out into the city for tea and a look at the shops and maybe even a film."

With that she gave her husband a kiss to show that there were no hard feelings and, taking Shirley by the hand, sailed out into the garden.

"Don't be late back. I'm on ambulance duty tonight!" Jim called after them.

Outside, fading chrysanthemums were sending their last bursts of colour up into the dreamy blue of the autumnal sky. The lawn, however, truly showed signs of being the worse for wear after Jim's earthworks, though it had to be said that the Anderson shelter, down a short flight of steps, was impressive. It was impossible to ignore it and, despite her earlier grumbles, Edith was genuinely proud of her husband's achievement.

"Jim's a wonderful husband, so don't you worry if we appear to have our differences; we're only teasing," she assured Shirley, "and really when the War's over this shelter might come in handy as a spare room. It's a double shelter, really. I don't know how Jim managed to get hold of the second one. He says that if Granny ever comes to stay, we can put her in here!" She laughed and drew back the door of the Anderson. "See, it's spacious and comfortable – and look, Jim's even installed a flue for the heater and the camping stove, so we don't get suffocated by the fumes."

Shirley peeped in. It was certainly larger than Cousin Archie's shelter, because it was twice the width and housed a sofa and a bunk bed. In one corner there stood a water butt, ready-filled, and at the back a set of shelves held a small camping stove, a tin bowl, cups, plates and pretty much anything that befitted a tiny but well-equipped kitchen.

"So you see," Edith announced, "we would be quite comfy in here, though I'm sure we won't need it." She glanced at her watch. "I say, it's time to head off into town! It's ten to three and there's a bus in ten minutes, only two doors away," she announced. "Are you ready to go straight away, Shirley?"

Shirley's mouth was still dry, and she longed for a drink, but she forced herself to say brightly, "Of course – let me take you out to tea, Edith." She was still wondering with a certain sense of grievance, how, given all the deprivations and shortages in London, Jim had managed to come by two shelters and convert them into a sizeable property, so much larger, more comfortable, and better equipped than the cramped, stuffy, damp metal box that stood in Archie and Eileen's back garden.

Edith talked throughout the journey into the centre of Coventry, mostly about her house and her little boy, and about her husband as well. His job as one of the managers of the Aero Works, where aircraft parts were made for the RAF, was so much better than anything he could have hoped for in Birmingham. By the time the bus turned into the bus station, Shirley's head was lolling on her chest, for she was not sure how much more of Edith's monologue she could bear and still keep her eyes open.

"Well, here we are!" Edith declared. "I thought it would be nice if we went round the old streets to the cathedral first, then we'll have a look at the shops. We'll be ready for tea after that!"

Shirley was dying to suggest, "Couldn't we have tea first?" but Edith kept prattling on and there was no chance of interrupting her. Shirley was struck by her cousin's endless chatter and decided that she must have inherited it from her grandmother.

"Jim says there's no hurry so long as we are home by seven-thirty in time for him to go off on his ambulance duty," Edith was burbling on. "He drives ambulances, you see, and they practise on Thursday evenings for a major raid, like the ones you've had down in London. He's quite happy looking after Sam; he'll give him his supper and put him to bed, so if we want to go to a film, we'll have time for that too, if you'd like. I think they're showing that new film, *His Girl Friday* with Cary Grant. What do you think?"

Shirley saw that it was impossible to change the order of preferences, because Edith had it all planned and seemed so excited that she couldn't bear to disappoint her. Anyhow, the film was one that she had missed the first time round because of so many other distractions, and she very much wanted to see it.

Near the bus station, Edith pointed out the Old Grammar School and then led her cousin down alleyways and past old half-timbered houses to the city centre in Broadgate. Although her head was swimming and her feet in smart shoes were aching, Shirley was fascinated by the sights of a city which had preserved its medieval buildings, yet operated as a vibrant and busy modern shopping centre. She just wished that Edith would slow down and let her find somewhere to sit for five minutes. Finally they came to the soaring, majestic, rose-pink cathedral, which dominated the city from all angles. Inside the vast space with its towering columns, both of them were overawed by the magnificence and the silence of the place.

Here Shirley's wish was partly fulfilled: "I think I'll sit down for a moment," she whispered to Edith, "I need time to take all this in; it's so beautiful and peaceful!"

For once Edith's prattle was silenced. "Yes, I need to take the weight off my feet," she said in a hushed tone, for which Shirley was thankful, though "taking the weight off her feet" did not mean that Edith sat in quiet contemplation: she coughed and rustled around in her handbag for a cough sweet, unwrapped its noisy paper and then, having sucked on the sweet, blew her nose loudly. Shirley was both irritated and amused. It seemed that Edith could not bear silence, and felt obliged to make a noise to fill it. Nonetheless, she succeeded in ignoring the interruptions, because her brain was whirring with ideas.

"What a wonderful set for a ballet an ancient cathedral like this would be!" she thought, although she realized it would be difficult to come up with a suitably respectful story as a basis for such a ballet.

Edith, meanwhile, was tussling with the threads on the cuff of her woollen coat in which her watch was entangled. In a whisper that echoed off the columns and was much louder than her normal speaking voice, she said at last, "This coat is such a nuisance; my watch keeps catching on all the loose threads – but Shirl, we must be going if we're going to see the shops and have tea before the film. It starts at half-past four, so we only have about an hour or so."

Wondering how long Edith needed to look round the shops, Shirley stood up promptly, if a touch unsteadily. Edith's words were not exactly what she wanted to hear. She would have to keep going for a long time before there was any hope of that longed for respite in the tearoom.

"Let's go," said Edith, who was struggling to her feet. "We'll have a look in the department stores, and then I'll take you to a lovely little tearoom quite close by for a quick cuppa. Afterwards we'll just have time to see our famous clock, Peeping Tom, before the film starts."

In each of the department stores, Edith lingered long over every rack of winter clothing, from scarves and gloves to dresses and coats. Having bought herself two dresses, a coat and a hat, she insisted that Shirley should buy something. "The shops are all open this afternoon, and late at that, because they say clothing will be rationed soon, you know," she informed her cousin, "so you should buy something now."

Shirley did a mental review of her rather dismal wardrobe: over the past weeks and months there had been no time to go shopping for clothes in central London. In any case, after losing Alan, she did not feel at all inclined to dress up. He was the only person she would have wanted to show them off to, and as he was no longer alive, she had no enthusiasm for clothes or any other form of finery. If she were to buy anything, it would have to be a maternity dress, but back in London Eileen had promised to make one or two of those for her.

At last, over tea in the King's Head – which, as Shirley realized she should have expected, was high tea, complete with sandwiches, a few salad leaves, cake and a cup of tea – she was able to kick off her shoes under the table, while Edith scrutinized her anxiously.

"I'm surprised you didn't want to buy anything, Shirley. It might be a long time before we have that chance again. Are you all right?" she asked. "I'm sorry; we've been rushing around. That was because there was so much I wanted to show you, and you haven't bought anything while I've bought loads of lovely clothes. I'm sorry. I know I've been talking too much as usual, but that's because I was so pleased to see you and have you to stay."

"Don't worry," Shirley said, disarmed by Edith's warmth, "I'm fine, and I'm so pleased to see you too, but I shall be glad when they fill the teapot up!"

Edith's well-intentioned apology had given her the opening Shirley needed to talk about herself. "It's been awful down in London," she said. "The bombs have been raining down and Pa and I have been working as ARP wardens ever since it started; this is the first break we've had. As for Ted, he's gone off to work with the Free French, though you mustn't tell anyone about that, let alone Granny. You know how word spreads?" Edith nodded sagely. "My lips are sealed," she said.

Momentarily Shirley wondered if she should have trusted that latest piece of information to her garrulous cousin, but told herself that Edith was so preoccupied with her own situation that she wasn't likely to give Ted's activities a second thought, if indeed she remembered them. "I'm very glad to get away from all that," Shirley went on, "so I'm sorry if I seem rather tired. I hope Granny will let Pa have a rest, though I doubt it."

"You're right there!" Edith said with a grin. "She's so unstoppable she drives my poor father round the bend. But tell me about you, yourself; we've heard all about the London bombing and are so relieved we don't have that much here! What about your dancing? Are you still able to do that?"

One thing led to another and, after talking about the ballet, Shirley, before she knew it, found herself telling Edith the whole story of her all-too-brief and tragic romance. Edith's eyes widened, and tears of sympathy plopped onto her plate. "Oh, that's terrible, my poor Shirley," she cried, moved to the core by her cousin's story. "So, he asked you to marry him?"

"Yes, that's right, but he was killed before he could buy me a ring," Shirley stammered, conscious that her own eyes were filling with tears as they always did when she spoke about Alan.

"How sad!" Edith lamented. "So you don't have anything to remember him by, not even a photo?"

"That's right, not even a photo," said Shirley mournfully. After a minute's reflection she brightened up.

"Edith, I'll tell you a secret. I do have something though, even more precious than a ring, but I don't want Granny to know about it."

Edith was mystified, "Go on, then, tell me. You can trust me. Did he leave you a country house somewhere?"

"No, no, nothing like that!" Shirley exclaimed, annoyed at such a crass suggestion, but let it pass. Undeterred, she declared, "I'm going to have his baby!"

Edith was taken aback, and for once was rendered speechless.

When she had recovered from the surprise, she said, remarkably softly, "Shirley, that's the most wonderful news! I'm very pleased for you. Life hasn't been easy for you, and now at last something is going right. I hope I haven't tired you out this afternoon. You must make sure we look after you while you're here."

"Thanks – I'll be all right," Shirley said, brushing off her cousin's concern.

"I'm so lucky," Edith went on, "I have my Jim at home. He's in a reserved industry, you know, so he's escaped the call-up. It's not easy for him, though; he knows his work is essential, but people stare at him and often they ask him why he's not in uniform, even though he wears a badge as a sign of what he's doing. Some people hurl abuse at him and call him a pacifist. That makes him very embarrassed. So, of course, if I'm with him, I jolly well stick up for him, and I tell them straight that his work is crucial to the war effort – *and* he drives ambulances. But I can't help worrying that those Nazi spies will have mapped out the works and all the other factories, and they'll bomb us one day, maybe when he's at work and inside the factory."

Shirley acknowledged the truth of what Edith was saying. On the other hand, she could not help feeling envious of her cousin's fortunate circumstances, and well understood why Jim might not always receive the sort of reception that Edith evidently thought he deserved. She might have been very tempted to think the same.

"Well, let's be off to the pictures if you've had enough to eat and drink," said Edith, "I know I said half-past four, but that's when the adverts start, so it'll be fine, if we don't arrive till a quarter to five, to skip those. It's a pity we've missed Peeping Tom; he only comes out on the hour and it's getting too dark to see him. Oh, and it's getting cold." She shivered, but ever the optimist she comforted herself by saying, "Well, we'll soon be home after the film, and there's a nice stew in the oven for supper."

Shirley could not help wishing that her cousin had a better grasp of time: They had arrived at the cinema at a quarter to five, as Edith had said, but then they still had to sit through a few more advertisements and trailers, when she herself would have relished another cup of tea.

However, once inside the cinema, they settled down in comfortable seats for a welcome escape to the United States, where Cary Grant, a newspaper editor, was forced to think up ever more improbable ploys to prevent his former wife and best reporter from remarrying. Shirley's mood lifted as she was transported into the glamour and carefree world of Hollywood, thousands of miles away from the War in Europe in general, and England in particular. Her chances of becoming a film star were diminishing by the day, yet she still enjoyed glimpsing that other world where life was so easy, opulent and colourful.

At times such as this, she did not blame her mother for preferring America to Europe: indeed, she almost wished that her mother had taken her with her when she left London, her husband and her children, for then she, Shirley, might have been able to go into the film industry. Clearly that was something that was never going to happen, and perhaps it was better not to fantasize about it, because that would be unfair to her father and to Ted. And anyhow, if she had gone to the States, she would never have met Alan again, and she might have spent the rest of her life wondering about him, longing for him, without ever being able to make a relationship with anyone else. Emotionally she would certainly have been the poorer, and that spark of passionate creativity which informed her dancing would surely have died.

9

At around half-past six that Thursday evening, the two young women emerged from the cinema to a frosted city over which the moon shone brightly.

"Oh, it's dark already! I hate these winter nights!" exclaimed Edith. "But it is lovely and clear! That's unusual here. It's always so foggy!" As she pulled her gloves on, she remarked, "Ah, well, twenty minutes on the bus and we'll be home in time for Jim to go out on ambulance duty." She was satisfied the afternoon had gone according to her plan: she had shown her cousin the sights of Coventry, and a short ride would take them home.

"That's strange," said Shirley, pulling her coat round her and turning up her collar. "Why are all those dogs making such a noise?" The yelping, yapping, growling and full-throated barking which greeted them from all quarters was unsettling.

"I'm not sure. It's dreadful, isn't it? Quite scary," said Edith, frowning and casting her eyes anxiously about in search of some clue as to the source of the disturbance.

Then, stopping in her tracks, she cried, "Oh, Shirley! You're right! I've heard something like it in the distance, but we were always indoors so it's been muffled. It happens every time those bombers come anywhere near! But I don't hear any planes, do you?"

Shirley stood still, like the yapping dogs, all her senses bristling. "Edith," she said quietly, "I can hear a sound coming from miles off – from the south, I think, and I recognize it. I've heard it before in London. That's the sound of bombers!" She drew breath sharply and yelled, "Is there a shelter round here? We must get to it quickly!"

"I don't know," Edith whimpered miserably.

Exasperated, Shirley shouted, "Come on, give me your shopping; we must run! Those are Heinkels, I guess – and they're coming this way!"

"No! No! It can't be!" Edith screamed.

"Come on!" Shirley urged her, grabbing one or two of her cousin's parcels as the airborne rumbling and whining grew louder and louder until, like thousands of vibrating hammer blows resounding on a metal surface, it pulsed and screamed its way through the cold night air. The sirens started to wail while bursts of anti-aircraft and ack-ack guns echoed some way off, sending their flares heavenwards.

"Keep going, Edith!" Shirley shouted. "Look! There's the department store where we had tea. Let's hope they have a shelter! Hurry up; let's go over there and see, but be careful! Those are the pathfinders coming over; they send them first to drop flares, so the pilots can see what's on the ground!"

Before they could reach the building ahead of them, which might or might not have been the department store, the planes were right overhead, hundreds and hundreds of them, letting loose flares all over the city centre. Edith was in tears – "Jim! Sam!" she screamed – but Shirley, well-practised at dealing with this sort of situation, slipped automatically into the role of ARP warden, which had become second nature to her in the London Blitz, and she shepherded her distraught cousin away from the danger towards which they had been heading.

At that moment, a cluster of incendiaries, both flares and bombs, fell onto that structure a hundred yards away: up it went in a massive explosion sending vicious plumes of flame out in all directions, carrying chunks of masonry, wood, metal, china and glass, doors, windows, mirrors, coat hangers, clothes racks, windows, burning rugs and dresses up into the sky. Gravity then pulled all the burning debris down again onto the heads of the hysterical populace who had not yet managed to find cover. Shirley had pushed Edith into a doorway and there they sheltered using their handbags to protect their faces from the blast, which shook the ground beneath their feet.

Edith was hysterical and Shirley had no idea which road to take. "Edith, we must get away from here, so you must keep calm and tell me where to go!" she shouted above the din.

Her cousin tried to pull herself together: her teeth were chattering, and her hand trembled as she pointed to a street easily visible in the light from the blaze. "O-o-ver there," Edith stuttered, "but it's a long way home! Oh, Jim! Oh, my little Sam!"

"Never mind, how far it is," Shirley commanded briskly, "we must keep going and you'll have to lead me. Don't worry about Jim and Sam! Don't you remember that amazing Anderson shelter Jim built? They'll be in there already, of course! Or maybe next door with Jim's parents in their shelter."

Edith gradually quietened down as they set off at a brisk pace in the direction of her home, which was also the direction of the factory in the vicinity of which most of the employees, including Jim and his family, lived. She responded to Shirley's measured, authoritative tone and marched forward, trying to keep up with her. They attempted to run, but had to slow down when they stumbled over hot bricks, melting glass and the shards of burning wood and metal that were piling up in the road. Their feet hot in their shoes, they dodged the blazing craters, potholes and red-hot tar in their path. Clouds of evil-smelling smoke rose into the still air. Although the full moon had lit the way for the bombers, it also continued to shine brightly through the smoke, on the tremendous obstacles facing the escapees. Behind them another massive explosion sent shock waves throughout the city, making the ground tremble, like an earthquake beneath their feet. Shirley shuddered; this was as bad, if not worse than anything she had known so far in the London Blitz.

The barrage of planes in the initial onslaught eventually veered away, allowing the girls time to slow their pace. Shirley let Edith stand still for a moment to catch her breath. Edith bent double and then glanced up when her panting ceased.

"Look, Shirley!" she shouted above the din, pointing to a tree some twenty yards ahead of them, clearly visible in the cold, impassive rays of the moon. "Look at that parachute! There's someone dangling from it! Must be one of those pilots! You wait, I'll give him what for!"

Shirley followed Edith's pointing finger and gasped in horror.

"No, Edith, that's not a pilot, it's a parachute landmine up a tree! Run for your life!"

Edith did not stop to ask what a landmine was doing up a tree, but ran after her cousin as fast as her plump legs would carry her. They had no choice but to run past the tree and keep going for the next hundred yards. Then a blast struck them from behind and sent them flying face down onto the road. Shirley felt a sharp stab in her stomach, but picked herself up and went to Edith's aid.

"That was the landmine; it must have fallen out of the tree," she told her cousin as she heaved her up. "It's another one of their weapons: if you can't use them on land, send them up into the sky and drop them onto the people on the land below. And that's what they're doing here." She grimaced. "What more can they throw at us?"

The girls stumbled on, picking their way through the burning rubble. By Edith's calculation they were about halfway home when further squadrons of bombers came over, this time from the east. Not content with shedding their murderous load onto the city centre and its immediate surroundings, they spread further and further out into the suburbs. Shirley had a nasty suspicion that the planes were deliberately following her and Edith. In a sense she was right, because the aircraft overtook them and began dropping high-explosive bombs some distance ahead.

The whistling of the bombs as they followed their inexorable trajectory to earth was bloodcurdling. With an almighty roar, a huge blaze shot up into the star-spattered black velvet of the sky, blotting out the harsh silvery moon. The aftermath of a massive blast came rushing towards them like a mighty wind blowing hot in their faces.

"That must be the factory!" Edith panted, horror-struck.

"Let's run faster again for a bit, shall we?" Shirley suggested, urging Edith along while trying to hide her own rising panic and the pain in her stomach. "The faster we go, the sooner we'll get out of the centre and escape the fires spreading out from there."

For a mile or two before the next big blaze, the road, a dark hiatus between the targets outside the city centre, was as yet untouched by bombs or flares. Shirley, clutching the shopping, sprinted in front of her cousin; Edith, carrying considerably more weight, put on a spurt, impelled by the desperate desire to reach her home and her family.

All too soon, there broke out in their path another inferno, where on the other side of the road, houses and shops were collapsing like packs of cards, some all in one go, others more slowly, piecemeal; roofs caved in, walls fell outwards and floors gave way. The closer the girls came to the Aero Works, the more the road itself, though not alight, seemed to be about to ignite: the heat from it scorched their already searingly hot shoes, their hair and skin, and stung their eyes. The smoke-filled air choked them while hot ash fell about them, and a horrible acrid smell forced itself into their nostrils. The only blessing was that the road was wide enough for them to steer well away from the crumbling buildings on the other side.

Luckily the entrance to Edith's street was so far relatively unscathed by the bombs and the blasts, but as they turned into it, Shirley tripped, whether on a stretch of cable, a lump of rubble or a fallen branch she would never know, and fell flat on her face once more. When she tried to struggle to her feet, pain struck her again in the stomach. This time it was much sharper than before.

"Oh, Edith, help me up, please!" she cried out.

Edith lifted her to her feet and supported her as they stumbled on along the street. It had not escaped the raid, for some of the houses to left and to right were ablaze, and everywhere the noise of falling masonry was deafening.

It was Edith's turn to spur Shirley on. "We're nearly there, Shirley love; just keep going a little longer!" she said, panting heavily.

Remarkably Jim's parents' house was unscathed, and Edith's was apparently still intact, although the bomb blast had projected burning debris from other buildings onto the front lawns. The side passage to the rear garden was clear enough for them to be able to tiptoe gingerly through it, and ahead, through the smoky haze, the low hump of the Anderson shelter rose out of the lawn, silhouetted against the moonlight.

"We're there, Shirley; we've made it!" Edith sobbed. She helped her cousin down the steps with one hand and banged on the door with the other.

Inside, Jim rushed to open the sliding panel and yelled, "Oh, Edie, there you are! I was so worried about you. Sam's next door with my parents, so don't you worry about him!"

"Thank goodness!" Edith cried, falling into his arms, while Shirley collapsed onto the floor and passed out.

When she regained consciousness, she found herself lying on a camp-bed at the back of the second shelter, with her legs apart and bent at the knee. Edith was standing at the end of the bed looking at something. A searing pain gripped her stomach, her back, her thighs again and again in waves of excruciating, ever-recurring cramps. She gasped and screamed out in agony, drowning the external tumult of bombs exploding, buildings falling and aircraft thundering overhead.

In one of the few lulls, Jim, somewhat out of his depth in the developing drama, had ventured to make a dash to his parents' house to see to Sam, and left his wife to attend to her cousin. During the next round of bombing, Edith was standing over the stove boiling a kettle of water, when there was a frantic knocking on the door by someone outside appealing for help and shouting, "Please, please let me in!" She opened the door, letting in not only the frantic visitor but the full horror of the bombardment as well. Shirley heard her calling out, "Elsie, thank goodness you're there! We need you here! Come on in!"

Shirley had met Elsie, the local midwife, at Edith's wedding three years before; she had taken to her as one of the most likeable and sensible of the guests. Now in very different surroundings from the ostentatious glamour of that rather vulgar occasion, she, in her stupor, wondered why Edith was so pleased to see Elsie, the midwife. The blitzing raid was unbelievably awful, but they were safe, and no one was having a baby as far as she knew. But what was that searing pain in her tummy, and why had Edith been standing at the end of the camp-bed? For that matter, why was she herself lying there?

"The hospital's been bombed," she heard Elsie announcing, "and there's nothing anyone can do about it. I've been there for ages, and we've rescued as many patients as we could, but the rest of it is going up in flames. They sent me home because a new team has come to take over, but it's impossible to get through. Everywhere's on fire, so you were my last hope."

"Thank goodness you've come; you're *our* last hope," Edith whispered, ushering her friend to the back of the shelter. Elsie peered through her heavy glasses at the prostrate figure on the camp-bed.

"What's happening here?" she asked. "That's your cousin, isn't it, Edith?"

"Yes," said Edith, "it's Shirley and she needs your help! I've boiled some water."

"Poor girl!" Elsie exclaimed, "I can see she's in a bad way! Let me wash my hands and fetch my bag and I'll see what I can do. I've got some painkillers with me, so I'll do my best to help her."

When Elsie reappeared Shirley felt the sharpest pain yet.

"My tummy's fallen out!" she cried.

"There, there, Shirley, dear. I'm going to give you something to help. Just a little prick in your arm," Elsie said reassuringly as she plunged a syringe into Shirley's arm. She winced, but the pain eased off and soon she drifted into sleep.

After that long night, all was quiet in the morning when Shirley woke. She puzzled over where she was. She still trembled from a terrifying nightmare in which she had been caught in the firing line, and had been dragged out of a blazing city into an Anderson shelter where her stomach, which must have been wounded by a bomb, had fallen out. She reached down and felt her tummy. It was flat and unharmed.

She opened her eyes: she was indeed in an Anderson shelter, one that she had seen before, but had no idea where it was. She felt again and, on finding that she was wearing padding below her stomach, assumed that that was where her insides had fallen out. There was pain in that area which did not respond well even to her light touch.

She called out, "Hello! Hello! Why am I here?" But no one answered. She was tempted to try getting out of bed, but decided that if her tummy really had fallen out, that might be dangerous, so she stayed put and waited for someone to come. Surely they couldn't have forgotten her?

Slowly she began to realize that she was in Edith's Anderson shelter, built and enlarged by Jim, only now there was a curtain alongside her bed which she didn't remember from the previous day, but she did remember that the previous night there had been a terrible air raid in which bombs had fallen like huge, leaden raindrops. Perplexed, she thought that couldn't have happened, because the Blitz fell on London, and this wasn't London. Edith didn't live in London, but if not London, where was it? Somewhere safe outside London perhaps, but the name of the place escaped her. She heard a murmuring coming from the front of the shelter; it sounded like baby-talk. Whose baby was that? Was it her baby? Her baby! Where was her baby, Alan's baby? She felt her stomach again. It shouldn't be as flat as that. Where was the little bump she patted gently every morning when she woke?

She closed her eyes as her memory started to jolt itself into action. It told her that she was alive – but was asking what had happened to her baby in that storm of fire and bombs that had begun soon after she and Edith left the cinema? With sudden clarity she recalled the desperate rush to leave the city and dash home to Edith's house, the flaming department store, the explosions, the earth tremor, the burning roads, the huge flash as the aircraft works went up and her two falls, the second much worse than the first. She closed her eyes and fell back on her pillow. Surely that fall couldn't have killed her baby, her only remaining link with Alan, the love of her life, her only love, her fiancé, her future husband, dead and lying somewhere at the bottom of the sea?

"No, I won't believe that!" she told herself, defying her memory to come up with a better version of the events of the night. She would not, could not believe that the nightmare had really happened. She would not allow it to happen. On so many occasions in this War, she had risked her life, yet had never been badly hurt. It was unthinkable that she should be seriously injured here in this strange place which wasn't supposed to suffer from air raids. After all, her father did not seem to be here, and she expected that he was alive and well, so the same might apply to her child.

But the unanswered question persisted: where was her tiny child? Had she given birth to him already? Although she racked her brain, she couldn't remember when he was due. Had she reached full-term with him? For some unknown reason that seemed unlikely, but she didn't know why. Had he been hidden away perhaps, by Elsie, that friend of Edith's, who had arrived last night shouting and banging on the door, and had then stuck a needle into her arm? If Elsie had taken him away, which she had no right to do, she hoped he was safe. Why hadn't they told her where they were taking him? Nothing made sense. She would have to shout at the top of her voice until somebody heard and came to see what was wrong.

While she was summoning the energy to shout long and loud, a dust-laden draught blew into the shelter as someone opened the door, calling out, "Hello, it's only me, Jim!" Then that same male voice whispered through the curtains, without coming in, "Shirley, are you all right?"

"Yes, I think so," she replied drowsily, "but where am I and what's happened? What's going on?"

"You stay there; I'll fetch Edie. She's giving Sam his breakfast, so I said I'd come and check up on you," he said and went out again.

Edith came into the shelter a while later. She poked her head through the curtain. Shirley recognized her only by her voice, for she was covered in grime and looked like the old witch straight out of *Sleeping Beauty*. "Let me have a wash, Shirley, and then I'll come and talk to you. Jim told me you're awake. Are you all right?"

Shirley had no answer to that. She was in a state of total confusion, so she muttered simply, "I suppose so, but I would like a drink, please."

"Right, a cup of tea coming up!" Edith declared.

When Edith brought the tea in, Shirley was shocked at the closer sight of her. Not only did she look like a dust-covered old hag, but her face was pockmarked, and she limped. It was Shirley's turn to be concerned. Edith sat down on the bed.

"What's wrong, Edith?" Shirley asked. "Jim's all right, isn't he, and Sam too? And what about you?"

"Yes, they're fine, and so am I really, just rather scarred by last night's, um, adventure," Edith said. "The worst problem is," she explained, "that the windows; every one of them has been blown into our house upstairs and we can't live there. Anyhow we don't know if the structure is sound. Luckily my in-laws are all right. Our house must have protected theirs against the blast."

"Oh, poor Edith," Shirley exclaimed, taking her cousin's hand. "I'm so sorry – and here am I lying here, doing nothing! I'll come and help. I'm used to climbing about in bombed buildings; I can rescue some of the things from your house!"

She pulled herself up in bed, wincing as she did so. "No, you stay there – you're not well enough to get up," Edith smartly decreed.

"Oh, why's that?" Shirley asked. "I know I've had a fall, and that was painful, but I'm sure I'm all right now."

"No, dear," said Edith gravely, "you've had a miscarriage."

The truth was brutal, just as it was for so many other people that Friday in Coventry.

"A miscarriage?" Shirley questioned. "What's that?"

She knew perfectly well what a miscarriage was, but despite having surmised as much herself, she refused to believe that that was what Edith had said.

"You've lost your baby, dear."

Shirley sank back onto the pillows. "My little boy?" she asked timidly.

"Yes, dear, I'm afraid so," Edith said gently. "He *was* a little boy."

Shirley closed her eyes. "Where is he? Where is he?" she sobbed. "I must see him and hold him and bury him myself!"

"No, love, that's not possible," Edith said. "Elsie has already taken him away."

10

The hazards, the smoking rubble, the potholes and the craters made the residential streets of Coventry impassable to all private traffic for days, despite the efforts of the teams working all over the city to clear the obstacles. The morning after the overnight air raid, Reggie in Birmingham stayed glued to the wireless which Horace had rigged up in his garage. He sat in a state of shock, listening to every report from the devastated city of Coventry, where hundreds of people had died, but no news of his daughter's fate reached him. Although sitting on boxes out in the garage, he still had to keep the wireless tuned very low so as not to spark off another of his sister's hysterical outbursts, for she, Winnie, was convinced that her daughter, Edith, and Sam, her grandson, had all died in the attack. Her distress was not surprising, or even unreasonable, especially because she had already lost her younger daughter to Infantile Paralysis, but her loud and constant lamentations were extremely disturbing for her quiet, long-suffering husband, Edith's father, and for her brother, Reggie, who feared that his own daughter and her baby had also been the victims of the massive enemy bombing campaign.

In general, that Friday, Reggie gave Winnie as wide a berth as possible, although hapless Horace was frequently called to her side.

"Horace!" she called out accusingly. "Don't leave me! Don't you care about me? Oh, how I'm suffering! My poor Edith, my poor little Sam!"

This became the refrain that accompanied every one of her wailing dirges from morning till night. On the Saturday, however, Horace mumbled some excuse about having to go to his pie factory to resolve a problem; he went out, taking Reggie with him, and leaving his wife to attend to her mother. Reggie was glad of the diversion and Horace was proud to have the opportunity to show his brother-in-law the workings of his business, in the hope of taking their minds off the likely fate of their daughters.

They repaired to a pub at lunchtime, and there, drowning their anxiety in a pint or two of beer, and appeasing their hunger with plentiful pies from Horace's factory, they deliberately avoided referring to their true concerns, other than for one of them to sigh and remark from time to time, "Ah, it's a bad business, isn't it?" The other one would then respond with a nod of the head: "Yes, there's no doubt about that, but we must try to be optimistic and hope for the best."

Thus, Reggie had managed to stay calm and focused, telling himself that Shirley was a survivor. After all, to be reassured on that score, he had only to recall her bold – some might say rash – rescue of her brother from France in the face of the Nazi invasion. Horace trusted in the sound common sense of his son-in-law, Jim, who, he was sure, would do his utmost to keep Edith and Sam safe. This argument had cut no ice with Winnie, who as usual undermined his best ideas, but alone with Reggie, his confidence in his own opinions grew.

The Sunday of that long weekend was dire for both the men: trapped in the house with Winnie, there was no escape from her wild imaginings of what had become of Edith and Sam. Predictably her mother was no help whatsoever; her contribution to the fraught scenario was the oft-repeated, incisive observation that if only her daughter had not insisted on her leaving her mansion in the leafy suburbs of London, and moving to the Midlands, which, when she came to think of it, was an obvious target for German bombers, she would have been much safer. Reggie did his best to keep his mother quiet – in the equally leafy suburbs of Birmingham – but to little avail.

At last rumours filtered through that the some of the main streets of Coventry were clear, though still hazardous, and were open to traffic, whereupon Winnie declared that she was too exhausted with grieving to be able to travel anywhere. Reggie cleverly deputed his mother to stay at home to look after his sister, to which the latter only agreed after a lively protest.

"But what about my Bridge club?" Mrs Marlow complained. "It's this afternoon, and I'm sure Winnie can look after herself for an hour or two. She really doesn't have to make such a fuss!"

Winnie sobbed into her handkerchief even more loudly. "You're all going out and leaving me! How could you?"

It was left to Reggie to take charge, Horace having lost all authority in his own household.

"Winnie!" Reggie told his sister, summoning all his powers of command, which were not many. "We're going to find Edith and Sam – and

Shirley," he added since no one had bothered to ask after his daughter at all. "I'll bring you a tray with a large thermos flask of tea and some sandwiches, so you'll be all right, and, as for you, Mother, we'll call a taxi to take you to your Bridge afternoon and another one to bring you home afterwards."

"Well, I suppose I'll manage somehow, but a taxi will be expensive," Mrs Marlow conceded huffily, and Winnie, having vociferously instructed her husband to bring Edith and Sam home to Birmingham, retired to her bedroom, slamming the door firmly shut.

Weary with worry and with all the drama on the home front, Reggie and Horace set out in their cars, one behind the other, to test the unconfirmed reports of the road clearances in Coventry. All being well, Reggie was determined to collect Shirley and, God willing that she was still alive, would drive her home to London without more ado.

After parking on a relatively clear stretch of main road from which wisps of smoke from the hot tarmac still rose into the foul air, Reggie and Horace picked their way tentatively through the backstreets, avoiding bare, broken cables, huge blocks of rubble and the deep potholes.

It came as a huge relief to both of them to find Edith's house still standing, despite the rubble, the tiles, chimney pots and glistening shards of glass which had landed in the front garden and were littering the path. The doorbell was out of action, so they knocked loudly: it yielded no response. They stood, helplessly surveying the wreckage both in the garden and along the street, and wondering where their daughters were. Yet again they began to fear the worst.

Once more Reggie felt a wave of despair that his Poppet, that fragile little dancer, had been caught up in the bombing. Nevertheless, he allowed himself to take a modicum of comfort in the sure knowledge that, however insubstantial her bodily frame might appear, she possessed a will of steel. Standing outside a seemingly deserted house in the middle of a scene of unimaginable destruction, the two fathers were contemplating their next move, when Reggie, taking a step or two backwards, happened to look up at the first-floor windows.

"Look, old boy," he exclaimed. "If you look up there, you'll see there's no glass in any of those windows, so they can't be living at home. Where else could they be?"

Horace considered for a moment. "Oh, I've been so stupid!" he exclaimed. "Jim's parents live next door!" He gestured to the house on the left. "So as likely as not, they're in there, and look there's still glass in some of Edie's windows!"

Stumbling over the debris, they made their way to the next house.

Edith opened the door and, after a second or two of amazement at the sight of her father, she flung herself into his arms.

"Ooh, Father!" she cried, "You don't know how awful it's been!"

While they hugged and sobbed, Reggie stood by awkwardly on the doorstep, not daring to venture into a strange house uninvited. Why, he wondered, had Shirley not appeared? Where was she? She must by now have heard the voices at the front door and, with her sharp ears, would have recognized his voice and possibly Horace's deep tones. Little noises, as of a small child playing, issued from somewhere indoors, but there was no other sound. Reggie's blood froze at the suspicion that, after all, something really dreadful had befallen Shirley.

He cleared his throat to draw attention to himself. Horace turned to him at once and, as if in apology for ignoring him in his joy at finding his own daughter, said to Edith, "Here's your Uncle Reggie, Edie, he wants to know where your Cousin Shirley is."

Edith quickly wiped away the tears that were streaming down her face.

"Ah, well," she began, cautiously putting her hand to her mouth, "she's not very well."

Reggie's heart was beating so loudly he could scarcely hear what Edith was saying.

"Um, she's in bed upstairs. Jim carried her up there because it was too dangerous for us to stay in our own house. We were afraid it was going to fall down, there are so many cracks in it. Jim's parents have been so kind to us, and this house is quite safe... no cracks at all." Her voice petered out.

Reggie forced himself to pluck up the courage to ask why Shirley was in bed.

"Um, she's recovering, but I expect she's asleep at the moment," Edith said, as if that were sufficient explanation of her cousin's condition, before adding brightly. "Come in, do; I'll go up and tell her you're here."

In those few seconds Reggie aged visibly; he heaved his already cumbersome frame through the doorway and slumped onto a stool in the hall. "Whatever happens," he said to himself, "I mustn't let the shell shock hit me now." It was quite a while since, despite the horrors in which he and the rest of the country were living, he had been free of that terrible legacy of the Great War. Nonetheless, always in times of stress, he worried that it might return with a vengeance to haunt him, and this War was testing his resilience to its limits.

"Come up, Uncle Reggie!" Edith was calling down from upstairs, "she's awake and will be so pleased to see you!"

Reggie mounted the stairs ponderously, held back as much by a sense of foreboding as by his own physical sluggishness. His right hip, where he had been wounded more than once by German bullets in the First World War, hurt in a way that it hadn't in years, so that leg dragged behind him. On the landing he had to pause for breath, and then followed Edith into a pleasant bedroom, fitfully lit by a pale, uncaring sun.

Lying on the bed he saw a corpse, as white as the misty, dusty sky. He groaned, holding on to the edge of a chest of drawers for support and feeling faint. Only then did he see that the corpse had its eyes open. Surely someone would have closed them by now, if she were dead?

But then a tiny voice whispered, "Hello, Pa, is it you?"

Tears ran down the corpse's face as her father went over to the bed and lifted her in his arms. "Shirl, Shirl, you're alive! What a shock you gave me just now."

He pulled a blanket round her, and gradually a hint of colour appeared in her cheeks.

Edith tactfully tiptoed out of the room, leaving father and daughter alone together. She returned carrying a tray of hot drinks and a bowl of porridge for Shirley, which, to everyone's surprise, she devoured avidly. Reggie sat by her bedside until she fell into a warm, rosy sleep.

Edith beckoned to Reggie to follow her downstairs, where she had started to cook lunch.

"Uncle Reggie, you must have something to eat, and you too, Father, before you go back to Birmingham," she said, turning to her father, who was playing at toy cars with Sam.

"Oh, but Edie, I've strict instructions to take you and little Sam home to Birmingham with me," Horace protested, alarm written all over his wan features.

"I'm sorry, but there's no way I can do that. I suppose it was Mother who told you to do so," came the reply. "Well, you'll have to tell her from me, I'm not going to leave Jim! He's a hero! Out all day with his father, clearing the works, and then at night he does fire-watching and is on call for ambulance duty. His mother is out with the WVS, and I'm here keeping house and cooking whatever I can lay my hands on."

Edith was becoming heated. "And then there's Shirley – she's been very ill, and I'll have to look after her until she's fit enough for the journey home." This was not the first time that Horace had wondered why his womenfolk were so strong-minded, each in her own way. Had he voiced this unspoken question, Reggie would certainly have agreed with him. "Now, Father," Edith went on, "I've put the potatoes on, so Uncle Reggie and me, we'll go and have a little chat in the front room while you keep an eye on Sam.

In the privacy of the front room, Edith sought to reassure her uncle. Without going into too much detail, she outlined the events of that night, Thursday 14th November 1940, blaming herself for not taking more precautions and for keeping Shirley out later than perhaps was wise. Had she been aware that Shirley was expecting, she would have been more careful and wouldn't have taken her into the city. But what else could she have done?

No one had warned the population to expect an almighty air raid, when they thought it was going to fall on London. It was an air raid so almighty that it had destroyed their beloved cathedral and had taken everyone, including the forces – the Air Force, the Army, the Home Guard, the ARP, all of them – completely by surprise. And she and Shirley had been having such a nice time, going out for tea and seeing a film. She pulled out her handkerchief and blew her nose. The problem was, she continued, punctuating her account with sniffs, Shirley had fallen badly twice on the way home and then she had suffered a miscarriage after they had reached the safety of the shelter next door.

Luckily Elsie, the midwife, had come banging on the door to ask to be let in just when she was most needed. The three of them – that is, Elsie the midwife, Edith herself and Shirley – had to spend the night in the shelter. It was impossible to do anything more for her, but they tried their best to make her comfortable, and she gained some slight relief from having the camp bed. The next day, because his house was out of bounds, Jim had carried Shirley into his parents' house.

Reggie listened with his head in his hands. "Thank you, Edith. Don't blame yourself. For that matter, I might as well blame *myself* for bringing Shirley to Coventry, but, like you, how were we to know? There was no warning, was there?" he said, aware that Ted had unwittingly given him the false information that London would be heavily bombed. Alas, it was Coventry that was bombed catastrophically.

"You've already done so much, Edith, and I am very grateful to you, but what are we going to do now?" he asked, wiping his forehead.

"Don't you worry, Uncle Reggie, I have it all planned," Edith announced with the authority of the hospital matron she would like to become, as she outlined her plans.

"You can sleep in the little bedroom in this house; Jim will go to the shelter next door – it's much more comfortable than the one they've got here – and I will sleep on a mattress on the floor in Shirley's room. Oh, and my in-laws – you do remember them, don't you, from my wedding? They can sleep in their own bed, and we'll move Sam's cot into their room."

"That's very kind, Edie. You've thought of everything. I had hoped to take Shirley straight back to London, but I see that's out of the question," Reggie said, trying to express his gratitude with an unaccustomed stutter, which suggested that this was all too much for him to take in. "But what will we do if there's another raid?"

"They won't be coming back, Uncle Reggie; there's nothing left to bomb!" said Edith as quick as a flash. Of course, that had been Ted's opinion of the London Blitz, although that had been somewhat optimistic.

Thanks to her father's presence, Edith's care and Elsie's regular visits, Shirley began to recover her strength, so that by the following Thursday, a week after the bombing, she declared herself to be well enough to travel.

Edith drew a sharp intake of breath. "Ooh, I'm not sure about that!" she exclaimed.

Shirley sat motionless on a chair in the kitchen watching her cousin cook the lunch.

"We'll have to see what Elsie says about that," Edith carried on. "Remember, she said you should stay in bed for two weeks, and here you are, up and about already, and it's only just a week since... since the air raid."

"No, I feel fine, Edith," Shirley insisted, "and anyhow, Pa wants to be getting back to his business, and I've put you to far too much trouble already."

Edith fell silent, but when she opened the door to Elsie later that day, Shirley, who was resting upstairs, could hear an intensive bout of whispering being conducted in the hall. Edith was very kind, so was Jim and so were his parents, but she hated being the object of the wrong sort of attention. This was not the attention accorded to a ballerina on the stage. It was the solicitous, pitying consideration given to a very sick patient and was all too reminiscent of the wards in the Infantile Paralysis hospital. She was not sick, she told herself, she was grieving, grieving for the loss of her child, the child who would have kept his father's image and presence alive in her life. The Nazis had not only taken her future husband away from her, but they had also taken his child, leaving her with nothing. She had not even been allowed to bury him.

She heard Elsie's steps on the stairs and swiftly leapt out of bed, grabbed a book and settled herself in an armchair in the bay window.

"So how are you?" Elsie enquired on coming into the room.

This was a question that Shirley was tired of being asked every five minutes. There was no doubt but that all these people were trying to do their best for her in what was for them very difficult circumstances: food was in short supply, the water supply was unreliable with frequent cuts while the mains were being mended, the electricity supply was sporadic. She could not bear to put them to more trouble than she already had and resented being so dependent on them.

She gave Elsie the same answer as she gave to everyone else: "I'm fine, thank you, Elsie."

This time, however, she added, "You've been wonderful, and I was so lucky you appeared in the shelter that terrible night. I'm so grateful to you, but now I think it's time my father and I went home."

She expected Elsie to say, "No, you can't possibly do that!" but she did not. Instead, she said quite calmly, "Yes, I quite understand, Shirley, but please just allow me to bring a doctor to see you first. They've all been so busy – there hasn't been anyone available, but the crisis is easing, so perhaps I can find someone to see you."

Shirley shrugged. "Thanks," she said nodding. She really didn't care. Whatever a doctor might say would make no difference.

The doctor, a friend of Elsie's, guardedly pronounced her fit enough to travel on condition that as soon as possible after her arrival home, she would visit her own doctor. Shirley agreed, but privately told herself that going to Dr Forbes would be a waste of time. All she cared about was her baby: she had lost him, and nothing would bring him back. She sat in the car, blankly staring out of the window on the journey to London and ignoring her father's hesitant attempts to say encouraging things, such as, "We'll be home soon and then we can light the fire and make ourselves comfortable, or if you want, Shirl, you can go straight to bed."

The truth was she wanted to get away from Coventry as quickly as possible. Indeed, when on the way through the city, she saw the extent of the destruction, she was struck by the comparison on a large scale with her own experience, for both admitted of no recovery. This made her even gladder to escape from that nightmare, but on the other hand, nor did she want to go back to the shop in grimy South Cross, and she definitely would not go to bed; she had spent far too long in bed already.

It was dark by the time they arrived home, and were surprised to see lights on, both in the shop and the flat above. Downstairs, Cousin Archie was dealing with the accounts and, whether out of embarrassment or because he was busy with calculations, he simply nodded in Shirley's direction. The telephones were still out of action in Coventry, so Pa had stopped by a phone box and rung to let Archie know that they were on their way home. Upstairs, a glowing fire in the grate, the smell of baking and high tea on the table greeted them.

As insubstantial and wispy as ever, Eileen emerged from the kitchen and shyly put an arm round Shirley's shoulder. "Welcome home, dear," she said. "I know what it's like; it happened to me too a long time ago."

11

The drive home had been awkward, all too reminiscent of the dreadful journey from Brighton to London after that fall down the steps leading to the beach. "How are you now, Shirl? Does it still hurt?" her father had persisted in asking on that occasion, forever trying to make positive comments, whilst she herself had tried so hard to be optimistic although in excruciating pain. The worst of it was that she knew in her hearts of hearts that she had not lost her footing: the reason for that fall was the first sign of Infantile Paralysis. Similarly, on the way back from Coventry, Reggie had done his best to jolly her along, but his words rang hollow in her ears so she preferred to ignore them because she could no longer put a brave face on her grief.

In the relative safety of home, the situation was different. Her father spent most of his time down in the shop and, despite the risk of more blitzing, Shirley allowed herself to drop her guard. No longer did she have to pretend that she had come to terms with her loss to keep other people happy, or be endlessly grateful to them for caring for her. Here where nothing was expected of her, she could relapse into whatever mood suited her feelings, and for several weeks, those feelings were mostly of the most profound melancholy. She wondered why she was still alive – indeed she wished she were not – and rejected all suggestions that she ought to visit Dr Forbes. Here, alone and upstairs, there was no one to argue with her: her father was out of his depth in dealing with female problems, so he kept quiet, and when he had to explain his daughter's absence from duty to the Air Raid Patrol, he simply said that she had been injured in the bombing of Coventry, which of course was true. The expressions of astonishment that Shirley should have been caught up in such a catastrophe, and the sympathy for her injuries that this simple explanation evoked, were overwhelming in themselves, so no more details were needed.

Archie stayed well out of the way down in the shop, where he kept his cousin company with his usual well-meaning banter.

"Don't you worry about your Shirley," he assured Reggie. "My missus will look after her. After all, as I've said before, your Shirley's the daughter or granddaughter she never had, so she'll be in her element!"

Yet again, indeed, it was Eileen who filled a maternal – or grandmaternal – role in Shirley's life, just as she had in those horrible weeks after Alan's disappearance over the Channel at the very start of the Battle of Britain. Eileen flitted noiselessly from one task to another, never presuming to offer advice or unwelcome suggestions, but judging the mood of each day and reacting appropriately. For instance, if Shirley seemed drowsy, she sent her back to bed and took her a couple of hot-water bottles; if she wanted to cry, she brought her handkerchiefs and sat silently with her; if she wanted to talk – which she did only rarely – she listened. For the most part Shirley was preoccupied with that one recurring and persistent thought: she had lost her child before his life had truly begun, and there was no way of bringing him back from the dead, any more than there was any way of bringing his father back to the new, fully adult, married life that had beckoned to them both with its promise of hope and fulfilment whenever the War came to an end.

With these thoughts churning endlessly in her head, Shirley at first sat staring blankly into nothingness, although she seemed to be perfectly aware of what was happening around her. But one evening when her father was out on patrol, Archie, who in spite of his age had been co-opted into the ARP and was waiting on duty down in the shop, received the call to sound the siren. He shouted up the stairs to Eileen to warn her before he went out. Not long afterwards, the siren whirred into action, its spine-chilling moan pulsing through the night air from the top of the church tower. Then, quite close, the ack-ack guns started sending round upon round of ammunition into the winter sky.

There was a burst of noisy activity when Eileen's usually silent movements turned into a frantic, bustling search for coats, hats, gloves, bags and keys.

"Come on, dear, we must be going round the corner to our shelter – there's an air raid coming!" she cried out. "Yes, I know," Shirley replied calmly, "but you go. I want to stay here. If I die in this air raid, that will be the best thing that can happen to me!"

"Well, if you won't move, I won't either!" Eileen insisted with such an unaccustomed degree of defiance that Shirley was shaken out of her stupor, forced to face up to her responsibility to protect this elderly relative who had been so good to her. She took the coat that Eileen handed her, and followed her slowly out of the room, down the stairs, into the street, round the corner and into Archie's garden, where she shuddered at the sight of a dimly outlined shape in the lawn, a hump not unlike the hump in Edith's lawn, only much smaller. She edged away. Nothing would induce her to go in there. She could not go in there, not for anything!

Eileen had drawn back the sliding door and had already gone inside; there she struck a match to light a candle and called out.

"Come in, Shirley! We mustn't leave the door open and let the light escape, or we'll be in trouble!" but Shirley stood trembling on the step leading down into the shelter. The enemy planes were coming closer, their engines throbbing against the wail of other sirens and the bursts of fire from the guns. A hand grabbed her shoulder and a push from behind sent her headlong into the shelter.

"Now, young lady, look smart; there's a queue of people wanting to get in here and you're holding them up!" It was Cousin Archie who had given her a shove, but still had his hand on her shoulder to stop her falling. The queue in fact consisted only of Mrs Fothergill and Madame Belinskaya, who followed him into the shelter, and he closed the door. Eileen lit more candles and a paraffin stove. The shelter was airless and crowded, with scarcely enough space on the benches for all five of them to sit down.

Having acknowledged Emily Fothergill and Anastasia Belinskaya, who, from their appearance, must have been roused from a comfortable snooze in front of the fire, Shirley's one aim was to escape from the cramped, stuffy conditions and the pitying looks, for evidently the news of what had befallen her in Coventry had spread fast. Unable to avoid staring glumly at the four older people, she sensed that someone was missing; in no time she realized who that missing person was.

"But Pa! Where is my Pa? Why's he not here?" she screamed, startling all the ladies, for that scream was the loudest sound she had given vent to in more than a week.

"Calm down, young lady – those German pilots will hear you and either they'll drop their bombs on us, or they'll turn tail and flee for their lives! Anyhow, you'll pierce my eardrums at that rate!" Archie chided her with his own brand of droll humour and reassured her: "Your father's fine. He's standing in our porch keeping an eye on the road."

"I must join him – please open the door!" Shirley demanded.

Archie glanced at Eileen, who glanced at Emily who glanced at Anastasia.

She nodded. "Eef she weesh to go, you mus' allow 'er," she decreed.

Archie opened the door and, with many an injunction to take care, Shirley stepped out into the cold night air. She wrapped her coat around her and breathed in deeply. This was only dirty old south-east London air, but it was the best she had breathed since leaving the capital to go to Coventry on that fateful day. There were rumblings in the sky and flashes and explosions in the distance, but she knew in her heart that this was where she had to be. She joined her father in the porch. With his usual reserve, all he said was "Good to have you with me, Shirl! It's a busy night, but I think we can go home and wait there for the call to sound the all-clear."

Shirley still said little after that night of activity: either she sat all day in the window watching the traffic go by with unseeing eyes, or observed Eileen as she went about her tasks. At night, however, she was allowed to go out with her father, not on patrol but as far as Archie's house, where she stood in the porch for a while, keeping an eye on the area, until Eileen called her in for a hot drink. They would sit together by the fire saying little, until one evening, Shirley, almost without realizing what she was saying, but suddenly overcome by the urge to put the question to Eileen, asked: "Dear Eileen, when I came home, did you say that the same thing had happened to you? Did that mean you had lost a baby? I thought your son died in the First World War?"

Evidently startled, Eileen looked up from her knitting; she bit her lip, as her usual, imperturbable expression changed to one of infinite sadness, then she said, so softly that Shirley had to bend towards her to hear what she was saying: "Yes, dear, I did say that. It happened when I was giving birth to my twin boys. The birth of the first one was not easy, but he survived. The second one, his brother, did not."

She paused as if wondering whether to go on; then she decided to do so.

"As you know, dear, the older brother, Francis, died fighting in the Great War, but that was twenty years later." With that she turned back to her knitting.

Shirley found it impossible to believe that anyone could have suffered a greater loss than her own, yet here before her was this sweet, elderly lady recounting her own great tragedy, calmly and philosophically, suppressing her grief, which must still have been so keen.

She pulled her chair closer to Eileen and whispered, "Dear Eileen, you are so brave. You set me an amazing example."

Eileen turned to her and smiled. "Archie was brave too. We had no choice, dear. That's how things were. A friend of mine lost her three sons in the Battle of the Somme."

When she observed Eileen by day, the focus of Shirley's thoughts shifted dramatically. Instead of constantly regretting her own loss, she focused more on the losses other people had suffered in both wars – and there were many of them. Unwittingly, as she observed her relative, she grew fascinated by her movements: they were graceful, unhurried and more light-footed than many a dancer's. How was it, Shirley pondered, that she had not noticed this before? She doubted that Eileen had any experience of the ballet, but she held her slight figure with all the poise of a prima ballerina. How beautifully, thought Shirley, she would have played the part of a grieving heroine!

Gradually these observations began to reawaken her longing for the dance, though she did not feel inclined to resume her involvement in the ballet yet. Quite the contrary, some of her observations caused her to wonder why, if an elderly lady with no training in dance could move with such untutored elegance and style, had she herself spent so many years striving for the same effect?

Perhaps ballet was after all a waste of time. It certainly wasn't going to help her avenge the deaths of her fiancé and their baby. In the back of her mind, she was aware that this train of thought was not exactly logical, but it did help divert her attention from the morbid fixation on which it had been set. She decided that if Ted came home for Christmas as she hoped he would, she would discuss her next step with him. In the mean time, as she slowly recovered her drive and her interest in the course of events, she began to consider what paths were open to her. She had to do something effective: it was not enough to sit at home wallowing in grief and waiting for the War to end.

Christmas was approaching, but the question of her future involvement in the War effort continued to lurk at the back of her mind, although she appeared to be occupied with more pressing concerns. Since a trip into town was at present far too arduous, she was resigned to buying only sweets as Christmas presents for her father, Eileen and Archie. All that was required for that was to step outside and use her ration book with its accumulation of thirty-six unused points to buy whatever was available in Emily Fothergill's renovated sweetshop next door.

This she did one day in mid-December for the first time in five weeks, coming out to shop in daylight, as opposed to going out on patrol at night. Emily and Anastasia were of course surprised and pleased to see her, but were cautious in their approach for fear of upsetting her. Steering clear of all mention of air raids, the War, Coventry, illness, children, and of course babies, ballet and the theatre, there was little else to talk about, so they showered Shirley with such free gifts and samples as they had to hand. There were so many small items that Shirley was at a loss to find recipients for them.

"Have you thought of giving some of them to Tilly for her family?" Eileen asked.

"No, I'm not giving Tilly anything!" Shirley retorted.

"Why not?" Eileen enquired cautiously.

"I'm avoiding her, because I know that given the slightest chance, she will talk about all the details of little Albert's progress and all the funny things he's said and all the naughty things and the clever things he's done. I don't want to hear about them!"

Eileen said nothing to this tempestuous tirade and left Shirley to simmer down. She knew this was not the lively, generous Shirley she knew and loved like a granddaughter. This was a Shirley still suffering in a nervous, depressed state of mind, unable to control her emotions: only time and patience would heal that wound.

Tilly came to work in the shop as usual, but Shirley avoided her. The former naturally found Shirley's disregard hurtful because, as Albert's rescuer in the Blitz, Shirley was deemed to have a special role in his life. It was only when Eileen took Tilly aside and gently explained to her the reasons for Shirley's behaviour that Tilly understood the need for restraint. She was so upset for Shirley that she wanted to apologize for all her tactless remarks about her little Albert.

"I had no idea! I'm so sorry for Shirley; please let me tell her I didn't want to upset her!" said she to Eileen, but the latter managed to convince her that that was not necessary.

Unfortunately Tilly's reaction was to tiptoe around Shirley, glancing anxiously at her and speaking in a whisper, which was almost worse than all her parental delight and enthusiasm at little Albert's progress.

Slowly Shirley's depression wore off, so that in the run-up to Christmas, after much deliberation, Eileen persuaded her to relent from her original plan of excluding Tilly from her present list. Shirley duly felt guilty, but that was better than feeling depressed, so for her presents, an emboldened Shirley went further afield than the sweetshop, to the church Christmas bazaar, held in the hall of the primary school. There she found knitted gloves, hats and scarves, even a knitted rabbit for Albert, and prettily embroidered handkerchiefs and home-made lavender bags as well, so that her near and dear, including Tilly and her family, would have more than just sweets in their stockings.

She also found a touchingly warm and discreet welcome from the ladies running the bazaar and serving the teas. She was after all the heroine of the borough as a result of her display of extraordinary courage when the bombs had dropped on home territory. The beneficial effects of this sortie became evident that evening when she sat down to supper with her father and, to his astonishment, ate a hearty meal. Between mouthfuls she smilingly told him of the lovely atmosphere at the bazaar and even hinted that she might go out again sometime.

Nevertheless, the relaxation and the smile hid the re-emergence of another of her qualities, that steely will which was already contemplating its next move. She hoped to be able to discuss her latest plan with her brother, having contemplated the possibility of joining the Free French and being airlifted into northern France as an undercover agent. The problem was that no one knew whether Ted would come home for Christmas, so that plan could not be put into immediate effect.

In any case, frustrated by her own inactivity and wanting to keep all options open, she resolved to go down to the recruiting office in a further attempt to join the WAAF. She told no one of this resolve because of the inevitable attempts to dissuade her. At the same time she started practising her balletic exercises again, not with a view to taking up the ballet, but to be sure of recovering as much as possible of her athleticism and fitness for the interview, or whatever else she might be subjected to.

One morning in mid-December, spurred on by more wholesale bombing of the City of London, which she and her father witnessed from Archie's porch while the residents of the area were safely sheltering in their bunkers, she slipped out early, and went along to the recruiting office. There was no queue, so she went straight to the counter and asked to sign up for the WAAF, the Women's Auxiliary Air Force. Behind the counter a seemingly dignified man with a handlebar moustache, who had taken the place of the younger clerks – the men now away working in munitions factories, the women in the country as Land Girls – surveyed her with an ill-concealed sneer and a curl of his bristly lip.

"Are you really sure that's what you want, young lady?" he enquired loftily, as if uncertain that he had heard her unlikely request correctly.

"Yes, please, I said the WAAF," Shirley repeated loudly and firmly, suspecting that he might be deaf.

"Hm, of course many young women like the uniforms, but there's more to it than that," the white-haired clerk declared sternly. "There are forms to fill in and you have to have a medical, you know, and then they might, or they might not accept you."

"All right, but please would you bring the forms and arrange for me to see someone?" Shirley insisted, determined not to be put off by this man who had most likely been demobilized from the forces on account of his age, but still wanted to assert his authority.

He marched off to another room and came back some minutes later with a sheaf of papers. With obvious reluctance he handed the forms over. Since the office was otherwise empty, she grasped the opportunity to make good use of the time.

"I'm perfectly fit, so can I see the doctor straight away?" she persisted, to the man's annoyance.

"At present we don't have a doctor here," he admitted irritably. "He's away on, er... he's away."

Presumably he had stopped himself just in time from saying "he's away on exercises", or something similar.

"So *I* have to ask you if you have seen a doctor lately?"

"Yes," answered Shirley, ready for what was coming next, "only a couple of months ago."

"And what did he say?"

"He gave me a clean bill of health," Shirley replied, embellishing some-what on the verdict of Elsie's doctor friend that she was well enough to travel back to London from Coventry.

After that exchange Shirley simply filled in the forms, although she was concerned by the question of whether she had any experience of flying – and to that she felt obliged to answer truthfully: "No." Having known Alan so closely and listened to him enthusing about the Spitfire, she reckoned would not be enough.

"You'll receive an appointment shortly," the old man snarled through gritted teeth. He did not like this type of interview, nor this cheeky little blonde flibbertigibbet of a candidate for the WAAF. What did she think she was playing at? However, he had a job to do, and he was always proud that he did it well, no matter how troublesome the candidates.

That evening, Shirley was debating whether to tell her father where she had been that day when their supper was interrupted by the arrival of a visitor. The shop was closed but he let himself in through the private entrance and came up the stairs. Reggie and Shirley smiled at each other in happy anticipation of the visitor's identity. As they had judged by the footfall on the stairs, it was Ted, not an intruder, though his beard was certainly an effective disguise. He came into the living room, and as usual he was as tired and as dirty as ever.

Shirley was tempted to tell him to take his muddy boots off, but that would have been a poor welcome home, so instead she gave him a hug and asked only if he was hungry.

"I could eat a horse – I haven't eaten in two days," he exclaimed wearily.

"Well, we haven't got a horse for you, but we do have a black pudding hotpot that Eileen cooked for us. It's full of potatoes, carrots, onions and herbs." Then she added hastily, to ward off any complaints, "It will fill you up and it's really delicious, isn't it, Pa?"

Reggie nodded in albeit a rather unconvincing show of appreciation, so Ted, who in any case was too tired to complain, sat down to a nutritious meal.

Shirley washed his clothes that evening and left them to dry in front of the fire. Ted disappeared upstairs to his attic and by the morning was gone again, leaving only a scrap of paper, saying, *"Thanks for the meal and the clean clothes. Sorry I have to leave again so soon."* His early departure was annoying, because there had been no chance to discuss her plans for becoming a secret agent with him, but given past experience, it was not surprising that he had left so soon. Reggie hid his disappointment by going down to the shop earlier than usual and staying down there until lunchtime.

Christmas was by no means as dire as had been expected only weeks beforehand. Shirley's presents were received with genuine gratitude, whilst everyone among the small circle of friends and family treated her quite normally, without showing any traces of sympathy for her suffering, which she had expressly wanted.

In fact, she had told her father so, and he had told Eileen, who had conveyed the message as requested. Eileen cooked a goose from the family farm and Reggie provided paper decorations from the shop. Tilly and her mother, now temporarily re-housed after the collapse of their house in the Blitz, invited Mme Belinskaya and Emily Fothergill to join them in the evening, so Shirley, spared the presence of little Albert, was able to relax and summon a modicum of enjoyment again, as she and her father played whist with Archie and Eileen.

12

In late December, only days before Christmas, when still no communication from the RAF had dropped through the letterbox, Shirley in her impatience, had decided to pay a further visit to the recruitment office to give that unpleasant man a piece of her mind. Anxious not to be seen, because she still had a guilty conscience about going on this mission without telling her father, even though she would soon come of age, she chose to go out in the middle of the morning when she was sure that he was in the shop, safely out of the way. The truth was that she did not want to worry him – and she knew he would be worried about a course of action which, if successful, would inevitably bring its dangers, dangers that she herself embraced wholeheartedly.

The objectionable, elderly man with the handlebar moustache was no longer at the counter, where his place had been taken by a plump, middle-aged woman.

"I want to join the WAAF, the Women's Auxiliary Air Force, and I was expecting to have heard from them by now, so I want to know what has become of my application," Shirley declared in no uncertain terms.

Taken aback by the abrupt manner, the woman replied with due caution. "I'm sorry about that," she said with a friendly smile. "Let me fetch the files."

Relieved at the change of personnel and at this reception, so much pleasanter than on the previous occasion, Shirley's mood mellowed, but when, on the clerk's return, she announced cheerfully that there were plenty of vacancies for secretaries with good typing skills in the WAAF, for cooks to feed the pilots, for mechanics and practically anything else of use at the RAF bases, Shirley bristled with irritation.

"No, no, you don't understand, I want to fly!" she exclaimed. Startled, the woman stared at her.

"I'm sorry. You're right, I don't understand. You see, women are not allowed to *fly* in the WAAF." She slowly put down the unopened file and thought hard before coming up with a suggestion. "Perhaps you mean the ATA, the Air Transport Auxiliary, what they call the 'ATA girls'? Please wait a moment while I fetch those files."

During the wait Shirley realized that it was not the clerk who was at fault, but she herself. How stupid of her to have forgotten that it was the ATA, not the WAAF she should have asked for! Her mistake took her back to the days – which seemed a hundred years ago – before the catastrophe that was Coventry, before her miscarriage, even before her mother's ill-fated visit, when she had first applied to join up, and had been examined by a doctor who had told her that he could not approve her application because she was pregnant.

She drummed her fingers on the desk. Even if her memory had let her down, she certainly was not going to apply to cook for the Air Force – she had done enough of that at home – and despite her pa being an engineer, she did not fancy getting covered in oil. As for typing, that was out of the question because she had never learnt how to do it. Then she remembered that what seemed like ages ago, but was in fact only weeks or months at most, she had filched a newspaper cutting from this very office about the Air Transport Auxiliary and seen photos of glamorous girls leaning on the wings of aeroplanes. That cutting must have gone into the wastepaper basket and naturally enough had completely gone from her mind in the turmoil since then. It really was the ATA that she had intended to apply for, and she should have asked for that, not the WAAF.

The woman returned with more files, which she spread out on the counter. There seemed to be no reference to the earlier application. In all likelihood it had never been sent off: obviously that ex-army officer simply had not bothered with it. He had probably thrown it away.

"Oh, wait a minute!" said the lady clerk, poring over the papers. "It says here that the ATA is now separate from the RAF and is based at White Waltham. That's near Maidenhead in Berkshire, not too far away. Incidentally, you will have to take some form of identification. A passport would be best if you have one – do you?" This was a question that was not problematic.

"Oh, yes," Shirley said airily, "I do have one of those." She crossed her fingers behind her back, trusting that her passport had not expired.

"Then I think the best thing would be for me to make an appointment for you to go there and talk to them. Would you like that? I'll ring them straight away if you like."

This offer was music to Shirley's ears. At last she was making progress. "Yes, please!" she exclaimed, grateful for this woman, the first person in the recruitment office to have taken her seriously. "That would be wonderful!"

Confirmation of an appointment for the 2nd of January came through, enclosing directions to take the train to Maidenhead and then a bus to the ATA base.

"I'm going to see about a job in Berkshire," she told her father the night before the appointment while he was listening to the news.

"How will you get there?" he asked. "Shall I drive you?"

"No, it's not difficult. I'll take the train and then a bus," she replied casually, suppressing her excitement.

"What's it for?" he then asked.

"I'll tell you when I get back," she said with a mischievous smile.

He was too busy with his ear to the wireless listening to the reports of the bombing of Italy to take much notice.

Thus it was that on a fine day at the beginning of January 1941, Shirley took the train to Maidenhead and then a bus from outside the station to the airbase at White Waltham only a couple of miles away. So far, so good, she thought on showing her still-valid passport at the gate, from where she was directed to the main building. Outside the HQ she paused in astonishment, because she seemed to have stepped through her own particular looking-glass. She stood mesmerized at the sight of the humming activity on the green airfield, where planes of all shapes and sizes were parked; some were being readied for take-off, some were being fuelled, others serviced by an army of mechanics who ran in and out of the row of hangars adjacent to the main building.

Further away, across the field, planes were soaring into the sky from an airstrip one by one, filling the air with the roar of their accelerating engines. Her heart missed a beat when she turned a corner and saw a tall pilot, dressed in a brown leather jacket and trousers with goggles perched on his helmet, emerge from a shed fifty yards or so away. He walked over to a small plane on the concrete apron: the plane was unmistakeably a Spitfire! Was that Alan? She was about to run after him and grab him by the sleeve, but when he turned to wave to one of his mechanics, she saw his face. It was not Alan's; it bore no resemblance to his at all. How could it have been Alan's? He was dead. She took a deep breath to steady herself before entering the headquarters.

Her instructions were to ask for Flight Lieutenant Leigh. He proved to be a stout, elderly officer who welcomed her with a heart-warming smile, as though she were a long-lost friend, before ushering her into his office where the windows opposite the door, looking out onto the airfield, were criss-crossed with protective, white sticky tape. Otherwise the office was bare, furnished with only a couple of chairs and a desk on which there was a telephone. One of the three other walls was covered with pictures of every imaginable type of aircraft.

"We have to be well-aware of how to fly each and every one of these aircraft," the Flight Lieutenant said jovially. "They're all different and we never know in advance which one we might be required to bring from a factory or a repair workshop to an airbase." He pointed to a large aircraft, "See here, this is a Hurricane at one end of the scale. It's a fighter, you know." Then he indicated a small plane. "And I'm sure you'll recognize what this is?"

Her face fell, and the words stuck in her throat. "It's a Spitfire, isn't it?" she stuttered.

He turned to look at her and raised an eyebrow quizzically before pointing to the maps, marked with red dots and lengths of red string connecting the dots on the other two walls. "These are our routes," he said, "and they show the factories and the repair workshops and the airbases."

Gesturing to her to sit down, the Flight Lieutenant asked, "Well, Miss Marlow, I gather you are interested in joining up with the Air Transport Auxiliary? That's good news! We shall be delighted to have you with us! You do know, don't you, Air Transport Auxiliary is what the letters ATA stand for?"

"Yes, yes, I do know that," Shirley replied, irritated at such a basic question, yet she hid her irritation because the Flight Lieutenant was so pleasant.

"Well," he asked, "what can you offer to do for us? We need typists, cooks, even lady mechanics…" His voice trailed off when he saw the sheer indignation written across her face.

"I've come here because I want to learn to fly!" she retorted somewhat more forcibly than intended. "I thought this was where women could fly planes; I know they can't fly in battle, but as you said, I do know that they can collect and deliver planes to the bases where they're needed! I want to fly a Spitfire!" She waved a hand towards the map covering the two walls.

"Hold on, young lady!" he exclaimed with a laugh. "Women do fly planes, just as you've said, but not from here any longer. Here we only have men pilots; the women's branch of the ATA has moved to the De Havilland airfield at Hatfield." Then he added more gently, "I'm sorry, I should have realized; I can see that you aren't applying to be a cook or wash dishes."

Shirley gritted her teeth.

Flight Lieutenant Leigh proved to be perceptive and considerate: he folded his arms on the desk and leaned over to enquire in a confidential tone, "Can you tell me why this means so much to you, Miss Marlow? Flying, in the first place, and flying Spitfires in particular?"

Emboldened, Shirley told him about Alan, but only in outline, because she sensed that she might be making a fool of herself and thereby jeopardizing her chances of ever being allowed to fly.

"I see," said Flight Lieutenant Leigh. When eventually he spoke, it was with hesitation. "Er, was your fiancé's name Alan Harding?" he enquired.

Such was her astonishment that Shirley was rendered speechless, scarcely able to nod.

"I recall seeing him and hearing about him," he said. "I wasn't really acquainted with him myself, but he had been at the same base as me for a time before I retired, so we had hailed each other in passing, so to speak. He was a true hero, no question about that."

The brief recollection ended hardly had it begun; it invited no response, because the Flight Lieutenant quickly changed the subject.

"I tell you what I'll do: I'll ring the ATA in Hatfield and arrange for you to go and see them. You'll probably meet Pauline Gower there. She's in charge of the women's ATA. Are you free any time?"

Shirley forced herself to collect her stunned senses. "Yes, of course... I'm afraid it's all still too raw," she stammered by way of explanation for her shaking hands and evident pallor: her head spun bloodlessly while her body, particularly her left leg, went limp.

"Of course, I understand." His tone was sympathetic now. "Just go into the waiting room and sit down, would you, while I make a phone call and find out when they can see you?" he replied. "I'll ask my secretary to bring you a glass of water – or perhaps a cup of sweet tea?"

He came out ten minutes later.

"I've made an appointment for you to go to Hatfield in four days' time, that's the 6th of January. Is that all right for you?"

"Oh, thank you!" Shirley cried with a faint smile as she still struggled to recover from the shock of hearing Alan's name mentioned by this stranger, who had had some slight connection with him.

"Yes, that's fine," she said, on reflection. "Today's Thursday the 2nd, so the 6th must be Monday – is that right?"

"Indeed it is, young lady!" he replied. He glanced out of the window. "Look. It's a nice, fine day. I've half an hour to spare and there are plenty of planes standing idle out there on the apron, not much enemy action either. Would you like me to take you up for a quick spin if they'll give me clearance?"

Unable to believe her luck, Shirley's spirits revived; she could have fallen at his feet in gratitude. She took a sip of tea to fortify herself and murmured breathlessly, "I'd love that!"

"Right, I'll call my assistant to fit you out with a flight suit, helmet and goggles, while I see about clearance for us, and then off we go!" he said.

Shirley cut a comical, ungainly figure in the flight suit, the helmet and goggles, all several sizes too large for her, as she walked out, shuffling slightly, to a small plane, a Tiger Moth, standing in front of the main building.

"Have you flown before?" Flight Lieutenant Leigh asked casually. He was also dressed in a flight suit, his goggles perched on his helmet. Wishing to appear more knowledgeable than she really was, Shirley longed to be able to fudge an answer and say "Yes, with Alan" or "with my father" or "with my brother", or even "on one of those flights at the seaside", but none of these would be true and it wasn't worth being caught out in such special circumstances.

"No, not yet," she answered.

"Ah," was the only reply from the flight officer, eloquent in its brevity. "Well, never mind, we'll hoist you into the front seat, and you must strap yourself in," he said. "This is a training aircraft; I will be sitting behind you where the instructor normally sits. You'll get a really good view, because the engine is upside down out of the way. Don't worry, I will be manning the controls. You don't have to do anything."

He produced a tube and some headphones.

"Wear these headphones and speak into this Gosport tube if there's a problem. They're not very good, so you'll have to shout, and you probably won't be able to hear anything I say, even if I shout, so listen carefully now."

Shirley was certainly not going to allow herself to be hoisted; she had watched other pilots climbing into their cockpits and so, despite that annoying weakness in her left leg, leapt into the front seat, to the surprise of all the inquisitive onlookers of whom, by this stage, there were several. Trying to contain her excitement, as if she were on her first visit to Father Christmas, she did as she was told, but paying attention to the instructions was hard when all she wanted was to be airborne as quickly as possible.

The Flight Lieutenant climbed into the open cockpit, strapped himself in and, seconds later, a fitter began turning the propeller a couple of times, and then called "Contact!"

The pilot repeated "Contact!" and on the next pull on the propeller, the engine started. Shirley waited on tenterhooks for the plane to move, which it did soon afterwards with a jolt; then rather bumpily it headed, not on tarmac but across the grass, to the airstrip, where it joined a queue of small aircraft lining up for take-off. By her side there was a small mirror. She looked into it and saw Flight Lieutenant Leigh's reflection giving her a "thumbs up". Evidently, they were ready for take-off. The plane ahead of them in the queue revved its engine and began to taxi down the runway, sending gusts of air in its wake. Faster and faster it ran until it lifted effortlessly into the sky.

Next it was the turn of the Tiger Moth: the engine roared, the wind rushed in her face and Shirley clung on, willing the small plane to move faster and faster, to leave the ground and rise up and up towards the sun. When it rose from the airstrip, she cried out for joy: the earth was disappearing behind and below her, houses, churches, trees, cars, lorries and roads shrank to the size of toys, and her mind, her body and her soul grew wings with which to fly away from all earthly sorrows and constraints. At last she began to understand what Alan had experienced, and why he was so passionate about flying. If she never came back to earth, it really wouldn't matter, for this was tantamount to communing intimately with him: it was so much more momentous than anything that lay below.

The tears streaming down her cheeks at the wonder and the emotion of it all, were whisked away like raindrops on the wind, but her face was still damp, as though the droplets were blowing back onto it. She soon discovered where they were coming from when the plane entered a small bank of cloud which sent out its moist, wispy tentacles to embrace the airborne travellers. Shivering at the chill touch of the mist, she wondered how the pilot could navigate through this blank, whitish-grey sea of fog. In the mirror, she saw his hand raised as if he were saying, "Don't worry; we'll soon be out of this." She was not at all concerned: quite the contrary, she was ecstatic at finding herself up among the clouds, cold and wet though they were, and marvelled at the sublime sensation of being weightless in the heavens.

The plane shook off the coils of fluffy cloud and turned away from the sun, which previously in the south had shone directly ahead. Now it sent its rays over to the east, illuminating a blue seascape in the far distance, beyond which a hazy line, perhaps a coastline, came into view. Her heart thumped in her chest and her head spun: it had to be France over there, her beloved France, torn apart and suffering under Nazi domination! How deceptively calm that blue stretch of water between the two countries appeared today!

It was that stretch of water that she and Ted had crossed last year by night in Uncle François's little fishing boat, in advance of the Nazi invasion, and it was that same stretch of water that had taken Alan to his grave six months ago. Ted was over there somewhere in France, and Grandfather Pépé and Céline, Louise and Charlot. What had become of them all? If thoughts alone could have kept that one little plane airborne, Shirley's would have been sufficient to fly a squadron. How she longed to stay circling the earth, always close to Alan, in sight of France, never coming down to the horrible reality of everyday life on the war-torn planet beneath! But the plane had begun its descent, turning until it faced north-west, and the magic slowly evaporated.

She did not leap out of the Tiger Moth when it came to a halt outside the headquarters. Instead, moved to her very core, she stayed rooted to her seat, reluctant to separate herself from the physical contact with the machine that had opened her eyes to a drastically different view of existence. Everything on earth was paltry by comparison with all that she had seen and experienced above it. Even worse was the horror that the human race was perpetrating on the innocence of creation. That vision – one might even say a religious vision – of perfection that she had seen was unattainable in the greed and violence of life down below on the ground.

It was with a sober heart that she thanked Flight Lieutenant Leigh. With the greatest reluctance, she made her way home, still floating, living in a different world, way above the earth. All was quiet in the flat. Her father had left a note on the table telling her that he had gone out to an ARP meeting and would probably go for a drink in the pub afterwards. She was glad of the chance to sit quietly and relive the extraordinary events of the day without having to explain them to anyone else. Thanks to Flight Lieutenant Leigh she had discovered what it was like to fly: "out of this world", was the only way to describe it, yet it had been disconcerting because it had revealed a side of herself, a thoughtful side, with which she was not very familiar, yet instantly it dawned on her that this was an element which was ever present in the type of ballet, classical ballet, that she loved the most.

Good principal dancers were bound through their performance to make the audience think about the role they were portraying, and react in their souls to that role. The execution of the steps was simply not enough, nor was the presentation of a beautiful spectacle. She had, she remembered, had a similar revelation some time previously when she had become aware that there was more to ballet than a perfect technique. Today's discovery about herself began to sow the seeds of doubt in her mind. Did she really want to abandon the ballet, she asked herself, for, inevitably, joining the ATA would demand that sacrifice. She heard her father's footsteps on the stairs and went out to greet him.

"Ah, Shirl! So you're home!" he exclaimed. "Now, where did you say you were going today?"

"Well, since you ask, Pa – I've been up in an aeroplane!"

13

Four days later, on the train to Hatfield, she laughed to herself at the recollection of her father's astounded reaction to the news of her flight at White Waltham: he had almost lost his grip on the banister and narrowly avoided falling backwards down the stairs. Nonetheless, she had not been prepared for the disappointment on his face, nor his first question when he regained his balance.

"Oh, why didn't you tell me? I should have loved to come and watch even if I couldn't go up too!" Explanations, more explanations than Shirley had anticipated, were then required. She tailored them, admitting that she had applied to join the RAF and had gone to White Waltham for an interview. A nice officer had taken pity on her when he saw her disappointment at the limitations on women's involvement in the service, and had offered to take her up for a spin. She did not mention the ATA, preferring to leave that for another day – next Monday at Hatfield, perhaps.

"So what does the RAF allow women to do?" Reggie was anxious to know.

"Oh, that was disappointing – only menial tasks, cooking and cleaning and so on, and office work, typing and that sort of thing."

"I thought they mapped flight paths and positions," her father butted in.

"No, no one said anything about that," she corrected him. "Well anyhow, we women are not allowed to fly in the RAF and that's that!" she said with a shrug, which was not enough to satisfy her pa, whose interest was well and truly aroused.

"That's strange," he remarked, leaning on the rail on the landing. "I'm sure I've heard mention of a branch where women do fly, transport planes, or something. I think it was in the papers not so long ago, but I don't think I could lay my hands on that article. It won't be there among the old papers any more."

"Maybe you're right; maybe there is an air transport section," Shirley said cagily. "I'll keep looking."

Reggie evidently wished he had not been quite so spontaneous and promptly let the subject drop: it was bad enough losing that fine chap Alan – who, according to his daughter, was her fiancé – in an air battle, but the prospect of losing her in the same way made his blood run cold. Reading his mind, she was quite content to say no more.

Leaving home for Hatfield that next Monday morning, the 6th of January, was not straightforward. Shirley was guiltily aware of being even more surreptitious about this second venture than about the previous one, and not only that, but she sensed her father's eyes on her when she put her hat and coat on and picked up her bag. Although the shop was open, he had come upstairs: she knew that he was watching her.

"Out again, are you, Shirl? Off to some other airfield?" he asked, the unease audible in his voice.

"Oh, I'll tell you when I come back; I must dash, I'm late already," she called over her shoulder as she made for the stairs. Although her appointment was not until midday, leaving early was essential since she had to cross London to King's Cross to catch the train to Hatfield, and that would take for ever because wartime services were so unreliable. In the event, that early departure was justified because the journey across London did take a long time, first by overground train and then by Underground, with the result that on reaching King's Cross, she had to run for her train. Once aboard, she felt herself to be covered in grime and soot, so it was a relief to have a compartment to herself. She stood up to look in the mirror, combed her hair and applied more lipstick, which she then rubbed off because she wasn't sure that it was appropriate for the day's meeting. Her elegant appearance had not bothered her four days ago; indeed it might well have turned out to be an advantage in her encounter with Flight Lieutenant Leigh, but today seemed different, most likely because the interviewer would be a woman – had he said her name was Pauline Gower? – who might not take kindly to a recruit plastered in make-up.

Hatfield turned out to be a rather small railway station in an unexpectedly rural setting, but the bus ride to the airfield soon revealed the development of an urban area near the huge airfield. On the airfield itself, modern white buildings stood out against the unremitting grey cloud-cover and spoke of the wealth of activity in all aspects of warfare, as well as the progress in modern inventions taking place there. At the gate Shirley asked for Ferry Pool number 5, as instructed by Flight Lieutenant Leigh.

"You'll be wanting the ATA girls, will you, miss?" the gatekeeper enquired, grinning. "It's over there."

"Yes, that's right, the ATA," she replied, her head held high, already imagining herself to be one of the elite members of that coveted group. She made her way to Ferry Pool 5, where she was admitted to a waiting room which served both candidates and the established pilots of the ATA.

She stood in the doorway, suddenly unsure of herself at the sight of a crowd of young women in uniform, mostly well made-up, lounging in armchairs and on sofas, chatting or reading newspapers. Their clipped accents and nonchalant poses reminded her all too uncomfortably of that terrible evening at the Dorchester, when she had emerged from the ladies' room to find a group of similar girls draping themselves about her darling Alan's person. Her self-confidence, previously so clear and assertive, sank into a foggy morass of uncertainty, like the clouds overhead.

From time to time one or other of the girls would ease herself languidly out of an armchair and go over to the window to survey the sky.

"Hmm," a tall girl drawled, "it really doesn't look like flying today, if you ask me."

"Oh! What a waste of a day!" a pretty brunette joined in, "Why don't they make up their minds and tell us we can go home? There's a party in town I want to go to tonight."

"Oh joy! Whose party is that?" they all asked eagerly.

"It's Charlie's. Do you know him? He's my brother's best friend; he's on leave," the brunette replied with a dismissive air, which was meant to imply that she was not intending all her daytime colleagues to accompany her. Her dismissive air did not have the desired effect, for immediately there came a chorus in reply.

"Oh, of course," one girl exclaimed, "I had an invitation and must have lost it!"

"I haven't been home in ages, so I wouldn't have seen it anyhow," another declared excitedly. "Where did you say the party was going to be?"

Details of Charlie's party were passed around, so that even those who had not been invited found themselves with a delightful prospect for the evening. Nevertheless, they sprang to attention when an older woman, an officer, came into the room.

"It doesn't look like a good day for flying, girls, but you'll have to wait a little longer, then I promise you I'll let you know whether you can leave," she announced, while scanning the room. "Ah, Miss Marlow," she said to Shirley, whose well-chosen civilian clothes marked her out as not one of the team. "Please follow me."

The officer's room followed the same pattern as Flight Lieutenant Leigh's, except that there were fewer lines of red string crossing the map, which covered only one wall, and the map showed only the British Isles, not the whole of Europe.

"Do sit down, Miss Marlow," the woman said; her tone was cool, businesslike, a touch bored perhaps at having to interview yet another hopeful. "What brings you here?" she went on, keeping her eyes fixed on papers on her desk.

Shirley was caught off-guard. If she had been expecting a warm reception after that meeting with Flight Lieutenant Leigh which had gone so well, and if she were hoping that he might have prepared the way for her, she was mistaken.

"I would like to join the ATA," she ventured hesitantly.

"Have you flown before?" the woman asked abruptly, not only keeping her eyes on her papers but also flicking through them.

"Yes, just once," Shirley replied, her voice faltering.

"So you haven't had flying lessons, then?" came the sharp rejoinder.

"No, but I should like to: perhaps I might…"

It was impossible to get a whole sentence in edgeways, because the woman kept shooting questions at her and interrupting her replies.

"Do you know how much they cost?"

"No, but…"

"I have to tell you" – this final interruption was clearly intended to bring the meeting to a close – "they are very expensive, probably much more than you could afford, and we don't offer training here. What's more, you are just one of the two thousand applicants for twelve places!"

Her self-confidence fired by this rebuff, Shirley seethed with indignation, and was on the point of telling the officer what she thought of such a casual dismissal of her patriotic zeal and her willingness to risk her life in the cause of her country, when the door opened. An ashen-faced secretary went straight over to the seated figure at the desk and whispered in her ear. The expression of the seemingly imperturbable officer registered shock and disbelief.

"Show Miss Barlow out at once, please – and tell the girls they can go home," she demanded before dashing out of the room.

"This way, please, Miss Barlow," said the secretary. Shirley followed her, aware that this was not the time to correct the misspelling of her name.

On the way home, indignation and incomprehension combined to give Shirley plenty to mull over. Certainly, if that was how the ATA operated, she might find it very unpleasant, intolerable, even if she could resign herself to being an outsider among those girls, which would not come naturally to her. Of course, there had to be discipline in the RAF, just as in the ballet, though admittedly there did exist a huge disparity, that of danger, between the two disciplines. The RAF dealt with real matters of life and death, and no one could pretend that was true of the ballet. Shirley's disappointment was the greater because her hopes had been so high after Flight Lieutenant Leigh's friendly welcome, his admiration of Alan, and above all, the joyride he had so spontaneously offered her.

Then she reviewed the weird conclusion of that day's interview. Undoubtedly the officer was keen to dismiss her because she fulfilled none of the requirements, given that keenness to join up was evidently not a requirement, but what was it that the secretary had said to her to make her leave the room so hurriedly – with not so much as a by-your-leave? Shirley guessed that there must have been a crisis somewhere, but what could it be? It was unlikely that any minor crisis would hit the news headlines. Ruminating on this unfathomable situation, she resolved to listen to the BBC News in case there had been a catastrophe, a lost plane perhaps in the ATA. She wondered if she would ever receive any acknowledgement of her interview, and resolved there and then not to be disappointed if she never heard from the ATA again. If not, she asked herself, what other paths might be open to allow her to participate in the war effort more than she was already doing?

The journey back was slower than the one on the way out, so when she reached South Cross her father had already gone out on patrol. She made herself a bowl of potato and onion soup, turned on the wireless and sat down at the table to listen to the early evening news. It consisted almost solely of reports of the Australian victory in Libya, where the city of Bardia had been taken with 25,000 enemy troops and seven generals captured, but there was nothing about the ATA at De Havilland's in Hatfield, so whatever it was that had brought her interview to a close must have been a minor upset, although it had not appeared to be so at the time. She turned the wireless off. With some regret that she would not be dressing up in the Air Transport Auxiliary uniform, she took off her modest, everyday costume, one that her mother had made for her several years ago, and replaced it with her Air Raid Precautions fatigues and helmet.

She intended to go out into the dark night to look for her father, leaving Cousin Archie manning the phone in the shop, but he caught sight of her before she could slip out. "Had a good day?" he called out in his usual cheery fashion.

"No, not really," she said, "but I'd better not stop to chat, because I must go and find Pa. Do you know where he might be? I had to leave in a hurry early this morning and didn't have time to ask what route he would be taking tonight."

"I'm not sure," Cousin Archie was saying when the phone rang. He picked it up at once, beckoning to Shirley to stay with him. "Right-ho," he said to the caller, "we'll sound the alarm at once." But Shirley had grabbed the key to the control box and was already out of the shop, running over to the church porch to switch on the siren. It whirred into action and moaned its way through the chill night air, disturbing sleeping babies and annoying the local inhabitants.

Outside, the ack-ack guns were not firing and there were no barrage balloons overhead, as would have been expected if a raid were imminent, leaving Shirley uncertain whether to discourage the stream of residents from leaving their homes or to send them to the air-raid shelters, either the public ones in the park, or the ones in their own back gardens. The siren was howling at the top of its register when a tiny pinpoint of light from a torch appeared a few yards away, advancing towards her.

"Shirley! Shirley! Are you there?" she heard Archie's voice shouting out.

"Yes, over here!" she called back.

"Well then, turn the siren off! It's a false alarm."

Shirley did as he said, with an exasperated sigh in anticipation of the complaints there would be in the shop and the abject apologies she, her father and Archie would have to offer the following morning. She heard the voices of the local population out in the streets, where the residents were obediently making their way to the shelters, and ran to assure them that all was well after all, and they could return home, praising them for their quick reactions to a false alarm. On her way she ran into her father.

"What's going on?" he wanted to know.

"Just a false alarm," she assured him. "Thank goodness they don't happen very often, or we'd have a riot on our hands."

Once they had ushered their protégés back to their homes, father and daughter walked the rounds together.

"So, miss," Reggie remarked rather reproachfully, "that's twice you've gone shooting out of the house with not so much as a goodbye. I know you're nearly twenty-one and you don't have to tell me what you're up to, but I would like to know where you're going in case there's a raid, and then I would know whether you're safe or whether I should be worrying about you."

"Yes, I'm sorry, Pa, but I didn't want to worry you unnecessarily, so that's why I didn't tell you. Anyhow, you know enough about White Waltham last week, and today I went to Hatfield to the De Havilland airfield, because that's where the ATA girls are now stationed. I was hoping to join them."

"And have you?" came his immediate question.

"No, I think that's very unlikely," she replied, "but there was something odd going on there and I don't understand it at all." She recounted what she had seen and heard, but Reggie was not able to shed any light on the strange situation.

They walked on in silence, her father trying hard not to express his joy that his daughter was unlikely to take to the skies. They were nearly home when he broke the silence, exclaiming, "I knew that De Havilland's rang a bell! Isn't that where that woman pilot is stationed now? What's her name? Amy something, isn't it? Did you see her?"

"You mean Amy Johnson, the solo round-the-world pilot? No, I didn't see her, but I think she's based there."

She cast her mind over that visit. Was there anyone in the waiting room who might have resembled Amy Johnson? she asked herself. No, Amy Johnson was certainly not there. She would have recognized her, because her face was famous from so much press and newsreel coverage. Had Amy Johnson been there she might have been tempted to pluck up the courage to ask her for her autograph, though undoubtedly those other girls would have laughed at her presumption. Perhaps she was having a day off, or maybe she was out ferrying a plane to a depot or an airfield. It was odd, though, because all the other pilots had been grounded on account of the thick cloud cover everywhere. At last that was clearing and as it did so, it brought with it the fear of an enemy attack, which did not happen, but had given rise to the false alarm.

Although the threat of enemy action appeared to have receded, the day's dramas were not over. No sooner had she and her father settled down in front of the fire, clasping steaming cups of very watery cocoa in their cold hands, than the doorbell rang and kept on ringing frantically. Shirley, who had nearly fallen asleep, groaned. "Oh, no! What is it now?" she grumbled, pulling herself up out of the comfortable depths of a shabby, old armchair. There was nothing for it; her father was not agile enough to run downstairs, so she would have to answer the bell. There on the doorstep stood a forlorn figure, easily recognizable even in the dim light of a waning moon. Madame Belinskaya was leaning against the door frame, an old blanket round her shoulders, trembling and wailing.

Her attempts to speak English, which were still only haphazard, were unintelligible, so Shirley addressed her in French. Madame's reason for being there then came tumbling out in a curious hybrid mixture of French and Russian, which was scarcely more intelligible than her English. Ushering her indoors out of the cold, Shirley led her into the shop and sat her down on the chair from where Archie usually pronounced his droll observations when not working behind the counter. Eventually she succeeded in interpreting the gist of Madame's hysterical utterances: Mrs Fothergill next door had collapsed on the floor and did not appear to be breathing. Shirley grabbed the phone and summoned an ambulance.

The next morning, her pa came lumbering up the stairs no sooner than he had gone down to open the shop. "You'll be sorry to see this, Shirl," he said, spreading out the newspaper in front of her at the dining table: there was no escaping the news on the front pages of all the papers, and on the wireless throughout the day. Amy Johnson had disappeared on an ATA flight from Prestwick to Kidlington; she was thought to have strayed off course in the dense cloud and to have come down in the Thames. The search for her was extensive, but hope was fading for her survival.

Closer to home, Shirley phoned the hospital mid-morning and was given the news that Emily Fothergill had not survived the heart attack that had struck her in the turmoil after the siren sounded the false alarm, and had died in the night. Shirley grieved at the sad end of the poor old lady who at long last, after so much loss and sorrow, had begun to enjoy life with her new friend Anastasia Belinskaya.

14

In that month of January, while the nation mourned the loss of Amy Johnson, its pioneering aviation heroine believed drowned in the Thames, Shirley in a small corner of South London, was forced to put aside her own personal grief and her faltering ambitions to help with the arrangements for the funeral of her elderly neighbour, Emily Fothergill. Shirley was struck by the tragedy of her neighbour's life for her hopes had been shattered, and her well-being badly scarred by the brutality of one war. Only twenty-two years later, she had died as a result of the terrifying new technological capabilities of the second. She had indeed been played a very cruel trick by fate.

Her face covered by a black veil, and insisting on walking alone, Anastasia Belinskaya cut a stately figure as she led the procession into the church behind Mrs Fothergill's coffin at half-past three on a cold, dark Friday afternoon in midwinter. Shirley could not help but think that Madame was in performance mode, advancing as if she were on the stage in a court scene, perhaps from *Swan Lake* or *Sleeping Beauty*. She was followed in the funeral procession by Shirley and her father, Archie and Eileen, and a handful of the customers who once again had begun to patronize Mrs Fothergill's renovated sweetshop. The congregation consisted of some of the other shopkeepers in the neighbourhood, one or two contacts of Madame's, and more than a few locals who appeared to have come to take advantage of the wake, so all in all, the turnout was not as meagre as it might have been a year or two earlier when Emily Fothergill had lived the life of an embittered recluse. Without pomp and with the minimum of ceremony, she was laid to rest beside the grave of her husband in the churchyard, attended by a small group of mourners, the rest of the congregation already having gone off to the primary school hall.

Since the bombing of the church hall, the school hall had been put at the disposal of the local community at the end of each teaching day and at weekends. Here Eileen had assembled a group of volunteers from the Mothers' Union and the Young Wives who provided fish paste sandwiches, scones, home-made cakes, biscuits and tea. Madame Belinskaya continued to display a guarded, regal presence, although she showed scant emotion at the function. She communicated little with the local population who had come to pay their respects and sympathy, except to thank them in well-rehearsed, impeccable English for attending the sad occasion.

When the congregation had finished availing themselves of the generous provisions, Shirley and Reggie accompanied her home to the empty flat above the sweetshop: there her composure evaporated, and she dissolved into fits of weeping and lamenting.

"*Ma chère amie!*" she cried in French which even Reggie understood. "The first true friend I have known in a long time, and now after only a few months, she has been taken from me! How can I go on living? We had both suffered so much and we had so much to say to each other! War, war, war and loss, loss, loss were the constant themes of our lives! At last we had both just begun to find peace. Now I have lost a soulmate. There is no one and nothing left for me!"

Shirley and Reggie read each other's thoughts, and it was Reggie who, quite unexpectedly took the plunge.

"*Voilà*, Madame," he began, easing himself tentatively into French. "We think you should come next door and stay with us tonight."

His daughter, who had been on the point of issuing the invitation herself, was astounded that her father should be so forthcoming, even more so when Madame put up no resistance and went to pack a small bag.

"But where are we going to put her?" she whispered when Madame was out of the room. Reggie was unfazed.

"Oh, I thought you would sort that out," he said.

Ever resourceful, she put clean linen on her own bed and tidied up the bedroom. Then she ran up to the attic to make up Ted's bed for herself. Next the question of food for the visitor loomed ominously. Because stocks were low in the kitchen cupboard, Shirley hoped that Madame had eaten enough at the copious tea, although she had no recollection of seeing her eat a single sandwich, scone or slice of cake, or even take a sip from a cup of tea.

The canned goods that Shirley had stockpiled before rationing were running low; what little was left, she was keeping for Ted's return, so she left the tins intact. As for buying more, she was nervous of being arrested and fined or imprisoned, because hoarding food had become an offence. She rummaged around in the bottom of a cupboard and found four large potatoes, which she had been keeping for Ted's next appearance. She took out three of the potatoes; the larder yielded some scraps of bacon and a small onion, and hanging in a muslin bag near the air vent, were the remnants of a sliver of cheese.

"Well, that will have to do," she said to herself as she cut the potatoes in half lengthwise. "Just enough for this evening."

She turned the oven on and set to, grating the sliver of cheese. She chopped the onions into thin slices, and was cutting the scraps of bacon into even smaller portions when her father and their guest arrived. The wailing had ceased and evidently Madame was much calmer. Reggie showed her into the living room, after which he came into the kitchen.

"She's brought her bag, but she refuses to talk," he told Shirley, "so she's sitting in the chair by the window and staring out at nothing."

"Poor thing," his daughter remarked, "but I've made up my bed for her, so I'll take her to see it when I've put these potatoes in the oven."

Madame was not at all interested in Shirley's bedroom with its pictures of ballerinas on the walls; she simply nodded as if to say, "This will do." She then calmly announced, to her hostess's horror, that this was the time of day when she normally took tea with lemon. Shirley left her sitting on the bed and went out to the kitchen, where her father was brewing a pot of tea.

"I need a good cuppa after all that," he declared.

"No, wait! Take some of those leaves out of the pot! It'll be too strong for her. Don't waste them!" Shirley hissed. "She wants a cup of tea with lemon! Weak tea will do, if only I can find something like a lemon."

Reggie did as he was told. "I don't know where you're going to find a lemon," he observed helpfully. "I haven't seen one of those in ages."

Shirley looked along the shelves in the cupboard. "Well, I do!" she announced triumphantly and took down a jar of lemon marmalade bearing the date January 1937 – which was when Eileen had made it before the War. She fished out the sliced lemon, which she put in the teapot.

Madame was persuaded to sit at the dining table at suppertime and suddenly started to show interest in food. When the cheese, onion and bacon baked potatoes came to the table, she greeted them rapturously and, before Shirley had sat down, was attacking one half of her potato with gusto.

No sooner had Shirley sat down than she abruptly stood up again on hearing well-known footsteps on the stairs and went round the table to her father.

"Pa," she whispered hurriedly, "eat up your potato before she takes any more. I can hear Ted coming up the stairs!" With that she grabbed her plate with her own baked potato on it, and rushed out onto the landing. Ted stood there, unwashed, dirty, and grey with tiredness as usual.

"Come on, up to the attic and then I'll explain," Shirley urged him. Before he could ask what was going on, she pushed him to the upper flight of stairs and, carrying her baked potato, which would now be his, she followed him up to the attic. There, while he slumped on the bed that she had intended to sleep in, she explained the situation.

"Oh, no, that's the last straw!" He groaned. "I need a good hot bath and a decent meal! And I don't want to have to hide up here! Can't you send her home?" His annoyance was understandable.

"Well, look, eat the potato and I'll bring you something else later on. I reckon she'll go to bed soon. She must be very tired. Nip down to the bathroom now and have a quick wash, or go down to the shop and use the cloakroom out at the back there. I'll close the living-room door, so she won't hear you, but I don't think I'll be able to wash your clothes before tomorrow."

Too tired to protest, he followed his sister's suggestion. She rued her lost baked potato, but congratulated herself at having eaten well at the funeral wake.

Madame showed no signs of tiredness as she sat at the table addressing Reggie volubly in French. He caught only the odd word of her chatter, and when eventually Shirley came into the room, his expression gave her to understand that he couldn't take much more.

"Now, Shirl," he said hopefully, "I think Madame is still hungry; is there any more supper?"

Shirley glared at him. "I'll see what I can find!" she muttered and stormed out into the kitchen. A couple of old dry crusts lay at the bottom of the breadbin: these she broke up into small pieces, shook half a teaspoon of sugar and saccharin mix over them, and fried them in margarine. She reserved some for Ted and herself, and took the rest with a very small jug of the creamy top of the milk to her father and the guest. She was tired and longed to sleep, even on the sofa in the living room for lack of anywhere else, but Madame was now irrepressible and wittered on for ages about all the tragic events in her life, until Pa stood up and announced that he was going to turn in, because he had to open the shop early the next morning.

Only then did Madame bestir herself and decide to retire for the night. Shirley took the remaining sugared, fried breadcrumbs up to the attic to Ted, but he was already fast asleep, so she ate them herself and lay down on the sofa fully dressed.

Early the following day she was roused by a tap on the shoulder. She turned her back on the intrusion, but the intruder would not go away. Gradually as she came to, she recognized the voice.

"*Ma chérie, ma chérie!*" it was saying with the strong Russian accent that Shirley knew so well. "I must have my breakfast. The lawyer will be coming at nine o'clock!"

Shirley opened her eyes to find Madame standing over her. "What time is it?" she croaked, her voice lost somewhere in her dreams.

"It is eight. I do not have much time to prepare myself."

In Shirley's opinion, Madame had plenty of time, or indeed could have gone home for her breakfast.

Without a word she dragged herself up from the sofa, thankful that she was already dressed, even if in yesterday's clothes, and headed towards the kitchen where she put the kettle on, before stumbling into the bathroom to splash her face with cold water.

Madame had to be satisfied with tea and toast, and more of the precious lemon marmalade, some spread both on her toast and some dunked in the teapot. While she ate, Shirley tiptoed upstairs carrying a breakfast tray for Ted, who was in a deep sleep in his attic. She grabbed a pen from the bedside table and scribbled a note to the effect that Madame would be leaving soon, so it would be safe for him to come downstairs shortly before nine.

In fact, Madame hurried away at half-past eight, having devoured two slices of toast and marmalade, but soon after she had gone, Reggie came up from the shop with a message from her for Shirley.

"Hello, Pa," Shirley said with surprise. "You don't often come up here at this time of the morning – aren't there any customers today?"

"Oh, yes, plenty," he replied, "but that Madame of yours" – Shirley bristled at this, as if Madame was her fault – "that Madame, she insisted I should bring you a message she had forgotten to give you herself. She says you've got to be round next door by nine o'clock."

He glanced round the room. "Oh, is that a pot of tea there on the table? Now I'm here, I think I'll have a cup." He poured a cup from the now almost empty pot. "Mm, this tastes odd," he said to himself, but by now Shirley had disappeared and was putting her coat on, wondering what on earth Madame wanted now. She had not mentioned anything about her having to go next door for nine o'clock. Perhaps she had dreamt it.

"Did she say what she wants me for?" she called out to her pa from the landing.

"No idea; you'll have to go round there to find out."

"Well, I'm not going to sell sweets in the shop, if that's what she thinks!" Shirley burst out in indignation.

Reggie joined her as she was about to go downstairs and out to next door. "Calm down, Shirl, just go and see. Remember she's in mourning and doesn't know what she's saying or doing. She's confused, that was obvious in the rigmarole of chatter she came out with last night." He cut short his words of wisdom, probably recalling the dark days of his own bouts of confusion.

As he followed her down the stairs, he asked, "So, do I gather Ted's here?" he asked. "I realized something was happening last night when you dashed out with that potato!"

Shirley nodded. "Yes, he's hiding in the attic. He was pretty fed-up to find he couldn't have a bath and have his clothes washed, but if he stays a bit longer, I'll do them later and he'll have to take them away damp. Actually, maybe I'll leave them to soak in the bath while I'm out." She shrugged in a gesture of frustration at the endless stresses of wartime housekeeping, especially with a brother in the French Resistance.

"Make sure he doesn't slip away again before I can catch him, won't you?" Reggie begged her.

"I can't do that if I'm next door, can I?" Shirley retorted sharply, but then in a more conciliatory tone added, "Don't worry, though. You know him – he doesn't ever go out in daylight, does he?"

Shirley rang the bell of the sweetshop next door, which was closed when she arrived at two minutes to nine, although since its revival Emily Fothergill had always opened it regularly at a quarter to the hour. Clearly it was not to be business as usual, unless she was going to be required to take it over, which she dreaded. Having to help out in her father's business was one thing, and it could be fun part-time, but that was enough shopkeeping.

While she waited on the doorstep these thoughts plunged her yet again into a depressing assessment of her young life. As she saw it, whichever way she turned, everything seemed to be putting a greater and greater distance between her and what she really wanted to do, that is to say, participating actively in the War effort, ideally by flying in the ATA, or through the ballet. She had been given to understand in no uncertain terms that flying, which would bring her close in spirit to her beloved Alan, was not for her.

Habitually now, in moments of near-depression, she tended to reminisce about all the misfortunes in her life, both recent and in the more distant past, and this was the direction her thoughts were taking that chilly morning. As for the ballet, in her jaundiced view the result of all the searing chapters of events of the past months, the terrors of the Blitz, her heroic attempts to keep the neighbourhood safe, the bombing of Coventry and her miscarriage, not to mention all that had gone before – that is, her mother's departure, the Infantile Paralysis and Alan's death – she doubted she would ever regain the necessary skill and athleticism that had fostered her dream of becoming a prima ballerina. At the age of nearly twenty-one that cherished dream was already fading fast. Of late there had not been a single moment even to take out her ballet shoes, let alone put them on. She slouched against the door-frame of the sweetshop, not expecting any good to come of this early morning meeting to which she had been summoned.

The opening of the shop door startled her out of her depressing reverie. A middle-aged gentleman dressed in suit and tie stood in the entrance.

"Good morning. You must be Miss Marlow. My name's Charles Woods and I'm Mrs Fothergill's lawyer; I arrived a few minutes ago," he said with a smile, holding out his hand.

"Yes, good morning," Shirley said, returning his greeting and shaking his hand. "That's right, I'm Shirley Marlow. Madame Belinskaya left me a message asking me to come."

"Madame is waiting for us upstairs, so please follow me," said Mr Woods, courteously beckoning Shirley into the shop.

The transformation wrought by Madame and Mrs Fothergill was extraordinary. The shop sparkled with newness, its shining jars of sweets and glass cases lent it a magical appearance, the scene for a ballet, not unlike Louise's *estaminet* in France, which Shirley used to visit with her mother when she was a small child. There she would imagine all the tools leaping down off their hooks on the wall and the household provisions jumping out of their drawers, and dancing together among the coloured bottles of liqueur and the coffee cups in the empty bar late at night, and here she imagined all the sweets jumping out of the jars and pirouetting on top of the glass cabinets.

At yesterday's funeral, Madame had worn a long black dress, with the addition of certain items of finery – a feather stole, a gold necklace and ruby rings on her fingers – all of which contributed to her aura of majestic self-control. She wiped the occasional tear from her eyes, but held her head high and never snivelled. Today, still in the same attire, she greeted Shirley formally, as if she had never met her before, and invited her to take a place at the table. Shirley was both mystified and amused at the incongruity of this august personage playing out a role that she had conceived for herself in a flat in the rather dismal area of South Cross. Only then did her brain put together all the elements of Madame's story: her involvement in the Mariinsky Theatre in St Petersburg, her frantic escape from the Revolution, with the loss of her little son, the ease with which she spoke French, her commanding personality, even her stately bearing – all these elements suggested to Shirley that Madame might well have been, or was, a Russian princess.

She wanted to shout out loud at this revelation, but restrained herself because Mr Woods was speaking, and she had no idea what he was talking about. She forced herself to concentrate, trying to catch up, and eventually understood that he was clearly but lengthily explaining his role in organizing Emily Fothergill's estate.

"Now we turn to the terms of the will of the deceased," he said at last.

"So that's what this is all about," Shirley said to herself. "Perhaps they want me to be a witness – but I can't, because I'm not old enough."

She raised her hand to prevent Mr Woods from continuing. "Excuse me," she butted into his speech, "if you want me to be a witness to the will, I can't, because I'm not yet twenty-one."

He looked up from his papers and turned to her with a bemused smile.

"No, no, young lady, that's not why you're here. Signatures have already been taken care of in my office. Now, if I may continue with the terms of the will…"

Shirley sat back in embarrassment, even more baffled. What had this got to do with her? she wondered. Mr Woods was stating that since the late Mrs Fothergill had no traceable next of kin, she had left her house and business to the dear friend she had only just had the pleasure of meeting, Madame Anastasia Belinskaya.

Here there was a sudden crash when Madame fell off her chair onto the floor in a faint. Shirley rushed to her side and applied some of the techniques she had learnt in her ARP training to bring the unconscious round. Mr Woods fetched a glass of cold water from the kitchen and lifted Madame off the floor onto a chaise longue. Shirley searched in the drawers of a sideboard and found smelling salts which she applied to Madame's nose. She recovered her senses, saying "*Une petite malaise, c'est tout* – just a little turn, that's all" – and insisted on taking her place at the table again unaided.

As imperturbably as ever, she gave Mr Woods instructions to continue. He took up his thread by repeating what he had just revealed, that Mrs Fothergill had left her property to her best friend Madame, but here he was interrupted by the said Madame, who was abruptly saying, "*Nyet, nyet*, Mr Woods, we have heard all that. Please continue!" So Mr Woods did as he was told and carried on with his reading of the will. There were various bequests to charities, to victims of the First World War, to charities associated with helping Russian refugees, and finally he announced a personal bequest of five hundred pounds to "the dear girl who lives next door, Shirley Marlow". It was Shirley's turn to fall off her chair.

After Mr Woods's departure, Madame and Shirley sat staring into space, speechless. Given the stupendous nature of the solicitor's formal statement, there was a great deal to say and each of them attempted to talk, though unusually for her, Madame was lost for words in any of her preferred languages.

After some twenty minutes of silence, Shirley succeeded in formulating a question which sounded banal in the extreme when she uttered it.

"Might I have a coffee, please? Do you have any coffee here, Madame?" she enquired softly.

"Of course! Of course! In the kitchen cupboard. Make some straight away and a cup for me too!" Madame commanded urgently, restored to her customary form.

Automatically Shirley searched through the cupboards for a bottle of Camp coffee, but there was none.

"Madame!" she called. "I can't find the bottle!"

"Bottle? Of course there is no bottle! Look for the tin!" came the imperious reply.

"Oh! Of course," Shirley said to herself, Madame certainly did not drink Camp coffee; as if she would! She should have remembered that. She searched again and there it was – a tin of Fortnum's best coffee! How did Madame come by it, she wondered, when the rest of the country was having to make do with the sweet, sickly liquid, good only for making cakes or icing? What's more, her search of the cupboards and drawers had revealed a stash of food, enough to feed a family for weeks. How Shirley rued her well-meaning attempts to provide a decent meal the previous evening, not only for her father, herself and her starving brother, but also for Madame – probably Princess – Belinskaya!

Closing her eyes in pleasure at the rich aroma of the coffee grounds, she made a pot and took a cup to Madame.

"I am overwhelmed—" Shirley began, but was immediately interrupted by Madame, who cried out, "*You* are overwhelmed, *chérie* – but *me*! Emily was my dear, dear friend, for such a brief time, but I never expected, never wanted her to leave me her apartment and the shop beneath as well!" She paused to pull out a lacy handkerchief to dab her eyes, before continuing, "Of course, she knew that I would receive no compensation for my house when it was bombed, because the insurers are no better than thieves; they don't pay for acts of war. But she offered me a home free of charge for as long as I wished, because, she said, she was so glad to have a companion."

Here Madame wiped her eyes as the tears flowed copiously; these were genuine, she certainly was not acting a part.

Shirley fell silent for a moment's reflection, and then remarked quietly, "She was a truly generous person. I never expected anything from her at all. This money for me is a windfall. Do you mind if I leave you for a moment, because I must tell my father about it?"

"Of course you must," Madame agreed, "but, *chérie*, may I come to lunch with you? For the present I don't like to be here alone."

Shirley gulped: this simple request presented her with a huge problem, one that she had not anticipated. Ted would be up and about now, roaming freely between his attic and the other rooms in the flat, though not going out of doors for fear of being recognized; he would not take at all kindly to having Madame in the house again, limiting his freedom of movement and preventing him from talking to his father and his sister. Anyhow, there was so much that she had wanted to discuss with him. How was she to juggle all these competing, incompatible demands? There was Madame needing company for solace and food for sustenance in her grief, and Ted needing silence for sleep and food for refuelling in preparation for his next secret mission. What was she to do?

A sudden vision of all the tins in Mrs Fothergill's cupboard gave Shirley her answer.

"Yes, Madame," she said, "but perhaps you don't realize that you have lots of food in the cupboards here, and we don't have any next door. Please may I take a few of your tins home with me? And the other thing is," Shirley continued, embroidering on the truth, "Pa likes to have his lunch in peace and quiet, after a long morning in the shop, and then he usually has a snooze when he has eaten. If it suits you, I'll make lunch for him at home and I'll bring some round here for you."

Madame, completely unaware of what Emily Fothergill's cupboards contained, was more than happy to let Shirley take whatever she wanted, and moreover agreed to let Reggie eat his lunch in peace.

Ted was up and about, and was impatient for a more substantial meal than the half share of a baked potato his sister had given him the night before for his supper. Predictably, he was delighted when Shirley came in carrying a collection of tins. She emptied two of them into a saucepan and left them heating on the stove while she fetched the remaining potato and started to peel it.

"Hey, Shirl, this is a feast!" her brother declared, as he wolfed down serving after serving of Emily Fothergill's tinned beef stews.

His reaction to the provender, available only under strict rationing in England, was much less dismissive than it had been in the early days of his missions to France, when across the Channel rationing had not come into force, and there were still plentiful supplies of gourmet cuisine.

"Did you manage to wash my fatigues?" he asked with some justifiable hesitation.

"Yes, I have! If you look over there to the fireplace, you'll see they're hanging on the rack in front of the fire," came his sister's curt reply, with a gesture towards the hearth, where steam was rising from the fatigues. "They smelt and looked to me as if you had been wearing the same clothes since the last time you went away! And the mud on them! Anyone would think you had been working on a farm."

"Mm, well, I've been so busy," was his only mumbled excuse, and she knew better than to press him for more.

Although their pa joined them for his share of the lunch, Shirley stopped herself, despite her excitement, from talking about her inheritance from Emily Fothergill in case Ted came up with ideas of spending the money for her. Anyhow she suddenly remembered that she had promised to take lunch next door to Madame. Since she herself had already eaten, she hastened to prepare a plate of leftovers for their neighbour.

Madame seemed not to have noticed the passing of time when Shirley appeared with a tray of food. She was downstairs in the former sweetshop, walking round with a tape measure, deeply preoccupied.

She greeted Shirley with joy written across her otherwise severe features. "Ah, *chérie*, you have come at the right moment!" she announced.

"Yes, here you are! I've brought your lunch – it's hot, so I'll take it upstairs for you straight away," said Shirley, unhappily realizing that she had acquired a new role: as well as shopper, cook, cleaner and laundry maid, that of waitress could now be added to her list of menial tasks. Bridling, she headed for the stairs, but Madame called her back.

"No, *chérie*, that can wait! Put the tray down on the counter; I have a brilliant idea to share with you!"

Curiosity combined with Madame's manner won the day; Shirley put the tray down as ordered, and waited for Madame to explain.

"*Voilà*, *chérie*, I definitely do *not* want to sell sweets. We will give this stock to your father to sell next door. I do *not* want it," she insisted, waving an arm over the counters, shelves and cabinets. "We will put down a proper wooden floor, even a *barre* round the room, then we will have a dance studio! Not very large, but big enough for soloists and even for two classes if we also convert the stockroom. What do you think?" Breathless with infectious excitement, she paused, gazing at Shirley with a look of triumph.

"Amazing, Madame!" her one-time pupil exclaimed, shaken out of her doldrums. This was a change that she could never have imagined, for it altered not only Madame's prospects but her own as well: it would give her those wings to fly that she desperately longed for in the darkest, most terrifying days of that dreadful War.

"Let us plan this carefully. You bring my food up into the dining room and there we will discuss our projects," Madame decreed.

"But, Madame, your dinner is cold," Shirley remarked, pointing to the tray with its plate of formerly steaming, but now congealing stew and potatoes in gravy.

"No matter," she replied. "I will eat it while we talk about how to do this."

They sat in Mrs Fothergill's, now Madame's, dining room, for the whole afternoon, compiling a list of requirements for a new ballet school, discussing how to incorporate them into the former sweetshop, drawing plans on sheet after sheet of paper, and drinking pot after pot of fragrant Russian tea, while Madame picked at her food. Eventually she became so carried away with her planning, whereby the room where they were sitting would become a further studio, and the back yard another, and the attic yet another, that Shirley had to take heed of the questions that were surfacing in her mind. It occurred to her to wonder if Madame were expecting a contribution from her recently announced inheritance, a discovery so new that she had not even had a chance to share it with her father.

She ventured a note of caution. "Do remember, you will need somewhere to live, Madame," she exclaimed, "and where will the money come from for all this?"

At this latter remark the Russian princess regarded Shirley with a stare full of haughty contempt, mingled with the aggrieved pain of a small girl who has lost her favourite doll.

"My dear," she pronounced loftily, straightening her posture as she did so, "we must think on the grand scale. These things will sort themselves out, and anyway, I have money, because I still possess some of the jewels I brought from Russia in the linings of my coat and dress in 1917. They are safely stored away in a bank vault. I will collect them and take them to Hatton Garden tomorrow to be sold. I know there is a dealer there who will buy them. I sold some of them years ago to buy my house when I first came to this country. And there is also the site of my house. I will sell the land to a builder; there is enough space there for several houses when this War is over. I have plenty of money!"

Shirley was silenced, glad that her money was not being included in the calculations, but also amused at Madame's astuteness. However, there were other questions, needing answers.

"The problem still remains, where will you live during the conversion?" she continued.

She anticipated a torrent of invective if Madame were proposing to move in with her and her father – and Ted – yet she feared replying to Madame's anticipated request in the negative. The chaos of the previous evening, which she had had to stage-manage, left her in no mind to contemplate a repetition of that.

Madame fielded this question lightly. "Don't worry, ma *chérie*, I am not proposing to live with you and your father, if that is what you were thinking. He is a kind man, but not my sort of person, so I will find myself a small apartment somewhere close at hand. Then, of course, the whole house here can become the new ballet school, with an office, changing rooms, and a bathroom and everything else that it needs. Oh, and by the way, may I join you for dinner this evening? Take any food you need from the cupboards."

"Thank you, Madame, but supper will be late as I have to help my father and clear up his flat before I start cooking," Shirley quickly replied.

Night was falling when, in a daze, Shirley left the premises of the new ballet school, laden with more cans of meat and fish, fruit and vegetables, packets of tea and tins of coffee. She was glad that there was no one watching her because she would almost certainly be arrested for buying in bulk and hoarding; for the same reason she avoided the shop.

Ted was standing in front of the fire still trying to dry his clothes when she entered the living room. "These trousers, they just won't dry!" he grumbled.

"Er, about supper this evening..." she began nervously, wondering how on earth she would tell him that Madame would be taking his place at the table again, but he shrugged off that problem.

"I won't be here! It's getting dark now so I'm off as soon as I can get these trousers dry."

"Oh, so soon?" she said, hoping that the relief was not audible in her voice."

"As soon as it's fully dark," he replied, "and of course, when I've said goodbye to Pa."

"Would you like something to eat before you go?" she offered. "See here, Madame has given me more tins from Mrs Fothergill's cupboard. I think one of them is a tin of ham. Why don't I make you a ham sandwich?"

"Wonderful!" cried Ted. "That will do nicely. I don't know when I last had a ham sandwich!"

"And, if I put the oven on low and put your trousers in it in a baking tin, maybe they'll dry off more quickly than in front of the fire."

"That's a fantastic idea! So long as they don't burn!"

Ted's gratitude was touching. "I've hardly seen you," he said, "and I've some news I'm dying to share with someone."

"Go on, tell me!" she replied, hoping that this was good news – that he was leaving the Resistance to work in the General's office in London, perhaps, or that he had seen Pépé and Céline on the farm in northern France. The news, when it came, was not at all what she was hoping for.

"I know you won't say a word to anyone, not even Pa, but I'm going down to the south on a special mission, and with any luck I shall be seeing Hélène!" he announced jubilantly.

Shirley tried to appear pleased for him, but the news filled her with foreboding.

"I see; I hope it all goes well for you and Hélène," was the limit of her enthusiasm at this news. "I'll deal with your trousers and then go down to the shop to tell Pa you will soon be off."

Their father reacted glumly to Ted's departure. He had borne up so well for so long during the Blitz, and although the Blitz had in no way diminished, he maintained a heroically positive and disciplined attitude towards it, constantly encouraging his fellow Air Raid Precautions team and being at the ready to come to the rescue of anyone in his area caught up in the bombing.

What brought him low, near to panic, was the fear of losing one or both of his children. He had suffered with Shirley through the numerous blows meted out to her over the past few years, and these days the slightest mention of Ted's supposed activities in northern France was enough to make him tremble for the safety of his son. He hoped against hope that his daughter would not take on anything so death-defyingly awful, because then he knew that his shell shock would return.

That evening after Ted had left – for France without a doubt – he sank into his armchair in front of the fire, intending to eat his tea-tray of a ham sandwich and a scrap of salad that Ted had not had time to eat, while listening to the wireless. The last person he wanted to have at his dinner table that evening was the woman from next door who gave herself such airs and graces. If he was not her sort of person, she certainly was not his, even though she had given Shirley a lot of help with her dancing. It was with a bad grace, therefore, that Reggie greeted Madame when she arrived, and throughout the meal of more ham, now heated through and served with potatoes and a sauce Shirley had concocted from the remains of a jar of jam liquefied with hot water from the potato saucepan, he gave the impression of being a deaf-mute, sitting silently but loudly clattering the cutlery at his end of the table.

Shirley tried to make conversation by asking questions in general terms that would appeal both to her father and their guest, but unsuccessfully. "Pa," she would say, "tell us what has happened in the War today," or some such, but Reggie would only grunt and murmur something incomprehensible – probably that he had no idea – in his great frustration at being forbidden to listen to Mr Churchill's broadcast speech, promising "not to fail mankind at this turning point in our fortunes".

If ever proof were needed that Reggie was not Madame's sort of man, even if at first she had thought him a kind man, this was it. She, however, showed quite clearly that she was not Reggie's type of woman. With her back to him, she spent the whole evening chattering in rapid French to Shirley about even grander plans for her new ballet school. By the end of the evening Shirley was tired of them both, and was waiting impatiently for Madame to stand up, ready to leave.

Madame did stand up, like a ramrod, and asked, "Ma *chérie*, may I stay here tonight again? I do not like to go home in the dark. I have brought my little bag with me." Reggie had understood this request and gave Shirley an unmistakeably hostile glance, but she, remembering that Ted's bed would be empty, nodded a weary, diffident assent and showed Madame once more into her own bedroom.

Up in Ted's attic, snuggling up to her hot-water bottle for warmth, she tried to sleep, but all the events of the day, within only a yard or two from where she lay, kept intruding in on her drowsy slumbers. Ever since her meeting with Mr Woods, Emily Fothergill's solicitor, she had been longing to tell her pa her good news. Five hundred pounds was a huge sum: it would possibly be enough to buy a house – not that she wanted to buy a house, or that Pa or Ted would want to buy one, except perhaps to get out of Madame's way.

Somehow, to her constant irritation, everything had conspired against her telling her father the good news. Juggling Madame and Ted had been a challenge. She hoped that hereafter she wouldn't have to juggle Madame and her pa: that would be one long nightmare. Nevertheless, having a ballet school next door would be a great advantage and might with luck give her the opportunity to revive her love of and talent for the ballet. She fell to musing about *Swan Lake* and *Sleeping Beauty*. The music revolved in her brain and her feet began to tap, until in her dreams she found herself on the stage turning in the slow *developpés en pointe* of the *Rose Adagio*. Naturally Alan was the lead male dancer, steadying her and turning her gently. They looked longingly into each other's eyes and waved goodbye. Then the stage started to rock like a ship on a rough sea as a storm blew up and threw the leading dancers into the ocean. Shirley woke with a start, crying out for her lost fiancé.

16

Madame Belinskaya began working on her plans for converting Emily Fothergill's sweetshop into a ballet school straight away, consulting surveyors and chasing up architects on a daily basis until she drove them all quite crazy. To her annoyance she discovered that the shortage of available builders meant that she had had to nurture a hitherto unfamiliar virtue, that of patience, but this did not stop her loudly broadcasting her complaints about the British workman to anyone who would listen.

Shirley was so tired of having her ear bent in this mindless way, which Madame herself would not have tolerated, that ultimately, annoyance forced her to remonstrate with her in no uncertain terms.

"Look, Madame, you can see all the devastation around us and everywhere else. It's not surprising that the builders can't come to convert your property into a ballet school yet; they've got far too much work to do shoring up houses that are nearly falling down, and clearing bomb sites of houses like yours, and of shops and offices that have already fallen down. You were very unlucky when your house was bombed, but we are lucky still to have our home and you to have your new one, and frankly to be alive. What's more, you can still teach in the Methodist church hall. You spent a lot of money having a *barre* put round the room, and your pupils like coming there." Having vented her exasperation, Shirley turned on her heel and headed to the door to avoid the expected strong reaction to this tirade, but it never came.

"Yes, my dear, you are right," observed Madame meekly as Shirley, with her hand on the door handle, stopped in her tracks. La Belinskaya fell silent for a couple of minutes.

"Yes, yes, I shall continue to teach my pupils in the Methodist church hall for as long as is necessary, until my new premises are ready." She looked to Shirley for approval, which was readily forthcoming. "And" she continued, "I think it is time for you to dance again, *ma chérie*. I think you are well enough now." This was in no way a question: it was a statement of fact. "Yes, I think so too!" was Shirley's happy reply.

Since the loss of her precious unborn child, Shirley had put all thoughts of a return to the ballet behind her for many reasons, quite apart from the deep sadness that had left her listless, lifeless and numb: she told herself she was not fit enough and never would achieve the required level of stamina ever again; she was too old and war-weary; the roles of a prima ballerina were now beyond her reach; and moreover she should instead be concentrating on her contribution to the war effort – not that her applications had so far produced any very satisfactory opportunities.

Yet when Madame suggested that she should return to the classes in the Methodist church hall, her heart leapt so joyously that it was impossible to ignore its plea for a return to the ballet. In her room that evening she pulled out her gramophone from under the table, wound it up and carefully inserted a new needle. Next, she selected one of her favourite records, the overture to Act II of *Swan Lake*, and sat on the floor, closing her eyes at the sound of Tchaikovsky's spine-chilling opening chord. Then, reaching both arms out in front of her, stretching one leg out behind and bending the other under her body, she brought her head down onto the floor in the attitude of a dying swan. "Yes!" she said to herself, "Yes, I can do it!"

The next morning saw her striding along the road, fearless of whatever might fall from the sky, ready armed with ballet shoes and leotard, in the direction of the Methodist church hall. There Madame would be embarking on her small advanced class for prospective ballerinas, most of them girls who had already left school and were applying to join Sadler's Wells, just as Shirley herself had done three and a quarter years ago. Heads turned when she opened the door and came into the hall, and she felt the gaze of twelve unknown, critical eyes upon her. "What did they see?" she wondered. "An old woman hobbling, fit only to play the witch in *Sleeping Beauty*?" She held her body erect, head high, shoulders down, tummy in, and stood looking for a space at the *barre*.

"Zees ees Shirley!" Madame announced in her own brand of broken English, "make way for 'er and 'elp 'er, girls! She 'as been very coorajooss, and ees coming 'ere to dance again."

The dancers at the *barre* made way for Shirley at once. Feeling her way like a beginner, she started to enjoy the session, though at first some of the exercises were challenging in the extreme. Gradually her muscles, even the muscles in her left leg, adapted to the moves, which were not new but habitual, learnt long ago. To her delight she found that those moves were still present in the physical memory. Not only did she recover some of her old self-assurance, but soon she began to perform as if she had never missed a class, let alone been absent, ill and unhappy, for such a long time.

Afterwards she tried to slink away from the hall, not wanting to hear Madame's critical commentary on her performance; it was enough for her that she had danced again and had recovered a little of her confidence. To her surprise Madame held her back, and far from criticizing any lack of agility or precision, congratulated her with a contented smile in a torrent of effusive French.

"*Voilà, ma chérie!* I knew you could do it! I told you so! There are a few minor things to correct, but your technique is far ahead of the others, so for the present I propose to teach you alone early in the morning every day, if you wish and can come to the hall at eight o'clock." Eight in the morning – that was rather early for tired limbs and a sleepy brain, but Shirley jumped at the chance. Madame's wish, so generously offered, was her command.

She was well aware that eight in the morning was prime time for the newspaper delivery and the shop was always full of customers then, but no matter: Pa was forever grumbling about having too many people on the payroll, so here was his opportunity to reduce the bills: she would renounce her pay and escape to her dance lesson, leaving him, Cousin Archie and Tilly to get on with serving the customers. The plan was perfect in every respect, except that she herself would be short of ready money, apart from her inheritance from Mrs Fothergill. Only then did she remember that she had forgotten to tell her father about her windfall, but there simply had not been enough time for that. However, given the amount of work she did in keeping the home running, shopping, washing, feeding whoever needed food, she reckoned that it would be reasonable to ask her pa to add a pound or two to the small allowance he already paid her. That would only be fair.

The problem was that her father did not see it quite, if at all, in the same way that evening when, after supper, she put the question to him. In fact, he was most indignant and raised his voice untypically loudly.

"I don't believe it!" he almost shouted. "Don't you know, young lady, there's the War on, and I'm working hard all day to give you a good home and keep you fed? And I already give you an allowance for helping out in the shop! What more do you want?" His hand raised, he only just stopped short of banging the table.

Shirley pulled a face and entered the fray with grim determination.

"Well, Pa," she countered angrily, "I don't think it's fair that I'm spending all my time shopping, cooking, cleaning, washing clothes, making beds without any money for all that hard work!" she retorted, and added, "Not to mention all the extra work when Ted comes home!"

"Your mother did all that without complaint," retorted Reggie, "and anyhow that's what girls are supposed to do, not all this gallivanting off to dancing classes!" He could not have chosen worse arguments if he had tried. This was a red rag to a bull; Shirley was incensed.

"Oh, come on! Why do you think Maman left us? She was fed up with having to do all your washing and shopping and cooking without any reward, and I'm not putting up with that! Why should I?" she fairly shouted at him.

The mention of his former wife made her father's blood boil, but he contained his anger. That niggling fear that perhaps he had been to blame for her sudden departure, though not for the reasons Shirley had suggested, constantly beset him. In his heart of hearts, there was no escaping the suspicion that she had abandoned him and her family because of the terrifying effects of his shell shock and the stress of coping with it, and now Shirley had added to his guilt with a list of all his other faults. Instead of continuing the shouting match with his daughter, he put his head in his hands.

Shirley at once became contrite: the argument was completely out of control; she regretted what she had said. She went over to her father and patted him on the shoulder. "I'm sorry, Pa," said she. "I shouldn't have said that."

"No, no, I do understand, my poppet. Let's see if we can come to some arrangement, but first let me explain how things stand."

Reggie launched into a long, tedious explanation of his financial affairs, first of all that he had not inherited any money, and only had what he earned, then how the takings from the shop were paid, not into his own bank account, but into a company which he had set up on good advice in case the business failed, so that he and his family would not be liable for debts. That being the case, the takings from the shop, which were paid into the company, were not readily available except to pay for the stock, the salaries of the regular employees, including himself, the upkeep of the premises and the general running of the business and the taxes.

The money he had paid to Shirley came from his own private bank account – which, he said, simplified matters. There was no spare money from the shop's takings, nor was there from his own personal earnings, so, much as he would like to increase Shirley's allowance, that was not possible at present.

"And, oh," he added, "I think I should tell you that I also give Ted a small amount each month, because it's not clear whether he's paid at all, and if he is, it's sure to be basic; what's more he never seems to have enough to eat."

Shirley could not argue with this, but it still was obviously not the right time to tell him about her good fortune, and it did mean that until the inheritance came through, she would have to work hard at the ballet, in the hope that, before long, she might be teaching a few dance classes, if and when Madame's plans for the conversion of the shop and flat next door into a new ballet school came to fruition.

Happily, the spat with her father soon blew over, especially when he announced that yet again, he had tickets for the cinema for her birthday celebration. She jumped at the prospect of an evening out, having put her twenty-first birthday to the back of her mind, deliberately suppressing all thoughts of the special occasion, which she had expected to spend with her beloved Alan. Now, she decided, was the time at last to tell her father the news of her inheritance. Reggie was delighted and relieved that his daughter would be well provided for. There was no need for any further mention of payment for her services in the shop.

Reggie's thoughts returned to the birthday party. "You'll be glad to know Bert won't be there," he said cautiously, still haunted by the memory of his gaffe the previous year.

"I should hope not!" Shirley replied caustically. "You know I don't ever want to see him again, and I'd rather you didn't mention him, Pa. Please don't spoil the occasion!"

"No, no," her father said apologetically, "all I was going to say was it was his friend, the projectionist, who let me have the tickets, and I just wanted to reassure you Bert's still somewhere up in the north and will be for some time to come."

"Fine, that's good. Come on then, tell me what we're going to see," Shirley begged him.

"Aha, it's a surprise – you'll have to wait till the day," he said.

"Can't you tell me who else is coming, please?" she begged again.

"Let me see, there's Archie and Eileen, and Madame from next door, and... oh, I wondered if you'd like to invite your friend – I forget her name?" was as much as he was prepared to say.

Shirley had several friends locally but none of them very close; those were the friends she would chat to in the street and sometimes invite in for a cup of tea, but they were not friends one would necessarily invite to a special birthday celebration. Such were the effects of the War. It didn't allow much time for friends. What's more, she doubted that any of those casual friends would have the slightest inkling of what she had been through. There was no way she could even attempt to explain to them the tragedies in her life. The dance was the only adequate means of expressing the depth of her emotions.

"Oh, I remember now! Her name's Celia," Reggie declared a couple of seconds later, pleased with his powers of recall.

"No, it can't be! I don't know anyone called Celia," Shirley said, shaking her head. "Ah, wait a minute, perhaps you mean Cynthia? Yes, that would be lovely – I haven't seen her in ages!"

"In that case I'll leave it to you to get in touch with her, shall I?" said Reggie, relieved that the subject was settled.

"Won't you tell me what we're going to see?" Shirley pleaded.

"No, it's a surprise."

Reggie was adamant. That evening, intending to phone Cynthia, Shirley was perplexed on finding no number for her mother in the phone book, and had to send a telegram to ask her to call her from a phone box in an hour's time, which, for want of a home phone, she did.

"Shirley, dear!" Cynthia's mother declared. "Cynnie will be so disappointed to have missed you! She's away on tour at the moment, but can I help?"

Shirley was baffled: she had never heard Cynthia being referred to as "Cynnie", and then was so intrigued to hear that her friend from ballet days, years ago, had gone on tour that she nearly forgot why they were talking.

"Oh, really?" she exclaimed when she had collected her thoughts. "I didn't know she was going on tour. That sounds lovely! Where has she gone to?"

"Well, she went on tour somewhere in the north, but I don't know exactly where," Cynthia's mother replied. "I'm not sure where they are at the moment," she said. "They're on the move most of the time, I believe, but I gather they're working for ENSA, you know, the organization that arranges entertainments for the troops. I think she said ENSA stands for Entertainments National Service Association, and she's hoping she might be able to find work with them. I've no doubt she'll be back soon, and I'll tell her about you. I know she'll phone you straight away."

"I see, I wanted to ask if she could come to my birthday celebration on the 20th?" Shirley explained. "Pa is taking us to the cinema, and I do so hope Cynthia (she couldn't bring herself to say Cynnie) will be able to come!"

"Don't worry, let me just look in my diary." There was a lull while Cynthia's mother rummaged in her handbag for her diary. Eventually she picked up the receiver again and said, "It says here in my diary she'll be home by the 18th. I'll tell her to ring you as soon as she comes in. This phone box is just opposite our house, so that's easy."

The conversation, which was inconclusive as far as the invitation was concerned, nevertheless set Shirley thinking. If Cynthia was somehow involved with ENSA, then maybe she might be able to join the organization as well. It would be precisely what she longed for: helping the War effort and dancing at one and the same time.

During the day of 18th February, snowflakes began to fall out of heavy, dark clouds.

"Oh, no! Please no more snow!" Shirley murmured as they dropped gently to the earth, where they did not melt but stayed in shape on the already cold, hard ground. A major snowstorm in January had brought the nation to a standstill, making life in wartime Britain even more taxing than it had been before: a snowstorm in the Blitz only added immeasurably to the nation's problems.

By the evening there was so much snow that she and her father had to start shovelling it away from the pavement outside the shop. It continued to snow the following day and the next. Cynthia did arrive home in time for the birthday celebrations, having spent most of the day valiantly struggling across London to the cinema through piled-up drifting snow.

"I thought I'd never get here! I could've done with a snow plough!" she exclaimed, shaking the snow from her coat when she arrived. "But I didn't want to miss your birthday, Shirl, or the film."

Reggie's surprise was yet another major film, the recently released *Citizen Kane* by Orson Welles, the young director only a few years older than Shirley, a fact that was not lost on her as she watched the story of an ambitious, ageing, successful but mysterious journalist unfold on the screen.

"How," she asked herself, "could anyone of near enough her own age be possessed of such deep insight into someone so much older?" The ending affected her deeply, when up in Kane's attic, the camera focused on an empty cot, the cot presumably of a lost child, a baby by the name of Rosebud.

"Why," she wondered, "had she not given her own child, her own dead baby a name? Would that have eased the pain of her miscarriage? Why, oh why, hadn't she been allowed to bury him? Then she looked along the row and saw Eileen dabbing her eyes, and remembered that she was not the only person present to have lost a child.

She came out of the cinema in a daze, forgetting all the urgent questions she had intended to put to Cynthia. There had not been much time to talk, apart from the exchange of greetings and birthday wishes as they filed into the auditorium, and now after the show, Cynthia was about to leave on the return trek through the snow to the Underground and from there, at the end of the line, another trek through the snow to her home.

"Cynthia, you can't go home in this weather! Stay with us! We can put you up and I can lend you a nightdress," Shirley said, trying to persuade Cynthia. "We're planning to go to the pub: it's halfway home and at last I'm allowed go in there legally!"

Cynthia did not need much persuasion. "Yes, thank you, I'd love to! I told mother not to worry if I stayed overnight, because I hoped you might invite me but, please, Shirley, call me 'Cynnie'! Everyone else does, even Mother, and I'm used to it now! Anyhow, I prefer that to 'Cyn', which I have heard my name reduced to, and I don't like it! It's insulting!"

"Fine," said Shirley. "In that case, call me Shirl!"

Thus the renewed friendship between the two girls was sealed.

Reggie glanced down at his watch and issued a formal invitation. "It's not yet closing time. Cynthia and everyone else, come and join us in the pub, won't you? They're expecting us in there," he said, encouraging the ditherers who thought perhaps they should be heading for home considering the weather. The party adjourned to the pub, where Shirley sat down at a table and beckoned Cynthia to sit beside her. Eileen, who had earlier in the day presented her "adopted" granddaughter with a beautiful cake and three of her precious china figurines, sat down on her other side.

"What's happened to Madame?" Shirley asked. "Isn't she coming too?"

"She said she'll be along in a minute but had to pop home for something; I hope she doesn't slip on the pavements," Eileen explained anxiously.

Shirley poked Cynthia in the ribs and whispered. "Come on, tell me about your touring! I'm dying to know!"

"So, Mother has been talking, has she?" Cynthia replied, laughing, but as she was about to speak, she was interrupted by a stately figure making an entrance behind a vast bouquet of early-spring flowers.

"'Appy Birfday, *chérie!*" Anastasia Belinskaya announced triumphantly, placing the bouquet on the table directly in front of a delighted Shirley, and took a seat on the remaining empty chair at the table, surveying the surroundings with an air of perplexed astonishment.

She scarcely registered Shirley's effusive thanks for such a lovely present, exclaiming, "Zo zees ees a poob, ees it? I 'ave nevair been een a poob before. So eet ees 'ere zat zee men come to dreenk, ees eet? Like an *estaminet?*"

"*Oui, bien sûr!*" Shirley assured her.

The other guests nodded in amusement. No sooner had Madame sat down than Reggie and Archie brought drinks for the ladies and Archie proposed a toast to Shirley, whereupon everyone sang 'Happy Birthday' and gave her three cheers, after which Reggie and Archie retired hastily to prop up the bar.

"Go on! I'm dying to hear about your touring!" Shirley begged Cynthia, nudging her.

"Oh, there's not much to tell: our troupe worked with ENSA; you know, the Entertainments National Service Association. It was fun, but we ran out of money and our London theatre was bombed, so suddenly it all closed down. That was that; we all had to make our own way home."

She sat staring into the middle distance and blinking. "Our own touring company would have been good, not just for me but for the rest of the cast as well," she whispered, "but none of us could afford it."

All eyes were fixed on Cynthia, who looked down at the floor in sad embarrassment.

It was of course Madame who broke the ensuing silence.

"But, my dear, zat is a wonderfool idee! You mus' follow eet up! I shood lof to 'elp you! I 'ave many choreographees zat I browt from Russia, and zay were the only zeengs I browt out from my 'ouse when eet was bombed! And I cood train zee dancers!"

Madame's enthusiasm knew no bounds, while Cynthia gazed at her as if a fairy godmother had dropped down from the skies.

Then Eileen chipped in shyly, "And I could help with costumes, if you need them".

"You are very kind," Cynthia said. I'm afraid, though, I only have my savings from the musicals I've danced in, and Mother only has her pension, so we couldn't possibly afford to finance a ballet troupe."

There was another pause during which the raucous conversation from the bar became loud and clear: a group had formed round Archie and Reggie, and they were debating the conduct of the War, a constant preoccupation of menfolk in pubs.

Eventually, after doing some mental calculations, Shirley said, "I've had an unexpected windfall, so I could put some money in!"

She glanced nervously at Madame, who remained impassive. "That's not what I meant!" Cynthia exclaimed. "It's your birthday, Shirl, and you should be enjoying that, not worrying about putting money into my project!"

"You don't understand; I want to be an active part of it!" Shirley declared, her face glowing at the prospect of dancing on the stage. "I would like to dance, if you would have me?" she added quietly.

"But of course!" Cynthia said, "I thought of asking you if you would dance, but, as it all seemed a pipedream, I didn't want to disappoint you, and anyhow, if you put money in, it would have to be your company, which would be fine by me, but it would cost a lot."

The buzz of excitement which rose from that group of four ladies drowned the talk at the bar, as each of them offered more and more suggestions for the formation of a new ballet company. Reggie came over to enquire if there were any more orders for drinks as the pub would be closing shortly, but his offer was refused.

"Goodness, how time flies!" Eileen, flushed with a small amount of alcohol and a great deal of exhilaration, exclaimed. "But it's not really late, so why don't we leave the men here and go to our house to carry on the discussion there?"

The party of women, young and old, emerged from the pub into the snow, ruddy-faced and warm with excitement.

By the end of the evening, Madame had laid plans for training the dancers in her new ballet school when it was ready, or, for the time being, in the Methodist church hall; Eileen had produced yards of material, curtaining, gauze, velvet and silk from her sewing room, saying that there was more in the attic.

Meanwhile, Shirley and Cynthia had discussed what type of dances it might be appropriate to include in their programmes. They had agreed that theirs would be a fairly small group, so it would not be possible to produce complete classical ballets, only excerpts, and they might have to include some popular dances as well. Cynthia had several friends who might well be interested in joining the troupe, though unsurprisingly, she had not as yet come across many men who were free to do so.

Shirley would have waltzed the short distance to the shop, had it not been for the treacherous conditions underfoot, and she feared breaking an ankle. Madame, striding along beside her in true Russian style, oblivious to the snow, kept up a running commentary on all the possibilities for suitable dances. What had started out as a rather run-of-the-mill birthday in unpropitious circumstances, had developed into a dream world of thrilling prospects such as Shirley had not enjoyed for ages. She allowed herself to float into that dream world, where once again she might find the fulfilment and happiness that wartime had denied her.

17

From that evening of her twenty-first birthday, the excitement of throwing herself into cooperation with Cynthia awakened in Shirley a renewed enthusiasm, not only for the ballet but for life itself. The two girls decided early on that engaging a provisional cast of dancers would be Cynthia's responsibility, primarily because she had a far wider acquaintance in the theatre, while Shirley and Madame would select programmes suitable for a limited number of participants, albeit with a marked shortage of men. Shirley was in heaven: she spent all day and every day searching through her growing collection of gramophone records, discussing choreographies with Madame and practising at the *barre* and in the centre of the floor at the Methodist church hall, until her feet were sore, and her limbs ached all over. Fortunately for her, in her left leg there was not so much as a twinge of the Infantile Paralysis that had dashed all her hopes of being a prima ballerina in 1937.

The Blitz, raging again with London its prime target, fired her determination to fight the enemy that had killed her fiancé, even more defiantly. With never a thought to her own safety, she went on her rounds as before by night, nights still mercilessly punctuated by the wail of sirens, squadrons of enemy bombers thundering overhead, and the occasional discharge of a stray bomb from an aircraft, as it shed its remaining load on its return to base in occupied France. Only when the first rays of a wintry dawn appeared in the east, would she run home and fall into bed, dropping into a deep sleep for a few hours until it was time to rush off again to Madame's new ballet studio, which had at last been completed and was conveniently next door, or, occasionally, to the Methodist church hall, which was larger.

Madame was equally fervent in her application to the new project. Her precious choreographies, based on those of the famous French choreographer, Marius Petipa, who had made his name devising the Tchaikovsky ballets for the Mariinsky Theatre in St Petersburg, were rescued from the bank vault to which they had been consigned for safe keeping, when La Belinskaya first came to England. She pored over them each evening, made notes and the following day subjected Shirley to the fruits of her toil, producing more and more dances, steps, and sequences for a solo ballerina from each of the Tchaikovsky ballets, *The Nutcracker*, *Sleeping Beauty* and *Swan Lake*.

From those three ballets alone she selected an abundance of possibilities: *The Nutcracker* yielded the well-known *Dance of the Sugar Plum Fairy*. From *Sleeping Beauty* there was plenty of choice: there was the Lilac Fairy coming to the rescue after the uninvited witch, Carabosse, had cursed the new baby, Princess Aurora, at her christening. There was also the mesmerizing *Rose Adagio* celebrating Aurora's sixteenth birthday. There were yet more dances from *Swan Lake*, though Madame decided to keep most of those for later. In the end there was more than enough for a single soloist, considering that she might also often be supplementing the as yet non-existent *corps de ballet* in their dances.

There remained one problem for Shirley: as usual she had kept her father in the dark about this new departure, and a departure it really would be, because her work, if and when it came to fruition, would take her away from home frequently, and for long periods. Cynthia, who previously had tried to tackle this problem with her mother when she was first going away on tour, warned her of the difficulties.

"How do you think your pa will cope, being on his own, without your company and help at home and in the business, often and for several weeks at a time?" she enquired when they met one afternoon in central London.

"I ask this because my mother is not too happy about being left alone. The difference is, of course, your pa sees plenty of people every day, so perhaps it wouldn't bother him so much."

Shirley pulled a face. "To tell the truth, I'm getting to the stage when I don't really care!" she burst out peevishly. "Well, that's not true, I do care about him, but I can't be responsible for him all the time. I need to dance and there's not much chance of that at home, *and* I want to be involved in the War effort in a meaningful way, and all I do is go out on the same old patrol night after night. Oh, and there's a bit of fire-watching that I do sometimes too, but that's either so cold on top of the church tower, or so boring when I sit up in the little turret on the corner of that house on the hill, beyond the station for hours, that I find myself going over the past, and that's not helpful." She hastily wiped away a drop of moisture that was forming in the corner of her right eye. "The old people who live there are very kind and keep bringing me cups of tea, but it's hard not to fall asleep. I shouldn't complain, but I have to get away from here or I shall go crazy!"

Cynthia patted her arm. "I do understand," she said. "I feel the same, and I've been thinking: for a start, why don't we have some of our rehearsal sessions in the West End, so your pa would get used to being on his own more often? It works with Mother; she's used to me being out for performances and the occasional tour, and now she's getting used to me being away altogether."

"Yes, maybe that would be a good idea." Shirley greeted Cynthia's suggestion with downcast eyes, doubting that it would work, but out of courtesy tried to show due interest. "Do you have anywhere in mind for rehearsals?" she asked.

Cynthia dismissed this mumbled query with a wave of the hand. "Oh, there are lots of places – but do you think your Russian lady would be prepared to come into town to rehearse the company sometimes?"

"I'm sure she would be delighted!" Shirley replied as quick as a flash, her face lighting up as she emerged from behind the cloud of frustration. "What a clever idea! You are brilliant, Cynthia!"

"Anyhow," Cynthia went on, "you should come and meet the other performers I've managed to line up. What about next week?"

It was hard to hide her excitement from her father that evening. "You seem very cheerful," Reggie observed as Shirley served their meagre supper while humming the waltz that had been revolving in her mind all the way home.

"Yes, Pa, I'm fine," she said, glad for once that this was the truth.

"Have you been somewhere nice?" he enquired in a gruff attempt, between mouthfuls, to make conversation.

"I went into town to meet Cynnie for tea," she replied airily, without giving anything of significance away.

"What's Cynthia up to then?" he asked, keen for once to show an appropriate degree of interest in his daughter's activities outside the home and the shop. His awareness that she was very talented in, not simply passionate about, dancing had grown of late, thanks to "that woman" – by whom he meant Madame Belinskaya. She had made sure he was in no doubt about that after she had taken over quiet, unassuming Emily Fothergill's place next door.

It was bad enough that Madame was always popping in to talk to Shirley, but when she started to berate him for limiting his daughter's freedom with menial household tasks, he struggled to maintain his self-control. Nevertheless, that domineering woman's insistence had worn down his resistance to the extent that he regretted his angry refusal to increase Shirley's allowance, and was ready to make amends, because, as a methodical inspection of his bank statement had revealed, he could well spare an extra pound a week to keep his daughter happy. As for that inheritance from old Mrs Fothergill, there was no doubt in his mind that it should be reserved for her future and her ballet projects, for, as things were going, it seemed that they would be very expensive.

The result of Madame Belinskaya's constant harping on Shirley's innate talent, was that he felt himself compelled to view that talent in a radically different light. It was the same light in which his former wife had viewed their daughter's potential as a dancer, and the reason why she had devoted so much time and effort to encouraging their small child to pursue her dream of becoming a prima ballerina, rather than a front-of-house usher, which *he* had expected might be her likely future occupation. After all, it was as an usher that she had met that fine chap, Alan, the RAF pilot. He had reckoned that the Infantile Paralysis had put a stop to any fancy notions of a career on the stage, but now with his newly revised appraisal of his daughter's talent, had come an uncomfortable sense of guilt that in his anxiety to make a success of his business, and give her a secure home after all the tribulations of her young life, he had overlooked an essential part of her being, those persistent dreams and ambitions. The consequence was that with the undeniably selfish wish to keep her at home, he had attempted to clip her fledgling wings. Because the subject had come up again, he resolved to try to grasp the nettle and show a more conciliatory interest in whatever she and Cynthia were concocting, even if his interest was, as always, ill-informed.

On her side, since the opportunity had come up, it occurred to Shirley that this might be a good opportunity casually to ask her pa if he knew anything about ENSA, in the hope of leading to a deeper discussion of Cynthia's plans. So, she began: "Pa, have you heard about ENSA, the Entertainments National Service Association?"

He frowned. "It rings a bell. I've heard something on the wireless about it, something to do with an organization in the forces set up to entertain the troops, but more than that I don't know, except that they say ENSA stands for 'Every night something awful'." He laughed, but his daughter was not amused.

"Is Cynthia involved in it?" he enquired, trying to mend his ways. This was precisely the opening that Shirley needed. "Yes, actually she is, and she wants me to be involved too!"

The truth had burst out. She waited with bated breath for her father's reply. Would he sink into a slough of despond at the prospect of her leaving home and no longer keeping house for him, or would he respond angrily at her for abandoning the business, on which the family finances depended, a consideration he had from time to time impressed upon her?

"Tell me more about it, then," he said, to her astonishment. "How are you going to be involved?"

"Pa, it's so exciting! Cynnie wants me to take part in it and dance some of the principal roles!" she exclaimed, no longer treading carefully or avoiding potentially contentious subjects.

From then onwards, it was easy enough for Shirley to launch into a lengthy account of Cynthia's ideas for the new company, which as yet did not have a name. Reggie listened duly with serious attention, nodding here and there as if he understood the gist of his daughter's enthusiastic torrent of information: there was Cynthia's contact within the organization, Madame's involvement and Shirley's own excitement at finally being invited to dance the roles she had longed to perform since childhood.

Her excitement was so infectious that he scarcely registered the fact that she would probably be away from home for long periods at a stretch, and imperceptibly found himself being carried away by the project until he heard himself saying, "I daresay I could lend a hand, building and painting simple sets, or furniture, or that sort of thing, if you need it!"

Later that evening after listening to the Nine O'clock News, he called Shirley, who was practising *pointe* work in her room.

"Shirl, come here!" he called. She ran in her ballet shoes into the living room, afraid that he might have fallen over, but no.

"Shirl!" he exclaimed excitedly. "What a good job you're establishing your ballet company! You'll never guess what I've just heard on the news! Ernest Bevin has just announced a massive mobilization plan for young women of your age, twenty- and twenty-one-year-olds, to work in armaments factories! That would be you if you didn't have your company! Let's hope it gets going quickly – the sooner the better!"

After that evening, it was much easier for Shirley to slip out of the house, without subterfuge, either en route to the renovated ballet studio next door or to the Methodist church hall which Madame insisted on keeping in reserve for rehearsals, or to central London: it didn't much matter where she was going, since her father's reaction was always the same.

"Don't forget your gas mask! Have a nice time, but be careful and whenever the sirens sound dash for the shelters if you can't get home! If that's the case, I'll hope you will have been sensible and taken shelter," he would shout as she ran down the stairs.

"Don't worry, I will," she would reply as she made her escape. The sense of freedom, despite the constant threat of bombing and all the restrictions and very real dangers of bombing in the all-out War was a freedom she had not experienced since those blissful few days, full of love, promise and hope, spent with Alan before his disappearance over the Channel in July 1940. There was no longer any point in searching for his face in the crowds in the West End, because she knew she would never find him there. He was lost for all time, as was their baby, both innocent victims of the cruelty of warfare. Her future now depended entirely on her own endeavours, her own commitment and her love of the art form that she would make her own. Increasingly, under Madame's guidance, rehearsals took place in a convenient studio in central London where Shirley got to know the other members of Cynthia's blossoming troupe.

At first she felt cowed, because so many of the dozen or so dancers were professionals who were used to performing on the London stage, but when Cynthia told them in confidence about the tragedy in Shirley's life that had prevented her from taking up her place at Sadler's Wells, but had not dimmed her passion for the dance, they warmed to her and admired her tenacity – all, that is, except for one girl, Doris, a tall, lanky girl with prima-donna ambitions who resented the threat to her own position.

"I'm not very happy about having that girl in the troupe," Cynthia had told Shirley. "I don't know who introduced her; she just appeared and said she wanted to dance. In fact she is quite good, and when she dances, she's much more graceful than when she walks, but I can't see any suitable roles for her: she's so much taller than anyone else. I can't think of a way to fit her in."

"Something's bound to turn up," Shirley observed without much enthusiasm. From the outset, she had sensed Doris's hostility and decided to have as little to do with her as possible. Otherwise Shirley's personality and good nature ensured her an immediate place within the company, which after long and arduous rehearsals would repair to a pub for animated discussions about the arrangements for the launch of the new ballet. The most important and the most discussed seemed to be the question of the company's name.

One evening, while various banal suggestions for a name – *Ballet in the Blitz, Ballet in War* and so on – were being debated and becoming heated in the pub after rehearsals, the sirens sounded, and everyone made a dash for the door and from there to the nearest Tube station, where crowds thronged in the direction of the escalators, which had already been turned off. The station attendants prevented a dangerous free-for-all by barring the way and allowing only two people at a time to step onto the stationary steps and proceed down to the depths in a quick but orderly procession. More attendants stood at the foot of the escalators and controlled the surge onto the platforms, where a supply of sleeping bags was issued to the lucky first-comers, and vendors stood ready at their stalls to provide food and drink. At the far end of the platform stood a couple of chemical toilets. Shirley was glad that she had used the facilities in the pub only shortly before the sirens sounded.

"We're lucky to be down here," Cynthia remarked. "The last time this happened to me, I had to sit on the escalator all night because the platform was already full, and up there you couldn't move up or down. This is luxury by comparison."

Shirley was not so sure about the "luxury", but was fascinated by this extraordinarily positive consequence of the Blitz. A singsong had already begun further down the platform, as had a sense of comradeship and defiance. Strangers were talking and laughing together in the warmth of the Underground, which was so much cosier, more fun and certainly more comfortable than standing fire-watching on the top of the church tower in the middle of winter, or sitting bored in the turret of the house on the hill. Now someone had started to sing a well-loved song and in no time the whole station was joining in with it:

> Pack up all my cares and woes,
> Feeling low here I go.
> Bye, bye, blackbird.

Where somebody waits for me,
Sugar's sweet and so is she,
Bye, bye, blackbird.

No one seems to love or understand me.
What hard luck stories they all hand me.
Make my bed and light the light,
I'll be coming home tonight.
Blackbird bye, bye.

No one would be going home that night, and no one seemed to mind; they were all enjoying the novelty of the situation, safe in the knowledge that German bombs might be falling overhead but not on them. The much-loved song was repeated *ad infinitum.*

Cynthia stopped singing after the third repeat and nudged Shirley. "This has given me an idea," she said.

"Another one and down here?" Shirley asked raising her eyebrows at Cynthia's unstoppable imaginative flow.

"Yes, I think we need a compère for the show; someone who would introduce the show and tell the story of each ballet to the audience; that might help get them engaged item by item, especially if they haven't seen a ballet before. And it would give us a breathing space, and create a really good atmosphere." Cynthia's idea came flooding out in a flow of enthusiasm which was matched by Shirley's reply.

"Mm, that's a jolly good idea," she remarked, "and it would keep the audience involved. I was wondering whether an evening of ballet without any introduction or explanation would be entirely to their taste. But for now we have to get our troupe going." That settled the matter.

At that moment a train drew slowly into the station, shedding a brighter light on the recumbent figures on the platform, and bringing more provisions and blankets.

Shirley yawned. "This surface is hard, much harder than my bed, but I am very tired, so I think I'll try to get some sleep."

She was about to lie down and close her eyes when an unmistakeably gawky figure came towards them along the platform.

"Oh no!" she whispered to Cynthia. "Here comes Doris. What on earth does she want?"

"I fear she's looking for us," answered Cynthia, propping herself up on an elbow and deliberately looking in the other direction.

"Oh, there you are!" Doris exclaimed, "I hoped I'd find you while the train's still in the station. It's much easier to recognize people in the light, isn't it?"

"Yes, is there something you want?" Cynthia's tone was deliberately curt.

"Yes, there is – or rather no, there isn't, because I have something for you!"

"Oh, yes, what's that?" Cynthia asked, making no attempt to hide her annoyance. "We were about to try to get some sleep."

"If you make a space for me, I'll sit down and tell you," Doris replied, planting her decidedly unballetic frame between Shirley and Cynthia.

"You see, I've had an idea for a name for our company."

"Really?" Cynthia remarked, as if there were nothing at all, even a name for their ballet company, that could interest her at that time of night, sitting on a platform in the Underground while bombs fell overhead. "OK, tell us what it is, quickly – we are so tired, aren't we Shirl?" Shirley nodded and yawned again very conspicuously.

"Well," Doris continued with more enthusiasm than she had ever shown for anything ever before, "it's just come to me. Why don't we call ourselves the Aurora Company!"

Cynthia and Shirley both sat bolt upright. "Ooh, how lovely! The princess in *Sleeping Beauty* is Aurora! It's a beautiful name, just right!" they cried out, their faces lighting up with excitement while Doris basked in their approval.

Noises of disapproval from up and down the platform put a halt to their exclamations, so the three of them had no choice but to settle down for the night. Doris parked herself between Shirley and Cynthia who, with this obstacle between them, could not whisper to each other about the surprising development which, thanks to Doris, had given new life to their venture. Independently each of them acknowledged that Doris had assured her place in the company.

Shirley closed her eyes but did not sleep; her mind was too busy churning over Doris's idea and admitting that she could not have thought of a better name herself. Eventually, long after the station had fallen silent, she dozed off with the music of *Sleeping Beauty* floating through her subconscious; she did not wake up until the early hours, when an attendant came to rouse the sleepers, calling out that the all-clear had sounded and they could leave. Bleary-eyed, they emerged into the freezing early morning temperatures and were met by a dust-laden scene of devastation, the sort of scene that had become all too frequent, making them grateful for the protection they had enjoyed underground. A workforce was clearing the streets of broken glass and rubble to make way for fire-engines and ambulances, their bells clanging, to pass through to the ghoulish remains of buildings where residents, nightbirds or partygoers were trapped.

Shirley shivered; the horror of it, not only of the visible, physical damage but also of the fact that the devastation had been inflicted by human beings who were intent on killing whole populations, was all too reminiscent of Coventry. Like many of her night-time companions she turned back into the warmth of the Underground and found that the trains were running more or less normally again. She took the first one and reached home as daylight was breaking. The morning star twinkled brightly in a clear sky and the air was clean and fresh by comparison with central London. For the first time there was a sense of comfort in coming back to this area, to the tall grey building, the shop and the flat which she had called home out of habit, but never with any affection.

Her father was awake, having been up all night waiting for her. It was impossible to tell who was the more relieved, Shirley to be home or Reggie to see her alive and well. She hugged him. On her insistence, over a cup of strong tea, he gave way to his exhaustion, emotional and physical, and agreed to break with his customary routine by leaving a note in the shop for Archie telling him that he would not be at work that morning and nor would his daughter.

"You won't believe how relieved I am!" Reggie declared later that day when Shirley appeared after a long sleep. "You probably haven't heard that last night, they tried to bomb Buckingham Palace, starting with incendiary flares. Luckily, they missed. They did, though, bomb a dance hall somewhere! What will they do next?" He shook his head in despair at the evil that was dropping from the skies.

With its name established, the Aurora Ballet Company, known for short as Aurora, gained an identity that united all prospective participants. It gave them not only a sense of being part of an exciting project, but also held out the promise of contributing significantly to the War effort by affording the troops a magical respite from their daily toil. Cynthia and Shirley, the founders, were recognized as the leaders of the company, while the other potential participants expressed a willingness to assume roles in which they already had some useful experience. For instance, all the girls possessed their own ballet shoes and were used to repairing them; some of them had a few old costumes in their wardrobes that could be reworked and spruced up for performances, others were willing to paint backdrops, and all knew how to apply make-up and dress hair.

At first the advertisements for male dancers yielded few results, because so many men were away in the armed forces, but those numbers grew when word spread that a ballet company really was in formation. Not all were trained dancers, although of those who were, some had been put out of work by the closure of theatres and companies, and others were colonials, New Zealanders and Australians, not subject to mobilization but stranded in Britain by the War. There were refugees from occupied France, Holland and Belgium, or Spaniards escaping from Franco's Spain. There were one or two who volunteered to dance when on leave to "keep in training", and one was a conscientious objector. The only problem with the male dancers was that they were always very much in demand elsewhere: companies were always on the lookout for men to fill roles at short notice, or to make up the numbers when their teenage dancers were conscripted.

Also, there were men simply in search of jobs, some young and others older, who brought much-needed skills other than dancing. They ranged from van-driving and carpentry, stage management and scene shifting, to drawing and printing. There was one exceptional young man, Dmitri, a nearly-blind candidate, who was introduced by Madame as the son of friends of hers who had escaped to Britain just before the Revolution, bringing with them their new baby. Dmitri proved to be a genius with all things of an auditory nature, particularly with gramophones and gramophone records. He knew how to amplify sound and how to combine different versions into one as the programme demanded, thus avoiding the need to keep changing records. When asked by admiring colleagues how he did it, he simply shrugged his shoulders and said that from birth he had been much more sensitive to sound than was normal, perhaps because of his very poor sight, and so it was obvious for him to train as a sound engineer. He painted different, embossed letters onto the centre of the records so that he could recognize each one by touch. Fortunately, he was very knowledgeable about music. His status in Aurora was that of a hero, since catering for the continuous flow of appropriate music loomed as one of the biggest headaches for the organizers. Another recruit to the workforce came in the shape of Rocky, a large American stranded in Britain by the War.

With such an enthusiastic troupe, the most urgent problem staring Shirley and Cynthia in the face was finance: how were they going to raise enough money to keep their fledgling company afloat without, as yet, having a single engagement in the diary and with only a vague promise of work for ENSA? The dancers would have to be paid for the time spent training and rehearsing, let alone performing; the cost of studio rental would mount up; old costumes and ballet shoes would wear out quickly, probably within a week, and new ones would be needed. Moreover, rail fares to distant venues would be expensive. Then there was the question of payment for Madame Belinskaya, the *regisseur*, director, choreographer and dance mistress, who had already taken up her part unsummoned, resuming the strictness and rigid authority in rehearsal that Shirley remembered from those early days when she had first nervously gone to ask her for lessons.

"If we don't find some money soon, we'll lose all our dancers and our backstage staff. As far as the dance is concerned, we are doing very well, but we can't expect the group to keep coming for rehearsals if we don't pay them. They've been very obliging so far because they know we're trying to get things going, but they don't live on air." Cynthia's tone was desperate one afternoon when she and Shirley were discussing the situation so far, after a particularly rigorous dance session.

"I've been thinking of that too," Shirley agreed. "We can't afford to offend them, so we had better try to raise some money."

"Easier said than done," Cynthia said with a shake of the head.

Silence fell, until Shirley's better nature overcame her and she blurted out, "I did tell you, didn't I, that Mrs Fothergill left me an inheritance? It was such a surprise! I'll put some of that towards Aurora, and I'll ask Pa for a loan – that sounds better than asking him outright for money. He's not mean, but he's always anxious about paying bills."

Having made her offer, she enquired tentatively, suspecting that she already knew the answer, "Is there anyone *you* could ask for help?"

Cynthia shook her head. "Thanks for your offer, Shirl; we shouldn't use your money but, as you know, Mother's not very well off since my father died, and she appreciates whatever I can give her to keep the home going. You know, don't you, that Father never recovered properly after being shot in the Great War, and we only have Mother's war widow's pension and what I can earn?"

Shirley nodded in sympathy. "Yes, of course, I hadn't forgotten about that," she said, thankful that her father's wound had not rung his death knell. "Don't worry, we'll find a way. I'll put my thinking cap on and ask around. Maybe I can drop a few hints here and there."

On the Tube she set her mind to work to find ways of raising a minimum of two thousand pounds, because, before parting, she and Cynthia had done a few approximate sums and agreed that two thousand pounds was the minimum needed to set Aurora off on a reasonably sure footing. Hopefully once the company was well established, the money would flow into the coffers and any loans could be repaid, but two thousand pounds was a huge amount of money and, apart from her own contribution, Shirley had no idea where it would come from. The question was, how to raise the subject. There was no point in asking people outright; the shock at her impertinence would produce a horrified "No!" She recalled how not so long ago, when she had asked her father to raise her allowance, his reaction had been an outright no, so she would have to be more subtle and appeal to a sense of fair play, if indeed one existed. She racked her brains for a solution.

In the middle of the night, after a particularly long day of rehearsing, her brain was still buzzing when it occurred to her out of the blue, that perhaps the community, though not wealthy, might like to show its appreciation to her for all the dedication she had given through her valiant ARP duties since the beginning of the War, and her fire-watching as well. She had, after all, saved many lives, not just those of Tilly, her baby and her mother, but also the lives of the many people she had warned of attacks, shepherded into shelters and pulled out of their houses, even out of their beds, at the last minute as the planes were fast approaching. There were occasions too when she with her father had tended the injured until ambulances arrived, and put out fires that were encroaching on properties. On the other hand, how could one even broach the subject without appearing to be mercenary?

She tested her more diplomatic approach that evening: it was definitely milder than her usual way of doing business, so much so that at supper her father, troubled by her lack of communication and her downcast air, suggestive of a weight on her mind, which of course there was, asked, "What's the matter, Poppet?"

His concern was genuine, since he never ceased to worry that her left leg, the Infantile Paralysis leg, might be giving her trouble.

"Oh, I don't know, Pa," she answered glumly. "I don't think our new ballet company is going to work out. I've been talking to Cynnie this afternoon, and to tell the truth, we just don't know how and where we are going to raise the money!" She waited in hopeful expectation.

"Oh, that's a shame!" her father exclaimed. "You were so excited about it!"

He contemplated his plate of sausages, a rare treat from the butcher, and said no more. Whereas in the past she would have followed this up with an impatient request for money, she kept quiet, and she kept quiet for the rest of that evening until footsteps on the stairs aroused her from her hopeless plans for making money, and her father from his habitual fixation on the Nine O'clock News.

They both recognized those footsteps, albeit that they were heavier than usual, as if the well-known person were dragging himself up the stairs in a state not just of extreme weariness and hunger, but also of despondency. He staggered into the room and fell into a chair. Although he was dirty, unkempt and exhausted, as was to be expected, Shirley sensed at once that there was more to it than that.

"Ted," she cried out and went over to give him a hug, but he pushed her away roughly. "I'll get you something to eat," she said. "There are a couple of sausages left from supper, and a few potatoes."

"No, I don't need anything," he said sharply, pulling a bottle of beer out of his pocket. "Well, then, a cup of tea, perhaps?"

"No, I already said, I don't want anything! *Tu ne comprends pas?*" he rebuffed her, resorting to French as if that would make it clearer.

"Ah, bon," she replied, and went upstairs to check that her brother's bed was made up, for evidently he was in dire need of a good night's sleep.

On her way down again to the first floor, she was alarmed to hear the gist of a conversation in the living room where Ted was talking to his father about the situation in France and sobbing. Rather than interrupt them, she tiptoed into the kitchen and put the kettle on just in case her brother had changed his mind.

"Had something happened to Hélène, the love of Ted's life?" she wondered, taking a cup and saucer down from the cupboard.

After all, he had more or less told her that Hélène was closely involved with the disparate Resistance groups in the area of the Vichy regime, free only in name, in the south of France, and was conducting dangerous undercover operations against the all-pervasive grip of the enemy. If Hélène had been captured or killed, then she alone, Shirley, could give Ted the comfort he needed, because having lost her own beloved Alan to the War, only she could know what he was suffering.

She loaded a tray with a plate of cold sausages, some bread and butter and a pot of tea, carried it into the living room and set it down beside her father.

"Pa, I thought you might need something, even if Ted doesn't," she said. Her father took no notice of what she was saying; his expression was grim.

"Shirl, I think you should sit down and hear what Ted has to say," he said with a deep sigh and then put his head in his hands.

"Tell her, Ted," he went on.

Ted turned a red face and swollen eyes to his sister.

"Yes, sit down, Shirl," he said more gently than his previous pronouncements. "Prepare yourself, because what I have to tell you is terrible."

"Is it something to do with Hélène?" she asked immediately, her heart pounding in her chest.

"No, Hélène's fine. She's over the border in Switzerland at the moment, lying low and having a rest." He paused. "I'm sorry to say, it's about Trémaincourt," he continued. Shirley shuddered. Images flashed through her mind of Grandfather Pépé, and Céline, her step-grandmother, and all the dear friends she had known in that tiny French village since child-hood. A surge of sudden guilt overcame her at not having thought about them lately because there had been so much happening on the home front.

She did not want to press Ted for more information; instead she wanted to ward off the moment of revelation, because that was obvi-ously going to be dreadful. It was not necessary to press him: the words were beginning to tumble out.

"They…" (Shirley knew that he meant the Nazis) "…discovered that Charlot had been helping himself to petrol from that shed on the edge of the wood. You remember where that was, don't you? He filled up his van and a can for Pépé there that night he helped us escape."

She nodded. Of course she remembered – how could she forget that night when Charlot had been so brave and had guided them almost as far as the coast during the German invasion? For all his deformities, she was very fond of him and was well aware that he worshipped her.

"It seems that someone in the village gave Charlot away. So, what did those Germans living in the chateau do? They took him out and shot him!"

Shirley gasped. "No, no, please say it's not true," she cried. "I can't bear it! And poor Louise, she must be heartbroken! What has happened to her? Did they shoot her as well?"

"No, they didn't shoot her because they liked to drink the *estaminet* dry too often, but of course, she's heartbroken. She closed up the *estaminet* straight away and she said she would never open it again, because she didn't want to find herself serving the person who had been responsible for the death of her son. And she's gone away, I think, to stay with her sister but no one knows where that is, which is probably just as well." Ted fell silent.

After a moment or two during which he bit his lip hard to avoid weeping, he added dourly, "And no prizes for guessing what they did to the *estaminet*: they torched it! Luckily some of the neighbours saw what was going on and came out with hoses, so it's still standing if she ever comes back."

Shirley's brain was whirring and was blank at one and the same time: it churned over the dreadful news of Charlot's brutal death, trying to believe, hoping against hope, that there was some mistake, yet knowing that was impossible. Ted had very rarely, if ever, spoken about his activi-ties in France, and had sworn his sister and father to utmost secrecy, so it was unthinkable that he would play a cruel joke like this on them. The news was so dreadful that he had had to drop his guard and share it with them. He was visibly shaken to the core, and so was his audience. Shirley sat nursing her grief, like an impassive statue.

"I think it's time we all went to bed," their father was saying. "There's enough hot water for you to have a teacupful for a bath, Ted, so why don't you go and take off those muddy clothes and have a good wash. You'll feel better for it."

"But, Pa, there's…" Ted began, but Reggie had anticipated his reaction and gestured to him to keep quiet.

Shirley's eyes were on the floor, so she did not notice this exchange. She bade her father and brother goodnight and went to bed completely drained of all energy, all hope, all emotion. She lay in a stupor for hours, casting back over memories of Trémaincourt on those long summer days when the sun shone, and she and Ted rode home atop the sheaves of straw on the cart after the harvest. And then there were the harvest suppers out in the yard where they all sat out on long tables, feasting far into the night on the delicious food prepared by Grandmother Mémé, and on Pépé's cider, in celebration that the harvest was safely gathered in.

Later, after Mémé's death, Pépé's housekeeper, Céline had taken on the role of cook and hostess for these delightful parties. Of course, Louise and Charlot were always at these gatherings, joining in as if they were part of the family, which probably they were, because family relationships were kept alive through many generations in the French countryside. Charlot could not talk, but he could communicate by writing down what he wanted to say, which was usually a droll comment on the situation, as for instance when one of Pépé's barrels rolled over and flooded the yard with his precious cider. "Oh, well," wrote Charlot in his notebook, "no need for glasses tonight, we'll just get down on our hands and knees and lick the ground!" Everyone laughed. There would be no laughter in Trémaincourt at present, except for the Nazis in the chateau, who were probably enjoying the retelling of the killing. Shirley buried her face in her pillow and sobbed into the black night.

Breakfast the next morning was a sombre affair; no one had any appetite either for the leftover sausages or for conversation. Reggie, to Shirley's surprise, had, contrary to his usual procedure, reappeared back upstairs after opening the shop and sat at the table with his children, who drank only a cup of tea each and ate nothing.

"Is that all you had to tell us last night?" Reggie enquired of his son, somewhat naively, because it quickly became obvious to Shirley that Reggie knew already what was to come, and that the horrific news of Charlot's murder was not the end of Ted's tale.

Reggie glanced at Shirley apologetically. "We didn't tell you everything yesterday evening, because the shock of Charlot's murder was quite enough, but there is more. Shall I tell her, Ted, or will you?" Ted shook his head. Shirley gripped the table. She sensed what was coming next.

Ted began to speak very slowly and deliberately.

"I was telling Pa while you were upstairs last night, that, having shot Charlot, the Germans went looking for other villagers who might have been receiving free petrol, supplied by him from their store in that shed." Shirley's blood froze. Both she and Ted knew full well that Pépé had received a plentiful and regular supply of fuel to keep his tractor running from that same source, that is, from Charlot. "The Nazis found cans of petrol on practically every farm, including our grandfather's and simply took all the farmers out and shot them. I'm sorry there's no gentler way of putting it." Shirley keeled over as the blood drained from her head. Ted rushed to her side to hold her upright on her chair when she passed out. He lifted her onto the sofa while their father looked on helplessly.

On regaining consciousness, she raised herself up and whispered, "I've had a really bad dream. In it Pépé was shot. Did that really happen?"

"Yes, I'm sorry to say that's right," her father mumbled, "but Ted says Céline escaped – though, just like Louise, no one knows where she is."

Shirley sank down into the soft cushions in search of comfort, but then quickly raised herself up again when a further question occurred to her.

"Ted, how do you know all this?" she demanded in fright.

"I know it because I was there in hiding," her brother answered candidly. "You see, I was on undercover operations, but I was on my own, and couldn't do anything to help against a crowd of armed Nazi soldiers. You won't tell anyone, will you?"

"Of course not!" his sister exclaimed. "As if we would. Isn't that right, Pa?"

He gave a weary nod. "Don't worry, we won't tell a soul; we've too much to occupy us here."

Ted went back to bed and slept for the rest of that day and night while his father worked in solitary confinement in what he called his "counting house" at the back of the shop, with strict instructions that no one was to disturb him.

Shirley went out without a word to anyone, intending to go on her ARP rounds to check that all was as it should be, and to inspect the siren on the church tower to make sure that it had not been tampered with. It was far better to be out of doors doing useful work than staying inside mulling over the horrors that had befallen Trémaincourt and its inhabitants, including dear Charlot and her own grandfather.

The memory of them and the report of their awful fate made her weep internally, though she tried unsuccessfully to maintain a professional façade. In spite of her intentions, her footsteps strayed first in the direction of the railway and Tube station where, to her dismay, she discovered that the piles of sandbags were tipping over and had to be put back in position. She stayed there longer than she intended, reprimanding the stationmaster and his staff, and setting them to work as a matter of urgency. She did not leave until the work was done to her satisfaction. Consequently, it was not until the afternoon that she reached the church tower. The control box for the siren in the church porch was open: it could not have been blown open by the wind, because the door was still so stiff that it always took some effort to force it to yield. This meant that someone must have been messing about with it – probably a band of idle teenage boys, who would be in for a shock when they were called up.

Cousin Archie and Tilly were surprised when she appeared in the shop. "Oh, Miss Shirley, are you all right?" Tilly enquired. "We thought you were asleep or unwell upstairs."

"No, I'm fine," Shirley said without her usual smile, "but I *am* furious: I've been checking the district all day and found the siren control box has been tampered with, so I must make a phone call to get it fixed before tonight."

In the evening, although she served her father a poached egg on toast, she had no appetite herself, and instead of sitting with him while he ate, she simply went straight to bed. She lay awake until the early hours, tossing and turning to keep the nightmares at bay, ready to jump up if the phone rang. The phone did not ring and the siren did not sound that night.

19

All was quiet when Reggie took his tea and toast into the living room at 7 a.m. There was no sign either of Ted or of Shirley, though in the circumstances, he was not surprised. They were both probably still sound asleep. On the table he found a folded piece of paper and, expecting it to be a note from Shirley asking him not to disturb her because she couldn't sleep, he picked it up and opened it out. At first, he was puzzled by what he saw, since it was in French. Although his spoken French was – or had been – adequate, the written language had always presented him with a challenge. The note was in Ted's handwriting.

The first phrase was easy enough: "*Ma chère sœur*," it said – "My dear sister" – he turned the paper over and saw that it was addressed to Shirley, not to himself. "*Nous avons fort besoin de toi en France*" – Reggie had no problem with that – "We really need you in France" – but he had to reach for the dictionary for what followed: "*Il nous faut nous venger de l'ennemi et puisque tu es si belle et si chic, tu pourrais nous aider à tendre un piège pour les attraper. Pense à Pépé et à Charlot et à tous les autres! Viens vite!*"

Reggie was shocked, then angry, at what he managed to deduce. Here was his son, Ted, urging his sister to go to France, and with her glamour seduce the enemy into a trap to avenge her grandfather, Charlot and the farmers of Trémaincourt, who had been taken out and shot for helping themselves to petrol to keep their farms going! What on earth was Ted thinking of? Didn't he realize that Shirley had suffered enough in this ghastly War? Hadn't she already done enough by rescuing him, her hothead of a brother, from France at the time of the invasion, and yet was now working with the utmost courage in the ARP patrols.

Of course, he reasoned, the opportunity for her to support the war effort through her dance company was so recent that Ted had not heard about it yet, and it certainly had not come up in conversation the previous day. The dancers would be working with ENSA and would wear the ENSA uniform, a sure sign that they were committed to the battle on the home front. That in itself would have its dangers, for who knew where they might be going, but it would be infinitely preferable to her acting as a bait to lure German soldiers into traps in occupied France. Yes, if ever he, Reggie, had had any doubts about this dance troupe of hers, he resolved there and then that it was to be encouraged, especially in light of the present circumstances, evidence of which he held in his shaking hand. He crumpled up the message and used it to light the fire.

Shirley did serve in the shop that morning, although she was not at all communicative. She had nothing to say either to Cousin Archie or to Tilly, for even if she could have told them the truth about the little French village that meant so much to her, they would have no understanding of the horrors or the sadness to which she was prey. Their sympathy might have been heartfelt, but to her it would have been artificial. Nonetheless, when Eileen came in mid-morning to make dandelion coffee for the workers, she summoned a shadow of a smile.

"Do you remember, dear, I said I'd look up in the attic as well as in my sewing room for some material for costumes?" Eileen asked.

"Oh, yes, I remember," Shirley replied apathetically. "Did you have any luck?" She had not given the ballet any thought and was not in the mood to show the slightest enthusiasm for anything so seemingly fanciful. In any case it was unlikely that Eileen would have found anything useful in her attic.

That was one of the problems with wartime: you took two steps forward, thinking you were making progress, but then circumstances determined that you had to take one, or even ten, or twenty, or a hundred backwards – so she was surprised when Eileen's face lit up.

"Yes! I've found masses of material that would be just right for your ballet costumes! I'll have to ask Archie to get it down from the loft this evening, but there's my old wedding dress, my bridesmaids' dresses, a roll of silk left over from the dress my mother had made for herself for my wedding, and heaps more! There are yards of tulle and taffeta, and none of it has faded because it was all carefully packed away in tissue paper in huge cardboard boxes – not a cobweb in sight!" Her face glowed with satisfaction. "Oh, and I found a roll of purple silk as well. That must have belonged to my grandmother, because the Victorians were mad about purple. Everything had to be purple when they discovered how to make purple dye from coal tar. I reckon we could turn it into top layers for skirts for the *corps de ballet*, and also a top layer of purple silk over stiffly starched net for your tutu. Net should be easy enough to find and not expensive."

Shirley was astonished; she had never heard Eileen wax so lyrical. "How extraordinary! That's wonderful!" she said in a sudden burst of delight at such infectious enthusiasm.

"Come to supper, you and your pa," said Eileen, "and I'll show you some of it, and then we can decide how to make it up into ballet costumes!"

"That's very encouraging," said Shirley, smiling. "I'd love to come, and I'll tell Pa. I have to go out on ARP duty this evening, but that's not till nine o'clock, so there'll be plenty of time."

"My brother has sent us a piece of pork from his farm, so I'll put it in the oven this afternoon!" Eileen promised, before dashing off to take another look at her treasure trove, and concoct more ideas for using it to good effect in a variety of ballet costumes.

Tilly had been in the shop during this exchange, and after Eileen had left, she shyly asked if Shirley had a moment to spare from sorting magazines.

"Why, yes, Tilly, of course. What can I do for you?" Shirley pushed the magazines to one side, tut-tutting. "Some of these are out of date – Pa hasn't been keeping track of them properly. Maybe, Tilly, we can carry on sorting these while we talk. Is something the matter?"

"No, nothing, apart from this War. When will it ever end?" Tilly replied with a woeful sigh, but then, picking up a handful of magazines, she started to explain.

"It's not the War I wanted to talk to you about. The thing is, Mother has been telling me for ages that she wants to find some way of thanking you for saving her life, well, not just her life but all our lives, mine and little Albert's as well. And she keeps going on about it. 'Tilly,' she says to me, 'we must find some way of thanking Miss Shirley for saving us when we were bombed; she was so brave!' Practically every day she asks me if I've come up with something, and I never have, but just now I couldn't help hearing you and Mrs Archie talking. I didn't want to eavesdrop, but there wasn't anywhere else for me to go. You were talking about making costumes for your ballet, and I thought to myself, 'Mother could help with that!' She'd love to help you if you'd have her. She used to be a dressmaker, and she's very good at sewing. Oh, and if you're wondering, she won't want to be paid. She'd be offended if you even so much as mentioned it! It would be her way of thanking you for saving us."

Shirley listened, hardly daring to believe her ears. She might not have had any success so far in raising funds, but help was to hand in another priceless form: yards of beautiful material and two willing dressmakers! If Eileen and Tilly's mother were able to make such a contribution, they would save Aurora a huge amount of money and thereby reduce the amount she and Cynthia would need to find.

That evening, after an ample dinner of healthy farm produce, Shirley enjoyed a blissful respite from mourning for France, and Eileen from wartime preoccupations: they opened cardboard cartons and old suitcases to reveal beautiful dresses from a more opulent age, and rolls of unused material, silks and velvets, which were seemingly just waiting to be turned into ballet skirts for the girls and courtly robes and jackets for men. With a liberal dose of starch, there would be gauze for perfect tutus, and also silken bodices. Eileen was only too happy to share her role as dressmaker with Tilly's mother, because, as she said, she would have her work cut out to make costumes for as many as fourteen dancers or more, on her own, and hoped that some of them could be reused in different programmes. She supposed that, as far as court costumes were concerned, some of the beautiful dresses with their tiny waists from the Victorian period stored in her attic might easily be adjusted without having to make new ones.

Reggie had not entered into the dressmaking spirit, apparently having other, more worrying concerns on his mind, and was clearly relieved when Archie took him off to the parlour for a quiet smoke and a glass of his secret supply of whisky, leaving Eileen and Shirley immersed in handling gorgeous fabrics and discussing their possible uses. So immersed were they in their delightful task, they hardly noticed when Reggie put his head round the door to announce that he was going back to the flat. Not wanting to spoil his daughter's moment of joyful relaxation, he did not say that he was going to man the phone line in case of an air raid. Evidently Shirley had completely forgotten that she was supposed to be on ARP duty too, so he considered it kinder simply to be ready for action himself if the need arose.

Half an hour later, the delightful evening was brought to an abrupt close when the dreaded noise of the siren whined into action from the church tower.

"Goodness," Shirley cried, leaping to her feet, "I'm supposed to be on duty! I must dash!" Grabbing her coat, she ran out of the house and reached the shop at the same time as her father, already in uniform and wearing his helmet, arrived back from setting the siren off.

"I've brought your helmet and uniform downstairs, Shirl," he said, beckoning to a pile of clothing on the counter. "I was sure you'd come back as soon as you heard the siren. They reckon it's going to be a big one tonight, so on with your uniform as quick as you can! We must hurry!" Shirley struggled into her uniform, and off they went, out into the dark night once again to rouse the neighbourhood and send the residents into the shelters before the distant hum of the advancing aircraft became a threatening, throbbing, deafening roar overhead.

Archie and Eileen would have certainly taken shelter as soon as Shirley left, but she was not so sure of Madame, with her imperious ways and tendency to sleep soundly. She sent her father to bang on her door, ring the bell and shout up to the window, while she herself made her way to the streets where people were already coming out of their houses, finally well aware of the dangers they faced. Those who did not have shelters in their gardens allowed themselves to be herded in an orderly file to the public shelter, scared of what might await them if they resisted. It took Reggie much longer to rouse Madame and hurry her round to Archie's Anderson shelter. Naturally she would not consider going to the public shelter.

The night was one of the most terrifying of the Blitz, stretching father and daughter to the utmost limits of their endurance. Although their own area escaped almost unscathed, they were asked to help out in a neighbouring district, where they climbed up ladders to help trapped residents to safety, pulled people out from under rubble, summoned ambulances, assisted the crews as they tried to rescue terrified inhabitants from burning buildings and, worst of all, held the hands of and talked gently to the dying in an attempt to keep them alive and conscious until the ambulances arrived, which was often too late. In all this time debris and fire rained down on them, as did jets of water and hissing steam from the hosepipes.

Scarcely had they time to glance towards central London; when they did, they saw those terrifying red pillars of fire and flame, the hallmark of the Blitz, reaching once more to the heavens.

Shirley closed her eyes, and her father sighed. Clutching his arm, she struggled to stammer, "It's worse than ever, isn't it, Pa?"

"I reckon there'll not be much left after this," he murmured darkly.

Some hours later, when they turned the key in the lock of their own front door, their faces were blackened and burn-speckled, their uniforms torn, their helmets dented and their hair scorched.

"We're lucky to be alive!" was Shirley's rueful and only comment through her tears. Her father said nothing.

He was so traumatized by this raid, which had evidently been designed to take the heart out of London, both the city and its people, that he sat slumped in his armchair the next day, brooding over yet another catastrophe. Although he relayed, to anyone who would listen, every disaster reported in the news bulletins, from the attacks on the Houses of Parliament, Westminster Abbey, St Paul's and the British Museum to the bombing of the four main railway stations, he did not speak otherwise.

Shirley, meanwhile, had no desire to discuss fabrics and costumes, or even the ballet itself, although Eileen, bringing half-a-dozen fresh eggs, called round to see how she and her father were. In any case, it was obvious that such frivolous considerations would have to be put on hold, because there was yet more bomb damage and devastation to be recorded and missing persons to be accounted for. First impressions suggested that the worst damage was limited to a neighbourhood a mile away, where they had worked on rescue operations the previous night. Later it became clear that the main targets this time had in fact been the railway and the Underground. These, the main arterial links from the borough into central London, had taken a direct hit. This was indeed bad news for Shirley: more than ever, that link was the indispensable lifeline to the development of Aurora and the ballets that Aurora was going to perform for the troops all over the country. There was nothing for it: hereafter she would have to take the bus into central London to join the other dancers for rehearsals, and how tedious that would be! It was some consolation that Archie and Eileen's house had not suffered, nor had that precious collection of materials.

Reggie called an emergency meeting of the ARP the following week to discuss future involvement in neighbouring areas; it was generally agreed with the wardens from those areas that there should be more cooperation between the neighbourhoods, starting at once, in anticipation of future raids. More recruitment was also a top priority, particularly because, Reggie said, his daughter would be leaving the patrol shortly as she was working on other ways of supporting the war effort, namely by setting up a dance company to entertain the troops. She would most likely be leaving, he added, as soon as she had raised enough money to put the show on the road.

This news was greeted with "ooh"s and "aah"s of admiration. A well-dressed man stood up and began to speak. "Mr Marlow, I think I am representing not only the wardens from our borough here present, but all our residents, when I say how grateful we are to you and your daughter for all the support you gave us that fateful night, and on many other similar occasions. You and she acted tirelessly, and without regard to your own safety, to help us. You saved many lives in that inferno; without your courage the death toll would have been much greater than it actually was. It is quite remarkable that a slight, young, ballet dancer should have come to our aid, and we wish her well in her further efforts to save the country at this most critical time." There was applause, to which Shirley stood up and curtsied before going out to make the tea.

During the following weeks, it took an army of workmen to repair the Tube and railway lines. In that time Shirley and Madame Belinskaya spent all day and every day in the Methodist church hall, when not taking the bus into central London, which in any case was depressing in the extreme, and difficult to negotiate because of all the clearing-up activities on the way and at their destination.

"Zees, *ma chérie*, ees a great opportunity for us," Madame announced in her heavily accented English. Shirley was about to interrupt that it was not an opportunity but a disaster when Madame stopped her. "What I mean, ees zat togezer, since we can only travel eento London occasionally vairy slowly by bus, we 'ave ze chance to perfect our ballets, our programmes, our choreographeez and zee details of your performance wizout ze ozers interfering. In ze evenings you can speak to Zeenzeea on ze phone and tell 'er what we are doing."

Shirley nodded and smiled wanly. As ever, Madame was right; this was indeed an ironic though excellent opportunity to talk about and concentrate on all those things which otherwise would take ages to hammer out in the company rehearsals. There, each of the other parts and each sequence had to be tried out separately with each group of dancers, the men, the *corps de ballet* and the soloists. Instead, at the end of this enforced protracted period of isolation, she and Madame would be able to present various *faits accomplis*, and these would be so good that no one would be able to quibble with them.

Madame's boundless enthusiasm in selecting dances and excerpts from the great ballets, both for the whole company and solos for Shirley, was in danger of running away with her, although as yet her ideas were not destined for any particular programme. Shirley was none too sure that she agreed with all of Madame's choices, some suggested on the bus ride, and some kept for later discussions. One afternoon, over Russian tea in Madame's flat, Shirley brought up the worrying matter of Doris's attitude. Despite being keen to dance till she dropped, she was aware that if she hogged all the main roles herself she would become very unpopular, especially with Doris, who, after all, had proposed the inspired name of the company. Therefore, with a certain reluctance, she steeled herself to relinquish certain parts – for example, the role of Odile, the daughter of the wicked baron Rothbart, who seduces Prince Siegfried away from Odette, the Swan Queen, in *Swan Lake*. "If I'm going to dance Odette, someone else should have a turn at dancing Odile, I think," she told Madame.

"Hmm, ze black swan is usually played by ze same ballereena who dances Odette," Madame responded, in her still halting English, "but you will 'ave such a lot to do, I zeenk per'aps it would be bettair for you if someone else, maybe Dorees, dances Odeele."

Shirley knew that despite her reservations, this was the best solution, because her left leg, though strong now, might if overworked, let her down, so she reconciled herself to sharing a little of the glory. Nevertheless, she had other doubts, which she took the opportunity to voice. "I am happy to let Doris take a solo role, Madame, and you're right that Odile would be perfect for her, but I think *Swan Lake* is too ambitious for the moment. Why don't we start with *Sleeping Beauty*, with Aurora's christening, perhaps? It's less demanding than *Swan Lake* and more manageable for a company like ours. After all, we are a small company, so everyone has to dance like a soloist."

She could hardly believe that she was speaking with such authority, but Madame took it in good part, and agreed with her, saying that *Swan Lake* could wait for the next tour.

"Anyhow," Shirley said, "our company *is* the Aurora Ballet Company, so to begin with the Princess Aurora's christening is really appropriate."

"Yes, zat ees true, but I 'ave 'ad anozer idee," said Madame, unstoppably, though for once in a remarkably pliable frame of mind. "I zeenk we should perform zose ballets you eenvented for us. You remember, no? Ze Spanish ballet or ze French market dances? Zay were lovely and so *populair*. We need to 'ave a change from only performing ze classical dances. Do you ave notes for zem? My notes and my gramophone records were lost een my 'ouse when zay bombed eet."

Shirley did indeed have her choreographic notes for her Spanish ballet and for the French market ballet, and also the dances for the *Seasons*, a ballet which she had partly choreographed seemingly an age ago, but in fact only a couple of years before. Memories of those days at the market in France with her grandmother, Mémé, and her Maman came flooding back. Who could have anticipated then what was happening now?

She wiped her nose and stuttered, "I'll look for those notes, but I don't remember what music we were dancing to."

"Do not worry, I weel find some muzeek for zose dances," said Madame.

Then, to Shirley's surprise, Madame switched into French and slipped in yet another, rather different idea, which Shirley, happily contemplating her own choreographies, was not expecting. "I think the programme should begin with the village dance from *Giselle*," La Belinskaya suggested, "because that engages the audience right from the very start. After that will follow the first act of *Sleeping Beauty*, the christening of the Princess Aurora to launch your company of the same name with you dancing the Lilac Fairy. Then we will have the interval, and after that one or two of your Spanish dances for a soloist – you, probably – before a shortened version of *Coppélia*."

"That is such a funny ballet; people will love it!" Shirley burst out in raptures. "They will forget about the War and go home feeling they have really enjoyed themselves!"

Shirley was taken aback that Madame had dismissed all of their previous discussions, and there she was, coming up with a whole programme of new ideas! She admitted that they were good ideas, but she would need time to adjust to the change. She nodded weakly, though she realized that Madame was thinking about audience reaction, which of course was essential to the success of any performance, or indeed to a tour. "Yes, thank you, Madame. I will talk to Cynthia about this." She picked up her handbag and shuffled towards the door.

Cynthia's reaction was sensible. "Well, I do think she has a point," she said, "because if we just start with the beginning of *Swan Lake*, we would then have to abandon that ballet as the plot starts to develop, but the village dance from Giselle is a stand-alone piece. It's an energetic introduction to the story, but is not much more than villagers having fun. It's quite a good lead-in to another ballet – in this case, *Sleeping Beauty*, with Aurora's christening, the perfect way to launch our company! One or two Spanish dances would certainly be a lively opener for the second half, and a scaled-down version of *Coppélia* would be a great way to end!"

Cynthia's words of wisdom persuaded Shirley to see the sense of Madame's planning. As a result, she passed on the information to Eileen and Tilly's mum whose fingers were itching to start working on costumes, beginning with Shirley's.

"If we have our prima ballerina's costumes done, it will be simpler when we come to work on the *corps de ballet*," Eileen announced, "because for the *corps*, we shall be making the same costumes over and over again, and mostly they will all be more or less the same size – well, I hope they will be."

"Yes, you don't need to worry about that," Shirley assured her. "We are all about the same size, except for Doris, who is much bigger than the rest of us."

Each evening she conferred with Cynthia, who rang from a call-box, telling her what had been achieved that day. Cynthia agreed more or less with everything that Shirley told her, having no ambitions to dance starring roles herself, for she had other matters to deal with.

Cynthia was rehearsing the troupe, most of whom were trained in classical ballet, for *corps de ballet* dances, which were already in their usual repertoire, but there were others whose experience of dancing was limited to variety performances. Cynthia had not yet met a prospective compère for the performances, but her worst headache was still the question of funding.

"I haven't been able to raise any money at all, but Mother really would like to help with the costumes; she is also a very good seamstress, so I suggest she makes the costumes for the men and your aunt Eileen and Tilly's mother make the costumes for you and the *corps*. There are more girls than men, so that should work out well. Mother also has a lot of fabric up in our attic, and I'm sure some of that would do."

"But that's wonderful," said Shirley. "Between your mother, Eileen and Tilly's mother, we'll have our wardrobe, and we'll save so much money! We won't need to raise two thousand pounds after all – much less than that!" She paused while another thought formed in her brain. "But," said she to Cynthia, "we must pay your mother!" She did not say, "because she needs the money," but that was uppermost in her mind.

Cynthia was opening her mouth to protest, but Shirley was quicker off the mark. She simply nodded and said, "We'll talk about that later."

Her father's seeming lack of interest in funding was still troubling Shirley. She dared not ask him for money outright, but she did hope that by now he might have offered even a modest contribution to the endeavour, which undeniably was in a good cause.

One evening, as he was listening to the news, the doorbell rang, and Shirley ran downstairs to answer it. On the step there stood the well-dressed man who had come to the ARP meeting and had praised her and her father so warmly. He was carrying a bag. "May I come in, Miss Marlow?" he asked.

"Yes, do, come upstairs, will you please?" she replied. He followed her up and into the living room.

Reggie was surprised to see the visitor. "Mr Bartlett!" he exclaimed. "It's good to see you! Come in, do! Have you come to arrange another ARP meeting to follow up our suggestions from the last one?" he asked.

"Yes, of course, but that can wait a day or two; that's not why I'm here," Mr Bartlett said, seating himself on one of the dining chairs by the table. He put his bag on the table. "You and Miss Marlow here were extremely heroic in that last raid, which did so much damage and caused so many casualties, and we wanted to thank you, so we arranged a house-to-house collection. There was not a house among those still standing where the occupants did not want to thank you and give you a contribution, however small, for your work. So here it is! It comes with our heartfelt thanks and our best wishes for Miss Marlow's dance company. We hope it will help her get it going!"

Shirley dropped onto the piano stool in astonishment. She heard her father saying, "That's most kind; we were only doing our duty and were glad to help, weren't we, Shirl?"

"Yes, of course, but I had no idea that everyone would be so generous," she stammered, her voice fading away. She felt rather dizzy with surprise.

"I haven't counted the money, but I hope it will come in useful," said Mr Bartlett, rising to his feet.

"Oh, yes, it will, thank you very much. And please thank all those kind people. Here, let me write a little note for you to put up in your post office or newsagent's." Shirley scribbled a thank-you note and handed it to the visitor, who took it, put it in his breast pocket and departed, leaving Reggie to count the takings.

"I'm not sure we should accept all this," said Reggie, gesturing towards the bag on the table.

"Oh, Pa! Don't be ridiculous! It's not for us or for me personally, but for Aurora. Look, do stop grumbling and get on and count it, please!" She tipped out the shower of brass, copper and silver coins and a few notes onto the table, and left her father to stack them into piles, his usual method for adding up the day's takings. She went into the kitchen to wash up the supper things and then into her room to practise a few pirouettes.

"Shirl!" he called out eventually. "Come here. I haven't finished counting all these threepenny bits and sixpences, but there's well over thirty pounds!" In fact, there was much more than that. The final tally amounted to thirty-seven pounds and some small coins, halfpennies and farthings.

Pa surveyed the table with satisfaction. "There, you see," he said, "you are very much appreciated, and I'm proud of you!"

Shirley was overjoyed, although at the same time she experienced a niggling hope that her father might use this opportunity to offer to contribute to the fund, perhaps to raise the takings to a hundred pounds. He did not do this. Instead, he offered to put up a notice in the shop asking customers to show their appreciation for his daughter's sterling efforts to safeguard the community, by dropping some money into a box provided just inside the door, as a contribution to her new venture, the Aurora Ballet Company, which would be performing with ENSA for the troops to aid the war effort.

Nonetheless, the piles of coins and notes on the table eventually prodded Reggie's memory into recalling his fury at Ted's preposterous suggestion of a role for Shirley by luring German soldiers into traps in France; he also recalled his own realization that this new ballet company would be the best way for her to do her bit for the country without endangering herself more than was absolutely necessary. When he had thrown Ted's message into the fire, he had told himself that it was time for him to contribute to the company, but so much had happened since then that it had gone completely out of his mind. It was still not too late.

He brought the matter up when she came into the room carrying a sheaf of papers and spread them out on the table.

"We're going to use my ballets in our programmes, Pa!" she declared jubilantly, bending over the scribbles and patterns on the sheets.

"That *is* good news!" he said, hoping he sounded appropriately enthusiastic now that the moment had arrived. "I've been thinking, Shirl," he said, "I know your project's important, and it will encourage the forces. You'll be fighting on the home front! So, I want to contribute to it!"

Taken aback, Shirley looked up, her face a picture of surprise, joy and confusion. "That's wonderful, Pa! Thank you very much – whatever you can afford!" she said.

"I was thinking about fifty pounds," he said, with some hesitation in case she might have been hoping for more.

She stood up and danced round the room. "Oh, Pa, thank you so much!"

Only two days later in a quiet moment in the shop, Archie gravely ushered Shirley into the "counting house" to tell her that the collection in the shop for her ballet company had raised twenty-six pounds. She rang Cynthia that evening to tell her that with her father's money, some of her own from Mrs Fothergill's bequest, and the contributions from the grateful neighbours and other inhabitants of the area, she would be able to bring enough money to Aurora to put the company on its feet.

Cynthia was overjoyed. "We're in business!" she exclaimed. "We really don't need to look for more. What we've got will certainly get us going! Now I'll try and find out more about ENSA, how we apply and so on!"

20

A reply from ENSA to her application arrived much sooner than Cynthia had expected, as she told Shirley over the phone. She read out the letter:

"We are glad to hear that Aurora, your troupe, is well-established. It ought to be possible to arrange for you all to put on shows for us in the summer, in July or August. If you can suggest a suitable programme, our valiant soldiers would enjoy being taken out of their rigid lifestyle in army barracks, and transported into distant parts."

Shirley's faced glowed as she listened; Cynthia was overcome with excitement. "That's wonderful, isn't it? It's going to happen, Shirl!"

It was now Shirley's turn to be overcome.

"Yes, but come on, Cynnie, read on!"

"Please give us details of your troupe, how many participants there are in it, and we'll try to accommodate them on one or more of our Army bases," Cynthia read. She paused for the letter to take effect, as it did, with Shirley laughing over the phone. She then continued with more good news,

"Please be aware our bases are rather isolated. Therefore, it is much easier for you to eat and stay on the spot. This is less expensive than finding accommodation in towns, always assuming that you have no objection to sleeping on camp beds in our empty Nissen huts."

Here the glow in Shirley's cheeks faded and her brow puckered.

"Ah," said she, "Nissen huts. Have you ever slept in a Nissen hut, Cynnie?"

"No, I can't say I have," Cynnie answered, "but I expect it'll be all right."

"I hope so!" Shirley exclaimed fervently. Nevertheless, her impatience to know more overcame other considerations, so she put Nissen huts to the back of her mind.

"Do they say anything about payment and travel?" she asked.

"No, not yet." Cynthia was guarded now. "We haven't got as far as that yet, and I didn't want to put them off."

"Would it be better for someone else to deal with that sort of financial nitty-gritty? Someone like my Pa, perhaps?" Shirley suggested.

"Oh no!" Cynnie cried out defiantly. "I don't expect there'll be a problem. I can handle it, and, in any case, we don't want to have to find our own lodgings. We had to do that sometimes for our variety performances, and it was awfully complicated and expensive when we weren't actually performing for ENSA. The food was dreadful, and the landladies treated us like tarts! In one place we actually had to share the bath water, which was horrid when you think of all that perspiration and grease paint already in the water when you step into it!"

Shirley squirmed; this was an aspect of touring that she had not anticipated. "Oh, well then, if ENSA has something better than that, we should accept their offer," she said, trusting that her co-founder's confidence in ENSA was well-placed.

In the mean time, while waiting for the completion of repairs to the railway line, Shirley continued under Madame's guidance to apply herself to the major balletic roles in readiness for rehearsals with the company. All those steps which in the wake of her paralyzing attack of polio she had thought never to be able to dance again, had firmly re-established themselves in her repertoire: the *bourrées* across the stage *en pointe*, the *pas de Basque*, the *frappés*, the *fouettés*, the *sissonnes*, the *developpés*, the *grands jetés*, the *ronds de jambe*, the *fondus*, the *posé* turns, the *piqués* and above all the *pirouettes* – all those were old friends, conjured up much more easily than she had dared expect, so that reviving them *en pointe* to Madame's satisfaction, indicated merely by a nod of the head, gave her the heady sense that the major roles were well within her reach.

Finally, on completion of the repairs to the line, she and Madame took the train to London three days a week for the intensive rehearsals of the whole company, in preparation for Aurora's inaugural public performance, as they all supposed, on tour. There was a buzz of excitement when the dancers heard that Cynthia had lined up their first engagement, though the concern of many was how much they would be paid.

"I'll let you know that as soon as I have all the information," Cynthia informed them apologetically, "but we do now have confirmation of our fixed booking through ENSA in Yorkshire, to be followed by several more in the north. Please reserve the end of June and the whole of July for the tour." She was also able to tell them that they would be issued with army uniforms to wear on the bases where they performed, and travel warrants to enable them to buy cheap rail tickets, for which they would be refunded. For the time being, she asked them to trust her, confident that all would be well. After conveying all this information, Cynthia whispered to Shirley, "And there's more. I'll tell you later!"

Madame had been in the studio, listening intently, when Cynthia gave her speech at the end of a rehearsal. After the dancers had left and while she waited for Shirley, who was helping Cynthia to tidy up and sweep the floor, she enquired, quite out of the blue, if she would be wearing a uniform too. As one, the two girls stopped what they were doing and turned to look at her, their jaws dropping in a mixture of shock and horror. Shirley was quick off the mark and answered La Belinskaya in French.

"But Madame, no, of course not. Don't worry about that. You won't have to wear a uniform; that's only for those of us who will be visiting the bases. We're not expecting you to come with us because you are doing so much for us already, and we haven't paid you yet for all the training you are giving us. Without your help we wouldn't be able to put on the shows, but we do need to earn some money before we can begin to pay you."

Then she added a fatal afterthought: "And all the travelling will be very tiring, and it could be chilly in Yorkshire even in July, especially in army accommodation."

At this Madame bridled and then exploded in a mixture of French, English and Russian. "You treat me as if I am very old! I am not as old as you think, and I am quite capable of travelling to Yorkshire or wherever it is you are going. Remember I left Russia in the winter with only a small bag. Then from the Finnish frontier where the train stopped, I had to walk into Sweden – yet I survived, so this country in July will be warm compared with that! I insist on coming with you to supervise the performances and continue the training. And as for payment, I do not want any! I am doing this to fight the Nazis!"

Shirley did her best to translate this tirade into coherent English for Cynthia, whose face fell the more she heard. She did not answer at once, but gave the appearance of giving the question serious consideration. Then, with a smile, she intervened.

"Please tell Madame, in French so that she understands properly what I'm saying," she said to Shirley, "that it is very kind of her not to expect payment; we do appreciate the training she is giving us in so many dances,

THE FIERY PILLARS OF WAR

and what's more she really is making us into a company, rather than a collection of random dancers. It's nice of her to want to come with us. I will get in touch with ENSA to ask if it might be possible to accommodate Madame in a hotel somewhere, rather than on a camp-bed in a Nissen hut, but it's unlikely they will be able to find a hotel, because the base is so far from any town."

Shirley found it hard not to laugh out loud, but did as Cynthia had asked, although she had difficulty in translating "Nissen hut" into French. On hearing the words for the two sorts of Nissen hut, "*une hutte préfabriquée en toile ou en tôle ondulée*", Madame quickly changed her tune. She then said to Shirley, meekly, lapsing into French, "Yes, I should prefer to stay in a hotel if that is possible; but if not, then I shall prefer to stay at home," and fell silent.

Plunged into this unforeseen crisis, Shirley came up with another idea: "Perhaps, Madame, you would like to come with us when we perform nearer London?" She shuddered when she heard herself saying, "There are so many airbases within easy reach, and that would only involve a day trip."

Madame ignored this well-meaning idea, and walked off to the Underground station alone. Shirley remained behind to collect herself up. Had she really talked about airbases near London, the very bases from which Alan had flown? How would she ever be able to bring herself to perform on an airbase? She was shaking from head to toe, but only succeeded in pulling herself together when she heard Cynthia laughing, and uttering a sigh of relief.

"Phew!" she exclaimed when Madame had disappeared out of earshot, "Oh, my goodness! That was a narrow escape! Just imagine what it would be like with her with us! We'd never have a moment's peace!"

"You don't have to tell me," Shirley replied. "I do hope no one will find her a hotel; you never know where she might have friends. They seem to be all over the place."

Cynthia chuckled. "I don't think that will happen," she said, before pausing to reflect. "We must take care not to offend her again; she really is such a valuable support. We wouldn't be doing this if it wasn't for her."

They agreed to buy a suitably large and colourful bouquet of flowers for Madame.

"Oh, and by the way," Cynthia continued, "I didn't have time to tell you earlier on, but I've found out we could also be adopted by CEMA, the Council for the Encouragement of Music and the Arts. They don't have uniforms, but they do pay better than ENSA. After all, we need to make sure we are paying the going rate for our dancers. And CEMA is a more prestigious organization!"

Madame attended rehearsals over the next week or two, but avoided travelling into London with Shirley; she maintained a huffy, though not openly hostile, attitude, which was upsetting nevertheless, and had a depressing effect on the company: the fragile magic of Aurora was dissipating fast – not on account of Doris, but of Madame.

"We are going to have to do something about this situation," Shirley observed.

"I agree, but what? She hasn't even mentioned the flowers we sent. Let's hope she just calms down eventually," Cynthia said, making an effort to sound more positive than she felt.

"She could have a strong influence on our dancers if she doesn't," came Shirley's rejoinder, casting doubts on Cynthia's optimism. "That will be even worse if she starts discouraging them more than she has already." She explained the reason for her misgivings. "You know that baton she keeps in her bag and uses to tap us when she's not satisfied with our posture?" Cynthia nodded. "Well," Shirley went on, "if she becomes more peevish and begins to hit harder, people won't like it and will leave, because we don't have any way of hanging on to them. I know what the full force of that baton's like: she used it on me when I first went to her classes!"

A despondent silence fell, broken only by Cynthia who observed, "On the other hand, I can see her point of view: she is very committed and wants the dancing to be perfect, so she has a right to see us in performance. The trouble is she doesn't understand the complications of having her with us on tour. It would be like having a strict head teacher in charge, and we're all adults; we don't want that. Anyhow, the others would rebel at it. We'll have to come up with some idea to please her pretty quickly – otherwise it's all going to fall apart."

"Maybe, maybe," remarked Shirley with a grimace, but then her face lit up. "I say," she said, "what about putting on a performance somewhere here before we go away?"

There was a lull while Cynthia considered this latest suggestion. "I think I see what you mean," she said. "We could put on our touring show in honour of Madame, and – oh, what's more, have you thought of this? It might bring in some *money* at the same time."

"Even better! I hadn't thought of *that*, only of pleasing Madame and keeping her on side, but money as well, hooray!" Shirley cried out, her face broadening into a huge smile. "We'd have to find a suitable hall with a stage, of course, and pay for the hire, but it might be possible; let's suggest it to Madame tomorrow, shall we?"

Madame applauded the plan and was touched that Shirley and Cynthia were so keen to please her. Deep down, although of course she would not admit it, she was not so sure that she really wanted to go on tour after all. Escaping from Russia all those years ago had made her vow that she would never allow herself to be placed in such discomfort ever again if she could possibly avoid it, and if the proposed tour involved staying in a hut with a canvas roof, it would certainly take her away from all her home comforts in the warmth and elegant cosiness she had created for herself in Emily Fothergill's flat.

The trains were up and running, Madame was placated, and, with the incentive of an imminent engagement, the company recovered from the setback and even increased its momentum, especially since Cynthia and Shirley agreed that if Madame were not going to expect any payment, they could afford to make advance payments to their dancers. For this Reggie was brought in after all, because only he knew how to handle the bookkeeping required. There was a spring in his step, and he felt equal to any challenge, especially after the attack on the newly launched, fastest, largest German warship, the Bismarck, on its attempt to break out of German waters into the Atlantic, with the aim of sinking the convoys crossing the ocean. On 24th May 1941 two British ships – the Hood, a cruiser, and the Prince of Wales, a battleship – intercepted the Bismarck near Iceland. The Hood was hit and sank with a huge loss of life, but the Bismarck, damaged and leaking fuel, escaped. It was heading for Brest in occupied France, but on 26th May, three hundred nautical miles from Brest, it was bombed by the RAF and attacked by three British warships. It lost its steering, and sank quickly, too far out of Brest for U-boats to come to its aid.

Reggie was ecstatic on hearing of the sinking of the Bismarck. It gave impetus to his new role as the bookkeeper for his daughter's ballet company, itself part of the fighting force. As he saw it, his support of her company was, in a small way, another of his contributions to the welfare of the country, which, it had to be remembered, was by no means defeated. Indeed, with more victories like the Bismarck, it might well pull through. His willing help in taking an unwelcome load off their shoulders, freed Cynthia and Shirley to complete the programme for a possible London show, as well as the Yorkshire venture. For the latter it was decided at a full meeting of the company that the programme should not be too complicated or ambitious, so that the dancers would be able to acclimatize to the challenge of dancing to an audience, mostly of men, from all grades of army personnel in an unfamiliar, possibly uncomfortable, army barracks.

The male dancers were particularly anxious not to find themselves subjected to jeering from the audience for not being in active service. One of them suggested having brief notes about each section of dancers on the sheet of paper that served as a programme. These notes would detail why the men were performing on the stage and not fighting in the forces, either because they were refugees far from home, or because they were stranded in Great Britain, or simply on leave. There was general agreement that this was sufficient information to cover the whole cast of male dancers, plus the four stage-hands, Rocky the American, Bill and Jeff, his rather elderly helpers, plus Dmitri, the short-sighted master of the musical accompaniment played on Shirley's gramophone. She reluctantly agreed to take on the task of writing the programme notes, not only explaining the situation of the men, but also giving brief accounts of the ballets from which excerpts had been taken. No sooner had she agreed to do this, than she thought of asking Madame to write out the notes for the ballets in French, which she would then translate into English, thus saving herself valuable time. Perhaps, therefore, it would not be necessary to engage a compère as well.

By general consent the show would open with the energetic village dance from *Giselle* for the whole company, as suggested by Madame; this truly magical scene would stifle any catcalls and whistles. The scene-changing, which in fact only amounted to replacing the backdrop and adding a few items of furniture, would just give the cast time to adjust their costumes, the girls exchanging their green overskirts for mauve ones, and the men changing their jackets, before appearing in the christening of the Princess Aurora, an abbreviated act from *Sleeping Beauty*. In this, five of the girls would have solo roles, a reduction from the original twelve of the fairy story, each dancing the part of a flower fairy bearing gifts and promises for the baby's future. The flower fairies would be followed on stage by one of the men playing the hideous, uninvited Carabosse, casting her wicked spell on the baby princess. Shirley, wearing a purple tutu, would then appear as the saving grace in the role of the Lilac Fairy, using her power to alleviate, though not dispel, the strength of the curse, which would be limited to one hundred years of sleep, instead of death. There would be roles for the rest of the company as courtiers and servants, not forgetting the distraught King and the Queen, the latter being a suitably imposing role for Doris.

The second half of the performance would begin with the comical, lively act from *Coppélia* where Franz creeps into the workshop of the old inventor, Dr Coppelius, after dark in search of the beautiful image, Coppélia, he has seen sitting in an upper window. Swanhilda, his jealous fiancée, breaks into the workshop ahead of him with her friends, and they amuse themselves setting Dr Coppelius's mechanical dolls going. Swanhilda, on finding that Coppélia is nothing more than a life-size doll, throws her to the floor, dresses up in her clothes and takes her place in the window. To his horror, when Franz approaches Coppélia, alias Swanhilda, she wrecks the studio, and both are caught red-handed by the old man on his return.

The evening would end with one of Shirley's own choreographies, two of her short Spanish dances, a finale designed to give the army audience a glow of colourful, southern sunshine. Dmitri, the expert in recording matters, was brought in to make gramophone records of appropriate excerpts from all the ballets on the programme, including a combination of movements from Bizet's *Carmen Suites* for the Spanish extravaganza. Shirley went shopping for props – fans, castanets and the like – and at home, she made *papier-mâché* oranges to be put round the edge of the stage in baskets. Meanwhile, Eileen looked out red, yellow and black silks from her supply for Spanish-style overskirts for the *corps de ballet*, and made red floral decorations to pin on the general-purpose bodices. No one would have guessed that the company did not have a copious wardrobe of costumes for each individual ballet.

Tilly's mother set to work with Eileen, creating these striking costumes for the girls, while Cynthia's mother took on the considerable task of making the elaborate costumes for the men, all of whom luckily had their own tights. Once a week, armed with suitcases full of half-completed garments and their sewing kits, the three ladies travelled to the London studio to take measurements, arrange fittings, snip with their scissors and stick pins in their creations, which grew by the day into such glorious concoctions that no one would have guessed that the basic fabrics, silks, velvets and cottons, had lain forgotten for decades in dusty attics. Eileen, Cynthia's mother and Tilly's mother, all kept on refusing payment, insisting with one voice that they were glad to have the opportunity to contribute to the war effort.

In spite of all this dedicated work, Shirley, although thrilled that all was going well, failed to see how it might be possible to accomplish so much in such a short space of time. First and foremost, there was the training to be considered: Madame was only too keen to take charge both of that and the choreographies. Fortunately, although it was not huge, Madame's new studio, in the place of Emily Fothergill's old sweetshop, proved the ideal venue for training all the solo artists, both male and female. After losing not only her own house in that horrendous bombing raid, but all her equipment, costumes, recordings and everything that was not already safely stored away in a bank vault, La Belinskaya was overjoyed that her secret dream of establishing a ballet company was being realized, and, as Cynthia had expected, forgave both her and Shirley for excluding her from the tour.

A couple of the men, including Rocky, the huge, good-natured American scene shifter, came to Archie's back garden on Sundays to help him and Reggie build structures from which backdrops could be suspended. These, designed by Reggie, were hinged so that they could be folded up and easily altered to fit any size of stage and also to fit into the van that was to transport all the props and the costumes to Yorkshire and anywhere else. Two other men and Doris spread out old curtains over large, overlapping sheets of newspaper on the fine, sprung wooden floor in Madame's recently opened studio, and carefully applied paint to create scenic backdrops, whether of a medieval country village, a royal court, a mad genius's workshop or a striking vista of a white-painted Spanish town. It was all very exciting, but inevitably it all cost money, and then there were records and needles to buy, as well as a gramophone to take on tour. Shirley had very reluctantly parted with her own gramophone because it was needed in the London studio; now she was anxious to reclaim it. Nobody even dared suggest borrowing Madame's new gramophone for the tour.

Even with such generous support, the money kept slipping away in spite of Reggie's careful bookkeeping: the hire of the London studio, which they needed to use when the whole cast was involved, was not cheap:

the dancers' pay reduced the funds drastically by the week, and Shirley began to wonder whether the money, including her own inheritance from Mrs Fothergill, would run out before the company ever reached Yorkshire, even with their travel passes. There would also be the cost of petrol for the van, which Jack, who also danced when needed, was borrowing from his father to transport the sets and the costumes.

Things were not looking good. She asked her father one evening if he had any suggestions for salvaging the situation. As usual he was inseparable from the wireless.

"Maybe, Shirl," he answered without interrupting his listening, and then burst out, "Thank goodness your company is set up! I remember you said you already had an engagement at an army base and would be in uniform, is that right?"

She nodded. "Yes, Pa, that's why I wanted to talk to you, but you were glued to the wireless. I said we're running out of money and asked if you had any ideas."

"Yes, yes, I heard that, but I wanted to tell you more about that call-up for women first. Aneurin Bevan is now saying he *is* mobilizing women, and they really will work in armaments factories! That's shocking and dangerous. I can't tell you how relieved I am that everyone will see you're working – as if you haven't worked hard enough here already, but memories are short, and everybody has to do their share."

Shirley waited impatiently for her father to get to the point.

"Let me see… you had said you were going to put on a performance to keep your Madame What's-her-name happy before setting out on tour, is that right?" he asked.

"Yes, that's right," said Shirley.

"Well," he said, "if you put on a show somewhere round here – say, in early June if you can be ready by then – I reckon a lot of people would come to see it and be prepared to pay good money to do so. I'm always hearing complaints in the shop that there's nothing much to do here. People are too scared to go into central London in the evening these days, and since the cinema was damaged when the railway line was hit, they can't even go to see a film."

"Yes, Pa, we've already thought of that to keep Madame happy, because she's definitely not coming on tour with us, but the trouble is I can't think of a theatre, or even a suitable hall, round here," said she, her reply speaking loudly of frustration.

Reggie's quick reaction not only swiftly dispersed her frustration, but astonished her by its relevance.

"I reckon you could fill the cinema," he remarked. "The repairs on it are almost finished. It wasn't damaged structurally, but they can't get a new projector, so it's standing there waiting to be used; it does hold a large audience and there is a big stage behind the screen, which of course is not in place at the moment. I'll go and talk to some of my friends to see if they might be able to put on your show. You'd have to hire it and that would cost something, but there is enough money in the account for that."

The cinema was the perfect solution to Aurora's problems. It had undergone sufficient basic repairs and redecoration after the bomb damage, to render it cleaner and pleasanter in all respects than it had been in a long time. The flooring was smooth and safe for dancing, and the empty stage was large enough for the ballets on the programme. The owners were prepared to offer it for hire at a reduced price, and the technicians were pleased to offer their services, also at a reduced rate, because this was a performance for local people being put on by a heroic and enterprising young resident.

Madame was delighted that the show was being produced in her honour, as was announced in the programme, although the ulterior, monetary reason for it was kept secret from her. She was confident that the performance would be up to scratch and ready for early or perhaps mid-June. Eileen and her team worked even harder at their sewing machines. Reggie was relieved that his poppet would not be conscripted to work in an armaments' factory – or even worse, sent to France as a special agent.

21

Although all appeared to be going according to some sort of plan, a never-ending flood of administrative issues, threatening to sweep both Cynthia and Shirley away, poured into the limited hours on Tuesdays, Wednesdays and Thursdays, between the end of the day's dancing in London and bedtime. Those issues also took up any free moments between sessions in Madame's studio on Mondays and Fridays. Because there was no time to shop even for the limited provisions available, meals were so scant that both father and daughter began to lose weight, something he, but not she, could well afford to do. Eileen watched anxiously as Shirley shed the few spare pounds that in any case were scarcely visible on her, and when her normal healthy complexion began to fade into a ghostly pallor, the elderly relative took the law into her own hands.

"Shirley, I'll cook the evening meals for you and your father, if you can commission Tilly to do your shopping. I have my hands full with the costumes, otherwise I would shop for you as well, but my dear, I simply don't have a second to spare. We are on course with our sewing, but if I take even a moment off for other things, I won't be able to finish by June. When did you say the show was going to be here, up the road in the cinema? If it's mid-June, that will be all right, but any earlier than that, we can't manage, not without staying up all night and Archie won't let me do that."

"It *is* mid-June, and I'm hoping we'll manage it," Shirley replied, scarcely audible on account of her low blood sugar levels. "I can't thank you enough; dear Eileen, you are such a marvellous fairy godmother to me!"

Eileen laughed. "I would do anything to keep you fit for your dancing, and it doesn't take a doctor to see that, gasping like that, you are short of good, healthy food. You need building up, dear, not to put on weight, but to strengthen you for this new challenge. Let me put my thinking cap on…"

The next day, Eileen came back, saying, "I've had my thinking cap on, Shirley, and I've come up with a better idea. I think you and your pa should come to supper with *us* when you get back from your training, on those mid-week evenings at least, and then at the weekends when you are based at home, you can cook for yourself and your father, and let's hope you'll enjoy doing so as a change from all that exercise. It won't make any difference to me, because feeding four is scarcely any more effort than cooking for two."

Shirley was overcome by such generosity of spirit, although how Eileen was really going to manage doing all that when she was so busy with Aurora's costumes was not obvious, despite her being a wizard with a needle and her sewing machine. Reggie, on the other hand, much as he wished he were a more accomplished cook, was greatly relieved and grateful that his daughter would be spared providing meals for both of them. He also always looked forward to Eileen's cooking and resolved to pay her for her time and trouble.

Cynthia had the advantage of having her mother at home to cook hearty meals for her, not only every evening but every morning as well, setting a full English breakfast before her at eight o'clock, before she left home for a day's training. Cynthia was also in contact with all the forthcoming venues for Aurora's performances, and passed on most of the arrangements to her business partner, which was how the two girls described themselves these days.

"Everything is arranged for Yorkshire," she told Shirley cheerfully one Monday when the latter had spent the weekend struggling with organizing, pricing, ticketing, air-raid precautions and posters, let alone the printing of an, as yet, unwritten programme sheet for the cinema production.

"Ah, good!" Shirley replied, doing her best to sound enthusiastic. "I haven't had time yet to translate the programme notes that Madame has kindly written out in French for us, but that will be quicker than writing them myself from scratch. Nor for that matter, have I written the notes about why the male dancers are not in the forces."

She let out a sigh of exhaustion, before continuing her to-do list. "What's more, I still have to arrange rehearsal times in the cinema. The staff there are very obliging, but their times don't always coincide with ours, especially because some of our *corps de ballet* work in other places on Fridays and Saturdays."

"Oh, what a nuisance!" Cynthia groaned. "I thought it was already arranged that our show would be on a Saturday."

"Yes, don't worry, it will be," Shirley reassured her. "Two of our male dancers who are already engaged elsewhere are going to find deputies for that Saturday, but most of the cinema staff also have temporary jobs on Saturdays while they wait for the new projector to arrive, so they'll have to find substitutes as well. Let's hope they can!"

Such were the problems that beset Shirley, when all she wanted to do was concentrate on the ballet. In that fantasy world of love and passion, beauty and horror, life and death, sadness and joy, wordlessly conveyed in sublime music and movement, she found the full expression of all her own experiences and all her hopeless longings. Immersed in ballet, she could, when time and space allowed, shut herself off from the terrors of the real world outside, where sirens, alarms, enemy aircraft overhead, bombs, destruction and killing were not only an ever-present threat, but also a frequent occurrence. In the ethereal world of the ballet, she could imagine being with Alan, with him defying wickedness and evil, and together reaching for eternal happiness either in life or death – it did not much matter which.

The interruption to such dreams by the tedious day-to-day running of the company, the success of which depended not simply on her and Cynthia, but also on the willingness of the cast to cooperate, was annoying in the extreme. There were inevitably occasions when members of the troupe had commitments elsewhere, or developed ailments, twisted ankles or sore toes – all justifiable reasons for absence, but problematic in view of the tight schedule. Shirley occasionally was on the verge of displaying her irritation, but, mustering an uncharacteristic restraint, she refrained from speaking her mind, because she was aware that would only make matters worse.

However, the band of willing helpers from the neighbourhood and the goodwill of the local community encouraged her not to lose heart altogether. When rehearsals moved to the huge performing space in the cinema in a couple of weeks, posters went up thanks to the paper boys, who took them out with the morning round and pinned them up on hoardings or fences in the area. Tickets were already going on sale in the cinema box office; programmes had been printed; costumes were ready for their final fittings, and the sets, at least for the first performance, were in place – with Reggie and Archie, plus a handful of their friends from the pub, acting as scene shifters.

"Cor," said one aged, bedazzled helper, "bless me soul, I never in all me life expected to see meself ushering in a theatre and watching the show! I think I'll look out for more opportunities. It's great! Me missus can't believe it. ''Arry,' she says, 'You've taken on a new lease of life. I'll 'ave to come and give it a try too. Mebe they'll find a role for me on the stage, in among them there dancers!'"

Harry was even more exuberant after witnessing the show to which he had been giving of his time. "I'm goin' to change me lifestyle," he announced. "I'll come out of retirement and take up a new profession, on that there stage! Just imagine me dancing like that! It'd get me poor ole legs goin' again! No doubt about it!" Mrs Harry was not so sure, but agreed that, judging by the rapturous applause from the audience, the show was a resounding success.

If ever they had needed that impetus, the performance certainly, in Harry's words, got Shirley's legs going again. She danced as she never had before: in control of her posture, the support from her inner core, the precision of all her steps and movements. Attentive to the rhythms of the divine music and the demands of the drama, she gave herself to each part as though she were the Lilac Fairy, or Swanhilda, or Giselle, or even a Spanish Gipsy. At last, after so many setbacks, she was fulfilling her dream of dancing the roles she loved on a real stage before a real audience. The experience was thrilling, enabling her to anticipate the forthcoming tour with a sure confidence that she would be able to dance to perfection without a hitch. Perhaps one day she would be able to fulfil that cherished dream of dancing on the stage at Sadler's Wells after all! The applause at the end of the performance lifted her high on a wave of exhilaration, and as the final cinema curtain fell, she ran, crying with joy, into the cupboard which served as her dressing room.

The cast were also overjoyed, as were all the helpers, except for tall ungainly Doris, the inspired author of the company's name, whose face was as dark as night. She stormed out of the communal *corps de ballet* dressing room, a large store cupboard, as soon as she had changed. Cynthia observed this hasty exit, but resolved not to spoil Shirley's fun that night. The boss of the cinema was so delighted with the show that he immediately asked if the company would repeat the performance a week later. All were in favour, as there were still two weeks to go before their departure to Yorkshire, and the more practice they had performing in public, the better for them.

Madame, however, was not wholly in favour of a repeat performance in the cinema. In her view, having succeeded in producing one highly successful show, the company should proceed to perfecting a new programme. She provisionally suggested it should be made up of dances from *The Nutcracker*, with Shirley dancing the part of the Sugar Plum Fairy. She would also take the lead in her *Scenes from a French Market*, and the dance of the *Black Swan*, from *Swan Lake*; they would not necessarily be performed in that order, but were already being practised and nearly learnt, though by no means yet up to performance standard.

"You see, *ma chérie*," she explained, "we must have another programme ready to perform, because you and Aurora will be greatly in demand. This performance will be mentioned in all the newspapers, so we will have plenty of publicity material to advance your company and give you promotions throughout the winter season."

Shirley protested that just one more performance at the cinema would not do any harm and they could all still be rehearsing for the new programme. She did not mention the huge takings from the cinema performance, which, although shared with that venue, would set the company up nicely for the coming year and might even permit Cynthia to draw a salary. Madame sensed that there was more to it than just the success of the performance: she had seen the full house and the unbelievably glorious dancing, and was astute enough to realize that the returns must be considerable, and might even be doubled within the week. She therefore relented and allowed the second performance to go ahead, content in the knowledge that there were still two weeks to go before the Yorkshire visit, which had now become a tour, so one more night on a London stage, if not in the city centre, could do no harm.

Nonetheless, ructions within the company were threatening to harm its success. Cynthia fielded them as best she could, always calm, always diplomatic, and always trying to protect her friend, whose dancing astounded her, but the latest issue was one that eventually she reckoned she had to bring to Shirley's notice before more damage was done. Doris, sometimes a willing helper but still harbouring a grudge because she was dissatisfied with her part in the *corps de ballet*, had been currying support among the dancers in that section and setting them against Shirley: it was all the more disturbing because she did not complain openly, only under cover.

Already jealous at still not having a solo role herself, more than a bit part as the Queen in *Sleeping Beauty*, Doris's indignation grew when she failed to convert any of the men to her cause: they, as one, adored Shirley; they admired her skill, her lightness, her suppleness and the depth of emotion she brought to her performance. Among themselves they concluded that there was much more to Shirley than met the eye: undoubtedly there had been some profound tragedy in her life that enabled her to plumb and portray such heart-rending feelings. It was not hard to imagine what that tragedy might have been, given the horrendous state of the War, yet despite all that, she was still fun to be with and easy to talk to. In their view Doris had none of those advantages, and what's more, they laughed among themselves at the prospect of one of their number having to lift her high above his head.

In the *corps de ballet* there were several of Cynthia's friends whom she had co-opted, both before and after the formation of Aurora. These friends had been put out of work by the bombing of their theatre and the collapse of their variety company. They in turn had introduced other friends, not all of them previously known to Cynthia: Doris had been one of them. Cynthia was sure that she could trust her own friends to respond reliably to Aurora, but did not have the same confidence in the others. It was not until a rehearsal one Tuesday morning after the first successful cinema performance, when Maria, one of her true friends, approached her, asking for a quiet word, that she began to realize that a serious issue was at stake.

"You're terribly busy and don't want to be bothered with this sort of thing, but I really think I should warn you there's real trouble in the company," Maria said apologetically, as they sat in a tearoom near the studio.

"It's that Doris. She's the cause of it, and she's jealous of Shirley because Shirley has the starring roles – and so she jolly well should!" she stressed. "Shirley is amazing! Only a few of us had ever met Doris, and none of us had seen her dance when she joined us, but she seems fine in the *corps*; she is a good, reliable dancer and never makes mistakes, although of course she has to dance at the back of the stage because she would be too tall at the front."

Cynthia folded her arms around herself as if to protect herself from an unpleasant, unforeseen threat to Aurora and to Shirley.

"We know there's trouble," she said to Maria, "but we don't really know what Doris wants. Have you any idea?" she asked Maria.

"I haven't heard her saying anything outright," Maria replied, "but I've been told she wants to dance one of Shirley's solos. What's more, she wants the Lilac Fairy's part from *Sleeping Beauty* that Shirley is dancing so beautifully. I don't know whether to weep or laugh when I think of her taking that over." She paused to allow her words to sink in – not that Cynthia needed any time for that: she already was well aware of the severity of the problem. "She has a grudge because, as she says, she thought of the name for the company but is not being given any recognition for it," Maria carried on, "and as I see it, if she doesn't get her way, she'll leave and take half of the *corps de ballet* with her."

Cynthia took a deep breath and blew it out slowly. "Thanks for putting me fully in the picture," she told Maria. "I'm not sure what to do; I'll have to think it over. Don't tell anyone else what you've said to me, will you?"

Cynthia went home and spent the rest of that day and a sleepless night searching for a solution to this major problem. She was angry that it had arisen, that it was Doris who had caused it, and yet she had to admit that perhaps Doris had been unfairly treated. The question was how to resolve the situation. Not until light came through her curtains at three in the morning did she fall asleep.

As it happened, she need not have been so worried, because when Madame Belinskaya came to the rehearsal in the centre of town that Wednesday, it occurred to her that here was someone she would be able to confide in, instead of Shirley. She had a sixth sense that she might understand.

Therefore, after the morning rehearsal, while Shirley was changing and getting ready to go out shopping for a new suitcase in the lunch hour, Cynthia approached Madame, unsure how to address her since French, apart from balletic terms, was not her strong point. Nonetheless, she valiantly mustered a couple of simple sentences, which were sufficient to capture Madame's attention.

"*Chère Madame,*" she began nervously with a pronounced English accent, "*si vous plait, je veux parler avec vous. Il y a un problème.*"

Madame guessed from Cynthia's hesitant approach that this must be a serious problem, which undoubtedly involved Shirley, unbeknown to her, otherwise she herself would have brought it to her notice. Madame responded graciously in her broken English, inviting Cynthia to take lunch with her.

"I weel see you een my favoreete restaurant, ze Reetz, for a queek lonch," Madame whispered to Cynthia when Shirley was out of ear-shot. They left the studio separately – Madame went out before Shirley dashed off on her shopping expedition, and Cynthia after her. Had she had warning of this occasion, Cynthia would have worn her best dress, which in fact would quickly have aroused Shirley's interest and given rise to questions, so it was as well that the invitation was so spontaneous.

Madame showed appreciation of all Cynthia's hard work behind the scenes for Aurora and complimented on her performance. "You shood take a small solo role, Zeenzeea," she said. "I shood be 'appy to 'elp you, becose you 'ave 'elped *ma chérie* so much."

Cynthia smiled at the compliment, while wondering how she was going to eat the mountainous salad set down in front of her, and still have time to outline the situation to Madame. She need not have worried; no sooner had she begun to speak than Madame interrupted her, saying that jealousy in the company was no surprise to her.

"Eet always 'appens, Zeenzeea, my dear! Zere ees always someone who zeenks she is bettair zan someone else," she explained. "I 'ave nevair known a company where zat does not 'appen. So, what ees zee problem?"

Cynthia explained that Doris was jealous of Shirley and wanted to take her solo roles.

"But, as I soojested a long time ago to *ma chérie*, Dorees, she ees a good dancer – not of *ma chérie*'s standard of course – and she shood be given ze role of Odeele in *Le Lac des Cygnes*, and a few ozer solo parts. Leave eet to me; I weel arrange eet."

As Madame divulged no more of her plans for "arranging" the prob-lem, Cynthia was left in the dark until the following morning, when, even before warm-ups had begun, Madame announced a change of plan for the second programme, which they were already rehearsing. She said she had been considering the sequence of dances and had decided that the show should open with one or other of Shirley's ballets. Then there would follow excerpts from the *Nutcracker* ballet, beginning with the *Dance of the Sugar Plum Fairy*, danced by Shirley, and this would be succeeded by the men performing the *Cossack Dance*: at this the men cheered. The *Dance of the Flutes* for the *corps de ballet* would come next.

After that – here Madame paused for her words to have full dramatic effect – Doris would perform the *Arabian* – or *Coffee Dance*, to give it its popular title, as a solo. Doris's mouth opened, and a surprised smile spread across her sullen features. The *Chinese Tea Dance* would follow, and then the *Dance of the Flowers*. The *divertissements* from *The Nutcracker* would end with Shirley and one of the men, probably Andrei, performing the *pas de deux*, the duet, at the end of the *Sugar Plum Fairy* sequence.

In the second half, when it came to *Swan Lake*, not yet on either of the programmes and not yet fully rehearsed, Doris should dance the role of Odile as the Black Swan.

Everyone seemed happy with the change of plan, which came as no surprise to Shirley, because she remembered discussing it previously, when she had suspected Doris was beginning to cause difficulties. La Belinskaya said that she would give the rest of the programme more thought and let them know her conclusions the following week. She did, however, inform Cynthia that she would be given the part of the female soloist in the Chinese dance, the *Tea Dance*.

The more she thought about it, the more Shirley found Madame's announcement perplexing. Although they were already rehearsing various possibilities, as suggested by Madame, there had not as yet been any firm decision on a programme for the second show, so she could not understand why she had decided to put her own ideas forward so quickly as a *fait accompli*, before discussing them with either her or Cynthia.

"A bit odd, isn't it?" she remarked to her friend. "I don't understand why it's all so cut and dried already, without her even discussing it with us."

Cynthia gave an innocent shrug, as if it was all news to her too. "I expect she wants us to get on with it because we will soon be off to Yorkshire," she said, "and there won't be time to practise for the second programme if we don't rehearse it now to get to know it properly. Then, if there's a chance, we'll be able to practise it while we're away. Lately we've been too busy with the cinema show to give the second programme the attention it needs to be really good." She changed the subject slightly. "Don't you like her programme? I think it's very good."

"Yes, it's fine," said Shirley, "and I'm glad she's given Doris a solo – well, two, in fact; we owe her that, perhaps more, but I was thinking she might like the *White Adagio* from *Swan Lake*. It seems Madame thinks differently and is giving her the *Black Swan*'s routine. What do you think?"

Cynthia, trying to appear totally indifferent, but in fact taking Madame's part, replied, "Don't you remember, we talked about this before and agreed that Doris should dance Odile, the Black Swan, in the excerpt from *Swan Lake*?"

Shirley frowned. "Really?" she said, in disbelief that she might have forgotten something so important.

Cynthia nodded. Then, to sweeten the pill, she innocently asked, "Why don't you dance the *White Adagio* from *Swan Lake* yourself?"

"I'll think about it." Shirley retorted rather frostily, aware that she had been caught off guard. "Anyhow, I have plenty to do already, so for now I don't really want to take on any more, thanks!"

Cynthia hastily reported the essence of this conversation discreetly to Madame, whose reaction was: "Ah, so what was a zundairstorm, ees now only rain een a coffee cup!"

Aurora's second performance of the first programme took place before a smaller but still sizeable and equally enthusiastic audience in the cinema. Additionally, to the satisfaction of the founders, it also brought in more money to the coffers. The owner of the cinema promised Shirley and Cynthia that he would be delighted to host their company, should they wish to bring a new programme to his cinema between tours. Thereafter, in the remaining weeks before the start of the northern tour, the dancers began to practise the new programme, which Madame had expanded since making her initial declaration of its contents to the company. It would begin as previously suggested with the *Dance of the Sugar Plum Fairy* opening the *Nutcracker divertissements*. Shirley's *Spanish Scenes* would follow. The second half would open with an abbreviated version of the first act of *Swan Lake*, the court scene, in which Prince Siegfried's mother, played by Cynthia, insists that he should choose a bride before he goes out on a shooting expedition. However, he meets and falls in love with the Swan Queen, Odette, to be danced by Shirley, suffering under Baron Rothbart's curse. Doris seemed sufficiently satisfied because, in Act Two, also abbreviated by Madame, she was promised the role of wicked Rothbart's daughter, Odile, the Black Swan, who seduces Prince Siegfried. This would bring the performance to a close.

"I think we need to change our plans; that won't work. I'll have to tell Madame!" Shirley declared petulantly. "And we really must find a compère because it's all getting too complicated. It was all right with the first show with the programme notes I wrote, but for a shortened version of *Swan Lake* it's too confusing without a fuller explanation! Anyhow, it would be good to have someone to introduce each of the ballets."

She folded her arms across her chest as if in defiance of all that Madame had devised, then sank into a sulky silence from which she eventually emerged in a more positive frame of mind, taking up her idea for a compère again.

"After all, those soldiers have probably never seen a ballet in all their lives," she said, "and even though we might persuade an officer to compère the show perfectly well on the base in Yorkshire, that would mean having to engage someone new at each venue."

"Well, then, let's ask one of our back-up team to read the explanations of what's going to happen on the stage," Cynthia suggested tentatively. "There's big Rocky, the Texan; he has a booming voice and would do it well."

"Fine, you ask him, then," Shirley retorted, and flounced off, feeling that she was no longer in charge.

Rocky, the Texan, had applied to Aurora, saying that he had once danced in a school pantomime, which was hardly the sort of experience the founders of the ballet company were looking for. Nevertheless, although his true role in life back home had been selling farm machinery, which he had also been commissioned to do in Europe, he was keen to have any form of employment. He was very willing to take up the role of compère for the ballet, to ease the tedium of being stranded far from his homeland. In fact, he volunteered to do anything to help Aurora. His offer was unanimously accepted on condition that he should accept a modest extra fee for his services. Thereafter he more than proved his worth, never complaining, however great the demands made of him. As the principal arranger of all backstage manoeuvres, he shoved props, whether market stalls, carts, furniture or thrones, on and off stage, changed the backdrop between ballets, and still slipped seamlessly into his new role as compère.

Reggie mopped his brow when he heard of the varied programme that evening at suppertime. "Your Madame What's-Her-Name, is unstoppable. Doesn't she understand that scene changing is a strenuous business, even if it is mostly only backdrops, and it's not something you can do in two minutes?" he complained.

"Not to worry, Pa. Our new scene-changer manages all that. He's huge, and he's fantastic! He's an American engineer, and now he has a new role as our compère," Shirley reassured him, having recovered her better nature.

She was interrupted by the familiar sound of footsteps on the staircase. Ted was home! Over the past weeks she had been so preoccupied with the organization of the show, which now had engagements in two other venues apart from the army barracks in Yorkshire, that she had given only the occasional thought to her brother and his whereabouts, assuming that after the horrible events in Trémaincourt, no news was good news. In this she was to be disappointed.

Ted crashed into the living room, looking more dishevelled and grubbier than ever, flung his tattered rucksack down onto the floor and without so much as a glance at his father, he scowled at his sister.

"So, here you are, living in luxury with Pa! I've seen the posters of you tripping about the stage, pretending to be a fairy! What use is that? Don't you know there's a war on! You should be out there with us in France, fighting!"

Their father stood up. "That's enough, Ted!" he shouted. "How dare you come home and behave like this?" Pa grew redder and redder in the face, carried away with indignation, "Shirley is working very hard preparing to go on tour for ENSA, and she still helps with the patrols, so don't you speak to her like that!" He stopped to catch his breath and then in a calmer voice said, "Sit down, old chap. I expect you're tired and hungry. Look, there's plenty of Eileen's rabbit stew in the pot."

He turned to his daughter. "Shirl," he said, "you go to your room for a bit while I deal with this."

Shaking, Shirley stood up and limped into her room. She lay down on the bed shivering. "Why, oh why had Ted behaved so cruelly to her?" she wondered, but then she heard the phone ringing. The raids were no less severe than they had been in the winter, and it was unlikely to be a call from Granny Marlow, because she rarely rang these days, therefore the phone call could only mean one thing. She jumped out of bed, pulled on her uniform, picked up her helmet and ran down the stairs to the shop, where the emergency phone was still ringing. She answered it, then grabbed the key to the siren box and dashed out to the church porch to set the siren in motion. Her father came stumbling behind her.

"What are we going to do about Ted, Pa?" she asked.

"He refuses to come out to a shelter, says it's more important to protect his identity, so I've told him to take a bath and go to bed," he said dourly.

Enemy planes thundered overhead seemingly for hours, without dropping bombs, but that was scant comfort, because they would be sure to discharge any unused payload indiscriminately over the suburban areas on their return to their bases in France. A couple of incendiary bombs fell onto waste ground where the scarred remains of previously bombed houses finally fell to the ground, thus leaving it clear for reconstruction, but not before sending clouds of burning dust and ashes into the night air.

Among the ARP workers there were a handful of casualties, but they had not suffered badly, since minor burns from flying sparks were quickly treated, and the population in the shelters were safe. When the all-clear sounded they emerged, and many of them called out, "Loved your show, Shirley!" as she ticked their names off on her list.

Ted was waiting for her and Reggie in the flat. "I'm so sorry, Shirl," he said. "Please forgive me! I really hate behaving like this; I suppose it's because of all the tension caused by the War."

There was no reason for him to say anything more. Shirley fully understood; she sympathized with his situation and said so.

22

Shirley kept studying the map of the British Isles to find out exactly where Yorkshire was. Uncertain where she should be looking, she resigned herself to seeking her father's advice.

"I hope Yorkshire's not too near Birmingham, is it, Pa?" she asked her father, while in the living room she folded her clothes about to be packed for the journey north.

Her father had his ear to the wireless. "Good gracious!" he exclaimed, ignoring his daughter's question, but addressing his remarks to her. "You know I told you the Nazis have broken off their pact with the Soviets?"

Shirley nodded, not sure whether in all the flurry of preparations for the tour she had actually registered this snippet of information. "Is that important, Pa?" she asked.

"It most definitely is! It means that Hitler is taking his forces eastwards and he's invading Russia, so let's hope he'll leave us in peace for a bit!" Reggie laughed and rubbed his hands together with evident glee.

"Ah, I see," said Shirley uncertainly, and then repeated her question about the precise location of Yorkshire.

"Didn't they teach you anything in that expensive school I sent you to?" he replied with a resigned grin. "No, of course it's not! It's nowhere near Birmingham! It's north of Birmingham!"

"Ah good!" she exclaimed, "I must have been looking in the wrong place."

Her father assumed that she was scared of going anywhere near Coventry, considering what a disaster that earlier visit had been. Understandably she would not want to be reminded of that and its tragic consequences. Birmingham was not that far from Coventry but miles from Yorkshire. What's more, he recalled, Birmingham itself also held dire memories for his daughter, because that was where she had come into contact with Infantile Paralysis – polio – and its near-fatal consequences in 1937.

However, that was not what Shirley had in mind. She was hoping that Yorkshire was far enough away from Birmingham to spare her the irritation of finding Granny Marlow in the front row of one of the shows. According to Cynthia, these had been arranged for Aurora with support from CEMA, the Council for the Encouragement of Music and the Arts, in towns and cities nearer other army bases than their immediate destination in Yorkshire. She was consoled to hear that Yorkshire was not near Birmingham.

She spoke often over the phone to her cousin Edith, who had reluctantly returned to Birmingham, on account of her husband, Jim's change of job.

"Does Granny ring you?" Edith asked hopefully.

When she heard that Shirley was spared that inconvenience, she sighed, saying, "I have Granny ringing up every evening just when I'm putting little Sam to bed, and sometimes coming round here for supper by taxi to ask why I haven't been to see her! I keep telling her I'm working in the hospital again, but she doesn't listen, and she says there's a nice little dress shop where there's bound to be a job for me. I don't want to work in a dress shop! I love my job in the hospital!"

Poor Edith! Shirley was well aware what a pain their grandmother was, forever wanting to install her granddaughters in dress shops or department stores, totally against their wishes. Consequently Shirley considered herself very lucky not to be going anywhere near Birmingham.

The troupe travelled further north-east than Birmingham, so Shirley was safe on that account. Nevertheless, although all was going nicely as planned, the journey was interrupted by the discovery of an unexploded bomb beside the railway line two hours out of London. Shirley was enjoying the ride through pretty, unfamiliar countryside, when the train ground to a halt and the passengers were hastily herded, without their luggage, onto the tracks. For the dancers, the drop from the carriage steps down onto the line was easy – all in a day's work, as one of the men remarked – but for the elderly and infirm passengers it was a struggle. Rather than obey the railway workers' instructions to head straight down the steep embankment, the Aurora men valiantly helped the old people off the train and then carried them down the slope to wait for buses to take them to a pub in the nearest village. "So much for Hitler leaving us in peace," thought Shirley.

The wait seemed interminable since the train was stranded miles from anywhere, but the sun was still high in the sky and the air so much fresher than in London. There, even in summer, residual particles of houses, shops, schools, churches, office buildings, theatres, roads and railway and Tube lines, all blitzed, still hung in an evil fog, supplemented by the smoke and smut from trains. Shirley filled her lungs with the country air and basked in the sunlight: it reminded her of France, except that a shiver ran down her spine when she recalled the stark truth that Trémaincourt would never be the same rural idyll that she had known in childhood. She doubted that she would ever be able to contemplate going back there after the horrendous murder of her grandfather and dear Charlot. The place would be haunted.

Although it had hurt her deeply at the time, she had forgiven Ted for his recent angry outburst against her, because it was obvious that he was engaged in heroic activities, working with the Resistance under the noses of the Germans. Sometimes she felt twinges of guilt creeping over her, since she was at last enjoying herself so much in the ballet. In such moments of soul-searching, she asked herself whether she too ought to be in France. She feared that, were she to cross the Channel, she would no longer be able to muster the courage to face the dangers, and if her courage failed, she would be easy prey for the Gestapo.

When in the dark at midnight the travellers at last arrived at the army barracks in deepest Yorkshire – in possession of their luggage – the welcome they received from a captain was heart-warming. He gave Cynthia a beaming smile as she stepped off the bus, and introduced himself as Pete, at which she grinned. He then took them all straight away to the officers' mess where they were served a good meal, so much better than anything available, except in the best restaurants in London.

Afterwards they all expected to be shown to their accommodation. However, to their surprised dismay, Captain Pete had other ideas. As the plates were being cleared, he stood up, called everyone to attention and announced that there would be an air-raid practice which they, the dance company, would have to join in before going to bed. The troupe groaned as one: they had brought their gas masks as instructed by Shirley, and considered air-raid practice quite unnecessary, out here in the dark and the dead of night in the back-of-beyond.

Captain Pete noticed their glum faces. "It's all right," he assured them, "it won't take long, but here, in an army camp, we are a sitting target. They do come fairly close sometimes – we hear their engines – and they only have to drop flares to be able to see us here, even though we are as blacked out as you are in London, so we have to be well-prepared and extra careful."

There were grumbles in the company. "We thought we were here to dance, not to go on exercises," one wag commented. "We know enough about air raids already!"

"It's for your own safety and ours. If you don't like obeying orders, I suggest you leave at once!" Pete retorted brusquely, and led the way out into the night.

When at last the dancers were shown to their accommodation in two small Nissen huts, they were relieved to find them well appointed with camp beds and clean linen, though the essential facilities, consisting of two small sheds outside each Nissen hut, left something to be desired: one was for washing – in cold water – and the other was for bodily needs.

"Thank goodness it's summertime! Madame wouldn't like this!" one of the girls observed drily, whereupon they all laughed.

"Just as well we persuaded her to think better of coming with us!" remarked Cynthia, to more laughter.

The basic accommodation reminded Shirley of France, so she took it in her stride, unlike some of the others who had never encountered anything like it before, and said so rather vociferously.

Shirley addressed them curtly, saying, "Look here, you city dwellers, it's not perfect, but it is clean, and this is the way many people live all the time. Remember, this is *our* contribution to the war effort! It's cushy by comparison with what some people are having to put up with in this War!" The message was not lost on them; thereafter either they did not complain about the army barracks, or if they did, they kept their grumbles to themselves.

That night most of the girls slept soundly, although another complaint was voiced in the morning, expressed not by the girls but by the men. Apparently the trouble was that it was too quiet out in the country, and they missed the noise of the traffic at home. Shirley simply laughed at this. "Think yourselves lucky," she said, "that all you have to worry about is the cock crowing, and not about bombs falling on you!"

Pete was standing close by and heard what she said. "Watch out," he whispered, "Remember, you were late because of a bomb by the railway."

"Yes, but that was a long way away," she retorted.

"Not if you're flying one of those bombers," he said. "Yorkshire is not out of their range. Hull has been blitzed to smithereens and Leeds has taken a knocking, so it's highly probable they'll come here sooner or later."

Pete and Cynthia had, it emerged, met during one of her tours with her previous company, and they had fallen for each other, a fact she was no longer able to conceal once the Aurora brigade arrived in Yorkshire. It also explained why it had been so easy for her to make Aurora's first booking. Pete's was an endearing personality. He was not very tall, but his mischievous smile, bright eyes and curly fair hair made up for what he lacked in height, and gave the whole company, men and girls, confidence that they were all assured of an enthusiastic reception for their performance. He did have an annoying habit of calling Cynthia "Cyn", which made her blush and gave rise to sniggers among the company.

Shirley was irritated on Cynthia's behalf, but she didn't know whether Pete did it deliberately or unconsciously, so although she would have liked to put a stop to it, she didn't want to cause trouble between her friend and her otherwise very likeable boyfriend. All she said to Cynthia was,

"Hey, you are a dark horse, Cynnie; I suspected there was something like this happening when you made the booking so quickly."

Cynthia blushed. "No," she said, "there was not really anything happening, as you say, between us; it was just that we liked each other and wanted to meet again. After all, Pete was the person best placed to help Aurora get going!" Shirley laughed.

While the others breakfasted, Pete took Cynthia and Shirley to inspect the stage. Cynthia had insisted in her correspondence with him, that the stage must be absolutely even and smooth. No dancer would risk his or her career by dancing on a rough set of slanting, wobbly planks that could lead to a broken ankle or worse. A large Nissen hut had been reserved for the show that evening: already rows of chairs were lined up inside, and a table bore glasses and drinks for the interval. Pete pulled back a curtain to reveal a sizeable stage, reached by a set of wide steps.

"Here we are!" Pete announced joyfully. "I hope you like it. Our engineers have set up the stage and we've worked hard to smooth out all the rough bits, so you won't notice even the slightest join in the wood. Oh, and we've polished it for you too! Look how shiny it is!"

Shirley and Cynthia glanced at each other, horror-struck. A slippery, polished floor was the last thing dancers wanted! A fall on a polished floor might mean the end of a career, quite as quickly as an uneven plank. There would be a rebellion.

Wearing their ballet pumps, Cynthia and Shirley climbed onto the stage. "It's lovely, Pete," Cynthia began uncertainly, hoping that Shirley would think of something to say that wouldn't offend him.

Shirley tried out the surface, executing a perfect pirouette, and then another, which was a disaster: she slipped and fell, her straight supporting leg, her right leg, sliding out from under her as she spun round.

"Shirley!" Cynthia cried out in alarm and Pete rushed to pick her up from the floor.

"Are you hurt?" he asked anxiously.

Shirley groaned in pain. "The floor is so slippery. I lost my balance when my leg slid away!"

Cynthia was distraught; she came across to where Shirley lay in a heap moaning, "Oh no! My ankle hurts! Oh dear!"

"Stay there; I'll get help," said Pete, dashing off, while Cynthia fussed round trying to make Shirley comfortable.

"I'm so sorry; I'm so sorry," she kept repeating.

Pete returned with a crowd of young soldiers, eager to lift the patient off the stage and carry her back to the Nissen hut on a stretcher.

"No, that's all right," she said. "I'll walk if you can support me and just carry me down the steps." Next to arrive was a medical team, who felt and prodded and pulled her ankle about, asking if this movement or that hurt. She winced and said "yes" to each and every one.

"No dancing for you tonight, young lady," the doctor decreed.

"Oh, but I must!" Shirley cried out, attempting to sit upright. "The company needs me!"

General consternation ensued and Pete and the medical team went off to confer, leaving Shirley and Cynthia alone.

Very quickly, and to Cynthia's amazement, Shirley took charge again in her customary fashion. "Don't worry, Cynnie – they'll have to scrape all that polish off the floor before the rehearsal this afternoon, that's obvious. I will probably be better by tonight and able to dance, but only for the Lilac Fairy. I was thinking that Doris might like to take over Coppélia. I know it's your part and it's a bit late in the day, but Doris would love it; she's been to enough rehearsals to know the part by now. After all, there is supposed to be the rehearsal this afternoon, though I'll have to give that a rest, and maybe everyone else will have to too, if they haven't sorted out the stage by then."

She shrugged her shoulders before continuing. "Anyhow, you're really too light and too small for the doll, Coppélia, Cynnie. You don't mind if Doris takes it over, do you?"

Cynthia bit her lip, and said, "No, that's all right; I'd like to dance one of Swanhilda's friends, though."

"Fine, that would be just right for you," said Shirley, now in organizational mood and carried away with a new idea. "Let's give Maria the solos in the Spanish extravaganza," she said. "I like the way she dances, and I'm sure she knows what to do. She'd be better at it than me."

Shirley had deliberately refrained from telling Cynthia that the fall was not quite as bad as it seemed, and the sprained ankle was beginning to feel better than it had at first. She needed to exaggerate the problem because, above all, the stage had to be scrubbed clean of all that polish, otherwise the whole cast would go down and then that would be the end of the tour and of Aurora, so the worse her fall appeared to be, the more care to have the stage in proper order would have to be taken in future.

"I'll tell the cast to be prepared for the rehearsal this afternoon, hoping the stage is ready," said Cynthia, edging towards the door. Shirley sometimes was so bossy, she said to herself, thinking it best to keep out of her way. It was bad enough that she had fallen on Pete's stage and that she, Cynthia, was to lose the technically undemanding part of the doll, Coppélia.

"I don't want Pete to be upset by this," said Shirley, issuing more instructions as Cynthia opened the door, "but if he asks what he can do to help, tell him to have the stage floor scraped and scrubbed immediately, ready for the rehearsal, and he should also get in touch with the other venues to warn them definitely not to polish their stages!"

"I'll tell him at once," Cynthia replied meekly, on the point of trotting away to find her boyfriend.

Shirley's apparently speedy recovery of her senses after such a shock was puzzling, yet she did not doubt for one moment that the fall had been genuine, because Shirley herself had opted not to dance all of her roles that evening. Her friend, however, called her back. "And by the way, Cynnie, my ankle still hurts, so you can dance Swanhilda, not just one of her friends, tonight!" This was the principal role, Shirley's role. Cynthia gasped and ran out of the door.

It was not a great loss for Shirley to miss out in every item that evening, because, with her ankle hurting but firmly bandaged, she was still able to dance a reduced version of her part as the Lilac fairy in *Sleeping Beauty*. After mitigating Carabosse, the witch's curse on the baby Princess, she watched the second half of the performance from the audience, a novel experience for her. She applauded whole-heartedly with the crowds of servicemen around her, but with an eagle eye, examined every aspect of the show – from the sets, which inevitably were rather basic but perfectly serviceable, to the costumes, which were beautiful, to the footwork, which on the whole she found very satisfactory, except that she detected a slight lack of coordination in the *corps de ballet* dances, especially in their *fouetté* and *pas de chat* sequences, and made a mental note to point that out the following day.

On the whole she was proud of her company, especially of Maria, whose flamenco dancing to the excerpts from a selection of Bizet's *Carmen Suites*, had the touch of authenticity and flair that could only have come from her Spanish background. As was to be expected, Cynthia was a charming and lively Swanhilda.

Still ostensibly limping after the performance, though not really sure whether she was limping on her right or her left ankle, Shirley joined all the dancers in the officers' mess for drinks, and congratulated each one of them, every member of the *corps de ballet* and Doris, who was clearly quite pleased with her own portrayal of Coppélia. Maria beamed with delight when Shirley suggested enlarging her part and asked if she knew of a male flamenco dancer who would be willing to join the cast and dance with her.

"*Pero sí!*" Maria exclaimed, her eyes wide with excitement. "Yes, of course I do! There's Pedro – of course you know him… he is already dancing with us. He's the one who escaped from Franco at the end of the Spanish Civil War."

"Well, then," came Shirley's delighted reply, "would you ask him to dance with you?"

"No problem," Maria replied, "we already do a performance in a Spanish nightclub in London. Not at the moment, of course, but when we have time off from Aurora. We have been dancing at weekends to earn some more money."

Shirley was surprised and relieved, not only to find that there would be a dramatic new element in the future programme but also that she herself would not have to dance the Spanish dance again: in all honesty, she doubted that she with her blond curls was suited to the role, and she hated wearing a black wig. Moreover, she was aware that her movements were exclusively those of the ballet, and not dramatic or angular enough for flamenco.

As for Swanhilda, she regretted giving up that part, but Cynthia had acquitted herself admirably in it. Although Shirley praised her to the skies, Cynthia was not happy at finding herself in such a prominent role. She begged Shirley to let her dance one of Swanhilda's friends if she couldn't go back to dancing Coppélia, because, she said, she would enjoy that, but hadn't enjoyed dancing the part of Swanhilda at all: it was too stressful.

It was much easier to be fervently complimentary to Maria than it was to Doris, who took compliments as if they were owed to her. Nevertheless, the unexpected change of plan furnished Shirley with a new idea, which would resolve any future problems at a stroke.

"It seems to me," she said to Cynthia, "that because we don't have understudies, everyone in the company should learn the other parts; that's to say, the men should learn the other male parts and the girls, whether principals or *corps de ballet*, should learn the other female roles."

"That's rather ambitious, isn't it?" Cynthia queried.

"Mm, maybe," Shirley replied, before revising her plan. "Let's say they should learn all the other roles, but perhaps each member should learn at least two other parts, so that, if a dancer in their section falls down or drops out, there will always be someone to take over. It worked tonight and I don't imagine it'll be too difficult. We have all seen all the parts time and time again, so I reckon everyone could manage it. Let's hope we don't have an air-raid warning…"

Aurora's first performance on tour had clearly pleased the men on the army base, and was a talking point the next morning. While the company waited for the bus to take them to the Georgian spa town where they would be dancing that evening – in a proper theatre before a public audience – everyone was allowed to relax for a while, though Shirley was not best pleased when she saw several of the girls walking off, arm in arm with soldiers. She went looking for Cynthia to ask what they should do, but she was nowhere to be found, so she asked herself what Madame would do in such circumstances. She imagined Madame drawing herself up to her full height, straight-backed, shoulders down, but beyond that inspiration escaped her, so she had to let the matter rest.

It was as well that she did, because Cynthia reappeared mid-morning, her face shining a smiling, rosy red. She was arm in arm with Pete. For a second Shirley thought, "Everyone's having fun except me!" And then pointedly asked, "Cynnie, where have you been? I've been looking for you!"

"Never you mind," laughed Cynnie. "Look at this!" She stretched out her left hand, where a diamond sparkled on her third finger.

Shirley was taken aback. "Oh, oh, congratulations, Cynnie!" she exclaimed, hugging her friend.

She turned to Pete. "Now, Pete, take care of Cynnie, won't you?" she stressed Cynthia's nickname as often as possible in the hope that he might catch on and stop addressing as her friend as Cyn. Cynthia smiled: she understood what Shirley was trying to do and was grateful.

Their hired bus arrived shortly afterwards. While the girls came out with their suitcases and climbed on board, the stage-hands brought the van to the performance hut to collect the props. Eventually the convoy set off on the tortuous journey over the moors to the next venue. Cynthia turned her ring this way and that, smiling dreamily at it.

Fearing for the future of Aurora without Cynthia, Shirley, sitting next to her, said, "It's a lovely ring. Does this mean you're going to get married soon?"

"No, not yet – not until the War's over. We'll have to be patient," Cynthia replied, "but I hope you like Pete. I fell for him the moment I saw him, but that was some time ago when we were touring with the variety show. He kept in touch, and then I saw him again when he came to London on leave. I didn't tell you at the time, but he actually came to stay with Mother and me! So, when he proposed this morning, there was not the shadow of a doubt in my mind."

Shirley tried to quash the wave of envy surging through her, and simply said, "Yes, he's very nice; just right for you. I'm sure you'll be very happy, but you won't leave us, will you?" The audible anxiety in her voice grew, as she said this.

"No, don't worry – I'm here as long as it takes!" Cynthia reassured her yet again.

According to Pete, the theatre at the next venue attracted large enough audiences to be able to treat the dancers properly, and with a full house already booked and paid for, the management would be able to accommodate the company comfortably and feed them well. Shirley's spirits rose at the prospect, hoping there would at least be a proper bathroom with hot running water. Both her legs were fine, as if they had never been anything else, and she was looking forward to resuming her role as the prima ballerina in the performance.

"I would like to dance all my solo roles tonight," she told Cynthia, who was not surprised, "but, twice a week, I'll have a rest, and you can dance Swanhilda. Oh, and Maria can take over the Spanish dance altogether. I knew I wasn't right for the part. In any case Maria and Pedro can add more authentic Spanish touches. How does that sound? I shall be glad of a break and don't want to have to fall over to achieve it!"

"That's fine," said, Cynnie, more intent on her ring than on Shirley's deliberations.

The spa town did indeed receive Aurora rapturously. "It's not often we have a show like yours these days to lift us out of the doldrums and carry us away to happier places," the manager of the theatre said appreciatively to the company backstage after the last curtain call. "We've put you up in the best hotel," he went on, "so we hope you'll enjoy staying there."

On the outside, the hotel indeed advertised itself as the best in the town, and probably it was because there was not much competition. Inside, one might have thought that the management had assumed that a simple advertisement was enough to convert a mediocre lodging house into a deluxe establishment. The cast had to sleep four to a room, two on proper beds and two on camp beds, and the bathrooms were few and far between. Nevertheless, they were all so tired that sleep quickly overcame them.

The problem arose later in the night when in each room one snorer woke everyone else. No amount of shaking would wake them, and it was a grumpy cast that came down to breakfast the next morning.

"Welcome to touring, Shirl," Cynnie greeted her. "Who was your snorer?"

"Better not say," said Shirley, "but I've made a mental note, and next time we'll put all the snorers in the same room – that is, snoring men in together and snoring girls in together. Strange, wasn't it, that we didn't have that problem on the army base?"

"Oh, I'm not surprised after that long journey and the show!" said Cynthia, who did not add "and the excitement of seeing Pete again" – though that thought was definitely uppermost in her mind as she turned her ring to and fro to admire it sparkling.

23

Although convinced that true happiness would never be hers again, the delight, satisfaction and fulfilment that Shirley derived from that tour gave her an enhanced reason for living. The delight increased from venue to venue: she danced many of the principal roles, and had full confidence in the skill of her other principals, of whom there were now six – three men and three girls. Sometimes, "to keep them on their toes", as she laughingly put it, she chose who would play which role only on the day of the performance – apart, that is, from Doris, who could not be squeezed into any borrowed costume other than Coppélia's, which in any case had been swiftly enlarged for her at the army barracks, or, when the programme required, the loose-fitting regal costume of a queen. Usually the dancers were content with this arrangement, often even proud of their own versatility and their performances. The reception they were given was a gratifying response to their balletic skill. Nevertheless, as the first flush of summer roses was starting to fade and June yielded to July, Shirley began to withdraw into herself. She still danced beautifully, some might have said more beautifully than ever, and took rehearsals with a rigour that would have made Madame proud, but with the dying roses her smile lost its radiance.

"What's worrying you?" Cynthia asked her one day.

"Oh, nothing much – I expect I'm getting a bit overtired," replied Shirley, in the full knowledge that this was not true. She was extremely fit physically, not at all tired, even though she gave so much of herself on the stage – yet mentally she was carrying a huge burden that she would not on any account share with Cynthia for fear of dampening the blissful euphoria of her engagement to Pete.

Cynthia, meanwhile, smiled at everything and everyone; she took menial chores lightly, sorting and mending ballet shoes or torn costumes. Financial matters were well within her scope. She dealt with them seriously, issuing invoices or paying bills, always with a cheerful but modest disposition. Shirley, on the other hand, was becoming more anxious and more sorrowful by the day, wanting to hold back the advance of time as it brought the dreaded dates in her diary closer and closer. There was no way of escaping those dates; they jumped off the page at her, and each date brought back the precise memory of the unforgettable events of a year ago. That the days of the week were different was insignificant. Only the date, not the day, mattered, beginning on the 1st of July 1940, when Madame had suggested that she should work as an usher at Sadler's Wells to acquaint herself with the performances there, in the hope that she might reapply to Ninette de Valois's ballet company.

Three days later, on 4th July, she had entered the hallowed portals and was immediately given her orders and her uniform by strict but kindly Gladys, who told her to have a look round to familiarize herself with the layout of the theatre. In a dream she had wandered along corridors and had dared to peep into the theatre where a rehearsal was still in progress, before going down the passage to where dear old Tom, the stage doorkeeper, remembered her from the time of her ill-fated audition nearly three years before. After sharing his tea with her, he had sent her back to the foyer to take up her position by one of the doors to the auditorium. She had watched the first half mesmerized, deeply moved by Act Two of *Swan Lake* with its spine-chilling opening chord. Then, in contrast, she was amused by Ninette de Valois's own creation, *The Prospect Before Us*, danced with great agility by Robert Helpmann.

In the interval she had set to work at the fraught business of sandwich-selling, with not a spare second to glance at her customers until one addressed her in French. Then she did look up; to her astonishment, there, standing in front of her, was the vision she had worshipped night and day since their meeting on a cross-Channel ferry in a storm in 1937 – before her illness, before her mother left the family for good, and before the outbreak of the War. The vision was not a fleeting trick of the imagination, but was real and alive and handsome: there before her stood Alan, whom she had searched for day in, day out, ever since the fleeting moments of that first encounter. For the second time their eyes met and the gaze that passed between them obliterated all other considerations of time and space, confirming a passionate bond between them, a bond that he, too, had apparently felt as strongly as she had.

In the ten days that followed the 4th of July, despite dire misadventures and misunderstandings, the relationship grew so quickly and so power-fully that in the euphoric bliss of their love, they were already laying plans for an idyllic post-war married life together, plans overshadowed only by the fact that Alan had signed up as a fighter pilot. Then came that fateful day, the 14th of July, when Shirley and her father went in the morning into central London, to watch Ted on parade with General De Gaulle and his Free French troops. That evening Shirley, with sinking heart, waited by the phone for Alan to ring, but in vain. Later, there came only the stiff, formal letter from Alan's sister, Elizabeth, announcing his disappearance and presumed death over the Channel, while protecting convoys from enemy fire on Sunday the 14th of July.

The anticipation of the 14th of July 1941 in Yorkshire, the first anniversary of Alan's presumed death, had cast Shirley into a pit of melancholy. She tried her hardest to present a positive, smiling façade to the company, though she did not know how she would manage to dance that evening when all she wanted to do was hide away alone, conjuring up images of her fiancé, of their time together, of drives in his yellow Jaguar, of blissful visits to the Downs, of stays, sanctioned by her father, in country hotels, of their long talks and their passionate embraces.

Interrupting those images was the horrible memory of Bert and his attempt to assault her one night when she was out on an air-raid patrol. Alan had unexpectedly come to her rescue, punched Bert and sent him flying into a rose bush. They laughed about it then, but how she resented Bert's ugly intrusion into her last meeting with her darling, the love of her life! Bert had a habit of popping up unexpectedly, even on her twentieth birthday, when her pa had unwittingly invited him to join her birthday party. How she hated him – Bert, that is, not her father! Life was and always had been like that: the sweetest memories tainted by the sour, bitter ones.

The afternoon before the anniversary, when Shirley, sitting head in hands after the rehearsal, was deep in such meditations, Cynthia burst unannounced into her dressing room. "Shirl, guess what! I have some really good news! You'll be…" – she had been about to say – "so pleased", but stopped short when Shirley turned a woeful, tear-stained face up to her. "Oh, Shirl, what's the matter? I was going to say, we have two more engagements – in Birmingham and Coventry! They've built a makeshift theatre there and want us to go and lend some sparkle to it."

"No, no!" Shirley cried out. "I'm not going to either of those!" Not only had she lost Alan precisely a year ago; his loss was compounded a million times by the loss of their unborn child in the ruthless bombing of Coventry eight months earlier, and here were people wanting her to revisit that area! Never would she go there again!

Cynthia stood stock still, speechless. Eventually she meekly said, "Shirl, I thought you'd be pleased. What *is* the matter?" But no sooner had she uttered those words, than she changed her tune. "How stupid of me! I'm so sorry! Of course, you lost your baby when Coventry was bombed, and it's the anniversary of Alan's disappearance about now, isn't it?"

Shirley nodded. "Yes, it's tomorrow, and I don't know how I'm going to dance tomorrow evening. And as for Coventry…"

"Yes, I'm so sorry," Cynthia said gently. She sat down beside Shirley and put an arm round her shoulder. "Look, you don't have to dance tomorrow if it's too much for you; and as for Birmingham and Coventry, well, you don't have to go there. You can go straight home, if you like. Those engagements would only be an extension of the tour."

Shirley dried her tears and summoned a faint, courageous smile. "Cynnie, you are so kind," she stammered. "Don't worry about me. With friends like you, I'll be all right. Maybe I *will* dance tomorrow. It's nothing too emotional; the *Giselle* opener is straightforward enough and I can manage the christening in *Sleeping Beauty* – I love dancing the Lilac Fairy – and I'll do that naughty Swanhilda as well, if you don't mind. I know it's really your night for Swanhilda, but that would cheer me up! And, of course, Maria and Pedro are excellent in the Spanish *divertissement*, so that takes care of everything." She heaved a sigh. "Thank goodness we're not doing *Swan Lake* yet. That would really tear me to pieces!"

"Oh, I don't mind about Swanhilda; that still gives me stage-fright! You'll be fine once you get on stage – I'll make sure of that – and Birmingham and Coventry can wait till after tomorrow for a decision," Cynthia said comfortingly. "Now why don't you go back to the hotel and lie down for a bit?"

Shirley went back to the hotel and slept for the rest of the afternoon.

Cynthia, meanwhile, rounded up the cast to tell them about Shirley's predicament. They were shocked to hear what had happened to her, although the more sensitive of them had already detected the signs of a profound sorrow in the sudden change in her personality. They were unanimous in agreeing to whatever arrangements would suit Shirley best. Cynthia did not mention Birmingham or Coventry. That could wait for later.

Once on the stage on the evening of the 14th of July, Shirley cast aside the unhappiness which had overshadowed her so darkly over the past couple of weeks. Hers was at times a dual personality: one was the individual who conducted all her projects with determination and enthusiasm, but the other was a fragile young girl who, in reality, had been subject to so much heartache and tragedy, that a lesser person would have broken down under the weight of them. There was, too, the stage presence who lived in a dream world of fairy tale and music, governed nonetheless by strict discipline and control of movement, creating a magical impression of beauty and emotion. The stage presence won out over reality that evening, spreading some of her magic over the many troops who, for all their bravado, faced an undoubtedly treacherous future.

The prospect of dancing the same programme in Birmingham no longer held any of the horrors that Shirley had predicted. In fact, she hoped that her cousin Edith would come to the performance, and was confident that if her granny decided to come too, Edith would take charge of her. She decided to ring Edith from a phone box and offer her free tickets. The joy in Edith's voice when she heard Shirley at the other end of the line was touching. "I'd love to come, Shirl! And to think of it! You'll be on the stage!"

Shirley did not intend immediately to extend the invitation to her granny nor, for that matter, to Edith's mother, Aunt Winnie, hoping that if she left it a while, they would have other things to do, but Edith disillusioned her of that. "I'm sorry, Shirl, but I have to ask if you will be inviting Granny to the show," she said. "You see, I never go out in the evening, so as soon as she learns that I *am* going out for once, and Jim's babysitting, she'll pester me until I tell her where I'm going. If I don't tell her the truth, she'll soon find out somehow. You won't believe it, but there's no hiding from her beady eye anywhere in this city! She has her spies on every corner. Jim says she should be sent to Germany to spy for us there, but that wouldn't work because she can't keep her mouth shut, and she'd go round telling everyone she's a spy!"

Shirley laughed, "I do understand; I'm really sorry for you, Edie. In that case, you had better invite Granny to come too – and Auntie Winnie if she'd like to," said Shirley, who had had enough encounters with their mutual grandmother, to be quite sure that Edith was not embroidering on her boundless propensity to interfere in other people's business – nor was she embroidering on her indiscretion.

"I'll ring you back in a day or two to find out how many tickets I should reserve for you," she told her cousin. "Please, though, on no account allow *her* to come backstage to my dressing room before the performance."

"Don't worry – I'll lie across the doorway, if she tries that!" Edith replied.

Shirley smiled at the thought of portly Edith lying down on the floor to block the doorway and her nimble but diminutive granny trying to step over her. If ever she had to dance the part of an old busybody, she would have a good role model for it. Perhaps she might include a similar character in one of her own ballets one day, even in her French market *divertissement*.

Granny Marlow's appearance at the Birmingham venue was exactly as Shirley had predicted: she of course wanted to go straight to her granddaughter's dressing room. However, Shirley had primed the front of house staff to stop her, Winnie, and poor Edith, who was vainly trying to hold the party back, and send them off in the opposite direction: they found themselves lost in a warren of corridors. Finally, just before the bell rang, an usher went to fetch them and brought them to their seats, not in the front row but several rows further back, where they would be invisible to Shirley. Fortunately, the music was loud enough to drown Mrs Marlow's endless comments on every aspect of the show – the scenery, the dresses, the props and the dancing.

"Would you ever?" she remarked to no one in particular. "I don't believe those girls are really dancing on the tips of their toes. I think they're suspended from the roof!" Then, when the men appeared on stage wearing tights, she gasped, "Where are their trousers?" Not surprisingly, when Shirley came on, her remarks were fully audible: "Ooh, there's our Shirley! She's my granddaughter! Isn't she lovely?" Edith, sitting between her mother, who whimpered at the slightest opportunity, and her irrepressible grandmother, had a hard time keeping the two of them quiet. She told Shirley afterwards that she wished she could have muffled them both.

Shirley need not have worried about Coventry, because the show there was cancelled on account of newly-discovered structural weaknesses in the theatre, with the result that Birmingham marked the end of a very successful tour. All participants were satisfied with the results: the promoters because the programme was extremely well received by packed audiences, the troops because they were uplifted by the spectacle, the dancers because they all enjoyed their roles and felt appreciated. Cynthia and Shirley had good reason to be pleased because everything had gone according to plan: their company had developed into a unified entity with everyone working to the common good. Moreover, Aurora's bank balance was left in a gratifyingly healthy state, all of which made it possible for the company to develop the second programme further and bring it to perfection for the next tour after two weeks' holiday and a month's rehearsal period back in London.

24

For many, including Cynthia and Shirley, the return to London was a dismal blow in other ways than simply finding themselves back in the blackened ruins of the capital city. Everybody wished they could have stayed in Yorkshire until the end of the War. Certainly, after the clean air and green moors of North Yorkshire, London, even in August, was depressingly dark, just as they had left it, still veiled in that grey fog of soot, smoke, ash and particles of debris from bombed-out buildings. The latter loomed out of the fog like skeletal ghosts. When a fitful sun came out, the fog turned yellow. But there was more to it than that: after well-nigh four weeks of the excitement and exhilaration of regular performance, they had all disciplined themselves to dance at every opportunity until, suddenly, there appeared to be nothing in their diaries. In fact, plans for the next tour, beginning in late September, were already well advanced, but that seemed a long way off.

Although they would all have preferred never to leave the stage or stop dancing, they were at heart aware of the need for a rest to replenish their strength and energy. Madame, who came to meet them at Euston, was indeed keen to hear every detail of every show, yet she refused absolutely to allow any dancing in the first two weeks of their break. What they did in their own time, was their business, she said, but training for Aurora and the next tour would have to wait until the end of that two-week holiday period, after which they would have to be prepared to work *very* hard.

Despite Shirley's attempts to persuade her that it was better to keep up the momentum, while they were all fit and eager to dance, she would not hear of it, declaring that they should stretch and exercise each day, but no more than that: she did not want *her* dancers to suffer from overexposure, strain their muscles and lose their radiance and flair. She herself was going away to visit friends in the country for the next ten days, so would not be available to meet them or train them. With that, she picked up the small suitcase she had brought with her and marched off in the direction of the Circle Line, heading for Paddington.

Shirley was more depressed than most by her return to the blackened shells of buildings and the gaunt, grey house with its shop on the ground floor that she had learnt to call her home. Inside that forbidding house, the situation was dire, and the reception she received in the shop was not exactly welcoming.

"Oh, there you are, Shirl," her father said by way of greeting. "You've been away much longer than you said; I thought you were coming home weeks ago."

Shirley bridled and was tempted to walk out of the door to go straight back to Yorkshire. Instead she said coolly, "I rang to tell you, Pa, that we were going to be away for longer because we had other bookings, but maybe you've forgotten that. What's more, we performed in Birmingham, and I had to put up with Granny whispering and talking right under my nose while I danced on the stage!"

"Yes, well," Reggie retorted sharply, "I was out, and Tilly took that message. I did expect that you would call me again later."

"I couldn't do that, because I was on the stage later. Anyhow, I'll tell you all about it over supper," Shirley replied wearily; she turned her back on her father, and went upstairs.

There a scene of chaos met her eyes. In the dining room, which also served as the sitting room, a heap of grimy clothes lay on the floor. They obviously belonged to Ted, who must have come home, perhaps more than once, in her absence. In the kitchen dirty pans and greasy plates were piled up higgledy-piggledy on the draining board, while knives, forks and spoons that must have slid off the plates lay on the floor.

The cupboard was almost bare: all the tins of stewed meat she had stacked up for the winter had disappeared, leaving only a half-empty box of eggs and one large potato, which would have to do for supper. Without a doubt, she would be cooking supper, and would be spending the next two weeks putting everything to rights.

Unable to face the chaos left for her attention, and secretly glad that her father had not been able to get in touch with her during the tour, she spent the afternoon emptying her suitcase, washing her smalls, rearranging her wardrobe and putting her luggage away until she heard him coming up from the shop at the end of the day.

"Where are you, Shirl?" he called out from the top of the stairs.

"Here in my room!" she answered curtly. He lumbered along the passage and stood in the doorway, leaning against the frame.

"I didn't want your return to be like this, but it's been very stressful since you went away," he began. "One thing after another, you might say. Ted came home soon after you left. He dumped that heap of dirty clothes on the living-room floor, and disappeared again the next morning before I had even had time to say goodbye to him. Eileen's sprained her back and hasn't been able to do any cooking or shopping for me, and Archie's had to stay at home to look after her because she can hardly move. Then on the day you rang, Tilly's mother fell ill with shingles, so Tilly left a scrawled note, and has been at home ever since, looking after her and little Albert. He caught chickenpox, and then Tilly caught it too: all of which means I've been on my own, trying to juggle all the balls and keep the business going. So, you see, I've scarcely had a moment to do any washing, any shopping or any washing-up."

He paused. "At least," he continued, "I reckoned, Ted wouldn't be coming back soon, so his washing could wait." He stood a helpless figure waiting for her reaction.

As usual, Shirley's kinder nature overcame her frustration. "Don't worry, Pa," she said resignedly. "I'm home now, and when I've cleared the kitchen, I'll fry up those eggs and mash that one potato. You can come and help me." Although she intended her father to do the drying-up, she changed her mind when she saw how grimy all the tea-towels were. "On second thoughts, Pa, you go and run the bath, put in some washing powder and soak Ted's clothes and these tea-towels while I straighten things up in here."

Far from having a rest or a holiday during those first two weeks at home, Shirley found herself obliged to divide her time between doing the domestic chores, waiting in one long queue after another for the meagre provisions available, and helping sort out the chaos that she found in the shop as well as in the living quarters.

While endeavouring to manage on his own, her father had been lax about bookkeeping and stock-taking, so she sent him into his office to sort out that side of the business, while she dealt with the front of shop, loading up the paper-boys' bags early in the morning, and thereafter selling newspapers, magazines, sweets, cigarettes and tobacco, and restocking the shelves. She eventually rather enjoyed running the newsagent's herself. It reminded her of those days long ago when, to earn some pocket money, she used to help Mr and Mrs Salvatore in their paper shop.

Her father, both relieved and grateful to have her back, agreed to take over the sales for an hour or so every day while she went shopping. One could never judge how long that might take because supplies were becoming even shorter and the queues ever longer. Disappointingly, without the bonus of fresh food from the country, provided by Eileen's relative, she had to make do with whatever was available.

One advantage of the domestic situation was that her father had used very few of his own rations; Ted's ration book was virtually untouched, and she herself had not had cause to use many of her own, since meals were generally provided for the cast of Aurora wherever they went. She was therefore able to buy rather more food than she had anticipated, and not only items that were unrationed, such as tripe and pigs' trotters, but more palatable foodstuffs if they were on sale.

There was of course also her role as an ARP warden. Reggie insisted that she had to take this up again in the interim between tours, to avoid being conscripted along with so many other women of her age in 1941. Either they were sent to work in armaments' factories, agriculture and industry, or they were employed in the services, in the Wrens, the ATS or the WAAF. As for the latter, Shirley had already discovered that there was no chance of taking to the air in the Women's Auxiliary Air Force: joining that would mean boring clerical work, cooking, waitressing, and probably delivering messages, which she had decided long ago was definitely not for her. Nor did she expect that the Wrens, the Women's Royal Naval Service, would suit her: it would involve becoming a radio operator, a meteorologist, or a bomb-range marker on land, whilst going to sea did not appeal to her at all. As for the ATS, the Auxiliary Territorial Service, her reaction to that was quite blunt: the uniform was horrible. In any case, as she kept repeating to herself, dancing in Aurora was her occupation and her war effort.

Nonetheless, she willingly resumed her role as a volunteer Air Raid Precautions warden, a role still considered essential because although the Blitz was easing off slightly, it had not ceased, and was as unpredictable as ever. She had taken her gas mask on tour, so she pulled it out of her suitcase, and took her uniform, complete with helmet, from the wardrobe. Returning to ARP mode, she laid everything out, ready to put on as quickly as possible whenever needed. Her father had continued his work for the ARP in her absence and had also taken on most of her patrols. In all probability that was one of the reasons why he was so tired and, it had to be said, incompetent.

The upshot of those weeks was that Shirley was fully occupied, upstairs and downstairs at home by day, and out patrolling the streets at night. She had no time to meet old friends; it was as much as she could do to visit Tilly, who was at home caring for her mother and son, and Eileen, whose back was slowly making a good recovery. Eileen was very happy to see her "adopted" granddaughter again, and was thrilled by Shirley's accounts of the performances, especially since, for her ears, those accounts dwelt mostly on the beautiful costumes in each of the ballets. Shirley assured Eileen that the costumes were wearing well and on stage had looked magnificent. There were, she admitted, one or two minor tears to be mended if Eileen's back would permit. Eileen was unexpectedly indignant.

"Shirley! I'm not an invalid!" she declared. "I've been making your new costumes – the ones for the French market ballet – since the doctor told me I could get out of bed, and they are all finished. Just look in my sewing room, dear, will you please? They're all there for you and your pals to try on!"

Shirley went to look and was overjoyed to see a whole array of colourful overskirts.

"I didn't make any green ones because you already have those from the *Giselle* ballet, and you still have the red and yellow ones from your Spanish dance," Eileen called out. "Have a look in the cupboard, because there are some of the costumes for the *Nutcracker* dances in there. I hope I'm right that those are going to be needed next?"

"Ooh, yes! They're perfect for our next performances," Shirley cried out in delight.

Using a walking stick, the elderly seamstress shuffled into her sewing room. She leaned on the door frame and whispered, "I don't know where Archie is at the moment, but I have to be a little bit careful in case he catches me in here. He always thinks I'm doing too much. Then he stops me, but sewing these overskirts has been a lifeline for me, otherwise I should have died of boredom from being cooped up like this all day and every day!"

She maintained that she was perfectly able to sit on a chair, with a cushion at her back, to use her sewing machine, and was sure she would be well enough in a couple of days' time to embark on more tasks. Meanwhile, she promised to ask her brother for a delivery of fresh eggs, vegetables and meat, and anything else he might be able to spare from the country, because she feared that Reggie had not been taking good care of himself while Shirley was away.

The days passed remarkably quickly because, despite the drudgery of some of Shirley's activities, there was so much to be done. As the "holiday" period drew to a close, she felt a quiet satisfaction that the home front was in a rather better state than when she had arrived. The flat was clean and tidy: Ted's clothes had been washed and dried, as had the bed linen, teacloths and towels. Since Reggie lit the fire only in the evenings, carrying the washed, wet clothes downstairs and out to the yard, where her father had fitted up a short washing line for use in summer, was as much of an effort as dancing a principal role on the stage.

She did not ask for her father's help with these chores, since his lameness had become noticeably worse in her absence. Nevertheless, his general health improved day by day after her return, thanks to regular meals and her efficient dealing with the shop.

He said so one evening after turning off the Nine O'clock News. "You've really put us to rights here, haven't you, Shirl?" he said. "I didn't want you to come home and find everything in such a mess, but it was more than I could do to keep everything in order, what with Tilly's problems and Archie having to look after Eileen. But I think they'll both be back soon, so there's no need to worry, but I suppose you'll be off again, won't you?"

Having muttered something about being glad to help, Shirley took the opportunity to tell her father of Aurora's future plans, reassuring him that she would not be going away again just yet.

"I'll be here for at least another four weeks while we rehearse the new programme, Pa, but I will be very busy," she said. "We started working on it ages ago, but there's still a lot to do. Cynthia's fiancé, Pete, has spread the word round lots of bases where he has contacts, and it sounds as if he has managed to secure bookings for us in the south-west, so it will be rather like the northern tour but in the West Country, which should be nice in October. Oh, you'll be pleased to hear that he has fully registered us with CEMA, the Council for Music and the Arts. They paid for one or two of our performances up north, and now we'll be on their books all the time. They pay much better than ENSA; we'll still do the ENSA engagements but combined with CEMA."

Her father, brooding on her plans for the West Country, nodded, without having taken any notice of her most recent news. "Yes, it's beautiful down there. I took your mother there when she first came to

England. It was our honeymoon, I suppose you might say, and we were so happy." He sank into a morose reverie.

"We're going to be doing my dance for a French market, Pa, and some dances from *The Nutcracker*," Shirley announced brightly, anxious to jolt him out of his melancholy.

"Ah, that's good!" he replied, though he had no idea what she was talking about. Instead, he became prey to resentment as recollections of his blissful honeymoon in the West Country surfaced one by one. Those memories persuaded him that, without a doubt, Jacqui should be there with him and their daughter, listening to and encouraging her plans for her touring ballet company! His bitterness towards Jacqui grew: she had no right to abandon her family, he said to himself, even if sometimes his shell shock re-emerged, although he did his best to contain it, and these days it was much more controllable than in the past.

Suddenly aware that his daughter was still talking, he roused himself. "And I'm going to dance the Sugar Plum Fairy in the Land of the Sweets where Clara – she's the little heroine – finds herself in her dreams on Christmas night."

"That sounds exciting!" he exclaimed, to his own surprise, as he found himself drawn out of the doldrums into his daughter's description of her new ballet. "Tell me more about it!"

Shirley was taken aback. Her father had never shown much enthusiasm for ballet before, so she let her own enthusiasm carry her away as she prattled on about the *divertissements* in *The Nutcracker*, the Cossack dance, the dance of the Flutes, the Arabian dance, the Chinese tea dance and the Waltz of the Flowers.

"By the way," she informed him, "the Arabian coffee dance is going to be danced by Doris, that girl who, Cynnie and I thought, was going to be a nightmare, but when I gave her the solo in the coffee dance she was really pleased, and she's turned out to be quite nice. She has already danced the title role in *Coppélia* several times. You remember, don't you? That's the ballet where Swanhilda, the principal dancer, gets very jealous of a beautiful girl sitting in the window of an old scientist's workshop. She raids the workshop only to find that the girl in the window, Coppélia, is a mechanical doll! I love that ballet; it's such fun! We took it in turns to dance it up north. Doris is a good dancer, light on her feet even though she's so large." When she turned to look at her father in his armchair, she saw his head lolling on his chest and his eyes closed.

She coughed and suddenly she heard him asking, "What else did you say there was in the programme? Something about France?"

"Yes! We've decided to open with my little ballet about a market in France; do you remember that one? I think you've seen it. It's all very colourful with the stallholders selling their wares, cheese, meat, fish, fruit and vegetables, and jams and jellies; there's a woman selling lovely clothes she's made herself, and another with knitted goods. And there's the town band and acrobats performing in the square. And, let me see, what else? Oh, yes, there are people selling chicks and goslings, and a man with puppies." She was carried away with the anticipated excitement of performing her own creations, and carried on despite her father's eyes being closed. "I dance the part of a young girl, standing at the side. At first I watch and then I go round all the stalls, dancing with the stallholders. It ends with a *tarantella* – that's a fast Italian dance – for the whole company. Eileen has made some more costumes, but don't tell Archie that, because she's supposed to be resting. Anyhow, she hasn't had to make too many because we can use what we already have for *Giselle*. I'm not sure if I've told you about that. No one's going to know they're the same. The problem is that we still have to find the right music for it."

Shirley's enthusiasm was infectious. Scarcely pausing for breath, she treated her captive audience of one middle-aged man to more of her plans, although with his head nodding on his chest, it was not at all easy to tell whether he was concentrating on the flood of information that was washing over him.

"And after that," she went on, "we dance some of the *divertissements* from the *Nutcracker* ballet, as I told you just now. They are so lovely, and I begin that sequence with a solo, the *Dance of the Sugar Plum Fairy*! Then, at the end of the first half, my partner and I finish it off with the *pas de deux*, the duet from the same dance."

"Oh, by the way, I've not had a chance to tell you," he said, changing the subject abruptly, having opened his eyes, "but your Cynthia is very good at keeping track of the finances. While you were up north, she kept sending me all the details of invoices and receipts, all the outgoings and the payments, so keeping the company's books was easy by comparison with my own, and I'm glad to say, there's plenty of money in the bank, enough to pay the cast and all expenses for some time to come. And in my opinion, you and Cynthia should pay yourselves a salary."

Shirley butted in: "No, Pa, I don't want a salary; Cynnie can have one, but I'll take a part-repayment of my loan to the company, and you should do so too."

"No, I don't need that, but I'll make sure you are repaid some of the money you put into Aura, or whatever it's called," he said.

"It's Aurora, Pa," Shirley corrected him.

"Yes, well," Reggie replied, happy to be on firmer ground, "I've just remembered something: did you know that the manager of the cinema is wanting you to perform there, before you go away again? I had a word with him a couple of weeks ago. He said they don't have the projector up and running yet, and it's still going take weeks if not months to finish all the repairs properly, the redecoration and so on, before the screen can be put in place, so the cinema will still be out of action for some time to come. He was very pleased to fill the seats last time; he'd be delighted to have you back, even if it's not until September."

"Good for you, Pa! That's wonderful!" Shirley responded. "I was going to have a word with the manager myself, but I haven't had time. September should suit us fine. By the way," she went on, "I didn't say, did I?... Madame keeps changing her mind and has now decided that the second half will be Act Two of *Swan Lake*, but it will start with the end of Act One by way of introduction – that's when Prince Siegfried goes out hunting at night and meets poor Odette, who is suffering under the wicked curse which turns her into a swan. Only if she finds undying love, can she be released from the curse, but the wicked Baron Rothbart is trying to stop that by disguising his daughter Odile as Odette; Odile's a Black Swan, and she seduces Prince Siegfried. Of course it all ends in tragedy."

Reggie's head was nodding on his chest again at this torrent of information, but suddenly he paid attention, nodding sagely. "There you are!" he exclaimed. "A woman making a pass at a man she fancies!"

Shirley stared at him, astounded that such a remark could have come from her father. "Sorry, what was that you said, Pa?" she asked him.

Whereupon he scratched his head in embarrassment at his own outspokenness, and said no more. His daughter frowned, thinking it unlikely that he could be speaking from experience. However, despite this interruption, she went on, "We've decided to let Doris dance Odile, the Black Swan, though I hope Eileen will be able to run up a costume for her. I would have liked to do that myself, but never mind." Reggie had by now dozed off again.

In spite of the fact that Madame lived next door, Reggie rather sheepishly said, when asked, that he hadn't seen "that woman" while Shirley had been away on tour. She found this strange, because Madame had come to meet the company on their return, before going away on holiday herself, which meant that she must have been at home during the whole period of their absence. Since her return, Shirley herself had only set foot out of doors for shopping, her ARP duties and to visit Eileen and Tilly's family, so had not noticed whether Madame had returned. In any case, she did not want to bother her until the end of the so-called "holiday period".

Madame had now been away for ten days, so once the early morning rush of customers had cleared from the shop, she tentatively knocked on Madame's door, but no one answered. While she waited at the door wondering what to do next, she became aware of a tall, stately figure, coming along the road. The figure stopped behind her. She turned to find Madame with a broad smile on her face and her little suitcase in her hand.

"*Ma chérie!*" she greeted Shirley with evident joy both at seeing her favourite pupil and at being able to speak French again. "Are you ready to begin again? Are you ready to dance again? I called on your father and invited him to come to dinner with me several times while you were away, but he refused!"

Shirley raised a bemused eyebrow on hearing this. Unsurprisingly, Madame's kind invitations had been rejected, probably outright, because, however hungry he was, her father would never dream of having dinner with her. Clearly he must have believed that she was making a pass at him! The temptation to giggle was all but uncontrollable, and the only way to suppress it was for Shirley to bite her lip hard. Thereafter she avoided all reference to this episode which her father had been at pains to conceal, but which explained a great deal about his behaviour and his remarks. She politely said that she couldn't wait to begin to dance again. For once, she reckoned that the shop could take care of itself, or at least that her father could take care of it, especially since she knew that his paperwork was all in order and carefully filed away.

"In that case, *ma chérie*, let us begin straight away," said Madame. "Come to the studio in ten minutes after I have washed the dirt from my hands and face, and then I think we should begin with the *Dance of the Sugar Plum Fairy*. You learnt that in one afternoon before you went to

Yorkshire, but you will have to work hard at your posture, because I can see you are out of practice. I trust you have checked the choreography while I was away." She looked enquiringly at Shirley.

"Yes, Madame," she replied, not at all sure that she had checked the choreography thoroughly enough to meet Madame's extremely exacting standards.

"Remember," Madame said ten minutes later, refreshed after washing the "dirt" from her hands and face, "remember to hold your upper body erect: straight back, shoulders down and strong *tendus* are your source of energy for every step. They will govern your whole performance. Let us begin with the opening, which is all *pointe* work, that sequence of *pas de bourrée* and *pas de chat* into an *arabesque*."

Shirley knew what was required from her – a light but strong airiness of movement from her fingers into the depths of her body, holding every muscle rigid, down into her feet.

Madame nodded approvingly, but held up a hand to stop her when she went into the *arabesque*. "No! You must hinge at the hips for your *arabesque*! Repeat it!"

This was Madame's favourite method: to approve half a minute of dance and then criticize, before going back to the beginning. Once satisfied with Shirley's reformed *arabesque*, she challenged her with a couple of *pirouettes* leading into the *piqué manège*. "Attack with speed," she instructed. "Step onto a strong, straight leg, then turn, turn, turn, all round the stage! Remember to treat the stage like a box and turn, turn, turn from corner to corner! Keep the upper body held and let it lead you into the *coupé-jeté*. Good! *Chassée* up – and there, you've done it! Now do it all again!" Shirley reached for a glass of water, swallowed the contents in one gulp, and then took a deep breath before beginning again.

There followed days and weeks of similar non-stop exercises, practice and rehearsals. Madame co-opted Andrei, a recent addition to the cast, to dance the *pas de deux* sequence with Shirley, including all the lifts. Practising this well-loved sequence from *The Nutcracker* gave a huge boost to her confidence. Andrei was the perfect partner for her: he was the most muscular, agile and reliable of the male dancers. When she sprang into his arms, he lifted her high above his head, or when he tipped her so that she was leaning down, her head almost touching the floor, she felt not the least pang of anxiety because his grip was so firm and reassuring.

She told him at the end of one rehearsal how safe she felt with him, and he replied, "That's easy, because you are so light. I could pick you up with one hand! I like dancing with you!"

Shirley certainly liked dancing with him, and as they danced in complete harmony, a chemistry developed between them, bringing them very close.

The chemistry disappeared as soon as they stopped dancing, which, Shirley told herself, was only right, because Andrei had a wife in some distant part of the world, and she herself was certainly not ready for a new relationship. Andrei was indisputably the male star of the show and, like Dmitri, a great favourite of Madame's because of his Russian background.

Other men had joined the company when, one by one, some of the original cast were called up. Pedro was bespoke as Maria's boyfriend and partner in the flamenco sequences, while Giorgio, an Italian refugee from Fascism, was extremely popular with the all the girls in the *corps de ballet*, but attached to none. Naturally enough Madame also favoured the two French dancers, Marc and Arnaud, both refugees from occupied France, who had recently joined the cast. Among themselves the men, including Dmitri, the music specialist, the stranded Australians and New Zealanders, a Dutch escapee from the occupied Netherlands and big Rocky the Texan compère, who had been promoted to stage manager, prized the common bond of all being strangers trapped in a foreign land.

This fellow feeling led to a good working ethos, which was evident in their approach to the company. Without exception, they gave of their best, since all were grateful to be employed, and yet were not required to go to fight. Rocky's English assistants back-stage had by now dropped out, considering themselves to be too old for heaving scenery and props about in theatres and travelling round the country. Rocky was not bothered by this defection since he was perfectly capable of managing on his own. When help was needed, he called upon one or two of the male dancers who were not involved in the current performance.

The tour to the West Country, after a very satisfactory first performance in the cinema, assured an elated cast of the certain success of the new programme, and indeed that was the case in theatres from Bristol, via Bath, Exeter and Plymouth, to Truro, in seaside towns and in army and naval bases across the region. Shirley loved the scenery, wishing there were time to go for long walks across an enchanting landscape where purple heather basked in the rays of a bright, autumn sun, streaming from an azure sky. The views were as impressive but softer, gentler than those of the North Yorkshire moors, and she wished her father were with her to see them. The new programme went down well with audiences because, in a single performance, it encapsulated the essence of the art of the ballet, from *The Nutcracker*, through *Scenes from a French Market* to excerpts from *Swan Lake*, although both Shirley and Cynthia were not sure that the programme was arranged in the right order, because *Swan Lake*, though beautiful, did not exactly offer very cheerful entertainment. Nevertheless, however they considered it, *Swan Lake* really provided the grand finale to the performance, despite the tragedy of its storyline.

As the anniversary of the bombing of Coventry approached in November towards the end of the tour, Shirley steeled herself. Memories of that night of 14th of November 1940, precisely a year ago, when she lost her baby, haunted her: that was one more horrendous tragedy of this ghastly World War: her child was the most innocent of its victims. Yet, as she told herself, many people were suffering as she had suffered, and it was up to her to set an example by containing her grief and playing her part, which after all was fulfilling her dream of dancing on the stage as a prima ballerina. She persuaded herself that by performing to the very limits of her capability, she would be honouring her fiancé and their lost little son.

25

Those two first tours of the Aurora Ballet Company, to Yorkshire in the summer of 1941, and in the autumn to the West Country, were memorable both on account of the standing ovations the dancers received, and also for the welcome relief from air raids, allowing everyone a good night's sleep – apart, that is, from the nocturnal interruptions caused by snoring. The effects of this reprieve were visible. The members of the company, from the principals to the stage-hands, smiled and exchanged greetings, rather than passing each other with scarcely a word; the dancers not only helped each other with their costumes but at the end of each performance cleared up each other's belongings as well, making sure that nothing was left behind.

The general atmosphere was becoming more congenial by the day. Even Doris appeared in a different light: hesitantly at first, she laughed and joked, and soon began to participate in communal meals rather than deliberately sitting alone as she had done previously. Some of her remarks were illuminating. When asked where she came from, she was heard to say, "Unfortunately I come from the East End." Everyone knew what that "unfortunately" signified, because the East End had withstood the full fury of the Blitz. Also, gradually it transpired that Doris came from a poor family of dockers who did not take kindly to her aspirations.

From the age of twelve, her parents had expected her to work all hours of the day, packing boxes of English provisions for shipment to the colonies, whereas she longed to dance. She said she felt it in her feet – because they wouldn't keep still. Even while she was working, they kept changing position, rising up and down in what she later recognized as *relevés*. Eventually her parents were so tired of this constant motion that they told her to stop it, but she couldn't stop it, so they threatened to tie her down. She refused to work, and they did tie her down, but she sulked and wouldn't eat for the best part of two weeks, so they had to untie her. Her father was all for giving her a hiding and threatened to chop off her feet, but her mother, who was gentler when in a good mood, told her that she had one chance: if she really wanted to dance, she could go to a class she had heard of in a church hall a bus ride away, and pay for it out of her wages. If she wasted that chance, she would have to go back to work.

Doris's natural aptitude for the ballet was quickly recognized by the dance teacher, who volunteered to train her individually for free, and like Shirley, she benefited from personal tuition for several years until her teacher told her that the time had come for her to apply to join a company, a variety company at first, to condition herself to different types of dancing.

This routine was going very satisfactorily until the beginning of the Blitz, which destroyed the theatre where she danced. Doris's mother was killed in one of the raids on the East End when their house collapsed, and her father was left handicapped. No longer able to work, he sat at home, dependent on Doris, who found herself being inexorably drawn back into the dismal circumstances of life in the bombed-out East End, having only just escaped from it. One day in the West End she saw and replied to an advertisement for a new but as yet unnamed ballet company. She was accepted into its ranks, and was immeasurably proud that it was she who had chosen its name: Aurora. The company provided her with the opportunity to dance professionally in classical ballet, and thus to escape from her background once and for all.

The tale of Doris's struggle was not lost either on Cynthia's generous nature, or more particularly on Shirley's, for now she understood both Doris's personality and her reason for wanting solo roles: they were better paid than those of the *corps de ballet*, and she needed the money to support her father as well as herself.

Doris's occasional sulks were not a pretty sight, but Shirley was prepared to overlook them, interpreting them as a remnant of the deep frustration she had suffered, and with that she sympathized, remembering the black cloud that had hung over her own aspirations to become a prima ballerina. She also vowed to help Doris as and when she could by giving her more solo roles, well aware of the sheer determination required to advance in the profession. After unburdening herself, Doris became more light-hearted and made friends in the company, and thereafter she no longer had any reason to complain. She acknowledged and appreciated all that Cynthia and Shirley tried to do for her, and in fact, she became their most loyal supporter, nipping all criticisms of whatever nature, in the bud.

Between tours, Cynthia and Shirley, with Reggie's blessing, decided to put on a Christmas party for their dancers. The minister of the Methodist Church, grateful for the rental income received from Aurora, was only too pleased to allow them the use of his church hall, which still, on occasions, served as an especially useful studio. Since Hitler broke his pact with Stalin and invaded Russia, the War had turned to the East, and to the Middle East, with the result that the German forces were overstretched and air raids on London had become less regular and more sporadic. Nevertheless, on account of the unpredictability of the situation, no one had much appetite for a party in central London.

Eileen, Tilly's mother and Cynthia's mother, the seamstresses, all clubbed together to contribute food, since they had completed enough of the costumes for the time being. Reggie commissioned drinks from the pub and Rocky agreed to bring ballroom-dancing gramophone records to be played on Shirley's gramophone. The date for the party was set for Sunday the 7th of December. The party, which everyone was determined to enjoy – from Archie and Eileen, now fully recovered, to Cynthia and Pete, who had turned up at the last minute greatly to his fiancée's delight – gained an added dimension from the announcement earlier in the day that the Japanese had bombed the American Pacific Fleet in its base at Pearl Harbour in Hawaii. In deference to Rocky, displays of jubilation were discreetly suppressed, given the horror of the attack on a still neutral power, and the loss of life, yet it was impossible to hide an overwhelming feeling of relief that the United States would no longer be able to maintain its neutrality but would be bound to enter the War. Rocky put his thoughts into words when he said, "Ah shall soon be able to feel proud to be an American!"

In the period after the party and before Christmas, Madame again insisted that the company should take a rest as before, but she also called regular meetings, sometimes with only Cynthia and Shirley, sometimes with the whole troupe, including the backstage workers, to discuss future programmes. Reggie absolutely refused to join in these meetings. Anything that involved "that woman", he said, was out of the question for him. For the forthcoming tour, the third – of the east of England – with performances in all the cathedral cities from Canterbury to York, "that woman" proposed a revised programme which consisted of dances already in the repertoire, that is to say, a medley of dances from the first and second programmes. This time the performance would open with the *Nutcracker* sequences, and would be followed by Maria and Pedro's flamenco dances. The second half would begin with Shirley's *Scenes from a French Market* and end with the second act of *Coppélia*, with the title role of the beautiful doll to be danced by Doris. The whole company was satisfied with this arrangement. The choreographies, the music, the costumes, the stage sets, everything was ready and to hand, and only a few rehearsals after Christmas would be needed to adjust to the routine.

Johan, the Dutchman, however, put a spanner in the works by pointing out that York, their ultimate destination, was not so very far from the venues where they had performed in Yorkshire on their first tour, so perhaps if the audience were made up of the same people as in the summer, they might feel cheated at seeing two of the same ballets, that is, repeats of the flamenco dances and *Coppélia*.

Madame considered this objection. "Ah, well," she said, unconcerned, "een zat case you will 'ave to perform some of ze West Country programme een York! Anee'ow, eet only concerns ze flamenco and *Coppélia*. I weel zeenk about eet."

Madame did think about it and came up with a solution which, she said, involved minimum disruption to the scheme of things: the programme would open with a few of the *Scenes from a French Market*, with Shirley in the principal role, and this would be followed by an excerpt from *Swan Lake* with Shirley and Andrei, as Odette and Siegfried dancing the *White Adagio*, the expression of their passion for each other. Doris would then dance Odile, the Black Swan, in an abbreviated court scene where she deceives Siegfried into mistaking her for his beloved Odette. After the interval the programme would be devoted to Act Two of *The Nutcracker*, but in an expanded version, opening with the *Dance of the Snowflakes*, before the dance of the *Sugar Plum Fairy* and the *divertissements*.

At first sight it all appeared too complicated: the changes appeared awkward, and the cast shook their heads. According to Madame, it would be easy to organize and would fill the time. Shirley was not happy about going straight into the *White Adagio* in *Swan Lake* after her principal role in the French market scenes, and said so in private to Madame.

"But *ma chérie*," said Madame, in French, "there will have to be a pause for scene-changing after your market dances, when you will have time to take a breath and change into your next role." There was no point in arguing with Madame, so Shirley was reconciled to steeling herself for that one performance. She reckoned that she was at the height of her career, a career which she had thought would never be possible, therefore it was up to her to take on whatever challenges were expected of her without complaint.

The dancers set off to a garrison near Canterbury in freezing temperatures in mid-February: the place seemed deserted when they arrived, even though their van had arrived ahead of the Company, and was already waiting at the gate for admittance. Rocky put his head out of the window. "Gee," he said, "I guess they've forgotten we are coming!"

Shirley left it to Cynthia to deal with the problem, because this engagement had been set up by Pete, so Cynthia had to argue with the guard when he appeared a quarter of an hour later, either to let them in or at least to call someone in authority, which he was extremely reluctant to do. Only when she mentioned her fiancé by name and rank, did he speedily call an officer.

When at last, a junior officer appeared, he frowned, uncertain of who they were, and went away to check. The bus that had brought them from the station left, and there they were, huddled together like a flock of penguins against the strong, chilly wind that blew off the Channel.

The officer returned after an age, saying, "I'm terribly sorry, there seems to have been some mistake, but do come along and we'll try to make you welcome!" The whole company, plus the backstage workers, followed him to the officers' mess, where they were invited to stand by some rather smelly oil heaters to warm up, while he went to find out what to do with this bunch of raggle-taggle itinerant ENSA entertainers.

"I could do with a hot cup of tea," Doris declared dolefully, an opinion that met with general agreement, except that Jack and one or two of the men said that a beer would suit them nicely.

Shirley, frozen to the core, suddenly sprang into life. "Oh, come on, everyone!" she exclaimed. "This is ridiculous – why are we just standing around moaning? Off with your coats and your footwear! We'll do our warm-ups in our stockinged feet, or bare feet if you prefer! Look if we move those heaters out of the way and push the tables to the side of the room, there'll be plenty of space and we'll pretend there's a *barre*. Come on, even you stage-hands can join in!"

Shirley pulled herself up to her full height and took the session as if she were Madame, calling the steps *demi-pliés*, *full pliés*, *tendus*, *grands battements*, *rondes de jambe*, *frappés*, etc., and counting out the beats.

Still no one had come to tell them what was happening, so she called the group into the centre and embarked upon *petit allegro* exercises: *relevés, échappés, changements, petits jetés,* and so on.

She was amused to see poor Rocky panting and trying to keep up at the back of the room, where, behind his towering figure, closed curtains caught her eye. "Those curtains must be concealing a stage," she said to herself and went over to look. Behind the curtains there was indeed a fine stage, large enough for all their dances. "Look, everybody!" she shouted. They all cheered, shouting out, "Come on! Let's take over this stage! It's here waiting for us!" and scrambled to get onto the stage as fast as possible. The floor was smooth and clean but not slippery. By the time a senior officer arrived, it was full of whirling dancers performing the French market scenes, without music, barefoot or in their socks and stockings. After that unconventional introduction to the garrison, the company received many apologies for what was referred to as a "secretarial" error. In compensation they were treated royally, and their performance that evening was pronounced to be "splendid", although they knew it was not their best because the freezing temperatures had chilled their muscles, and the uncertainties had unsettled them.

The inauspicious start to the tour was an omen of what was to come, especially as far as the weather was concerned. Snow was blowing in the wind when the dancers woke up in the morning, and it continued to fall while they breakfasted and packed.

"We must get to the station as soon as we can," Cynthia announced, "so please have your bags ready in half an hour when the bus arrives."

Since punctuality was an important part of the discipline of a dancer, they caught an earlier train than expected to Rochester, nervously wondering what the naval venue would hold. They all, especially Cynthia, who had been mortified by the confusion at Canterbury, clapped at finding a bus waiting to take them to the naval base at Chatham. There they encountered a ready admittance at the gate, and preparations of a lavish kind had been made. The comfortable, warm and dry accommodation in an impressive brick building put Nissen huts to shame, the food was excellent, and correspondingly the performance was much better than that of the previous evening. Even so, the following night spent at home in London after Chatham, before setting out again for East Anglia, came as an unexpected pleasure, because it allowed them to dry out their clothes and shoes, and relax, ready for the next stage of the tour.

The snow turned to light rain the next day, raising hopes of better weather. However, outside the metropolis, as they headed north-east, heavy clouds gathered, and snow fell persistently, until it cloaked the flat lands of the Fens in a pure white sheet. When they stepped off the train at Ely, a bitter north-east wind greeted them, yet again freezing the travellers to the bone. They waited, shivering outside the station, but no bus came to collect them, although Cynthia was confident that she had hired a coach to take them to the airbase a few miles outside the city.

"We can't stand here in this wind; we'll all catch pneumonia," was Shirley's assessment of the situation. She went back into the station to ask where her dancers might find shelter, and charmed the station master into promising that should their bus turn up, and for that matter their van, he would direct the drivers to a hotel he recommended in the centre of the city. A forlorn band trooped off to the city centre, which would have seemed quite close, had it not been for the snow piling up in the streets. Beyond the cathedral, they found the hotel, where they took shelter and waited, both for news of the rest of their party coming by road in the van, and for transport to take them to the airbase. Shirley and Cynthia put their heads together to decide how much money they could afford to spend on food for their group, and remain within their budget, afraid that they might have to pay for overnight accommodation as well. "I think one and sixpence a head for lunch would be about right," Cynthia said after doing her calculations. "But it might cost us six shillings per person if we have to stay the night here," she added anxiously.

Cynthia's worst fears were not fulfilled when later that afternoon an RAF bus pulled up outside the hotel, but what was to follow was not exactly what she and the company had hoped for. The driver could not be described as a bundle of joy. "The roads are really bad," he said grumpily. "It's taken me an hour and a half to cover five miles."

"What about our van with the scenery, the costumes and the props?" Shirley asked him. "It's coming from London!" The driver shook his head. "No way they'll get through tonight – all the roads are blocked." Not in the mood for further conversation, he stumped off back to his bus, calling over his shoulder, "Come on, get in at once, or we'll never make it to the base." The dancers swallowed the hot tea they had just been served, picked up their bags and ran to the bus.

The airfield was cloaked in white silence, all sound muffled by the soft, heavy blanket. No engines roared, no planes sped along the invisible runway, no voices shouted instructions and, above all, no sirens wailed out into the night. If the snow had brought the airfield to a standstill, it had also alleviated Shirley's qualms about visiting, let alone performing, on an airbase, which might have aroused such feelings of loss and sadness that she had feared she might break down while dancing Odette. Without her knowledge, the airbase had somehow crept into their schedule at Pete's suggestion, because an old schoolfriend of his was stationed there. Cynthia was so apologetic that Shirley felt obliged to put her best foot forward and conceal her anxiety. As it was, apart from the pale blue uniforms, there was little to suggest that this actually was an airbase; it could have been the garrison of any one of the armed forces in any part of the country.

The routine was the same as anywhere else – a welcome from the Commanding Officer, tea, then an air-raid drill, before being shown to their accommodation, this time in Nissen huts rather than the comparative luxury of the Chatham naval base.

"What shall we do now?" Shirley asked Cynthia. "By my watch it's nearly half-past seven, and we should be ready to go on stage."

"Let's do our make-up and have our shoes and tights on, so that as and when Rocky and co. get here, we will only have to put our costumes on. If he unloads those first, we can be ready to go on stage very quickly. It shouldn't take them long to unload the gramophone and put up the sets for your French dances – no longer anyhow than it takes to let the audience in," was Cynthia's wise reply. "What's more," she went on, "if they don't arrive tonight, we'll have to wait and see. We can't be the only ones to be held up by the snow."

The van did not arrive that night, and Rocky and his crew, including Jack, who was both the driver and a dancer, had to bed down in the Fens, in among the props and scenery in the back of the van, covering themselves with all the suitable costumes, the court apparel and so on – in fact anything they could find to keep warm. The cast shed their stage personae and returned to their civilian identities, but without bothering to remove their make-up, which caused considerable amusement at dinner.

Cynthia asked if Pete's friend was available, but to her disappointment was told that he was on leave, so instead of spending a jolly evening with him and his friends in the mess, she and the troupe were promoted to dining with the Commanding Officer, supposedly an honour. He was rather taken with Shirley's heavily made-up appearance and showed her to the seat next to his in the officers' mess, once it had been decided that there was no likelihood of a performance that evening. His attempts to charm her fell on deaf ears, although it was impossible to ignore what he was saying.

"I gather you are supposed to be travelling into the heart of East Anglia tomorrow – that's right, isn't it?" he boomed as if speaking through a megaphone.

She took a deep breath in, "No, we're supposed to be going to Peterborough. Let's hope the snow clears!" was all she had time to say before he butted in.

"I have it on good authority you won't be doing that; my reports tell me the roads and railway lines further north are completely blocked by drifts. There's no way you can get through," he answered, emphasizing the "completely blocked" with apparent jubilation. "But *I* have a plan!"

Of course, he had a plan, thought Shirley – his sort always did, much too full of themselves. She had already met several officers of his type.

"Let me have the details of which base you were supposed to be going to next, and I will send a message to let them know you won't be coming. You can hopefully perform for us tomorrow evening, stay here for another night before setting off due north. Then you will arrive for your next engagement in time for your performances there! The snow will be easing off, and the forecast is better for tomorrow, so the mainline trains will be up and running and with any luck the main roads will have cleared. I suggest you take as many of your costumes as you can in your suitcases, just to be on the safe side. I expect you can manage without scenery, or even costumes!"

He laughed, giving Shirley a knowing wink as he did so, then he twirled his moustache in satisfaction at his logical vein of thought, quite convinced that he had made a conquest.

Cynthia and Shirley conferred as they slid into sleeping bags in their Nissen hut. "He's very assertive, isn't he?" Cynthia said.

"Yes, I thought he was odious; I don't like him, and I suspect his motives," said Shirley. "Please make sure I'm not left alone with him tomorrow! At least it seems we won't have to do anything except perhaps a bit of extra rehearsal for the performance in the evening. Let's hope the van has arrived by then!"

Shirley spent most of the next morning trying to avoid the Commanding Officer, who either kept following her and Cynthia or popping up in their path wherever they went. Unnerved, Shirley foiled him finally by asking Rocky to accompany her wherever she needed to go, but, lo and behold! there he was again, sitting alone in the audience at the rehearsal, although he had not asked permission to attend, clearly deeming it to be his right.

"Ignore him, Shirl," was Cynthia's advice. Rocky was so irritated that, as a last resort, he went over to the officer and explained that, as an engineer himself, he was exceptionally keen to find out about different types of aircraft, and he asked if he would kindly show him the aeroplanes stranded on the snow-covered grass. Rocky's manner was so very genial that the officer could not refuse.

The van arrived at the base just in time, although twenty-four hours late, allowing a full performance with scenery, costumes and music to take place. The Commanding Officer was sitting in the front row, to Shirley's annoyance; his presence distracted her as she grew ever more nervous of his intentions. That night she changed places with Maria, whose bed was further down the Nissen hut, well away from the door. Although Doris and another of the girls on either side of Shirley pulled their beds closer, leaving no space for an intruder to come between them, she slept only fitfully.

In the middle of the night she heard the outer door opening and ill-concealed footsteps approaching the beds nearest the door. She sprang into action, grabbed her ARP whistle from under her pillow, and blew it loudly. The piercing din woke everyone in the hut and scared off the intruder, who left smartly, banging the door behind him. No one slept much after that interruption. All the girls were shaken and disgusted at what had happened. Shirley had visions of the horrible Bert, so did not sleep at all.

The following day the dancers and their paraphernalia set off post-haste, after Cynthia, Rocky and one or two others, but not Shirley, had gone to thank the organizers at the base. Trains were running on the mainline and they caught an earlier one than intended. The snow was gradually melting on the roads, though it was slow-going for the van. Despite the weather, the only casualty had been the disruption to Aurora's timetable. Shirley, still shaken from the night's intrusion, thanked all the girls individually for helping to save her. They made no bones about what they would have done to "that man" had he touched any of them or her. Peterborough, Aurora's next venue, was not far away. Occasional snowflakes were still falling, but did not settle, and the intermittent clouds allowed a ray of pale sunshine to brighten the road ahead. In the city, the streets were slushy and wet, presenting less of an obstacle to traffic than piled-up snow, so the company and the van arrived in good order at the theatre where they were to perform for troops stationed nearby.

"Phew! The last of the snow!" someone declared.

"Don't bank on it!" someone else countered.

However, the performance to a modest audience went well, and the dancers were given proper bedrooms and bathrooms in a local hotel.

Word had come through from Lincoln that the show the following evening was cancelled because that city was still cut off by snowdrifts. "We're not doing very well out of this tour, are we?" Shirley remarked to Cynthia, who shook her head.

"It's not too bad," she said. "According to my calculations we'll break even, though there won't be much of a profit. Thank goodness we didn't have to pay for hotel rooms in Ely!"

The financial situation was redeemed by York, where there were two performances: one for local people, and the second, to Cynthia's joy, for the troops from Pete's base, and from other smaller bases in the area. Pete said that this was an opportunity that he and his men couldn't miss, because they had all become balletomanes. They were even more delighted to find a new programme, when they had expected to see a repeat of the one given at their own base the previous summer.

26

Those beautiful places in rural parts of the country ranging from Yorkshire and the West Country to the south-east of England and north to Yorkshire again, places where the Aurora's dancers had given their early performances, came under attack in the appalling onslaught of the Baedeker raids, deliberately directed onto England's most historic cities, in April and May 1942, just after the completion of the company's third tour.

These senseless raids, serving no military purpose, were said to be the brainchild of one of Hitler's cronies, who had planned the attacks using the Baedeker tourist guidebooks. All the dancers had vivid memories of the cathedral cities where they had danced and been enthusiastically welcomed. Some even shed tears at the destruction wreaked on such innocently tranquil places. They reflected on how extraordinary it was that, during that period at least, they had been safer back in London than in any of those venues which had been wantonly smashed and had their inhabitants killed by a murderous, psychopathic enemy.

Nevertheless, by that spring of 1942 Aurora's reputation as a prestigious touring ballet company was well established, with varied programmes that received increasingly rapturous applause. Shirley was in her element: on the stage, the War seemed blissfully far away and out of mind, but the reality in London was that that was only an illusion. In the capital city she found herself plunged back into the War.

"We are still at the mercy of random raids," her father had warned her, as soon as she arrived home, "by day as well as by night, so you'll have to put your ARP uniform on again. There's plenty for us to do." Banging the table with his fist as if to inflict a bombing raid on a harmless, useful piece of furniture, he also repeatedly exclaimed, "The world's on fire!" at the nightly reports of battles in distant places from Russia to the Mediterranean, and the deserts of North Africa.

He was morose and dejected. This his daughter put down to the constant mental and emotional battering he received from the reports on the wireless. She decided there was not much she could do about that, except to try to take special care of him while she was at home. She also wondered how long the table, not in its first flush of youth, would withstand the onslaught given it almost daily, if not by her father, then by her brother, who also regularly vented his frustration on it when he came home. As this thought occurred to her, she knew there was something not right about it, but could not decide what it might be.

Apart from assiduously fulfilling her ARP duties, as well as being fully occupied with answering the requests for more engagements that kept coming in, from as far away as Glasgow, Edinburgh, Aberdeen and the north of Scotland, she now had that other responsibility on her hands again, her father, although he was not the sum total of matters which required her attention, other than practising the dance steps. In particular, their programmes were in a constant state of revision, with some items being added and others removed. Not only that, she was also trying to find the time to develop her own choreography for a ballet on the theme of the seasons, which she had sketched out a long time ago. Dissatisfied with her earlier version, she revised it and set it to Vivaldi's music, providing Aurora with a novel *entrée* into a balletic adaptation of baroque dances. She also intended to introduce Fokine's enchanting ballet, *Les Sylphides*, into the programme. It was a short ballet that hopefully would not involve long hours of rehearsal.

At the end of an afternoon spent in administrative wrangling instead of practising dance moves in Madame's studio, Shirley herself gave vent to an angry burst of frustration, and complained to Cynthia,

"Look, Cynnie, I'm fed up with this! We can't go on like this! It's just too much! We should be rehearsing for the tour of Scotland, and I should be putting the finishing touches to the *Seasons*. And by the way, I must talk to Eileen about the costumes for it, but I can't do any of that because there are all these letters to write!"

"I know what you mean," said Cynthia, "but what can we do? We're the victims of our own success!" Pausing in their work, they shoved aside the mass of papers covering the dining table and leant their elbows on the battered surface. They grimaced at each other.

"I'll make us a cup of tea," Shirley announced, "and maybe that'll help us come up with an idea."

After a great deal of banging and clattering in the kitchen, she returned ten minutes later with the tea-tray to find Cynthia smiling.

"I've been thinking, and I've had an idea," the latter said. "Why don't we take on a secretary? There's enough money in the bank, more than we ever expected, and we'll have a lot more coming in this summer!"

Shirley nearly dropped the tray. Out in the kitchen, she hadn't thought of anything except her own frustration; in any case, she did not handle the finances, because Cynnie and her father managed that side of things, so she had no idea that Aurora was doing well enough to pay a secretary.

"Wonderful!" she replied. "But there's one problem. We can't take over this dining room, because it's also Pa's sitting room. Poor old chap, he seems to be weighed down with anxiety at the moment, so what I mean is, we would need an office for the secretary – not a big one, just one room, but there's no spare room here."

"Hm, I see that," said Cynthia surveying the chaos, "and my house is too far away, so that's no good. It's a secretary *and* an office we need. And I reckon it needs to be near here so your father can direct the secretary when we're away and keep a check on the financial situation, paying her wages and any bills that come in, so she doesn't get too close to our finances, only dealing with bookings and so on."

Shirley was grateful for Cynthia's clear head and rational thinking. "Brilliant, Cynnie – you always come up with good ideas!" she said. "I'll call Pa and tell him to come upstairs so we can discuss it with him."

Reggie left the shop in Archie's care and came slowly up the stairs. He listened carefully to the plans, considered them, then nodded and said, "Well done, Cynthia! There's certainly enough money, because you've all worked so hard. I can perfectly well keep an eye on that and pay out whatever is needed, but finding a space and a secretary is not going to be easy in the current situation, now that women have to work for the war effort. Anyhow, I'll put up an advertisement for a secretary in the shop."

Upon which, he left the girls to carry on with their administrative business. To their surprise they heard his heavy footfall on the stairs again, only a quarter of an hour later. "I've news for you two," he announced from the doorway. "As I was writing out the advert for the secretary and talking to Archie about your predicament, he said, quite spontaneously, 'Oh, they can have a room in our house! Five bedrooms and only the two of us living there! There's plenty of room!' Of course he said he'd have to talk to Eileen, but was sure she'd approve."

"That's extraordinary, Pa! Now we only need to find a secretary!" Shirley exclaimed, and Cynthia applauded.

Eileen, who was busy making new costumes out of old ones, and mending tears in overskirts and tutus for the new ballets, did approve of turning one of the bedrooms in her house into an office. In fact, she said how pleased she was that at last one of those empty rooms would be put to good use as an office for the ballet company in which she had become so deeply involved. Moreover, she agreed to help find a secretary for Aurora. She did not have to look far for someone suitable, because one of her neighbours, who was too old to be employed in the forces, was desperate to be able to do something useful with her secretarial skills. She and Eileen had been good friends for years, and so, without more ado, Maud slipped into the role of secretary to Aurora, leaving Cynthia and Shirley free to compose their programmes and practise their choreographies, happy to be relieved of the burden of secretarial work and to leave it in Maud's capable hands. What's more, Maud had her own typewriter, but until Reggie could fix up a better communications system, he suggested that Maud should use Archie's telephone, and he would pay for it from Aurora's funds. Eileen and Archie scarcely used the phone themselves, so working out Aurora's share of the bills would be fairly easy. Cynthia and Shirley danced for joy.

There was another less positive dimension to Shirley's stay in London that spring of 1942. Eventually she realized her that her father's dejection was not entirely due to the reports from the battle fronts, terrible though they were. She herself had been so fully immersed in the fantasy world of the ballet on stage, and the intensely practical world of touring when not actually on stage, that the time had flown since she had found Ted's dirty clothes in a heap on the living-room floor. Surely that couldn't have been nine months ago! In all that time when she had been so busy, she had thought about him often, but had concluded that no news was good news. She counted up the months on her fingers, and found to her horror that it really was nine months since she had last seen her brother.

Suddenly it dawned on her that there was absolutely no sign of her brother's presence in the flat, and that was why that memory of Ted's treatment of the dining table ten days or so earlier, had made her anxious. Fear for Ted seized her, and when she asked her father if Ted had been back lately, his reaction was so intense that she was afraid of a re-emergence of the shell shock he had suffered as a result of the First World War.

"No! I haven't a clue where he is," he fairly yelled. "When he was in northern France, it wasn't difficult to imagine where he was and what he was up to, but since your *grandpère* was shot, he seems to have disappeared off the face of the earth!"

In fact, Ted's last appearance had been in the autumn, when Shirley had been away on tour in the West Country.

"There's not been a word from him for months," Reggie moaned with his head in his hands. "Not so much as a message through a contact or a colleague. Every night I think I hear his steps on the stairs, but there's no one there! Except, once or twice, I think he might have crept in when I was out – and you were away of course – or perhaps in the middle of the night when I was sound asleep. It looked as if occasionally a mouse had eaten the cheese and run off with a slice of bread and an apple. But there was no note to say he had been here. I suppose he's trained not to make any noise at all. Reggie was on the point of bursting into tears.

Having tried to comfort her father with words that sounded trite in the circumstances, Shirley went up to Ted's attic, where crumpled, unwashed sheets and a pile of dirty clothes did indicate the presence of a rather grubby visitor. With all the dirty washing she had discovered downstairs on her return from Yorkshire, it had not occurred to her to think there might be more up in the attic. As she pulled the sheets off the bed, a paper fluttered to the floor. She picked it up and found to her surprise that it was addressed to her – in English.

"Sis," it read, "I'm off on a new mission and have no idea when or if I will be back. I won't be in northern France any more." Those words sent an electric shiver up and down her spine. She read on, "Take care of Pa. He will need you." This was so unlike Ted, for usually his messages were brief and to the point, whereas here he was warning her that he was embarking on a very dangerous mission, probably in Vichy France, from which he might not return, and was commending their father to her care. What's more, he had not left his message on the dining table, but between the sheets on his bed, where he knew his sister, but not his father, would eventually find it.

Later Shirley served her father the best supper she could rustle up, and then, complaining of a headache, took herself off to bed. She lay awake wondering where Ted was. Was he still alive, or had he been captured by the Germans and taken prisoner or, more likely, summarily shot? Above all she prayed that he had not gone on a foolhardy mission to Vichy France to look for Hélène, because there his chances of survival were negligible on account of the increasing stranglehold of the Gestapo on that half of the country, although nominally it was free of invading forces. It was unlikely that Ted was in England, but she resolved to shelve all plans for new dances and also for the next round of tours, especially the Scottish tour, leaving that to Cynthia and Maud, and instead devote herself to searching for her brother.

Her first and most obvious port of call early the next morning was the headquarters of the Free French in Carlton Gardens, from where Générale De Gaulle issued his decrees. The door there was closely guarded. She managed to gain entry only by speaking French like a native, and charming the door-keeper, asking him what part of France he came from and how long he had been in England. She told him about her mother and her grandparents, adding that her grandfather had been shot by the Nazis, then she was admitted.

Once inside, she kept her ears open keenly to the hum of all conversations in the background, but she drew a blank: no one professed to know anything about Ted, nor did anyone seem to care about where he might be. It was a mystery about which no one around De Gaulle could or would give her any information: considering that Ted had worked, and possibly still did, intimately with the Free French, that attitude of indifference infuriated her.

Her annoyance grew when no one bothered even to offer her a freshly made cup of the real coffee in a pot on a table, from which wafted tempting aromas, unlike the Camp coffee or the dandelion, chicory or barley drinks that the British were having to make do with. That lapse in *politesse* was so unlike the French. The impression was unmistakeable: the staff were distancing themselves from her, anxious to show her the door.

She came away suspicious of nearly everyone in that organization, convinced that they knew more about Ted and his fate than they were telling her. There had been just one girl, in a green dress, who was moving towards the coffee pot as if to pour her a cup, when she had been called away by a supervisor. If only she could find that girl and talk to her!

She ambled up Lower Regent Street on the right-hand side, wondering what to do next, when she heard running footsteps approaching her from behind. The girl in the green dress who had almost dared to offer her a coffee, ran past her and, as she rounded a corner into a narrow street on the right, she turned to look back at Shirley, as if beckoning her, while checking that no one else was following them. Shirley followed her at a discreet distance, thinking that the girl might only be meeting a boyfriend for lunch, which would perfectly well account for her hurrying. It would be against all the odds for her to have news about Ted. However, it was worth pursuing her.

Unexpectedly there she was, waiting for Shirley in a doorway round a corner.

"I hoped you would follow me," she said in French. "You see, I have to be very careful because the boss" (she meant De Gaulle) "does not like us to associate with people outside the building for fear of German spies, and English ones too. He is offended that the British secret services and Mr Churchill do not share all their information about France, and does not trust them. It is top-secret in there. I do not know how you managed to gain entry, and I would lose my job if anyone saw me, but I do know your brother – he worked for us."

Shirley nodded. "Yes, we know that too," she said. "So, where is he?"

"I am not sure, but he was so angry when your grandfather was shot, I think he went underground, perhaps working with another organization as well," she said. "I do not know any details, but I have some ideas. I want to help you, and if you like, I will try to find out where he has gone. Please come back tomorrow at half-past twelve and wait for me on the left-hand side of Lower Regent Street. When you see me, walk up the street until you come to the first turning on the left, and you'll see me in the first doorway there. And bring your address and telephone number on a piece of paper, concealed in a handkerchief."

The girl walked off. She stopped in a doorway a few paces further on, waiting for Shirley to catch her up. Then she scribbled a note and dropped it on the ground before walking off. Shirley hastened to pick up the note and stuffed it in her pocket. Rooted to the spot, she gave herself time to digest what she had just heard and decide what to do next. Frowning, she walked on to Trafalgar Square, where she sat down on a bench, ignoring the pigeons and the people milling around her. The note on the paper simply said, "Wear ordinary clothes, not fashionable or likely to draw attention to yourself, and a brimmed hat, if you have one." She was unlikely to come across a solution to the puzzle in Trafalgar Square, so, having collected her thoughts, she stood up and headed for home.

The next morning, having reluctantly dressed up in her oldest, most unfashionable clothes, shoes and a hat – all mistaken purchases before the War, lying piled up at the bottom of her wardrobe, she made her way again to Lower Regent Street, and arrived punctually at 12.28. Two minutes later, a slim young woman appeared from the direction of Carlton Gardens: she was wearing the same green dress. Shirley hastily wrote her telephone number and address in her notebook. She tore out the page, folded it up in her handkerchief and put it in her pocket. The girl did not wave or call out – she simply gave a hint of a nod. As she approached, Shirley set off up Lower Regent Street on the left-hand side as if she had remembered something important she had to do. She turned into the first side street, and there she slowed down. The girl caught up with her.

"Are we safe here?" Shirley asked in a whisper.

"I think so," the girl said, also whispering, looking over her shoulder to make sure that she was not being followed. "Walk on a little way, get out your handkerchief to blow your nose, and let it and the paper fall to the ground."

Shirley did as she was told and walked on before reaching into her handbag for the ready-prepared scrap of paper folded up in her hand-kerchief. She blew her nose, then, as if by accident, let the hanky and the paper fall into the gutter. She did not stop to pick them up.

The girl called out loudly in English, "Excuse me, you have dropped your handkerchief!" She ran to pick up the handkerchief and hand it to Shirley; the scrap of paper she spirited away into her pocket. She crossed the road and took no further notice of Shirley, who, breathing a sigh of relief that the girl now had her address and telephone number, headed for home. How ridiculous this cloak-and-dagger subterfuge was! she said to herself.

While she was preparing their supper and Reggie was clearing up the shop and adding up the takings, Shirley heard the clatter of the letterbox downstairs. She dashed down and found an envelope on the mat; she picked it up and mounted the stairs two at a time. Instead of returning to the kitchen, she took refuge in her bedroom, closed the door, and sat down to read the note: "Your brother worked for us, the Free French, and in the F (French) section of the SOE in Vichy France as well. I think he worked in the Massif Central. I don't know what happened to him," she read, "but someone let slip that he is now in England in hospital somewhere. Sorry, that is all I can tell you." The letter was signed "Aline".

Shirley sat, pondering Aline's message. If Ted were in hospital, at least that meant he was alive. But where? Should she tell her father that he was alive but in hospital? When Reggie came up, having finished his day's work, she had not yet prepared any food, because she was still in her room debating how to handle the situation. She had come to the conclusion that it would be kinder not to mention yet that Ted was in hospital somewhere in Great Britain. He might be anywhere, and who knew what state he might be in – yet how was she to deal with Aline's information without help, considering the workload on her own shoulders?

"What's wrong, Shirl?" Reggie asked when he appeared. "You're very pale."

"No, Pa, just a little tired," she replied.

"Pa," she said guardedly after a scant supper, but before the Nine O'clock News, "what is the real situation in France?"

He shifted in his armchair and his expression became decidedly grim.

"Why do you want to know?" he asked.

"Well, I was wondering about Ted. I came across the letters SOE somewhere today, and wondered what they meant," she replied, trying to sound casual.

"I don't know much about it myself," he replied, "but it has lots of nicknames to hide its true identity. Some people call it 'Churchill's Secret Army' or 'the Ministry of Ungentlemanly Warfare'. I believe SOE really stands for Special Operations Executive. I'm not sure what they do, but I do know they go in for really dangerous operations. It's all top secret. It is said that their offices are in Baker Street, though that's possibly just a sort of decoy. You might as well call them *Secret* Operations Executive. Now, don't you go getting involved with that, will you, miss?"

"Certainly not, Pa!" she said. "As if I would!

A brief silence descended, until the implication of those letters struck Reggie. "You don't think, do you…" he was saying, when he stopped in mid-sentence. "Oh, no, please, no!" he cried out. He stared at Shirley. "Ted! He's working for the French abroad, isn't he – with the SOE?" he asked nervously.

"No, he's not with the SOE, Pa!" she reassured him. Despite her intentions of not divulging to her father all she had heard about Ted, she had to tell him about the odd encounter with the girl from the Free French offices in Carlton Gardens the previous day, and their second meeting that day, which had led to the good news that her brother was alive. She said she had been assured by that girl that Ted was alive, although she did not tell him that he was in a hospital somewhere, nor did she let on that the girl had sent her a message that Ted was working *both* for the SOE as well as the Free French.

Her father spoke more calmly, "Ah, if he's working just for the Free French, he's probably still with De Gaulle here in London, but in secrecy: that's why we don't see him very often." He gave his daughter a quizzical glance, as if awaiting confirmation of what he had deduced.

"Yes, I think that's probably right," said Shirley, relieved that she had managed to quell her father's anxiety with a white lie. "But don't worry, I'm going to find out exactly where he is. I've no idea where I'm going to start, but it certainly won't be at the SOE in Baker Street! Obviously, they wouldn't tell me anything at all, and I don't want to get involved with them!"

Shirley spent the night wondering where to start. If it really were all so top secret, none of the organizations would tell her any more than Aline already had, which was not very much, except that Ted had worked for the SOE as well as the Free French and was in hospital *somewhere*, which did really mean that he must still be alive. True to her intentions, she had not shared all that information with her father, for fear of bringing on an attack of shell shock, and, at the same time, giving him false hopes. The best chance of finding Ted would be to ring all the hospitals in London she could think of before anything else. Ballet would have to be consigned to second place.

Once Reggie had opened the shop early the next morning and was busily occupied downstairs giving the paper-boys their filled bags, Shirley rang Cynthia to tell her that she would have to take Aurora over because something really important had come up and she needed to concentrate on it.

"Oh, that sounds exciting!" was Cynthia's reply.

"No, it's not; but it is deadly serious. I'll tell you later," said Shirley, putting the phone down hastily.

She then rang every hospital in London, which proved to be a waste of precious time, because the phones were never answered. She resolved there and then, as a last resort, to visit every hospital in London in the faint hope that she might find Ted in one of them. Wearing flat, comfortable shoes, she went out every day for the next three days, searching for a mere hint of a clue as to where he might be. Every day she jumped on and off buses, trudged along rubble-strewn streets, past hollowed-out buildings, and asked at hospital receptions for her brother.

The receptionists always asked her the same question: "What was his name?" and then would look down the lists of patients for Ted, or Edward, Marlow. These searches always met with the same response: "No, I'm sorry, we don't have anyone of that name here." Weary and disheartened, she examined her list: St Thomas's, Bart's, King's College, Charing Cross, Middlesex, University College, The Royal Free and so on. She had waited at reception for attention in all of those hospitals and more, only to be told that her brother was not on any of their lists.

She searched through the long list again and found a hospital that she had missed: Guy's. How could she have missed it? she asked herself, especially because Guy's was right next to London Bridge Station, which was the destination for the overground trains she frequently caught into London. From there she usually caught trains home again.

Footsore and exhausted, she trudged back over London Bridge, past the station, to Guy's Hospital. Although the receptionist was obliging,

Shirley had difficulty in remembering why she was there, scarcely able to put two words together. "I'm, um... I'm trying to trace my brother. I've, er, tried, um, every other hospital, but..." (sigh) "with no success. I wonder if, um, there, um, is any chance, um, he might be here?"

"Tell me his name," said the receptionist gently, "and then I think you had better sit down – you look shattered."

"His name is, er, Ted or Édouard – non, I mean Edward – Marlow," Shirley stuttered.

Concern spread over the receptionist's face. "Sit down over there for a bit while I check the records – you need a rest. What did you say your brother's Christian name was? Is it English or some other language?"

"Yes, it's both, English and French," Shirley replied, then without much hope, she went to sit down.

She was on the point of dozing off when the receptionist came across to her. "What sort of passport does your brother carry?" she asked.

Shirley was about to reply "British, of course!" when she realized what a mistake that would be. It was most likely that Ted had only the French identity papers provided by Maman, and had thrown his British passport away, as that would be incriminating if he were caught by the Nazis! He probably spoke only French. No wonder no one seemed to know anything about him! What's more, he would be carrying his French papers under an assumed name, and would be operating under a code name. To be called "Edward Marlow" would be the most dangerous possible liability in France. How stupid of her not to have thought of that before! He might well be in any of the hospitals she had already visited! She was wondering how to frame this information when the receptionist said, "Leave it with me, would you – I'll see what I can find out" – and with that she was gone.

It was a good half an hour before she returned, trailing behind a large, straight-backed woman, her grey hair scraped into a tight bun. The receptionist introduced her as the Matron and then slunk away.

The Matron stood towering over Shirley. "Well, Miss, er... what is your name?" she began sternly. "We can't let you in here in these dangerous times without some identification. Please show me some form of identity."

Shirley stood up, rummaged in her handbag and pulled out her ration book. "Will this do?" she asked timidly, handing over her precious coupons.

The Matron sniffed. "Yes, I suppose that will have to do." She handed the booklet to its owner after examining every page with a certain disdain. "And you are British, are you?"

"Yes, of course!" Shirley exclaimed. The woman shrugged her shoulders and said triumphantly, "Well in that case, we can't help you!"

She turned on her heel and was about to stride off down the corridor when Shirley came to her senses and shouted, "No, don't go! My brother and I are half-French, and he has French identity papers!"

The Matron stopped in her tracks and retraced her steps. "You really are wasting my time, young woman," she snapped at her. "Why didn't you tell me that sooner? Come on now, hurry up! What *is* his name?"

Shirley had begun to wonder whether the Matron was to be trusted or whether this Matron was actually a fifth columnist. In the circumstances she decided that was unlikely, despite the harpy's intimidating manner.

Imitating Madame Belinskaya's English accent, quietly and with dignity, she said, "Ees name ees Édouard Pruvost."

This flummoxed the Matron, who had to relax her style and ask Shirley to repeat the name, which she did loudly and clearly, spelling out each syllable.

"I see," said the Matron slowly. "We do have a young Frenchman in here. His identity papers were torn and illegible, but it is possible that one of the names on them was Pruvusst."

The Matron took time to collect herself, not having ever had to cope with a situation like this one. She came down off her high horse, and spoke more gently. "He doesn't seem to be able to tell us his real name, she said, but keeps repeating something that sounds like 'cashew'. That's what he keeps saying when we ask him. Does that ring any bells with you?"

"Cachou in French is what we call a cashew nut," Shirley explained, reverting to correct English. "I never knew my brother's code name, but 'cachou' sounds perfectly probable. Is he badly wounded?" A mixture of joy at possibly finding Ted and anxiety at his condition overwhelmed her.

"I will take you to the ward," the Matron said, resuming her brusque façade, without answering Shirley's question, and charged ahead.

The long ward was eerily silent, although it was full of patients. As Shirley followed the Matron along the open space between the beds, she noticed that they were all asleep. Some had bandages round their heads covering their eyes, others had box-like structures over their legs and yet others had pulleys over their beds holding a leg up in the air. They came to a desk in the middle of the ward, where a nurse was writing notes. Whispering, the Matron exchanged a few words with her and then, in a loud whisper, said to Shirley, "I'll leave you with Sister Andrews – she will be able to help you."

Sister Andrews at once put Shirley at her ease, simply by smiling at her.

"Please tiptoe and keep your voice down, because this is the post-operative recovery ward. Follow me – I'll take you to the young Frenchman and you will be able to tell us whether he is your brother. He's in the bed on the left at the end of the ward."

As they approached the bed, Shirley was filled with dread. Like the others, the patient lay still. He was not wearing a bandage over his head, nor were his legs covered by a box-like structure; his eyes seemed to be half-open, and he looked almost normal. His arms were hidden by a sheet. It *was* Ted lying there.

"Ted!" Shirley cried out. Her natural impulse was to rush forward to hug him, but Nurse Andrews gripped her by the arm, holding her back.

"Ssh! Don't touch him!" she whispered. "He's comfortable and resting – you can whisper in his ear, if you like."

Shirley bent down and whispered, "Ted! It's me, Shirley!"

At this her brother groaned, "Hélène! Hélène!" and shut his eyes completely.

"Come away now," Sister Andrews said. "I'll take you to see the doctor, and then you can come back to your brother. He will probably wake up soon."

She led a trembling Shirley away to a side room, saying that the doctor would be only a couple of minutes. Shirley waited and waited until finally half an hour later a young doctor appeared.

"Ah," he said, "so you are the sister of the young Frenchman, are you? In his lucid moments he tells us his name is Cashew."

Shirley introduced herself, confirming that she was indeed Cashew's sister, but that his real, English name was Edward Marlow.

She then had to give details of Ted's age and his home address. She then went on to try to explain all the confusion surrounding her brother's identity.

"We are half-French, you see. My brother has been working in the French Resistance, but I have the impression that lately he must have joined the SOE, the Special Operations Executive. And in one or other of those organizations, his code name must have been Cachou."

"That makes sense," said the doctor, "and it explains some of his ramblings. Can you tell me who Hélène is?"

"She's his girlfriend, and the love of his life," Shirley replied sadly. "But please, tell me, what he is doing here? How did he get here?"

"All I know," said the doctor, "is that he was brought to one of our field hospitals in Kent by a couple of chaps who left him there in a terrible state, and rushed off into the night. They were probably involved in the secret services and didn't want to be identified. It's not the first time that has happened and, in their defence, I have to say I expect they had brought your brother back from France, presumably on a secret night-flight from a field somewhere."

"Do you have any idea what happened to him?" Shirley asked with frantic urgency.

"The field hospital sent him here because his case is a very tricky one," the doctor continued. "He must have been involved in some sort of ambush in France, because there was a German bullet in his left arm; strangely enough, there wasn't just the one bullet, a new one, but an old wound with an old *French* bullet, deep inside it."

Shirley knew exactly where the French bullet had come from: it was the self-same bullet which Jean-Luc de la Croix had fired into Ted's arm to warn him to stay away from his sister, Hélène.

"So, Ted, or Cachou, my brother, is here in Guy's. What are you able to do for him?" Shirley asked, trembling.

"Let me assure you," the doctor said, "we are doing our best for him, but his arm was badly gangrenous when he arrived in Kent, and we had to stabilize that as much as possible before we could operate."

"Operate?" Shirley queried in alarm.

"Yes," said the doctor gently, "we had to amputate that left arm of his, before the gangrene spread into the rest of his body."

Shirley passed out. She came round in the waiting room to find the same doctor, a youngish man, standing over her. He offered her a cup of sweet, milky tea, which she drank eagerly, although that was not her usual taste in tea.

"I'm Doctor Smythe," he said. "I apologize for not introducing myself sooner. I'm sorry the news came as a shock to you, but we have saved your brother's life: the gangrene was very bad. Unfortunately, we couldn't save his arm. We are rather puzzled, though, not knowing where he came from and what he was doing in France. Do you know any more than what you have just told me?"

"I wish I could," Shirley said. "All I know is that he has been in France, I suspect in the southern half of the country, where he must have gone to search for his girlfriend, Hélène. Before that, as I said, he was working with the Free French or the Resistance in the occupied north. Maybe he changed allegiances and went over to the SOE, I don't know. We haven't seen him for ages, and we don't know what he was doing, but something must have gone awfully wrong."

"Ah," observed the doctor, "I am getting a clearer picture. But do you have any idea how he came by that first bullet in his left arm? It must have been there for quite some time."

"Yes, I do know how that happened. Two or three years ago, I forget how long, he was shot by the heir to the local chateau. He was angry that my brother and Hélène, his sister, had formed a relationship, and he wanted to put a stop to it." How Shirley hated Jean-Luc when she told that story!

There was some comfort in the fact that Doctor Smythe was confident of Ted's chances of making a good recovery from his near-death experience, although it would be slow and arduous. He would be in hospital for another six to eight weeks, probably longer, until the stump of his arm had fully healed over. Then he would be allowed home, but only if there were someone present who could check the arm daily and apply dressings. Although Shirley tried hard to concentrate, the shock had numbed her brain.

"Please could you write all this down for me?" she begged.

"Of course, I'll do that right away," Dr Smythe replied, whereupon he scribbled on a sheet of paper he tore from a notepad, and gave it to her, while she racked her numbed brain for the questions she ought to be asking.

Only one came to mind: "Can we – that is, my father and I – visit my brother?"

"Yes, you may, when he goes onto the general ward. This is an intensive care unit, you know, and we don't normally allow outsiders to come in here, but on this occasion, we were anxious to verify the patient's identity, which you have done for us. Ring the reception in a couple of weeks, and then, I'd say, you will be able to visit. Is that all?"

"Yes, but can I see him once more before I leave, please?" she asked, glad to have recovered sufficient presence of mind to ask that one most important question.

"Normally the answer to that question would be 'no'," Doctor Smythe replied, "but in view of the circumstances, I will make an exception on this occasion."

He showed Shirley to Ted's bed where he lay still and pale, his eyes flickering from time to time. Shirley kissed him on the forehead and left hastily.

All the way home from London Bridge, Shirley's mind churned with the horrific reality her searches had revealed. Then the questions started crowding into her mind. The most difficult was: what was she to tell her pa? He would be shattered at the news. How was Ted going to live with only one arm? What would he be able to do to earn a living? Who would dress his arm on his return home?

Only as the train neared her station did she allow herself to wonder how this situation would affect all their lives – Ted's, their father's, even her own. She dreaded telling Reggie the truth. He would be distraught, she was sure, and yet the truth had to be told. With her heart pounding in her ears, she walked slowly along the pavement to the shop and crept in to the private doorway. She could hear a clamour of voices, a sign that the shop was full of customers, making it easy for her to keep out of the way.

When her father came upstairs for supper, he took one look at her and exclaimed, "Oh, Shirl, you are so pale! What's wrong? Please! Don't tell me that Ted has been killed over there!" He sat down heavily on a chair, staring at her pleadingly, as if to say, "Please tell me that's not true!"

It came as relief for her to be able to say, as reassuringly as she could, "No, Pa, Ted hasn't been killed."

"Well, then, where is he? Has he been taken prisoner?" her father asked with an unaccustomed urgency in his voice.

"No, he's here in hospital."

"Well, then, don't mince your words, Shirl, tell me what happened. You said something about a hospital."

The moment had arrived for the whole truth to be revealed. Nervously, for fear of the effect on her father, she said, "Ted's going to be all right, so don't get upset."

"Shirl, stop beating about the bush and tell me what happened," he insisted.

"As I said," she began, feeling her way, and speaking in a hush, "he's alive, and he's here in Guy's hospital, the one near London Bridge Station. It sounds as if he must have been rescued by the SOE, or some other organization, and brought back to England." She paused for this much information to be digested, and to give herself time to prepare for the next interrogation.

"Right, you've told me so much, now I want to know why he's in Guy's hospital and why you're being so secretive about it!" He was getting quite hot under the collar,"

She took a deep breath, and then, in a whisper, said nervously, "Once they got him into hospital, they found a bullet wound and gangrene in his left arm. It was so bad they were afraid he might die. So they took him to the operating theatre and amputated his left arm straight away."

There, she had delivered the news and could breathe again! She looked up at her father; he did not appear to have taken in the full import of what she had told him, and was concentrating on the fact that Ted was alive.

It was his turn to take a deep breath. "Well," he remarked, "he's here and he's alive!" He paused, aware that in his relief, he had missed an important element of his daughter's account. "But what was that you said about amputation?" he asked.

Shirley repeated what she had told him, and he took it unexpectedly well. He fell silent for a minute or two, "I have to say, I'm glad he got away from there with his life," he said quietly. "I never thought he'd come back alive from all those hair-brained schemes for stopping the Germans in their tracks. So long as he recovers, that's what matters now. One thing is certain: he won't be able to go back to France, northern or southern."

After further consideration, he said, "Losing an arm is terrible, I know, but many of my pals in the Great War lost a limb; some of them didn't survive, but others came home and went on to lead normal lives. One of them became a bank manager, I remember." He nodded at the memory.

"At one stage, I thought I was going to lose my leg," he went on. Trying to look on the bright side, as much for Shirley's sake as for his own, he declared, "Well, as I see it, Ted will need a lot of help to begin with, but he is right-handed; he will still be able to write, and I'm certain he will be able to do things for himself without *too* much trouble eventually. When can I go to visit him?"

Two weeks later, Shirley and her father travelled to London Bridge station, leaving Tilly and Archie in charge of the shop. On that occasion, the hospital authorities made an exception to allow the father and daughter to visit the patient, who was still in the critical care recovery ward. On their first visit, they were told to be very quiet and not to disturb the sleeping patient, although they were able to cling to the scant reassurance from the nurses that "he would be fine". Ten days later, Ted was transferred to a general ward and began to give signs of recognizing his family.

When at last he recovered full consciousness, he opened his eyes and drowsily asked where he was and what was happening. Those questions were easy enough to answer, although he scarcely registered the presence of his father and sister. All he did was to call out for Hélène, which baffled his father momentarily, until Shirley deftly fielded his cries with a half-truth: "Oh, I'm sure she's fine; she'll be in Switzerland by now in any case."

This was enough to calm Ted's anxieties for the time being. The real challenge came when, almost fully *compos mentis*, he discovered that he no longer had a left arm. "Where's my arm? Where's my arm?" he shouted in desperation. At this Shirley called the Ward Sister, because she knew dealing with the situation was beyond her or her father. On hearing the Sister's explanation, Ted cried out, "It *is* there somewhere, I can feel it, but I can't touch it!"

The Sister gestured to Shirley and her father to leave, whispering, "This is a point we come to with our amputees. Don't worry, we'll help him come to terms with his loss, but it would be better for you to leave now."

As the days and weeks passed and Ted went into rehabilitation, his situation reminded Shirley all too painfully of her own struggle to come to terms with Infantile Paralysis, as she told him one afternoon. This gave him pause for thought.

"Yeah, I remember coming to visit you in that hospital not very far from home. What was the name of that extraordinary woman who put you through all those exercises? The Australian woman who wore the funny hats?"

"Fancy you remembering that, Ted!" Shirley exclaimed, laughing. "Sister Kenny saved me, really she did! I wouldn't be on the stage now if it wasn't for her." Silence reigned between brother and sister until Shirley murmured, "I'm sorry, I shouldn't have said that, because I didn't *lose* my leg…"

"Don't worry. I'll tell you something," her brother replied, changing the subject, "it was a terrible shock at first, but I am getting used to it, and it's almost a relief to lose that arm, because lately, since it was shot in that ambush, it's been throbbing all the time. You can't imagine how excruciating it's been day and night. The Doctor told me that I had two bullets in that arm, one a German bullet of course, but also an old French bullet. I know where that came from. If I ever meet that wretch, Jean-Luc, again, I'll shoot him!"

"Hm, in that case I hope you don't ever meet him again. Look, forget about Jean-Luc," Shirley interrupted him, "he's a scoundrel, and doubtless one of these days he'll get his comeuppance; you concentrate on getting better. Anyhow, don't forget he is Hélène's brother."

Ted was musing on recent happenings. "I won't go as far as to say that the Nazis did me a service by shooting me in that arm, when they discovered our ambush, but the gangrene had already set in, and I might have died if I hadn't been airlifted back here."

Shirley didn't have to ask who had airlifted him back to England, for she was in no doubt that Ted had come home in one of the Lysanders used by the SOE for their perilous rescue operations. "I wasn't feeling at all well," he admitted, but brightened at a thought that had just occurred to him: "And in any case, no one can accuse me of cowardice for not being in the forces when I appear without an arm!"

28

Every day Shirley rose early to do her *barre* work before breakfast, and before going next door to spend the rest of the morning learning, practising and rehearsing in Madame's studio. La Belinskaya, as inventive as ever, said that she had been doing her homework while Shirley was at the hospital with Ted. Having considered *Les Sylphides* as an addition to Aurora's repertoire, she had come to the conclusion that because *Les Sylphides* had no storyline as such, other than the encounter of a young man with ethereal wood-nymphs in a forest at night, it could serve as a very flexible contribution to any programme. Set to various pieces of music by Chopin, the ballet could be performed as a whole, or the movements used to fill five-minute gaps in the repertoire.

It also had the advantage of having either a small cast, consisting of one man and two ballerinas, or a larger one consisting of the three principals and a *corps de ballet*. She assured Shirley that it would be beautiful and would lend itself to any performance and any number of dancers. Even better, she said, the movements could be rehearsed easily and separately, either with each single soloist, or in twos or threes, or with the whole company.

Nevertheless, for the forthcoming tour of Scotland, she recommended another ballet, which she said was often confused with *Les Sylphides* because of its name, *La Sylphide*. According to Madame, *La Sylphide* was a much older ballet, one of the first truly classical ballets, and had originated in Italy with the pioneer of classical ballet, Maria Taglioni. However, the more modern version had been developed in 1836 by a Dane of French origins, August Bournonville, and it was this ballet that she was proposing for Aurora's Scottish tour. She had contacts in Denmark who had promised to send her copies of the musical score, with recordings if they could find them, and even the choreography.

"Why for Scotland?" Shirley ventured to interpose, wrinkling her nose with uncertainty and interrupting Madame's unstoppable flow.

"Why, *ma chérie*, it's because it takes *place* in Scotland!" her teacher replied. "And all the dancers wear Scottish costumes, tartan kilts and so on, and they dance a *quadrille écossais...*" (which Shirley interpreted as a reel) "...that is to say, a balletic Scottish interpretation of a *quadrille écossais.*"

Shirley saw the sense in this but doubted that everything could be arranged in time for the tour, beginning in only one month. "How long is this ballet and what's it about?" she asked.

"It lasts only about an hour. And, like *Les Sylphides*, it's also about a young man falling in love with a wood nymph, but she dies when he captures her in a silken scarf given to him by an old witch. It is very tragic!"

"I see," said Shirley, the doubt audible in her voice, "but I will have to ask Eileen if she can manage to make the costumes with Tilly's mum in time. And of course, there is Cynthia's mother too."

Madame pounced on the mention of Cynthia's mother and airily announced, "So, *ma chérie*, there won't be a problem then!" Having dismissed that matter, she was ready to charge ahead, saying, "We will rehearse intensely!"

After lunch either Shirley or her father or both headed off to Guy's hospital and spent the best part of the afternoon at Ted's bedside, and later, as his health improved, by his chair. Subjects for conversation were starting to run dry, so Shirley tried to encourage an interest in the ballet in her brother. It was hard going at first because, like his father, he had the annoying tendency to fall asleep when she was in the middle of a narration, describing the plot, or the choreography, the scenery or the costumes of the ballets in the latest tour.

Ted always apologized for his lack of attention, usually saying that he had had a hard morning doing physiotherapy. Clearly, he was interested in the tours, but only when she talked about the bases and garrisons where they had performed, and the untoward occurrences, like the slippery stage, so carefully prepared by Pete's men in Yorkshire, or their snowbound stay on the airbase on the eastern tour. Real people, like Doris and Rocky, and their roles in Aurora, also held his attention better than fairy stories.

The departure date for the Scottish tour was approaching fast, just a few weeks away. Shirley was satisfied that her brother would still be safe in hospital for the period of her absence, and her father would be able to visit him frequently. The repertoire presented few problems because the programme was short and would be the same, with *La Sylphide* at each venue. Because it would undoubtedly appeal to the Scots, Madame was sure that the timing, only an hour plus the interval, would not matter.

A major complication arose when the hospital suddenly declared, unexpectedly early, that Ted was well enough to be discharged, as long as his wound could be dressed, and he could be generally cared for at home. Apparently the hospital was short of beds for wounded servicemen and civilians. Eileen had all but offered to attend to Ted's medical needs on his return, and, in spare moments from dressmaking, she was reading medical journals to bring herself up to date, but the announcement of his imminent release flung her and Shirley into a flurry of anxiety and uncertainty.

"I'm trying to make kilts for the men, but they are very awkward, and anyhow we don't have the right material for them!" Eileen lamented. "And I can't do that and look after Ted properly at the same time!"

Shirley was at her wits' end. There was no way she could stop Ted coming home, but the tour had been booked for ages and kilts were essential for *La Sylphide*. "I just don't know what to do! I'm at the end of my tether!" she cried over the phone to Cynthia, who, inexplicably but typically, did not seem at all perturbed.

"Look, Shirley," she said in her usual calm way, "you and Eileen have enough to worry about, getting Ted home for a start. I'll see about the kilts."

Shirley had no idea how Cynthia would be able to do this, but did not ask. Miraculously Cynthia did see about the kilts, or rather, Pete did so on her behalf. She rang him immediately after talking to Shirley, confident that he would have a solution to the problem.

In his characteristic breezy manner, Pete was confident that he could solve the problem. "Cyn, you've come to the right man," he announced. "I can arrange that for you. I'll get in touch with one of my Highlander friends straight away. I'm sure they're not short of a few kilts, though whether your male dancers would want to do all that spinning round in a kilt, I rather doubt!" He laughed.

Cynthia gritted her teeth: he still persisted in calling her "Cyn", which she found embarrassing, and in front of other people too! Nor did she appreciate Pete's jovial reference to Aurora's male dancers "spinning round in kilts", as he put it. Nonetheless, she overcame her irritation, because that was immaterial by comparison with the promise of much-needed kilts for the Scottish tour. Pete rang her that evening with the news that on arrival in Edinburgh, she should go with the male dancers to an address where spare kilts from the regiments were kept. They came in all sizes and would be ready for the men to try on.

She passed the news on to Shirley, who naturally was greatly relieved that Aurora's cast would be appropriately dressed, but had yet another even more significant concern to put to Cynthia.

"Oh, Cynnie," she said, using Cynthia's preferred nickname, "I honestly don't think I'm up to this! I'm so worn out with traipsing off to Guy's hospital to visit Ted every afternoon, *and* with trying to sort out care for him at home, *and* with moving all my things upstairs so he can have my bedroom, *and* with having to do my ARP duty most nights, that I've decided that you should dance the part of Sylphide in Scotland! Please say 'yes'!"

Cynthia's gulp at the other end of the line was audible. "But—" she was saying when Shirley cut her off.

"No buts, Cynnie, please! You know the part, so all you have to do is take my place in rehearsals and I'll take yours. I don't like to make you play the part of the jilted bride, so I'll dance poor Effie's role. Anyhow, I can do it with my eyes shut". Cynthia was not given a moment to protest. "Right then," Shirley declared, "we'll be all set to go in three weeks' time!"

There was no gainsaying Shirley, so the Aurora Company, with Cynthia in the principal role of *La Sylphide*, was ready to leave for Scotland early that summer.

One warm day in June 1942, Reggie and Shirley brought Ted home from Guy's hospital. Shirley was surprised to find him walking out of the hospital. As he was easing himself into in the car, she whispered as much to her father.

"What did you expect, you silly girl?" he said quietly with a grin. "He hasn't lost a leg!" Noticing his daughter's crestfallen expression, he put his arm round her. "I understand what you're thinking. You're remembering that freezing cold day in February 1938 when you came out of hospital, aren't you?"

"Yes, I suppose so," said Shirley with a sob.

Ted was certainly glad to be home after his ordeal and tried to show his appreciation firstly to his sister for finding him, and then to both her and their father for visiting him frequently in hospital, sometimes together, sometimes taking turns. Despite his attempts to present a positive attitude, that was a mere façade. The new Ted was a more sombre, more morose character than the bravado-filled young fighter who had gone to resist the German occupation of France. He spoke little, seeming to be lost in thought, even despair.

One day, in the week before her planned departure to Scotland, Shirley, remembering how conspicuous she had felt on account of her post-polio limp, and trying to judge his frame of mind, took it upon herself to ask her brother if he felt like going out for a walk.

"No, I don't think so; I'd rather stay indoors," he replied.

"That's a shame, why not? It's a lovely day, out there," she said, gesturing to the window. "You can't stay cooped up inside for ever, you know."

A sudden inspiration gave her an insight into Ted's reluctance. "And if you're worried about people staring at you, you don't need to be, because they'll realize you are a hero and have been invalided out of the War!"

"Do you really think so?" he asked.

"Yes, of course I do!" she exclaimed. "Look, *you* have been fighting in France since Dunkirk. Not many people have been doing that! Pa and I are proud of you! Let me tuck your left sleeve into your jacket pocket, so when other people see you without an arm, they will be proud of you too! They certainly won't think you're a coward or a conscientious objector!"

"All right," he said, "I'll go out and give it a try, if you'll come too."

They walked out into the war-torn area, ghoulish with its gaping remains of buildings and rough patches of land, where the only – but nevertheless welcome – signs of greenery, were weeds and brambles. They crossed the road, and, skirting the ruins of the hall, passed the church along the footpath which led to the recreation ground. There they sat down on a bench and let the sun bathe their faces in its warmth.

"Is there something you want to tell me?" Shirley asked gently. "For instance, what happened? How did your arm get so severely injured?"

Ted took a deep breath. "I don't really know where to start," he said, "but as far as my arm's concerned, we were setting up an ambush for the enemy on a road, but someone, an informer, had spilled the beans and they were ready for us. I was lucky: I escaped, but not before they had shot me in the arm. I believe that fifth columnist was captured by my pals. He will have got short shrift!"

He snorted, but stopped short. "I shouldn't be telling you this," he observed in a hushed voice. "I've signed the Official Secrets Act, so I'll be in even worse trouble if someone finds out I've been talking about what happened! You must *not* tell Pa!"

"No, I won't," Shirley promised, "but it's clear to me you need someone to talk to, so tell me a bit more. Where were you? And how did you come to be in the Special Operations Executive?"

He stared at her. "Are you daft? I can't tell you all that," he insisted.

"Well then, suppose I ask you a question; you stay absolutely silent if the answer is yes, but shake your head if it's no."

Ted said nothing, so she began by asking, "Did you move south into Vichy France?" No movement from Ted. "So, were you working with the Resistance groups down there?" Again no movement. Gradually Shirley pieced together an impression of his activities and tactics in occupied France.

Later, long after the end of the War, he would tell her that he had volunteered to go south to try to organize the resistance fighters there into a cohesive group, before the Germans moved massed troops in. His job was to show them how to use explosives and other devices to blow up vehicles, railway lines and convoys, which was what he had been doing in the north. On that sunny day sitting on a bench out in the recreation ground, Shirley had to persist with her hastily devised system for extracting information from her brother. She persevered, asking, "And was Hélène there with you?"

She perceived a tear forming in his eye and regretted having posed that question. He answered it by remaining stock still. She then heard herself pursuing the inevitable line of enquiry, by asking, "Did she escape?"

Her system of communication only allowed one of two answers, yes or no, but Ted abandoned the charade, and gave his answer vocally. "I don't know," he said, his voice faltering as the tears streamed down his face.

Shirley hugged him carefully, and together they sat in silence for a long time. She had gathered all she needed to know, while he had been able to share some of his anguish without, in his estimation, offending against the Official Secrets Act.

Neither of them mentioned their talk to their father, who clearly preferred not to know the details of Ted's escapades, but satisfied himself with the certain evidence that his son had acquitted himself with tremendous courage on duty in France. Head held high, he was proud to tell his customers that Ted was a local hero of the War. When they noticed Ted's left sleeve hanging loose or tucked into his jacket, they agreed wholeheartedly and applauded him enthusiastically. Their imaginations, stirred by the regular news reports, answered any lingering queries.

Ted gained so much in confidence from the praise heaped upon him that, when Archie suffered what was known as a "turn" and had to be taken home after lifting a heavy pile of magazines onto a high shelf, he offered to take his place in the shop.

"Are you sure? Are you strong enough?" Reggie asked doubtfully.

"Yes, of course I'm sure!" Ted replied in annoyance. "I may only have one arm, so I wouldn't be able to lift a heavy load onto the top shelf, but I could do other things and leave you to do that sort of lifting."

Thus it was arranged that Ted would take over a share of the lighter work in the shop until Archie was fit enough to resume work. This arrangement suited all parties, especially Shirley, who was beginning to doubt that she would ever be able to go on tour to Scotland, let alone dance in the performance, even though her role was reduced to that of Effie, the bride jilted in favour of the wood nymph, Sylphide. Everyone, Ted, her father, Eileen and Tilly, insisted that she must go, for they could manage perfectly well without her, and, in any case, she was essential to the smooth running of her company. Ted went so far as to joke that he could practise one-handed cookery, if in fact there was anything to cook. As he had already mastered the use of the till in the shop, his offer did not seem so very far-fetched, so Shirley joined her Aurora Company ready for departure at Euston station with a clear conscience and her anxieties assuaged.

If the dancers were expecting to have left the War behind in London, they were disappointed and shocked to encounter ruined buildings and Edinburgh, their first destination, bombed out. This was certainly an aspect of the War largely unknown to southerners, most of whom had never been that far north. It also proved to be a sobering reminder that not only was the War never far away, but was still being waged around the coasts and on the high seas. Before their first performance, the men were kitted out with spare kilts, belonging to the Highlanders, though some were not too happy about wearing them. Fortunately for them, the ballet was demure in its demands on them, since they were required to perform many high leaps but few pirouettes.

From the outset, *La Sylphide*, with its Scottish setting, delighted audiences from Edinburgh to Lossiemouth in the far north. In contrast to Edinburgh, the Highlands of Scotland gave a soothing and reviving boost to the itinerant Londoners. Nonetheless, the threat of bombing always existed, because of Scotland's extensive coastline and its many concealed inlets, which were ideal hiding places for British naval vessels. There was also an airbase on the coast, where Aurora was performing.

"You have to expect air raids up here," an officer warned them in a strong Scottish accent after their arrival, "because this is the closest point to Norway, and the enemy is determined to take that country over in order to launch their warships from there. Goodness knows what else they are planning – something even more sinister by all accounts. Aberdeen, after Peterhead just down the road, has been bombed more times than any other city in the United Kingdom, except perhaps your London!" He then took them to the shelters and their Nissen huts.

His was grim news, but it did prepare the ballet troupe to be on the alert, and the warning was certainly well timed, because more than one performance came to an abrupt end halfway through. On these occasions a whole row of airmen would hastily but discreetly slip out, presumably after receiving a silently conveyed message. Immediately after their exit, the siren would sound, and Shirley's ARP experience was put into practice. She had trained her company precisely for this eventuality, having instructed them to roll up and leave their coats and shoes in an orderly array in the wings, ready to be pulled on in an emergency.

Such an emergency occurred in their very first performance. The dancers hurried off the stage in a disciplined line to the wings, picked up their neatly rolled belongings and in no time were marching quickly in the direction of the air-raid shelters, taking with them the remaining members of the audience. They were accompanied by the roar of Spitfire engines revving up and taking off, rather than by the music of *La Sylphide*.

On the way across to the shelters, a frisson ran through Shirley's frame at the sound of those engines. She no longer flinched at the deafening din, because it brought her closer to Alan, and it reminded her, not of his death, but of his heroism. She longed to wait there to watch the aircraft take off, soaring into the evening sky, but this was no air-show, for the planes were leaving on a truly dangerous mission, while duty called her to lead her flock to safety. The departure of the aircrews did not mean that the show could go on, because the rest of the personnel on the base, the ground staff, had run off to attend to their responsibilities.

After the first air-raid warning and the sound of the all-clear, Shirley and Cynthia escaped to a quiet corner, after marshalling the dancers into their Nissen huts. "I hope we don't have too many more of these interruptions," Shirley remarked as she changed out of her costume and sat down, "but I suppose we have been lucky so far on the whole."

"That's true," Cynthia agreed, "We've come this far with very few interruptions, but since we're sitting here with nothing to do, let's go over a few issues we need to tackle. I don't have pen and paper with me, so I can't make notes, but I can roughly remember what we need to consider. For instance, what worries me is that we don't have any confirmed bookings for our autumn tour."

"Maybe Maud will have some news about that, or Madame will come up with something when we see them again," said Shirley, smoothing her dishevelled hair. "In any case, the phone lines from here are not good enough for us to ring them up, so maybe it's all waiting for us back in London. Anyhow, let's not worry too much about that for the time being, because, for now, we still have several more venues here in Scotland. But do you know if there is anything really important we ought to be discussing?" said she to Cynthia.

"As far as I can remember, the records show that all is in order," Cynthia reassured her. "When we were in Edinburgh, I sent the current detailed accounts by post to your father, who was going to pass on anything significant to Maud."

Shirley heaped praise onto her friend; "You are so clever, Cynnie – you have danced superbly, *and* you are so meticulous in keeping the accounts up to date. I don't know how you do it!"

"Well," Cynthia responded quickly, as if she had been waiting for this opening, "I really am tired, and if you would like to take over dancing La Sylphide and let me dance Effie, that would be a relief."

Shirley showed a suitably diplomatic reluctance, although secretly she was pleased to be able to take centre stage for the final lap of the tour.

29

Towards the end of Aurora's tour, the officer in charge of ENSA at the camp on the east coast of Scotland where the company had just performed approached Shirley, saying, "Well done, Miss Marlow! Your company has put on a splendid spectacle here for us this evening! The programme could not have been more appropriate for our chaps up here in Scotland. I was wondering if you would like me to get in touch with colleagues at other barracks, say, on the west coast, because I don't think you have toured there yet, is that right?"

Shirley nodded in the hope of a good reference for her dancers and bestowed a warm smile of gratitude on the officer.

He went on to say, "I would certainly be glad to give Aurora an excellent reference. Not many performers want to come this far north, I'm sorry to say, so we are rather short of entertainment, even though we need it badly to keep our spirits up, quite as much as the forces down south."

Shirley could have hugged him. Little did he know that since the subject had come up ten days previously, both she and Cynthia had become increasingly concerned about the lack of future engagements; meanwhile, there had been no news from Maud about promotions for the autumn season. With any luck the promise of new bookings in Scotland would mean that they and their dancers would now be able to fill their diaries.

That was the good news. The bad news came out of the blue only minutes after this encounter, when Rocky came to ask Shirley if she could spare him a moment. "Of course, Rocky, what can I do for you?" she said, expecting to discuss items of the scenery and backcloths – village greens, marketplaces, grand halls, woodland glens and domestic interiors – which, after multiple uses in a variety of ballets, were beginning to look tired and in places ragged.

She was not prepared for Rocky's request, although it was couched in the most sensitive of terms. "Ah so much love workin' with Aurora," he declared. "You guys have made ma extended and unexpected stay in Europe 'bsolutely wonderful!"

She quivered, sensing that this declaration was a prelude to a topic that would begin with a "but", as indeed it did.

"But," Rocky went on, "every day Ah feel Ah should be doin' sumethin' more. Now that we, that is, we Americans, have entered this ahful war, it's time Ah signed up, maybe to work for the USAF on an airbase somewhere in this great, little 'ole country, and save it from destruction – after we get back to London, that is."

Shirley tried to hide her dismay without succeeding. "Oh, Rocky!" she cried. "What will we do without you?"

Rocky attempted to pour oil on troubled waters. "Ah'm so sorry to be leavin' you all, but Ah know this is sumethin' Ah must do if Ah'm gonna be able to hold ma head high, when Ah go back to the US of A!"

Shirley pulled herself together. "I do understand, Rocky," said she. "You have been such a tremendous help to us and such an asset to the company." She struggled to find the appropriate words. There was no point in attempting to change Rocky's mind. It was clear that he was determined to save the world single-handedly, and it would be unfair to try to stop him working as an aircraft engineer in an airbase, or even fighting shoulder to shoulder with his fellow countrymen, especially since he had set his heart on taking an active part in the military. "We'll find it hard to replace you, Rocky, but I do understand how you feel, and I know everyone will miss you," she finally managed to stammer.

Word spread rapidly through the company that Rocky would be leaving. Nobody could imagine Aurora without his large, cheerful presence and loud voice; nor had anybody any ideas for a replacement for him.

Cynthia was as dismayed as Shirley was. "I daresay," she said, "we could find another stage-hand, but it's hardly realistic to expect anyone else to *compère* the shows with the ease and enthusiasm he brings to his introductions. We can't ask any of the men to do it, because they're all needed on stage, and even if they aren't, it would be too confusing; no one would know where they're supposed to be and when. Anyhow they wouldn't want to do it. Only Jack, bless his heart, is prepared to take on loads of extra responsibilities, driving, transporting all our stuff *and* dancing when needed."

"My feelings precisely," Shirley agreed with her. "Let's leave it until we get back to London, shall we? We don't have any immediate bookings, so let's just hope that something turns up. Anyhow, we must have a leaving party for Rocky to show our appreciation."

"Leaving it" until the return to London was easier said than done. Although they were both of a mind to "leave it" for the time being, Shirley churned "it" over in her mind constantly, and so did Cynthia. Where could they find a new *compère* or principal stage-hand at a time when all able-bodied men had been called up for military service and many of the "exiles", the Australians, New Zealanders and those of other nationalities, had devised ways of supporting their own forces, or had joined the British in the battles in the Mediterranean and North Africa? Rocky's departure and his replacement even came up as a topic on the long rail journey home.

The train was crowded with servicemen standing in corridors or sitting on their luggage. The dancers, looking professional in their ENSA uniforms, had no option but to do as the soldiers did, whilst the seats in the compartments were taken by the officer class. Shirley peered into each compartment as she and Cynthia made their way down the train; it was a search in vain, until they came to a compartment where the door was open. Inside an officer was addressing his men, all of whom had seats.

He looked up and saw Shirley and Cynthia slowly edging their way down the train, gingerly avoiding the baggage, legs and sleeping bodies strewn over the floor in the corridor.

He put his head round the open door. "I say, are you looking for seats?" he asked.

"Yes, but it's hopeless. The train is packed," Cynthia replied.

"Well, I see you belong to ENSA, so you deserve better than that." He turned back into the compartment and, without more ado, addressed his men: "A packet of cigarettes for whichever of you will offer your seats to these young ladies!"

The men stood up as one. "Yessir – I will, sir!" they all called out.

"Good! I only need two of you, but on second thoughts, two at a time in relays of, say, forty minutes, how does that sound? And the offer of the cigarettes still holds!"

There came a chorus of "Thank you, sir!" accompanied by a mad rush for the door.

"Not in such a hurry!" the officer commanded. "Philips and Davies, you go first and the rest of you sit down." Philips and Davies had been occupying the seats closest to the officer, so Shirley found herself sitting next to him with Cynthia on his other side.

"Thank you so much," Shirley gushed. "That's very kind."

Cynthia nodded but the officer did not notice, for his eyes were on Shirley. "I see you are wearing the ENSA uniform," he said. "May I ask where you have been and what you have been doing?"

Consequently, far from dwelling with Cynthia on the dire necessity of finding a replacement for Rocky, Shirley spent the best part of the journey regaling the officer with stories of Aurora's tours, and there were many of them. She enjoyed having an attentive audience of one good-looking, youngish man, tanned, with dark eyes and hair.

For his part, he was clearly enchanted by her engaging manner, strong personality and impish laughter at some of the tales she herself was telling. There was no mistaking that her small frame, blond curls and bright eyes added to her charm. Their eyes met frequently. When that happened, the electric flash that passed between them momentarily put paid to their conversation. Then, awkwardly, one or the other tried to pick it up where they had left off, but could not remember what they had been talking about. This happened so often that they began to laugh at themselves, and each sensed that an extraordinary magnetic force was drawing them closer together.

The hours passed so quickly that Shirley felt a twinge of disappointment for reasons she could not quite fathom when the train pulled into Euston. "I'm so sorry – you'll run out of cigarettes," she said, wondering if there were some discreet way she might pay for some of the many packets he would have to buy for his men. She hardly dared admit to herself that she was hoping that this might lead to another meeting.

"No, that's not a problem," said he. "I don't smoke but I do have an allowance, so I have plenty in reserve!"

"That's good," she said, racking her brain for another opening, for this man was someone she definitely wanted to meet again. Nervously she eyed the soldiers, who were already standing up and heaving their rucksacks onto their backs.

"Thank you for keeping me entertained," the officer said as he stood up. He was an impressive figure, tall and slim, straight-backed, and conveying an air of authority, especially when he put his peaked cap with its shiny badge on his head.

"I say, if you have any problems when next you are in Scotland, let me know. Here is my phone number at the barracks," he said, handing her a card. "I must dash – I have to get across to Liverpool Street to catch

the train home to Norhambury. We're on our two weeks' leave, you see."
He glanced at his watch. "Oh, wait a minute, though – I think I have
enough time to carry your suitcase for you!" he said with a smile, and
lifted her case down from the rack, and Cynthia's as well.

To Shirley's annoyance, Cynthia accompanied them to the
Underground. Before saying goodbye, Shirley intended to give him her
telephone number but, because Cynthia was still hanging around, she
could not bring herself to do so, for that would be making a budding
friendship public. They all parted company, each in his or her own direction. Shirley gave Cynthia a grudging nod and then hurried off, ostensibly
to the Northern Line, which would take her home – but in a last-minute
change of plan, she ran to the Circle Line to catch the Underground for
Liverpool Street and the main line station for East Anglia.

She scanned the platform for her new acquaintance, but the crowds of
soldiers on leave, all in their khaki uniforms, were so dense, that it was
impossible to pick out any individual. Just then, a recognizable man's
voice called out to her from behind, "Hello, hello!"

She turned, delighted to find that there, standing behind her, was the
person she had been searching for, the officer in the peaked cap.

"Hello!" he said again, "I didn't know you were coming this way, or
I would have waited for you!"

"That's all right," she said, with an assumed nonchalance, but unable
to suppress a smile of delight. "There are various routes home and this
evening I decided to come on the Circle Line. I didn't want to hold you
up, because you said you were in a hurry to catch your train."

This, of course, was not true. It had in fact been her intention to
take the Northern Line to London Bridge all along, but as soon as
Cynthia left to catch her train, Shirley had realized that she was making
the worst mistake of her life, the same mistake that she had made
nearly five years earlier on that rough ferry crossing back from France.
Then she had met Alan all too briefly, had been too shy to speak to
him other than to thank him for reuniting her with her mother and
brother, and afterwards had spent years searching for him, as he had
for her. She must not let herself repeat that mistake; she must find the
person who had just appeared, as if by magic, in her life, so, despite
the burden of her heavy suitcase, she ran to the Circle Line to catch
the Underground to Liverpool Street, the mainline station for East
Anglia, and had succeeded in finding him.

Breathlessly she stared at him. "How... how nice to see you again," she stuttered.

"Nice to see you too," he said, "though I don't know your name. Mine's John Platt."

"I'm Shirley Marlow," she answered. "Thanks for giving me your card, John. I haven't had time to look at it; I was going to give you my father's phone number, but there was no time to do that either, so if we get on the Tube together, I'll find a scrap of paper and write it down for you."

Rattling down the tunnel, pushing warm air ahead of it, a train came into the station. John cleared a space between the troops and beckoned Shirley into the compartment ahead of them; there she spotted two seats together. John was the last onto the train, but none of the soldiers had taken the seat next to Shirley.

"Why did none of them try to sit down there?" she enquired. "I thought they would grab any empty seat."

He laughed. "It's because I'm a major," he explained, "and they have to give way to me."

"How do they know that?"

"They saw my cap with its badge on it while we were waiting on the station," he answered, and then added, "and they realized you were with me!" She blushed.

John checked his watch. "Oh, never mind, I've missed the five-thirty, but that's not really a problem – I'll catch the next one," said he.

"No, you haven't," she contradicted him. "Look, the station clock says five twenty-three. You'll catch it if you run now!" She could have bitten out her tongue. What a stupid thing to say! Why hurry him away when she had only just found him again?

"That clock is always five minutes slow, so the train is bound to have left by now," he said with a total lack of concern. "Are *you* in a hurry?"

"No, not at all," she said, confident that her father and Ted could surely look after themselves for one more evening, possibly with a little help from Eileen.

"Why don't we go for a drink, even find somewhere to eat?" he suggested. "The blackout won't start for hours yet."

At Liverpool Street Station, among the grit, the smoke, and the incessant noise – engines letting off steam, whistles blowing, porters shouting – Shirley stepped on air into paradise for the first time since losing Alan.

"Here, take my arm," said her companion. "We don't want to lose each other in these crowds." In a dream, she took his arm and allowed herself to be led out of the station to a small restaurant nearby that had survived the Blitz.

By the time they had finished their meal, they had exchanged so many details of their lives, that they seemed to have known each other for an eternity. Shirley spoke freely about her father and his work in the shop, and with pride she mentioned Ted, but omitted all reference to her French background and her mother, simply saying that her mother had left the family, and they no longer had any contact with her.

Nor did she speak about Alan, his death and the loss of their child in the bombing of Coventry. An inner voice told her to free herself of the past by closing the door on it, and to keep all those memories locked away in the depths of her heart. What good would it do to burden and probably upset John with the agony of those years? Who knew, he might have had similar crises in his own life and talking about hers might only open old wounds for him. His vision of her was that of her new identity as a dancer and a performer, taking entertainment to the troops through ENSA with determination and vigour, which he considered admirable. There was no need for him to know about the Infantile Paralysis either. It might come up one day, but why spoil the present talking about that?

After their dinner, they strolled arm in arm, warm and animated, onto the platform from where a train was about to depart to John's home city, Norhambury.

"I've never been there," Shirley remarked. "Is it nice?"

"It's beautiful, but it was badly bombed in July 1940, and it was struck again in a Baedeker raid," he replied. "Perhaps you'll come to visit it sometime?"

"I'd like that – tell me more about it next time we meet. We will meet again, won't we?" she said, not wanting to let him go.

He gazed down at her and gently took her face in his bare hands, lifting it so that he could look into her eyes and she into his. Time stood still, as yet again that electric surge passed between them.

"Of course we will," he whispered. "As soon as we possibly can. I want to look into your eyes again and again. Now, where's that telephone number of yours?"

Swept off her feet, she exclaimed, "Oh, gracious! I had completely forgotten that!" and hastily reached into the depths of her handbag where she grabbed an old envelope, scribbled her home telephone number on it, and thrust it at John.

The guard was all set to blow his whistle as he leapt onto the train. He pulled the window down and called out "Till next time!" as the train slowly began to move. Shirley watched the head of dark hair and the waving hand until they were no more than specks in the distance.

She was in no hurry to go home, even though the sun was setting, and daylight was fading. It would soon be time for the blackout, but she carried her tiny torch everywhere in her handbag, and knew the rules relating to it by heart. All the way from Liverpool Street to South Cross, changing stations like an automaton, not registering where she was going, she carried the image of John's large, dark brown eyes, the very epitome of his unassuming, friendly personality, as he had lifted her face to look into her eyes, then had leant out of the carriage window, waving goodbye to her from the receding train.

She longed to see those eyes again, not in two- or three- weeks' time, not in a week's time, but at once, immediately. How could she cope without seeing them? She wanted him to be beside her, in front of her, everywhere around her always and for ever. In the space of a few brief hours, something had happened to her that had seemed impossible, something she had thought would never happen again: she had fallen in love at first sight! There was no mistaking it, for it was exactly the same feeling that had overwhelmed her on meeting Alan for the first time when she was only seventeen. This time she was determined to handle the situation differently.

Darkness had fallen by the time she alighted from the overground train. She was preparing to set off down the road when her idyllic reverie came to an abrupt end. Out of the darkness there came a group of policemen. They surrounded her and one of them accosted her. "Miss," he barked, shining a light in her eyes, "what are you doing? Why are you out at this time of night? There's a curfew on! We will have to arrest you and take you to the station!"

"No! You will not!" Shirley screamed at him, brought to her senses by this rude interruption of her dream. She was furious not simply because of the manner of her arrest, but because it had brought to a cruel end one of the most idyllic evenings of her life. She screamed, not simply at the policeman who had barked at her, but at the whole crowd of them. A flash of inspiration told her that she held a trump card: "Don't you see? I am in uniform!" She shone her tiny torch onto her brown skirt and jacket. "And I am going home after returning from exercises in Scotland! Look, you can see my house from here!" She waved a hand in the direction of home without actually indicating which of the houses, invisible in the dark, was her home.

"Apologies, miss," the policeman said, tempering his tone. "Perhaps you didn't hear the announcement at London Bridge station about a curfew in this area because of troop movements tonight?"

"No, I did not!" Shirley said in the stentorian tone of voice she usually employed when reprimanding errant householders for allowing the merest chink of light to escape from their houses at night. In her dream world at London Bridge, she would never have noticed such an announcement, even had she heard it. "What's more," she went on, "I am also an ARP warden, and I need to get home quickly to change into my ARP uniform, because I am on duty tonight, and you are holding me up!" Chastened, the policemen melted away, leaving their boss to issue an even more grovelling apology.

Shirley did not change into her ARP uniform on arriving home: the night was pitch black and there were clouds overhead, probably heralding an imminent thunderstorm, an indication that raids were unlikely. The house was as dark as the streets. Relieved to find that her father and Ted must have gone to bed, she crept silently up the stairs by the light of her tiny torch. She went straight to her bedroom and carefully opened the bottom drawer of her chest of drawers. There lay the precious letter that Alan had written to her in anticipation of his possible disappearance in a dogfight in one of the first engagements of the Battle of Britain on 14th July 1940. She read it, weeping at every word, although she already knew it all by heart:

If the worst should happen to me, my beloved Shirley, I insist that you do not waste the rest of your life thinking of me and dwelling on the past. Please make the best of your time on earth. (There followed a passage encouraging her to pursue her career as a dancer.) *Then, when the War is over, maybe you will meet someone good and kind, and you and he will have a family and live happily ever after. I wish this for you with all my heart... Do not let the memory of me ruin the rest of your life. You are too precious to me for that.*

The meaning was clear: Alan was in fact giving her his blessing to fall in love again, and then to marry and have a family. She held his letter close to her heart and gradually the tears were replaced by smiles. There was no one she wanted to, or needed to, share his letter with, so she carefully placed it back in the drawer.

Ted, when she saw him the next day, appeared stronger and much more positive than when she had left. "I'm working full-time downstairs now," he informed her with an air of satisfaction. "Not that I want to do that all the time, but it helps Pa out at the moment because old Archie's back is not better yet. You remember he sprained it lifting parcels of magazines, apparently just after Eileen recovered from her bad back, and we didn't know if he'd be able to work again. He grinned before announcing, "Believe it or not, Pa is paying me!"

Shirley was nonplussed – she didn't remember Archie having a bad back, but, although horrible for him, that didn't matter, because the shop had evidently been in good hands, and she would not be faced with sorting it out, or hopefully, finding piles of dirty washing and empty cupboards, like on her last return from a tour.

"If Archie does return, and I hope he does," said Ted, "I have decided to apply to work in decoding here in London." He added, as if in explanation, "I must still be involved in the war effort, and I think that would be fascinating! I learnt a lot about it when I was working in De Gaulle's HQ."

"Good idea!" replied Shirley encouragingly. "You should look into it now, so you can start as soon as Archie is better."

Two weeks later Archie was declared fit enough to return to work by his doctor, providing he did not lift heavy packages onto high shelves. Ted quickly made his escape, having promised Shirley that for the foreseeable future he would be working in London and would do his best to help run the home.

"Don't forget the washing, will you?" Shirley reminded him with a grin, as he left for his first day working for the Secret Service.

"Thank goodness he's in a London office!" Reggie and Shirley said to each other several times.

As for herself, she still had a couple of weeks left before the tour of the west coast of Scotland. Secretly she was looking forward to it more than she had ever looked forward to a tour previously. There was of course constant ballet practice and revision of choreographies, steps and sequences with Madame, who was as rigorous as ever in her demands for perfection. Checking costumes and ordering kilts were Cynthia's chores, and most of the administration had been taken over by Maud, though Reggie still dealt with the financial side of what had become a proper business.

Shirley still had time for long conversations with John when her father was out of earshot. He usually rang mid-morning from a phone box. Shirley raced to the phone before her father could pick it up downstairs.

"I'm so pleased it's you!" she said one morning.

"Were you expecting anyone else?" John teased her.

"No, but I never can be quite sure whether it might be a newspaper deliverer or the ARP, or something to do with Pa's business," she said.

"Are you terribly busy?" he asked. "Could you take a day off?"

"No, not very busy; this next tour is going to be easy, because we've done it in more or less the same way before, so yes, I reckon I could take a day off, especially in this lovely weather."

"Right then – I have to come to London for a meeting at the War Office in the morning, but will be free for the rest of the day."

"What? To London?"

"Yes, that's what I said!" He laughed. "Are you free tomorrow?"

"Tomorrow? Yes, of course I'll be free!"

John's visit to London quickly set the seal on a relationship that was to flourish in spite of wartime restrictions, whenever the lovers could meet, although that was not very often. John came to London a couple of times, giving his parents some pretext or other for spending only a day with them.

One evening towards the end of one of those periods, after dinner in the restaurant near Liverpool Street, he proposed to Shirley. He scarcely needed to ask, because marriage to him was what she longed for. She had already anticipated his proposal, and said "Yes, please!" before the words were out of his mouth.

He then presented her with a beautiful engagement ring. On that occasion it did not seem to matter that she had not met his parents, neither had he met her family of father and one brother, because they wanted to keep their secret until the War was nearing its end, as he was sure it would. Then they would announce their forthcoming marriage in the certainty that thereafter they would be together for ever.

Shirley had some reservations about this arrangement, remembering her dismay at not having had any contact with Alan's family before his death, but this time she was reassured by John's gift of a sparkling diamond and emerald ring, which she placed carefully hidden away in her special drawer at home. It would not be appropriate to wear the ring on the stage, she reasoned, and it could be unsettling for the company, giving them the impression that either her heart was no longer in the ballet, or that Aurora might be folded up.

Cynthia, of course, was the only person in whom she confided. She was pleased for her friend but perplexed. "Why on earth don't you wear your ring?" she asked.

"I've noticed that you don't wear yours on the stage, and I'm afraid that I'd lose mine if I kept putting it on and taking it off," came Shirley's irrefutable reply. "Anyhow," she added, "with all his liaison work between bases, and whatever else he does, John hasn't a moment to spare these days to think about a wedding, and nor do I!"

Shirley did not confide in Cynthia her several reasons for not wearing her engagement ring, but Cynthia was still puzzled. True, she had to take her engagement ring off before performances, and put it back on afterwards, and was always worried that she might lose it, but she could not understand why Shirley wanted to keep her engagement a secret, when the only subject that she herself wanted to talk about, apart from the ballet, was planning her own wedding, whenever that might be. Shirley shrugged nonchalantly; she was well aware that for the immediate present, while she and John were expecting to meet in Glasgow at some unidentified time, Cynthia and Pete were unlikely to see each other at all for the foreseeable future.

30

In 1942, the War continued its grinding path, on and on, spreading out and raging in more distant scenarios – Russia, the Middle East, the Far East and North Africa: undeniably the title of the *Second World War* was well justified. In England, preoccupations shifted from the dread of nightly bombing raids to anxiety about food shortages, the ever-widening spread of rationing with its diminishing allowances, and above all a deep-seated concern about the troops stationed abroad.

The dancers were now obliged to take their books of coupons on tour with them, because eating in hotels and restaurants, which previously had been exempt (and exploited by the wealthy who could afford to eat out), had become subject to rationing, like everywhere and almost everything else. Ever secretive, Ted lived at home and went daily into London to some secure establishment where his fluency in French, his vast knowledge of France, from north to south, and its people, his contacts, his extensive familiarity with the layout of the land and his first-hand awareness of the positions of German forces, were invaluable assets.

Shirley was almost certain that he was working with the French section of the Special Operations Executive, the organization that at least appeared to have rescued him from France, even if it had exposed him to immense danger by sending him there in the first place. With that information to hand, she was certain of being able either to stop him going abroad altogether or to rescue him, if rescue were required, which she fervently hoped would not be necessary. Nonetheless, she reasoned, he was highly unlikely to be sent back to France, if only because the loss of his left arm made him so conspicuous, though she still feared that he might volunteer for some crazy mission in the vain hope of meeting his beloved Hélène. Reggie was glad to have his son back home, relatively out of danger. Given his own dreadful experience of warfare, he was surprisingly calm about the loss of an arm for, as he said, that was better than the loss of a leg, and that in turn was better than the loss of life.

For him, the bonus was that, at least temporarily, he had both his children at home with him. Shirley would be off on tour, without a doubt, as soon as the plans for her trip up the west coast of Scotland with her ballet company were finalized, but even then both she and Ted would still be in Britain. He was proud of each one of them, Shirley because she had overcome the challenge of that frightening paralysis, and, despite losing her fiancé and her baby to the War, was deeply committed in her own balletic way to the battle against Nazism, not to mention her work as an ARP warden. As for Ted, Reggie burned with pride, because there was no disputing that he was a true and valiant if unsung hero: that was obvious for all to see.

Nevertheless, the threat had not gone away, as the daily news reports reminded the entire population. Every victory for the Axis powers – the Nazis, the Japanese and the Italians – reinforced their arrogant confidence, that they would eventually win out over the Allies, principally the British, the Americans, the Russians, and other free countries from within Europe, as well as in the British Empire, including Australia, New Zealand and Canada.

Even though the threat of the Blitz had receded, there was no room for complacency: the west coast of Scotland had suffered the devastating attacks of 1940 and 1941 on Glasgow, and the Clyde with its shipyards and engineering works. The surrounding areas, which were home to armaments factories and steelworks, also suffered. Moreover, there was no knowing when the enemy bombers might return, as they did occasionally, not for military gain but to intimidate local populations. Indeed, the small, remote, unsuspecting fishing port of Campbeltown on the Mull of Kintyre had suffered that fate twice in 1940. With this in mind and always aware that Hitler might have new tricks up his sleeve, the Aurora Company again packed gas masks in with ration books and railway warrants.

The interim between the tours of the east coast of Scotland and the west had been used by Aurora to revise the programme, as Shirley was not satisfied that their audiences were receiving full value for money, given that *La Sylphide* lasted only one hour. She, Cynthia and Madame, together with other members of the cast, including Andrei, the principal male dancer, put their heads together and decided to introduce a shortish, comic first half to the programme. For this purpose, one or more of the *divertissements* from *The Nutcracker* ballet were the ideal choice.

Then the problem arose over where to insert the interval, because it seemed that the programme would be unbalanced with a first half of only thirty minutes and the second of an hour. As usual, Madame solved the dilemma by decreeing that there should be an interval of, say, fifteen minutes, between the end of the *Nutcracker* dances – for scene changing and so on – and the beginning of *La Sylphide*. Halfway through *La Sylphide*, that is, at the end of the first act before the tragic forest scenes, there would be a short break, but not an interval.

After they had studied timings, there was general agreement that this would work, dividing the evening up into three parts, not only giving satisfaction to the audiences, but also demonstrating Aurora's versatility. An added dimension to Shirley's concern was that everything should be perfect, including her own performance, in case John really did succeed in arranging a lightning visit to the base where they were performing. She and he did meet when he made a very brief daytime visit to Glasgow, but, although they managed to spend a blissful afternoon together, to her disappointment and his own, he had to leave before the performance, so he did not see her dancing at all, neither the Sugar Plum Fairy nor Sylphide.

While the troupe was staying in a small port on the coast, a message came through by telegraph from Maud at her secretarial post in Eileen and Archie's house: she had received numerous requests from CEMA and ENSA for performances by Aurora during the winter and spring months at RAF bases around London, that is from January to mid-April 1943.

Cynthia was positively bubbling with excitement when she brought Maud's telegram to Shirley. "I say, Shirl, this is exactly what we need! No more waiting around to be admitted to freezing camps or finding ourselves snowbound, miles from home like last winter. We can travel by train or bus, and if the performances finish on time, we'll be able to get home before the trains stop running!"

To Cynthia's surprise, Shirley's reception of the news was as cold as any of the icy winds or the snow that had trapped the dancers on the tour of eastern England the previous winter. Her mind was firmly closed to the idea of dancing for the RAF ever again. She had agreed to that performance in the Fens last winter only because the venue happened to be the best and only option on their route north. The only good aspect of it was that the weather had prevented the aircraft, Spitfires and Hawker Hurricanes, from taking off, relieving her of the constant roar of those engines which after a lull were still such unavoidable reminders of her beloved Alan and his terrible fate. Despite her success in ignoring the fighter jets taking off during the first performance in Scotland, her emotional armour was still fragile.

These invitations for future performances, coming relatively soon after the blossoming of her relationship with John, plunged her back into a whirlwind of emotional pain and confusion. She knew perfectly well that she should no longer be thinking about Alan, since John had come into her life, but she was still haunted by the memory of her first fiancé and his death. The prospect of dancing the highly charged, emotive ballets, such as excerpts from *Swan Lake* and *La Sylphide*, at RAF bases, threatened to open the searing wound of heartbreak, and cause her to doubt her burgeoning love for John.

She foresaw that this was bound to be a confusing consequence of these occasions, despite that last treasured letter from Alan in which he had urged her to live a full life with a home and a family should the worst befall him. The truth as she saw it, was that she was still passionately and hopelessly in love with his memory, which left little place for John, however much she might have been attracted to him and thought she loved him. Either way, she would have to be unfaithful to one of them – but which was it to be?

Ignoring Cynthia, who was still excited by the good news of further engagements, Shirley turned her back on her friend. She stepped out of the makeshift theatre in the village hall where the company had been rehearsing for the evening's performance, into a fresh autumnal breeze blowing off the Irish Sea. Clouds were coming in from the west, bringing occasional preliminary droplets of rain which fell onto her burning cheeks, soothing both them and her inner torment. A gentle hand touched her on the shoulder.

"I'm so sorry, Shirl, I should have known better; of course you are upset," Cynthia whispered. "Let's go over to that little tearoom and sit there while the storm blows over, shall we?"

Shirley allowed herself to be led and sat waiting while Cynthia ordered tea and toasted teacakes for them both.

Cynthia said nothing until they had eaten and drunk their fill, then she murmured cautiously, "I know you well enough to understand how you feel about airbases, and if you don't want to come on the RAF tour, we will manage somehow, if we keep it simple and light, but I do believe

it's important to keep the company going. If we refuse these engagements we might not be asked again. Perhaps we could dance *Coppélia*,
for instance? Doris is used to dancing the doll and Maria is good as
Swanhilda." She ventured a nervous glance at Shirley's impervious
façade. "I might even give it a try myself!"

At this, Shirley summoned a wan smile and said, "Yes, you should,
you dance it well!"

"It won't be like having you lead us," Cynthia went on, tentatively
feeling her ground, "but maybe you could join us from time to time,
Shirl, coming to bases which don't awaken cruel memories for you?
What about the ones north of London like, um, Stansted and Northolt?"

"I'll think about it," replied Shirley, and then clammed up.

Cynthia kept quiet for a while until Shirley mechanically began col-
lecting up her possessions, her coat, hat and handbag, ready to leave;
then she plucked up the courage to voice her intuitive reading of her
friend's mood.

"If you ask me, Shirl, which you probably won't," said Cynthia, I
think your lovely Alan would be delighted that you and John have found
each other."

Shirley stood up, flung some coins onto the table and said brusquely,
"Here's the money for the tea," and left.

Once outside, though, Cynthia's words, uttered so softly and gently,
rang loudly in her ears. She waited a second or two for her friend and
partner in Aurora to join her, but as Cynthia, not surprisingly, had
thought better of doing so, she walked on in the pouring rain, along the
seafront and round the harbour of the little fishing port.

Although she knew that Cynthia was right, that did not help quell
her inner turmoil. Nevertheless, the suggestion of performing at bases
with which Alan had no known connection, had begun to appeal to her
undiminished longing for the dance, so she inevitably started to consider how it might be feasible. As for John, she wouldn't be seeing him
for several weeks; he himself had said so when they had met briefly in
Glasgow. Hopefully she might have sorted out her conflicting emotions
by their next meeting, if and when that were ever to happen.

On her return to London from Scotland, her father presented her with
an envelope, which, he said, had come weeks ago. She glimpsed the envelope and was surprised to see that it was postmarked "Norhambury".
She did not open it there and then, but put it aside for later. Obviously,

it was from John, although for the present, she had decided not to have any contact with him. Why he should have written to her when he had seen her, albeit briefly, in Glasgow, she could not fathom.

Later Reggie pointed to the envelope where it still lay untouched on the sideboard. "You haven't opened your letter, Shirl," said he. "It might be important."

She was about to pick it up, but at that moment Ted came in, announcing his presence by loudly declaring "*Voilà!*" and startling his sister and father.

"What is it? What's wrong?" they both asked.

"I guessed as much!" he shouted angrily, banging the creaking table with his right hand. "The Hun is taking over Vichy France and the whole country will be under German occupation in a couple of days' time! The Militia has been co-opted into working for the enemy, and the Gestapo won't waste any time in setting up its web of informers in the south – of course, they've already been doing that!"

He banged the table again. "And those informers are the worst threat, those French collaborators working for the Gestapo," he continued. "They create an atmosphere of terror everywhere, destroying trust between friends and neighbours, and building up a hidden army more frightening than tanks and guns." The table wobbled under his assault, giving Shirley to wonder how many more attacks it could withstand.

Reggie shook his head, his usual reaction to bad news, and Shirley cried out, "Ah, *non!*"

Ted stood bolt upright, assuming the air of a personage of importance, probably subconsciously acquired from having worked closely with General De Gaulle before joining the Special Operations Executive.

"Just as well I've managed to coordinate some of the underground groups down there in advance," he snorted. "They'll need to bury their differences and work together now!" There followed a sombre discussion about the plight of the country across the Channel, the homeland of their absent mother, that beautiful, rich, and varied land that they loved so much.

The niggling fear that Shirley had tried to suppress for some time was too strong to be contained, and it overflowed into the discussion. "Promise us, Ted, that you won't volunteer to be shipped back into southern France, will you?" she blurted out.

Ted turned on his sister in fury. "Shirl, I'm amazed that you could say such a stupid thing!" he shouted. "Are you blind? Haven't you seen the stump that was my left arm? Isn't it obvious there's no way I can go back to France, even though that's what I want to do more than anything else?"

"Now, now, Ted," their father interrupted. "We know how angry you are, but Shirley is only wanting to protect you from yourself. So don't blame her!"

Shirley in her turn fairly shouted at her brother in the lull after their father's intervention.

"What's more," she cried, "Ted, I don't want you to put Pa through any more anxiety!"

Ted said no more, but stomped off to his room.

Over breakfast the next day, Ted was contrite, as he usually was after his explosions of temper.

"I'm sorry," he said to his father and sister. "I was terribly angry; I shouldn't have taken it out on you. I know I keep on doing it. The trouble is, I feel so frustrated sitting in that office when I want to be on the move, flying into some field in the dead of night to try to save France from that dastardly enemy."

Reggie stood up. "We understand how you feel, old boy," he said, "but I'm afraid I must be going down to the shop. I'll leave you two to carry on talking if you want to, before you go to work."

Ted turned to Shirley when their father had left. "You can't imagine how grim it's going to be in France, Shirl," he said.

"I do have some idea," she replied, "and I'm jolly glad that we don't have a secret police to deal with here. It's bad enough seeing all the destruction the Nazis have inflicted on the cities and even small fishing ports in this country and, believe it or not, in Scotland, like the ones we've visited on our tours! She went into the kitchen, ostensibly to pour more water into the teapot, but in fact to have a breathing space for reflection.

"Having to be suspicious of the neighbours is dreadful," she said to herself, now that her thoughts had turned to France and the news that Ted had just given her and her father. On her return, carrying a tea tray, she cautiously asked the all-important question, which was bound to be at the basis of Ted's extreme frustration. "Tell me, have you had any news of Hélène?" she enquired, tentatively feeling her way into a possibly delicate subject.

Ted closed his eyes and muttered, "I can't bear to think what she might be doing. She has sworn to fight until the last, though I'm sure she doesn't realize how sadistic the Germans and the Gestapo can be. If she gets caught, she's bound to be tortured, because that's what they do."

Yet again, it was hard to believe that Ted was the younger of the two of them by a year. So heavy was the weight of anguish pressing down on him that he looked like an old man, even older than their father, who admittedly was well into middle age.

After Ted had left, Shirley sat staring into space; she could not even bring herself to clear the breakfast table, nor had she had any appetite for the ballet exercises she usually practised first thing in the morning, before going to Madame's studio. She cast her eyes aimlessly round the room and spotted the letter from John, still lying on the sideboard. She had not given him much thought since she came home, and wondered where he was. She reached out to pick it up and opened it with a margarine-smeared knife. The letter was dated the 14th of October, only days after their meeting in Glasgow, already over a month ago. She read:

My darling Shirley,

I was delighted to see you in Glasgow, but only sorry that I had to leave you so soon. I wish I could have stayed to see you dance! That would have been a new experience for me as I have never been to a ballet. You will have to tell me about it when we next meet.

Unfortunately, I cannot promise when that will be, because I have been seconded to General Montgomery's staff with the Eighth Army in North Africa, where we are fighting against Rommel's Afrika Korps forces.

I am at home with my parents now and leave tomorrow. I had hoped to see you again while you were in Scotland but there have been too many demands on my time.

I know you are still somewhere up north, but the official phone lines to the west coast are dreadful, virtually non-existent, however much I try to call.

Please do not worry about me, but I may not be back for quite a long time.

With all my love,
John

Shirley did not clear the breakfast table – she did not do her exercises, she did not go to Madame's studio. Instead, she wandered round the flat in a daze, not even able to lift a spoon or a fork from the table, not concentrating on anything except the significance of John's letter, which she saw as an ill-omen. How weird it was that it should have arrived at the precise time when she was doubting her love for him!

Unexpectedly, Ted came home at lunchtime and brought her back to a semblance of reality. "I need to listen to the One O'clock News," he said by way of urgent explanation, which was not an explanation at all, and it was still only half-past twelve.

He glanced at his sister and remarked, "I say, Shirl, are you all right? You don't look well – I mean, you don't look happy."

If Ted had noticed her forlorn state, Shirley told herself she must be looking dreadful. "Actually, I've had rather a shock," she said, wondering whether to confide in her brother.

"Come on then, tell me about it. You know we don't have any secrets from each other – well, not the ones that matter," he said encouragingly, putting his right arm round her shoulders.

"You see, I've fallen for someone," she whispered. "He's in the army. I saw him briefly in Scotland, and was expecting to see much more of him now that our tour's over, but I've just opened a letter from him saying he was being posted to General Montgomery's staff in North Africa, or rather he must have joined it by now, because the letter's dated the 14th of October from his parents' home in Norhambury."

She interrupted her narrative, closing her eyes. When she looked up again, her face was flushed. "It was only the 12th when we met in Glasgow, and that's over a month ago," said she, "so the posting must have been urgent. I don't think he knew about it then – or perhaps he already did, because he was in such a rush. Then he must have had a day or two's leave with his parents before setting out, while I was still in Scotland." She wiped the tears away with her sleeve.

Ted reacted by whistling between his teeth. Leaning on his shoulder, she pressed her face into his shirt.

"And what's worse," she whimpered, "I had begun to doubt whether I really loved him, or should stay faithful to Alan. We've had requests from ENSA and CEMA – that's the Council for the Encouragement of the Arts and Music, in case you didn't know – to perform at the RAF bases round London, and I couldn't face doing that because of *him.* Alan was my first love, and we were going to get married, as you know."

"Don't be daft!" Ted responded forcefully. "If you've met someone nice after all you've been through, think how lucky you are! Alan is not going to come back, you know that, and I'm sure he would want you to be happy."

He pulled away and stared her straight in the eye. "And you should concentrate on this new chap of yours. He will need you..." He was going to say, "if he comes home," but stopped himself in time. Instead he said, "Ask Pa about what's been happening in the Western Desert. You've obviously been completely out of touch."

He reached out to turn on the wireless, saying "I must listen to the messages that come through before the news", and settled down at the table while Shirley went to prepare potato and onion soup for lunch. Ted took out a pocketbook and pencil ready to take notes. From the kitchen Shirley could hear the messages: "Would Emily Parker please contact the Lancashire police about her father who is in hospital?"

"Mr Frederick Carter is trying to trace his son, Giles; please contact Essex police if you have any news of him."

"Mrs Elizabeth Kennedy has had an accident. Would her daughter, Susan, please get in touch with her father?" The messages went on in this vein, appropriate telephone numbers being given out with each message.

Out of the corner of her eye, Shirley could see that Ted was scribbling furiously in his notebook. The soup was coming to the boil and Reggie's heavy tread on the stairs was coming closer. Ted turned the wireless off, closed his notebook, stuffed it into his pocket and hurried to fetch bowls and soup spoons.

"Ted! I didn't know you were coming home for lunch!" Reggie exclaimed, his face lit up in a rare smile.

"Just passing, all in a day's work, Pa, so I thought I'd pop in." Ted gulped down his hot soup and then stood up to go. "Thanks for lunch, Shirl!" he said with a cheery grin. "See you later!"

"That was a surprise!" Reggie observed after Ted had dashed out. "I don't ever remember him coming home to lunch. I wonder what all that was about?"

"No idea, Pa," said Shirley, feigning ignorance, for she well knew from what Ted had confided to her long ago, that at least one of those messages would be a secret code for SOE drops into some dark field in France. She promptly changed the subject. "Pa, what can you tell me about General Montgomery and the Eighth Army and the Western Desert?"

"Hold on! One thing at a time, miss," her father exclaimed, as he raised a spoonful of hot soup to his lips. After swallowing that one spoonful, he enquired why she wanted to know about the Western Desert.

"Oh," she said airily, "it's just that Ted's been telling me how out of touch I am, and I feel rather foolish because he's right."

"I see," said Reggie, still none the wiser. He slurped another spoonful of soup and wiped his mouth on a napkin before embarking on his explanation. "I don't suppose you know that back in August the War was going so badly for us in the desert that the commanders were replaced by General Montgomery?"

"Yes, that's to say, I have heard of him," she replied, glad that only a couple of hours earlier she had read about Montgomery in John's letter.

"Montgomery, he's a stickler for discipline and the spartan approach – forced marches on only iron rations and all that sort of thing," her pa explained. "Well, anyhow, he whipped the Eighth Army into shape and at the end of last month took them into battle at a place called El Alamein against the German Afrika Korps. It was while you were away. Monty promised he would hit the Afrika Korps for six and he did just that!"

"Were there many casualties?" Shirley enquired.

"I don't know," her father replied. "The figures haven't been released yet, but I would hope not – except we did have 200,000 men out there and it was a huge battle; it went on for days."

Shirley tried to maintain an impassive façade, despite the pangs of tension mounting inside her. Her father waited for his words to sink in.

"Well, in fact it went on till only a few days ago, but there's still a lot of fighting all over north-western Africa." Reggie looked at the clock. "Heavens above!" he said. "It's time I was getting back to work." With that parting shot, off he went, leaving his daughter sitting lost for words.

Like Alan, John had given Shirley no address either in person or in his letter, and yet again there were prospective in-laws whom she had never met. Although this time she did have an engagement ring, a beautiful emerald ring, she would not contact them, even were she to have their address, for fear that the shock of hearing that she was engaged to their only son when he was so far away in the heat of battle, might be too much for them, or they might not believe her.

The fact that he was the only son was almost all he had told her about his family, except that he had a sister, Evelyn, who was a pianist. Anticipating another loss and more heartbreak in her life, she cursed herself for being crazy enough to doubt her love for her second fiancé. The three shocks, the first being John's letter, the second Ted's reprimand for her stupidity, and the third and worst, the news from the Western Desert, wherever that was, had woken her into a conviction that her feelings for John were deep and true. She really was passionately in love with him.

She turned the wireless on and found herself listening to Vera Lynn's programme, 'Sincerely Yours', conveying messages to the forces abroad and putting them in touch with their near and dear at home. The songs were unbearably moving, and by the end of the programme Shirley found herself humming the tunes: "Bluebirds over the White Cliffs of Dover" and "We'll meet again, don't know where, don't know when, but I know we'll meet again one day!"

The combination of the words and the music coming from that powerful, intensely moving voice, held her spellbound, and inspired her to do something she otherwise would never have dreamt of doing. She fetched pen, paper and an envelope from the sideboard and wrote a letter to the BBC asking Vera Lynn to send a simple message: "To John, in north-western Africa. I love you, my darling, and I want you to come home to me soon. Your own Shirley." There was nothing more to say, she sealed the envelope, kissed it, and then searched for a stamp in the drawer of the sideboard. She went out unnoticed and popped the letter in the nearest postbox.

The relief from this most simple of actions was instantaneous. Every day thereafter, she delayed going to her afternoon rehearsal at Madame's, in spite of Madame's uncomprehending annoyance, until about a week later, when she heard Vera Lynn say, "Here I have a message for John, in north-western Africa – it's from Shirley. She says, 'I love you, my darling, and I want you to come home to me soon. Your own Shirley.'"

Vera Lynn then went on to read other messages, uniting other lovelorn couples all over the globe. Shirley's heart missed a beat – she felt dizzy and lay down on the sofa for a couple of minutes until the shock had worn off. The wireless was still playing her favourite tunes, so she stood up and imagined that she was dancing in John's arms, which had never yet happened. She whirled around the room, certain that her message would reach its destination, and that certainty gave her the will and the determination to carry on fighting the enemy with her own particular talent. That will-power and that determination were reinforced the next day when she answered a summons from Maud, conveyed by Archie, asking her to visit her in her office.

Excitedly, Maud explained that she had called Shirley in that morning because she wanted her to see the pile of fan mail! It came from bases all over the country, praising her performances and asking her and the Aurora Company to go back and dance for them again! Maud apologized, saying she should have asked Shirley to come in to the office sooner, but knowing how busy she was, she told Cynthia about all those invitations over the phone instead. She hope that was all right.

Shirley assured Maud that she was delighted with the news, and certainly approved of her telling Cynthia about it over the phone.

"Oh, and by the way," said Maud, with detectable hesitation, "there are so many other RAF bases that want to invite you. How do you feel about that?"

Clearly in that call, Cynthia had warned Maud of the reasons for Shirley's reluctance to perform on airbases. To Maud's surprise, she replied, "That *is* good news. Do go ahead and accept as many of them as we can fit in!" Which is what Maud did for the period between January and April 1943.

No longer was Shirley perturbed by the sound of Spitfires or Hurricanes taking off, nor was there much opportunity for prolonged social contact with the pilots, the engineers or anyone who worked on those RAF bases. For an evening performance, the Aurora Company would arrive well rehearsed and well fed before leaving London, or if, as increasingly happened, the performance was to take place in the afternoon, they would arrive late-morning after a hearty breakfast.

While the scenery was being set up, some of the dancers would inspect the layout and the surface of the stage, others would check the lighting and the sound, while others would view the backstage arrangements, which were always basic.

Either Shirley or Cynthia would co-opt a willing officer, an airman or an engineer, to read the introductions to the audience, conveying the synopsis of each act of the ballet. The system had worked well on earlier tours after Rocky's departure, and was accomplished quickly and smoothly, with no shortage of able volunteers to read the prepared scripts, so long as no emergency arose.

Even better, after each performance, a specially commissioned bus would collect the dancers to take them back to central London, from where they would make their own way home, usually well before the curfew. The new system was so easy to operate that Cynthia and Shirley wished that they had adopted it sooner.

Although Shirley was as committed as ever to Aurora, she was less engaged in the performances than previously, though not in any way noticeable to the audiences. On every stage where she had danced the part of the fated beloved – in *Giselle* or *Swan Lake* – she had embraced that role as though it were real. In fact, it had been real to her, because she had forever imagined herself and Alan embracing as they danced.

Now Alan had assumed a more befitting role as a memory, a much-loved memory, yet no longer one to be conjured up in reality, because Shirley's reality had acquired a new dimension and that was John. He had fully taken Alan's place.

Nevertheless a huge question mark hung over *his* head: that of the future of their relationship. Was it doomed by the perilous situation he was, by all accounts, facing in the deserts of North Africa? The prospect of losing another fiancé to the War was unbearable. Were she to allow John's image to impinge on her dancing, the emotion of it might well cause her to break down on the stage.

31

After that breathtaking moment of undoubted, distant communication with John through Vera Lynn, and after reading many of the appreciative letters from bases in Scotland, Shirley threw herself back into the ballet every day, working at the *barre* in Madame's studio, doing her *petits allegros* until her muscles were stretched to their limits, and then practising her dance moves in the centre of the floor. The only free time she allowed herself was for shopping, which in the days of extreme rationing was a lengthy and depressing exercise, cooking, which she enjoyed scarcely more than shopping, and finally discussing plans for Aurora with Cynthia, which made everything seem worthwhile.

Since Cynthia had been present on the train journey home from Scotland at Shirley's first meeting with John, she had been kept up to date with most other developments, and had been taken into the secret of the engagement. The bond between the two young women grew stronger, especially because Pete, Cynthia's fiancé, was expecting to be posted abroad before long. Therefore, the two of them had been able to share their hopes, their anxieties and their fears. The difference was that Shirley's anxieties had become stark realities, soothed only by that imagined moment of contact over the wireless, whereas Cynthia's still lay in the future.

The challenge for Shirley was to keep her optimistic outlook alive. "I can tell you one thing," she declared over the phone to Cynthia, "I won't care if we go to perform at as many airbases as you like! I think that particular problem is over and done with. I won't worry about going to them any more. Anyhow, it simply doesn't matter because John is my fiancé now."

Then, with a catch in her voice, she added, "I know Alan is not going to come back, the War's still on, and I mustn't waste time moping. So I've told Maud to accept as many bookings as we can fit in." As an afterthought she conceded, "Though, of course, if you still want to dance some of the major roles, that's fine by me."

Cynthia replied that she had no wish to take the major roles but suggested that Maria might be keen to take on one or two.

"Fine," Shirley agreed.

At that moment it was enough to believe that because she had made contact with John and assured him, and herself, of the depth of her love, all would be well, although the months passed and there was little news from North Africa. The news there was, consisted of vivid reports of the interminable battles, both on the wireless every day, and on Pathé News at the cinema on Fridays. Propelled by an irresistible curiosity, she was unable to turn her back on either of these, yet they certainly made her doubt her own optimism, which often seemed entirely misplaced.

Why, she wondered, had there had not been a single letter from him in all those long months of waiting? Did that mean that he had died in one of those terrible battles in the scorching heat of the Sahara? When these dismal thoughts assaulted her, as they did more frequently the longer John was out of touch, she often succumbed to periods of deep depression. On those occasions Maria and Cynthia had to take over the major roles at performances while she stayed at home, her head buried in her pillow. Only Cynthia and Ted were aware of the reasons for Shirley's depression, although Ted did not know that she was engaged to John.

Eventually, late one evening in May 1943, when Shirley had shut herself in her room and Reggie had gone to bed, Ted took a call. The line was so crackly he had difficulty interpreting the message from the caller, who asked him to tell Shirley that he would be arriving at Waterloo Station on the boat train from Southampton at seven o'clock in the morning in three days' time. Ted had the presence of mind to realize that the caller must be John and responded accordingly, saying that Shirley was bound to be there to meet him. He dashed into Shirley's room, and shook her violently.

"Shirl, Shirl! Wake up! Your John is coming home!"

Shirley jumped up, rubbing her eyes and wiping her face.

"How do you know?" she gasped, clutching her brother. "Where is he? Is he here?"

"No, not yet, but he will be soon, and clearly he wants you to be there to meet him!" She burst into tears, no longer of sorrow but of joy.

In the early morning three days later, Shirley joined the crowds of other women, young girlfriends, fiancées and wives, and older mothers, aunts, sisters and cousins at Waterloo Station for the boat train to arrive. They all stood chattering in excited anticipation for their menfolk to appear, making a hubbub as deafening as a cloud of starlings. Then, at the first sighting of the engine as it pulled into the station, they swarmed onto the platform. When the train came to a standstill, they surged towards the wave upon wave of servicemen who came stumbling towards them. Like Shirley, the women were shocked into silence at the appearance of their loved ones as they came struggling along the platform, stooping under the overwhelming weight of their backpacks.

Shirley scanned the crowds for a glimpse of John, but it was a long time before she saw him coming from the far end of the train.

At first she failed to recognize him, because that tall figure wearing dark glasses and moving slowly in her direction was clearly much too elderly to be him. He was deeply tanned, haggard, painfully thin and drooping with exhaustion. It was only when the crowds began to disperse that she realized that the tall figure was in fact John. She pushed through the lingering groups of soldiers and families until she was only ten yards or so away from him. With beating heart she waved furiously and shouted his name, but he did not hear her. They drew closer together until finally he saw her and then, limping, he tried unsuccessfully to race towards her. She flung herself into his arms and held him close. Their tears streaming down their cheeks mingled, hers perfumed and dissolving her make-up – his, sweaty and bearing the grit of the desert and the grime of a long, hard journey.

"Shirley, my darling," he exclaimed, "is it really you? I've been dreaming of this moment for weeks, and then I wondered if you would run away when you saw me! I'm sorry I didn't see you. My sight suffered in the bright desert light, I don't hear very well because of the thunderous noise of all the battles, and I have a slight wound in my right leg." He took off his dark glasses: his eyes were red and watering in his brown face.

Holding him was like hugging a skeleton. "Oh, my love," she cried, "what has happened to you?"

"You don't want to know, and I'm not going to tell you," he said. "That can wait for another time – but I'm so glad you've come!" He was panting under the weight of his rucksack.

"Give me your rucksack!" she said. "Then I'm going to find a porter to carry it for you. You are exhausted!"

"No, no, I'm fine," he insisted. "Please don't do that. I can carry it. I would feel a fool in front of the other troops if they saw you carrying my luggage!"

"In that case, I'm going to order a taxi," she declared, "and you are going to come home with me!"

John muttered something about taking the Underground over to Liverpool Street to catch a train to Norhambury, where his parents would be waiting for him, but Shirley was having none of it.

"What! Not really! You are going to abandon me so soon, after all these months? Have you sent a telegram to your parents?" she asked.

"No, not yet, but I am about to do so; I really expected you wouldn't want to see me," came the weary reply.

Shirley took control. "You can't possibly go home to your parents looking like that! And I do want to see you! I've been longing for this moment for ages; I was afraid I might never see you again. You're going to come home with me and when you've rested and cleaned yourself up, maybe your eyes will be better in this softer light, and your ears won't be buzzing with the sounds of battle.

I'll have a look at your leg and bandage it up for you. Don't forget I'm an ARP warden and am trained to do all these things. Then we can go to Norhambury together. Wait here a moment – *I* have to make a phone call." She ran to a phone box, leaving John leaning against a wall, and was back in no time. "That's fine," she said. "My Pa will be expecting us."

She hailed a taxi – an unheard-of luxury, but these were unheard-of circumstances. John did not object. In the cab, as she stroked his damp, shaggy hair, his head lolled onto his chest. Her Pa had made no objection, when she told him over the phone, that she was bringing home a friend who had just returned from the battles in North Africa, and was too poorly and exhausted to travel any further, so could he please set up the camp-bed for Ted in his bedroom, and make up Ted's bed in the attic for the visitor. There was no question about it: this was not going to be a romantic stay.

Reggie had agreed without a murmur, with the result that by the time the taxi reached the door, all was ready for the visitor: clean sheets on Ted's bed, clean towels on the rack, and the kettle singing on the stove. Reggie had even managed to find some biscuits. Shirley was proud of him.

John was so tired he scarcely knew where he was or what was happening to him. He struggled to climb the dimly lit staircase, still carrying his rucksack, greeted Reggie and Ted with due politeness, had a quick, superficial wash and then a cup of tea before falling into bed. He did not reappear for fifteen hours, that is, not until the middle of the following morning.

Meanwhile, Shirley was aware that her father, if not her brother, would need some explanation. As it happened, not much was required, because they were both awestruck at having a visit from an officer who had fought with Montgomery, who had not only contributed to the victory at the Second Battle of El Alamein, but who also, with the newly arrived American forces, had captured north-west Africa for the Allies.

Tactfully, Reggie did not enquire how Shirley had come to know this officer, whom she had simply introduced as John, or what was the relationship between them, although of course, Ted had quickly put two and two together and concluded that this must be Shirley's new boyfriend, not that he knew of their engagement.

It was enough, Reggie surmised after supper when Shirley had also gone to bed, that there must be some close connection between the two of them, otherwise she would not have brought him home to stay. Ted maintained a discreet silence in the face of his father's speculation. He did however wonder how long their visitor might be staying, and generously said that he was content to share his father's bedroom, if he could have some cotton wool to keep out the snoring and occasional bursts of shouting.

His sister searched to the bottom of her ARP bag, where she found a wad of cotton wool which she gave him. Noises there were, though they came not from Reggie's bedroom, but from the attic, where John was having nightmares. Only Shirley was disturbed by them; she lay awake for several hours debating whether to go upstairs to comfort her fiancé or to leave the ghouls to evaporate from his fevered brain. She was about to get out of bed and put her slippers on, having decided that she would go upstairs after all, when the cries died down, only to be replaced by the noise of her father snoring loudly. She regretted giving Ted all the cotton wool.

Both she and John longed to be able to indulge in a deep embrace, to feel each other, to discover each other, but time together was elusive, and discretion was always the word, since Ted might burst in at any moment; even Reggie might come dragging himself up the stairs and catch them unawares. It had been their decision to keep their engagement a secret and this was neither the time nor the place to make it public, even to Shirley's family.

Father and son were wise enough not to pester their visitor with questions about the Africa Campaign, because they had seen enough on the newsreels to know that it had been unremitting and unforgiving: the casualties were enormous and clearly John was lucky not to have been a victim himself. Probably by the look of him, he had come close to that fate. They admired his courage and concentrated on making him feel welcome.

After a visit to the doctor, who commended Shirley for her expert care of John's right leg, followed by a treatment at an eye clinic to be followed up regularly, John pronounced himself better and immensely grateful to his hosts for their hospitality, but said that he must be setting off for Norhambury to visit his parents before going back to his base in Scotland.

"I don't think you are well enough to travel," Shirley announced when he appeared, painfully thin and wan, dressed in his crumpled uniform, still wearing his dark glasses. "I'm coming with you!" said she.

The surprise written over his face gave way to polite caution. "No, no, that's not necessary. It's, um, not a good idea. I'm sure you need to practise your dancing for your next tour, whenever that is."

For lack of opportunity, she had not told him that her Welsh tour was scheduled to start in only three days' time, on the 17th of May: she longed to postpone it but could not find a way, which meant he would have to be told, but not just yet.

The obvious disappointment, clear for all to see, on her face on being told abruptly not to accompany him, brought about a swift change in his reactions. "It would be lovely to have you with me, but it's a long journey and I don't want to put you to all that trouble, my love," he said.

"Don't be silly!" she chided him, and then, glancing round to make sure they were alone, said, in a tone so serious that it brooked no argument, "You are my fiancé, and don't forget it! I'm going to look after you now and for ever, so don't argue!"

He laughed and hesitated, apparently searching for the right words.

"All right then, but I haven't told my parents about you, so it might be a shock for them to see me in this state with a fiancée on my arm. They are rather traditional, you see."

"Don't worry, but I *would* like to meet them, and I promise I'll behave myself. I could say I've come as your porter if you give me your rucksack."

John would have none of it – instead he heaved his rucksack onto his back, and was bent double under the weight. Without hurrying, they set out for Liverpool Street Station, had lunch in the restaurant that was becoming their favourite haunt, and then caught an afternoon train, leaving London, its ruins and its fog behind them.

Although Shirley was anticipating cuddling up to her fiancé and chatting with him all the way to Norhambury, he fell asleep only five minutes into the journey, waking only when the train pulled into their destination, two and a half hours later, so she had to content herself with holding his hand and gazing out of the window as the countryside flew past.

She succeeded in hiding her disappointment when he dabbed the sleep from his eyes and smiled at her, apologizing profusely. "Please forgive me!" said he. "I was so much looking forward to being alone with you, my darling, and talking, but I felt so comfortable and happy that I just dropped off. Can you believe it?"

He grinned, put his arm round her and declared, "Apart from staying with you and your family, this railway compartment is the most comfort I've known in ages!"

His manner was so endearing and what he had suffered must have been so appalling that she had not the heart to complain. "Of course you're tired after what you've been through; I don't mind, so long as I can hold your hand," she replied, which was not quite a truthful reflection of her frustrated feelings, but it made him happy.

Even on the station platform, the atmosphere in Norhambury was fresher and more wholesome by comparison with the dirt and grime of the London air. "Come on," he said, taking her firmly by the arm. "No need for a taxi here – the bus goes from right outside the station." And look, there's a bus coming up to the stop.

To her amazement, John was greeted like an old friend by the bus conductor. "Bless my soul!" he exclaimed. "It's young John, all dressed up as an officer!" He stepped down off the bus and took the rucksack before John had a chance to protest. "I reckon as you've been out in that there desert we've been a-hearin' about on the wireless – you need a rest, young'un. Tha's what your ole father said when I saw him. You're our hero, young John!"

He put the rucksack down and directed John to a seat.

"Well, I am glad to be home, I *can* say that!" John exclaimed, brushing off his heroic status. "But I'd rather go upstairs and see the city from above. I'll leave my rucksack down here." Ahead of Shirley he set off up the winding staircase. She was bemused, for in London she scarcely recognized any of the conductors on the buses she caught, nor did they recognize her. Certainly, none of them ever helped her with any of the bags or parcels she might be carrying.

"I say, you are popular," she laughed, following him nimbly up the winding stairs.

"Oh, that's nothing," John called out over his shoulder. "The bus-ride takes us through some of the oldest areas of the city, medieval streets and alleyways and the cathedral. It won't be dark yet, so I'll point them out to you as we go past. Maybe if you can stay on for a few days, I'll take you on a tour; but be prepared for a lot of bomb sites," he said, ushering her into a seat on the otherwise empty top deck.

"That would be lovely, but really in my little bag here, I've only brought my overnight things," she answered him. "Never mind," he replied cheerily. "You're going to be my wife, so I will take you out to buy some new clothes!"

Norhambury was lovely in parts, except for the bombed-out ruins, the bomb sites, the barricading and the emergency posts everywhere she looked. John sighed. "Our city has been bombed within an inch of its life," he observed sadly. She laughed, then fell silent. She worried that she had not told him that it was impossible for her to stay longer in Norhambury on account of the tour, with its looming departure date. She had to go back to London tomorrow, at the latest, for final rehearsals, packing and checking that all the arrangements were in place.

Although Cynthia, together with Madame, whom she had also taken into her confidence, had been extremely sympathetic and had promised to double-check everything and put the finishing touches to the performances, she felt that the onus was on her to make absolutely certain. Not only that but she was not even sure how to tell John that she would be leaving very soon.

"Penny for your thoughts," said a voice softly in her ear, as the bus rumbled past more overgrown bomb sites, medieval buildings, numerous churches and the soaring cathedral, which John was pointing out to her, but of which she was oblivious.

"Oh," said she, hastily remembering a question that there had been no time to ask him earlier, "John, did you ever receive my message sent by Vera Lynn on her show?" she asked. "It's called 'Sincerely Yours'. She sends messages to the troops from their families and loved ones at home."

He frowned, and her heart missed a beat.

"When was that?" he asked.

"Oh, it must be several weeks ago now," she replied, already painfully aware of what was to come.

"No, no, I didn't, I'm sorry to say. We were right out in the desert and communications were dreadful, hardly anything at all came through. You know I would have written to you if there had been any chance of my letters getting through." He turned to face her and saw the dismay on her face. Tears plopped onto the handbag on her knee. "I really thought that was a point of contact between us, and the thought of it has kept me going through this horrible time," she sobbed. He held her close.

"Tell me what the message said, and I will reply now, if you like, but what matters most is that the thought of it kept you going, just as the thought of you kept me going."

"It said something like, 'I love you, my darling and I want you to come home to me soon! Your own Shirley,'" she whimpered.

Blowing her nose as she came to the end of that useless message, she fixed her eyes on the floor. Gently he cupped her chin in his hand, turned her face towards him, kissed her on the lips and said softly, "I love you, my darling; I am home with you now, and I am your own John."

They kissed passionately for the rest of the bus ride; she, but not he, was aware that it might be the only private, passionate embrace they would be able to indulge in until their next meeting, whenever that might be.

There was a late-spring chill in the air and the sun was lower in the sky, when the bus deposited them in a lane on the edge of the city. John pointed out a row of newish houses on the other side of the road and picked out one in particular: it was his home. It augured well, since outwardly it was remarkably like that lovely, sunny house in south-west London where Shirley had grown up.

She and her family had lived there until her mother left them, and her father had no choice except to abandon his job as a railway engineer to take up the less stressful role of a newsagent. The house across the road in Norhambury, however, was wider, with a long front garden and a more rural aspect; the first roses of summer trailed languidly over a recessed porch, while a bushy fuchsia was balletically displaying its mass of red tutus on every stem above a neatly tended lawn. They crossed the road to the gate.

"Here we are!" John announced cheerily. "We'll take them by surprise and go in by the back door. It's there, do you see, in the side wall of the house."

He walked on, but Shirley held back, suddenly in the grip of an inexplicable foreboding. John climbed the two steps up to the back door and opened it. "Anyone at home?" he called. There was a flurry of activity from within and shouts of "John! John! Our hero! Our own hero! You're home!"

He disappeared indoors, and a light went on. Shirley moved tentatively towards the door and quietly mounted the doorstep. From there she saw her fiancé caught in a hug with a bespectacled, plump lady, probably in her early sixties, her greying hair held back in a bun. Beside her was a man with his hand on John's shoulder, doubtless his father, who was beaming all over his face and muttering, "Our hero, our hero!"

In the inner doorway to the kitchen, a tall, young woman with long, dark brown hair and, like John, a tanned complexion, shyly awaited her turn to hug him. "She must be his sister," Shirley surmised. She watched unnoticed, wishing she were Alice and could take a potion to make herself shrink out of sight, and out of this family reunion, where already it was quite obvious, she did not belong. The chances were that her presence would not be well received. Would it be better to leave at once, she wondered, take the next bus to the station and catch the train back to London? But that would mean not saying goodbye to John, and she could not bear to do that.

She was about to turn tail and flee when John's father noticed her standing forlornly on the doorstep. "Ho, ho!" he exclaimed. "Who have we here? Come in, young lady! Come in!" Heartened by this friendly greeting, she took a step inside the door and everyone stared at her, the mother fixing her with a frown in an unmistakeably hostile manner, the sister perplexed and surprised – the only friendly, welcoming face, being that of John's father.

John himself looked decidedly awkward. "Shirley! I'm so sorry. I should introduce you to my family…" he was saying when he was interrupted by his mother who curtly enquired, "So, who are you?" to the slight, well-dressed, blonde figure, now standing only just inside the door. Shirley quavered at the hostility in the mother's voice, as well as in her expression.

Before John could utter anything incriminating, like "This is my fiancé", she, quick-wittedly and with an assumed nonchalance, forced a reluctant smile, and announced, "Hello! I'm Shirley. I, um, just met your son on the train, and thought he looked so poorly that I ought to offer to help him. Obviously he had been caught up in the War somewhere terrible. He told me he has been fighting in North Africa. Clearly he is a hero, and I was very honoured to be able to do something for him."

She paused, but her audience seemed to have turned to stone. "It's not far out of my route," she stammered, hoping that someone would say, "How kind of you!" But no one said anything at all. It appeared that they were statues, and were no longer breathing.

Shirley broke the silence in the only way she could. "Now that he's safely home, I had better be going," she said with a catch in her throat.

Fortunately, John had left his rucksack on the doorstep when he bounded into the house. She stepped outside, heaved it up onto her shoulder, as if she had been carrying it all the way from the station, and dropped it down inside the door. She stifled a tremor in her voice. "Bye – I hope all goes well for you, John. Nice to meet you too," she said to his parents. "Goodbye!" She waved and marched off into the early evening. Out of sight she began to run to the bus stop.

The situation was all too depressingly familiar, recalling a past dreadful experience which came easily to mind. Yes, that was it! It was that wet evening when, inside the Dorchester Hotel, she had seen girls draping themselves around her beloved Alan. Just as now, she had run away. Handsome men were far too attractive, not that John was looking his best at present, but his looks would surely come back. There would certainly be competition on that front. It was a hard lesson, which she was still learning, and in these circumstances, it might well be too hard, too painful, and too soul-destroying.

She was already standing, hunched up in misery, by the bus stop when she heard footsteps scrunching on the gravel in the driveway behind her. She turned round to see John, holding his arms outstretched.

"My darling, don't go!" he called. "That scene was horrible! I didn't know what to do; it was all my fault! I should have handled it better. I'm so sorry. Please come back indoors! My mother was just rather surprised to see you standing there, but you *were* right to give the impression that we had just met, and that you were helping me. If you hadn't, I might have told them that we were engaged and that might have been too much for a first meeting. Mother is very possessive of me and my sister, but she will love you when she gets to know you, of that I am certain."

Shirley was not so sure, for she had been reflecting, not only on the scene at the Dorchester three years earlier, but also on how much the cold shouldering she had just received was like the reception she had *expected* to be given by Alan's parents, had she appeared at their vicarage after his death, announcing her engagement to *him*.

"How I wish I could come back to London with you now!" John was saying. "Though I fear that would make things worse."

"Don't worry – I'll go back to London, and when you have spent some time here, give me a call from that phone box over there, and let me know when you'll be coming," said she with a notable lack of enthusiasm. She allowed him to hug her until the bus came into view.

"Please can I see you soon?" he begged.

"Yes, of course, whenever you can – but I'm off on tour to Wales in a couple of days' time," she replied, with a marked indifference in her tone. She gave him a peck on the cheek as a parting shot and climbed onto the bus.

Once seated on the bus, without having waved to John as it left the stop, she said to herself, "Oh, why, oh why did I do that? Will I ever see or hear from him again?"

By the time she reached the station, she was too tired to travel further. In any case she did not want to travel with red eyes and swollen eyelids, so she booked herself into the station hotel and there spent a restless night, churning over that disastrous first meeting with John's family. She had fallen in love with John, of that there was no doubt; but did her love for him extend to submitting herself to mother-in-law problems when she had already overcome so much in her life, relying only on her own will-power and her sense of independence? Was she prepared to make that much sacrifice for him?

"John safely home?" her father enquired when she arrived at the flat at lunchtime the following day. She nodded.

"*Quel héro!*" Ted exclaimed.

Shirley had heard that word so many times in the past twenty-four hours that she did not want to hear it ever again in any language. "Well, so are you!" she spat out in exasperation, then went to her room, collected her ballet shoes and leotard, and headed off to Madame's studio, where she danced vigorously. The next two afternoons and evenings she spent practising hard for the tour and going over all the arrangements with Cynthia and Maud, trying to close her mind to her emotional turmoil.

However hard she tried, thoughts about it kept creeping in. Had she been stupid in running away from John and his family? What else could she have done? Time would tell, although she feared that time had already run out in their relationship. In any case, there was always the question of her past, which was worrying her. Although she and John were engaged, she still had not found the right opportunity to tell him of her previous engagement or of her pregnancy by her first fiancé.

Closing the door on that aspect of her past had at first seemed the right thing to do, but now she was not so sure. Supposing John discovered, or someone told him about Alan and the poor little baby, how would he react? Would he be angry and break off the engagement, which, in any case, already seemed to be in tatters? Or was there a chance he would be kind and understanding? The latter was asking a lot, perhaps too much.

On the other hand, the conviction was inescapable: if only Aurora were staying in London, and dancing at local airbases, of which there seemed to be an infinite supply, then the possibility of being in touch with John again would still exist. She would probably be at home when he rang, as she hoped he might, and if she were not there, Pa or Ted would take a message, and then they would meet again. This was her only hope, because there was no way she could write a letter to him at his parents' address. His mother would pounce on it and hide it away or tear it up before he had any chance of seeing it.

32

During the winter months in the interval before the next tour further afield to Wales, Aurora had never been short of engagements at the numerous airbases around London. In spite of sometimes inclement weather conditions, but never totally impassable roads, it proved to be so very much simpler to take the dancers and all the equipment to venues within easy reach of London, than arranging distant tours. Although the two girls often looked back with nostalgia on those earlier trips in which they had discovered formerly unknown parts of the country, they were relieved that the new system by far outweighed the old one in its convenience and manageability. In any case, the airbases in the Home Counties vastly outnumbered those in other regions, so that Maud was instructed to continue making bookings not only to the end of April of 1943 but also for the following autumn.

Not surprisingly in the new circumstances, the prospect of a visit to Wales was not met with much enthusiasm either by any of the dancers, or by the leading lights of the company, that is, Cynthia and Shirley. The tour would take them a long way from their London base, doubtless completely out of contact with their near and dear. Nevertheless, since the bookings had been confirmed long ago, it was up to the ballet company to fulfil them, and thus be true to their commitment to the War effort – but how much they longed, with the rest of the population, for it to come to an end, the sooner the better!

How tired everyone was of all the privations, the rationing not only of food and water, but of clothing and fuel as well, the dark, cold, unlit winter nights, when survival had been the main aim of all families, the limitations on travel except in an official capacity, the gas masks, the threat of invasion, and above all the dangers of the terrifying air raids, which, although not as frequent as in the Blitz, could occur anywhere at any time, and wipe out whole communities! On those nights, the skies were alight with flames shooting at the stars, and the stagnant air was rent with blasts, explosions and gunfire.

According to Cynthia, her Pete could not offer much in the way of encouraging information, yet it was obvious that his troops were preparing for some sort of massive operation, otherwise why would their manoeuvres involve scaling sheer cliff or rock faces and such daredevil activities, despite the fact that some of the otherwise most courageous soldiers were terrified of climbing those high walls on ladders, let alone ropes? Pete once let slip to Cynthia that his unit was also practising disembarking from ships at sea, which she thought strange for a land-based army.

As for John, his work as a liaison officer might take him away from his regiment on the east coast of Scotland at little more than a moment's notice. Shirley dwelt on this probability with increasing anxiety as the time between the disastrous Norhambury visit and the start of the Welsh tour slipped by. During that interval, there came no phone call or message from him. Whenever the phone rang, she ran to answer it, but was always disappointed.

Although his mother's behaviour towards her had been very unpleasant, she still found it impossible in those two days to close her mind to her fiancé, wherever he might be, for he had invaded her heart and her soul, so thoroughly that she had to admit to herself that she could not live without him. Her overriding worry was that he might have decided that *he* could live without *her*. She berated herself for overreacting in giving him the cold shoulder at the bus stop, on that nasty occasion when she had made her hasty exit from his parents' house.

Now she longed to see him more than ever, to hear his voice, touch him, kiss him, or even simply receive a message from him, but none of that happened, and it was up to her and Cynthia to put a positive gloss on the upcoming tour.

"Think how good it will be to get out of London!" Cynthia told the company.

"And we'll really be able to enjoy the spring, out in the country, free of this fog!" Shirley said somewhat half-heartedly. That her enthusiasm was muted was not lost on anyone, least of all herself, because John was forever in her heart and uppermost in her thoughts.

Suppose, she thought, he had already been drafted to some ghastly war zone, as bad as North Africa, or worse if it were in the Far East, and he had been forced to leave quickly with no chance of getting in touch with her? Perhaps, like the last time, he had sent her a letter which had not yet arrived. She felt herself being drawn into that dark cavern, the cavern into which she had been thrown on hearing of Alan's disappearance, and which had become even blacker on the loss of their baby. Then, only her return to the ballet had brought her out of that dark space. Now, one evening in the middle of May, it was time for her to set out with the company for Cardiff with a very heavy and fearful heart, though aware that the ballet was the only possible palliative treatment for her.

According to the plan, the combined forces of Aurora would take the late train to Cardiff after a full day's rehearsing, make their way to a hotel booked through CEMA, fall into bed, and rise and shine early the next day to begin exercising in the theatre, where they were to perform for the troops and for the general public that evening, the 18th of May.

The journey was uneventful until the train crossed into Wales, where it slowed down, crawling along the track at a pace which would have lagged behind a snail: at Newport station it stopped altogether. After more than half an hour's wait, Andrei volunteered to go and look for the guard: he was away for a long time.

When finally he came back to his seat, the news he had to tell his companions, who were crowding impatiently round him, was not encouraging. All traffic by road and rail in South Wales had come to a standstill because, even while there was yet light in the sky, the German bombers had swooped over Cardiff, flown off and then returned to inflict a massive air raid on the city. The guard had said that the train would be marooned for at least another hour, or even longer, until all the lines in the area had been cleared. He would make an announcement as soon as he had more news.

"So why don't we all go along to the restaurant car and have something to eat?" Andrei suggested, as if to sweeten the pill.

"I've already eaten!" came a unanimous grumble from the company.

Undeterred, Andrei came up with another idea. "Let's go and have a drink, then, in the restaurant car," he proposed. "What's more, we men will pay for the girls!" There was general jubilation from the girls, though not from the men, at this suggestion.

"Off you go then," Shirley instructed her troupe in her most school-marmish manner, "and behave yourselves! Don't leave the train!"

This was an order that she herself was about to disobey. "You stay here and guard the luggage," she told Cynthia. "If we are going to be stuck here for at least an hour, I must find a telephone to ring Pa and tell him where we are, and what's happened, so that when Jack rings in, as I've told him to, Pa can give him the message, and he will know to avoid Cardiff when he reaches Wales with the van."

Since the East Anglian fiasco when the van containing the costumes and the props had been snowbound, and the dancers were stranded waiting for the RAF bus to collect them, Shirley and Cynthia had devised a way of being in touch with their base camp on long journeys. This was that, either Maud during the daytime, or Reggie in the evening, would man the phone, and take and convey messages, to keep the dancers, travelling by coach or train, in touch with Jack, and his helpers, not forgetting Dmitri the music master. Jack, also in charge of the precious props cargo, would ring in to London from any available phone box on his route for any new instructions and changes of route from Shirley, similarly conveyed through a phone box.

Shirley fumed, waiting in the queue to use the station phone. Most of the callers, conscious of the short time available, kept their calls brief, apart from one little old lady, who was giving her daughter somewhere outside Cardiff, an endless shopping list, and the daughter was clearly protesting that there would be nothing to buy the next day, if in fact she were still alive. At last Shirley's turn came, and Reggie's voice was music to her ears when he picked up the receiver.

"Look, Pa, we have a problem," she said quickly by way of greeting. "The train is being diverted because there's bombing in Cardiff, so when Jack rings, tell him to find somewhere to stay away from Cardiff, and to ring you again in the morning. I'll let you know where we end up."

"I'm so glad to hear you, Shirl," he exclaimed. "Word came through that there was a raid in the west somewhere, so I was very worried about you."

"Yes, yes, Pa, I'm all right. Must go!" She put the phone down and turned to face the line of glaring faces impatiently waiting their turn to use the phone.

After more delay, there was an announcement over the guard's loud hailer from where he stood on the platform. "I am informed the train will stop here overnight, because Cardiff station has been bombed." This was information that most of the passengers had already ascertained for themselves. The guard went on, "We hope to run a service to Cardiff tomorrow at about midday. Please get off now and come back with your tickets at eleven thirty tomorrow, the 18th of May."

The sighs and grumbles all round could have been heard miles away. The dancers took their luggage down from the rack, despondently joining the crowds as they disembarked from the stationary train.

"What now?" Shirley whispered to Cynthia.

"I've absolutely no idea," she replied.

The crowds had dispersed by the time the dancers, coming from the far end of the platform, reached the barrier, and emerged into the station yard, only to find that all the taxis had been taken. "Oh no!" one of the girls cried out. "There won't be a single hotel room left!"

Hearing that desperate cry, a woman stepped forward from a group of middle-aged ladies who stood outside the station. "Are you young people looking for somewhere to stay tonight?" she asked pleasantly.

"Yes," said Cynthia wearily, "we are dancers and were expecting to arrive in Cardiff tonight for our show tomorrow."

"Well, you won't be going there, my dears!" the lady replied. "But my friends and I, we can offer you shelter for the night. We did this when Cardiff was bombed before, you see. It happens quite often… Just follow us, it's not far. We're going to put you up in our church hall."

There was nothing for it but to follow her, and spend the night on makeshift mattresses in the church hall. Before leaving, the ladies kindly provided tea, spam sandwiches and cake, and invited the members of the troupe to help themselves to more. They also showed them the workings of the tea-urn, and suggested they should make their own breakfast with the bread, margarine and marmalade, placed ready on a side table.

"Could be worse – at least we're safe," someone observed, yawning.

"Yes, be thankful for small mercies! I'm nearly asleep," another agreed as they settled down for a rather uncomfortable and fitful, but safe, night's sleep.

Outside the church hall, Shirley had noticed another phone box, and made a beeline for it early the next morning. First she called her father, who confirmed that the news from Cardiff was appalling: the comprehensive raid the previous evening had indeed hit the railway station, but that had been only the start of a vicious campaign of bombing, which was still going on. "I doubt you'll be going there, and I'm glad," he said, adding, "You'll be pleased to know we've heard from Jack and the crew, and they are all right."

He elaborated on the situation of Jack and his crew. "They slept in the van somewhere out in the country, like they did last year in East

Anglia. They're just waiting to hear where to go next. So you had better ring Maud."

There was no queue outside this phone box, so Shirley rang Maud, who, efficient as ever, had everything under control. "I rang the organizers in Cardiff," she said, "and they've said, they can't put on the ballet tonight or any other night because the bombing is so dreadful, and it looks as if it will go on indefinitely, so they ask you to go straight to Swansea."

Shirley was about to explode, saying "But how are we supposed to do that?" when Maud cut her short. "Tell me exactly where you are, because I've been in touch with the Swansea base on Fairfield Common. In any case that's your next stop, and they'll order a coach to pick you up and take you there. And I'll ask your father to let Jack know that he's to go straight to Fairfield Common, Swansea, when he rings in. But now I need the details of where you are!"

Shirley was silenced, for she had no idea where she was, apart from being in Newport. Stranded there, she had been so tired the previous evening when they reached the church hall that she had failed to register even the name of the church, let alone the street names. "We are still in a church somewhere near the station, Maud, but I'll have to call you back; I have an urgent errand to run," she said sheepishly. She ran outside to check the precise details of the location, and rang Maud back straight away.

Then she returned to the church hall to impart the news to her dishevelled band of dancers. "When is the bus coming?" – "How long will the journey be?" – "I need more than a slice of toast!" were some of the unhelpful, exasperated comments fired at her when she reappeared inside the church hall. She was furious.

"Look here, you lot!" she shouted, "have you forgotten there's an almighty War on? Even now people are being killed in Cardiff *in daylight*, while we have been given food and lodging by those kind ladies. Remember, we might all be dead if we'd gone any further! And back in London, my father and our hard-working secretary, Maud, are trying non-stop to sort things out for us. So shut up and think yourselves lucky!"

A shocked silence met this tirade. Shirley was surprised too: she had never spoken to her company like this before, though often she would have liked to. Nonetheless, since she had a captive and subdued audience, she thought it worthwhile to carry on addressing them. "So when you've washed up the plates and cups and saucers, and emptied the teapot and packed your belongings, we'll do some warm-ups and a few routines. You'll have to imagine the music!" Nobody spoke and they all turned busily to their chores.

In her fragile emotional state, Shirley was at the end of her tether and made no apology for her outburst. This tour was turning out to be a disaster before it had begun. Although she had not yet asked her father if there had been any message from John, he would surely have told her. She nipped out again to the phone box and called home.

"Pa, has John rung up?" she asked.

"Where are you now, Shirl?" he asked.

"Still in the same place, Pa, but I asked if John had rung up," she persisted.

"Oh, yes, a little while ago, just after you called the first time this morning," he finally said, answering her all-important question.

"Well, what did he say?"

"He said he was worried about you in Cardiff, so I told him you were in Wales, but in Newport, not in Cardiff, and were safe."

"Did you tell him we were going straight to Swansea?"

"No, I didn't do that, because he was ringing from I don't know where, and the line was crackly and then went dead. But I will tell Jack where to go when he rings in."

Shirley banged down the receiver in deep frustration. On the one hand, she was overjoyed to hear that John had rung and was concerned for her. On the other, that joy was depressingly tempered by the realization that a phone call from him was unlikely, since he would not know where to find her, and she did not know where he was.

For that matter, she herself was not at all sure where she and the company were heading; to add to their troubles, they would be arriving at the Swansea base twenty-four hours ahead of time because of the cancellation of the Cardiff engagement. Ruefully she reflected, not for the first time, that the day's date should have been the evening of their performance in Cardiff, and tomorrow the day of their planned arrival and performance in the base outside Swansea. Would the base be ready for them? What's more, the dancers would all ask where they would be staying. How was she going to tell them that when she didn't even know herself? That question was resolved for her by the bus driver, who arrived at the church hall at the same time as she did. He announced cheerfully to the practising dancers, "Ladies and gentlemen! All aboard! Fairfield Common Airbase awaits you!"

"You'll have a good time at Fairfield," the chatty driver told the passengers at the front, "but the squadron is on patrol non-stop, trying to defend Swansea, join the battle for Cardiff and patrol the Irish Sea. The Commander has asked me to warn you that there won't be anyone to meet you, but he wants me to show you to your accommodation and to the officers' mess where there will be food for you. He says please do use the main hall for rehearsing for your performance tomorrow night, as planned."

"Thank you so much. That all sounds fine, but will there be a phone I can use for getting in touch with our office, please?" Shirley asked, thinking that "office" sounded rather grander than simply "my father" or "Maud".

"Yes, I'll show you where that is too," came the ready reply. Shirley conveyed the information to her troupe, who nodded silently, all chastised by Shirley's outburst the previous evening.

On the right-hand side of the bus, the passengers gazed out at scenery gleaming in the sunlit, innocent green freshness of spring. Those on the left had a more sobering view, that of a grey pall and red flashes over the sky, as the bus skirted Cardiff on country roads, at a safe distance from the city.

"That's our capital city over there," the driver said sadly. "It's smoke, not rain in that cloud. Our chaps will need some cheering up after that. I hope you'll have something lively for them tomorrow evening, if this Blitz is over by then. They say hundreds of people have died already. Mind you, in Swansea, they dropped 1,273 bombs on us in February 1941, and 230 people died. Our town centre was flattened, and I doubt it will ever recover. When will it all end?" He shook his head and wiped his eyes. The grey cloud over Cardiff was a sombre reminder that the War was never far away, and that Aurora had been lucky not to have been the corporate victim of that particular outrage.

Fairfield Common Airbase was in the middle of the Gower Peninsula, an area of such beauty in the morning sun that it raised everyone's spirits. At the base, once reunited with Jack, his companions and his father's van carrying the costumes, the scenery, the records and the gramophone, there was nothing to do except find the main hall and set to work rehearsing *Coppélia*, the ballet that the company had voted for, in preparation for this tour.

The vote for *Coppélia* was the result of a newly instituted democratic procedure that allowed everyone a say in the choice of ballets. This change had been wisely suggested by Andrei, who had become the spokesperson between the company and the bosses, that is to say, Shirley and Cynthia. The arrangement was rarely contentious and usually worked well, except when individuals were tired or disenchanted, as had happened the previous evening. Those individuals had resumed their normal positive outlook, especially when they all realized that, fortuitously, *Coppélia* was the best choice for cheering up the forlorn servicemen at the Swansea base.

The chatty driver gave them a guided tour of the deserted base on their arrival, directing them to their Nissen huts and to the officers' mess, where a cold lunch together with bottles of cider awaited them. He opened an office and allowed Shirley to use the phone. With the driver standing in the doorway, she felt obliged to make her calls – one to her father and the other to Maud – brief, long enough only to confirm that the van had arrived at Fairfield Common, and the rest of the tour was expected to go according to plan. There was no chance of a private conversation with her father, so she did not ask about John.

If the base was deserted like a ghostly garrison when they arrived, allowing the troupe to please themselves, to eat and drink, rehearse and go for walks undisturbed, in the afternoon it became extremely noisy and busy. Shirley bit her lip while she watched a squadron of Spitfires and Hawker Hurricanes coming in to land and their replacements taking off, as if in relay. Where had all those pilots who had rushed out of a hut and clambered onto the wings of their planes been hiding? she wondered. How was it that they had not seen any of them?

Her questions were answered by the base Commander, who joined the dancers in the mess that evening. He explained that the planes flew in relays to attack the marauding Germans and defend their area. While one squadron was airborne, the pilots of the other were asleep. It was the only way, he said, to keep up a constant attack until the enemy was seen off. Unsurprisingly, no one had much sleep that night, though strangely Shirley was lulled into a doze by the sound of the aircraft landing and taking off in a rhythmic pattern. In her dreams she was piloting a Spitfire and experiencing the heady joy of lift-off.

The following day gave the troupe a break before their performance. In the morning sun they walked out along paths over the Gower Peninsula, trying to avoid looking back towards Cardiff, where smoke hung in dark smears across the otherwise matchless blue sky. In the afternoon their rehearsal routine was relaxed, and in the evening their performance of *Coppélia* received a rapturous welcome from the airmen and staff alike. All were grateful for a spell of light relief from the traumas of the War which, in Wales, had been quite as harrowing as anywhere else the company had visited.

In fact the tour of South Wales was eye-opening for the members of Aurora, who had expected to discover a rural idyll, unaffected by the conflict. In fact they discovered a small country that had by no means escaped the dreadful ravages of warfare and had suffered more than its fair share. Their travels took them along the seemingly peaceful coast-line from airbase to airbase, each of which had its own story to tell, the worst probably being that of Pembroke Dock, the base of the RAF and US Navy flying boats.

As the locals were all too eager to recount, early in the War on 19th August 1940, the dock had been blitzed by three enemy aircraft. An oil tank, containing thousands of gallons of fuel oil suffered a direct hit, exploded, and set alight the neighbouring tanks. The fire was the worst in Britain since the Great Fire of London in 1666. Despite the efforts of armies of firemen from as far away as Birmingham, it raged for eighteen days. From the south up to Aberystwyth in the west, to Anglesey in the north, the story of large-scale bombing designed to intimidate the local populations, to destroy the garrisons and naval bases, and to put airfields out of action, was the same everywhere.

Ultimately, the return of Aurora to smoky London at the end of June was greeted with relief by all concerned, not least by Shirley herself.

33

On her return to South Cross, Shirley looked in at the shop to say hello to her father, but the queue of customers was so long, he only waved and called out, "See you later, Shirl!" Expecting the flat to be empty, she took her time mounting the stairs, dragging her heavy suitcase behind her. There was no need for hurry now. The lengthy flurry of touring activity was well and truly over for the time being, and she was looking forward to the luxury of a week of relaxation before practising and rehearsing for the autumn round of engagements. Surely her father must have heard from John by now, and would have told him that she was coming home. She would start by making herself a cup of tea and then collapse into the sagging cushions of the old sofa, waiting for the phone to ring.

She had not reckoned on finding Ted already at home. He was sitting at the table scanning the pages of the evening newspaper, probably searching for some hidden code essential to his work – or his love life – so she simply said "Hello, Ted!" and headed for the kitchen, where for once everything was remarkably clean and well ordered.

"I'll have a cup of tea, if you're making one!" he called out in his typical offhand greeting to his sister. Not best pleased with this offhand welcome, she gave him his tea without a word, and then took hers into her bedroom, where she lay down and fell asleep until her father's tread on the stairs at the end of his working day woke her up.

Reggie's welcome was more fulsome than her brother's had been. He flung his arms around his daughter, exclaiming, "Oh, my poppet, I'm so pleased to see you home! That bombing of Cardiff really had me worried. Thank goodness you hadn't gone a day earlier – you would have been caught up in it, and then who knows what might have happened to you!"

He pulled out his handkerchief and blew his nose noisily. "No need to get upset, Pa," she reassured him. "I'm home now and luckily we were never in danger, although we did see the cloud of smoke and ash over Cardiff from a long way off. It was dreadful, so that was why we went to

Swansea instead. Mind you, one thousand two hundred and something bombs had already been dropped there." She gave him another hug and said, "Oh! It's lovely to be home. I have to say, although the phone lines were unreliable it was a great help that we could keep in touch with you and Maud, and that you were able to keep in touch with Jack, otherwise we would have been in a mess. But let's not bother about that now. Believe it or not, I am quite looking forward to cooking the supper!"

"Hold on!" Reggie exclaimed. "I'll cook the supper while you have a rest. Anyhow, we have a friend coming to join us."

"I've had a rest already," she replied. "Anyhow, who is this friend?"

"Not someone I think you know, so it's rather inconvenient they've decided to come today," was Reggie's only explanation.

"In that case, let's cook the supper together and I'll tell you all about the tour, because I won't be able to do that with a visitor present," she suggested.

On a shelf in the larder Shirley found a large chicken. "Oh, what a treat!" she cried.

"Eileen knew you were coming home this week, though none of us knew quite when. She brought us this chicken as a welcome-home present from her brother's farm," said Reggie.

"It will be a treat for all of us, and look, there are new potatoes and carrots to go with it. And she also brought some fresh eggs. They're down there on the bottom shelf of the larder."

Shirley covered the chicken with lard before putting it in the oven. "You peel the potatoes and carrots, Pa," she bade him. "I'm going to make an egg custard to go in the bottom of the oven, and while we're doing that, I'll tell you all about the tour – but let me look for the nutmeg first."

They settled to their tasks while Shirley regaled her father with almost every detail of the Welsh experience, of all the performances from Swansea onwards, of the major successes and standing ovations in theatres in towns, and in village halls.

She also entertained him with an account of the hitches, not all of them minor, on stages in barns, halls and Nissen huts, the worst being a nail that emerged in the floor of the stage in a barn which had been converted to a large performance venue for all the local people as well as the troops from a nearby garrison.

"You wouldn't believe it! I saw it coming up through the floorboards, but there was nothing I could do!" she declared with due drama. "I just prayed that Maria wouldn't tread on it in the middle of her flamenco routine. But of course she did. It ripped through her ballet shoe and gashed her foot. So the performance had to be stopped while she was taken off stage.

Luckily there was a doctor in the audience, and he treated her, though the nail had to be eased out of her foot by a carpenter! It was a disaster, but the show went on. Fortunately, Maria's foot healed quite quickly, thanks to the doctor, but we had to have the interval there and then. Then I took over, although Maria insisted she was all right, but obviously she wasn't. I'm glad the doctor was there. After the show he came backstage to see her and said very firmly she shouldn't dance for the next week. Goodness, that was frightful!"

"That's dreadful, poor girl!" Reggie agreed. "But what about the travelling home? I hope it wasn't as bad as the journey out?"

"Well, we didn't have the same amount of disruption, thank goodness, but the trains were crowded with lots of troops, going on leave I suppose." She was interrupted at that moment, by a ring at the doorbell. "That will be your visitor. You'd better let him – or her – in," said she.

In all the excitement of telling him about the tour, she had forgotten about the unknown visitor. Perhaps, she speculated, it might be Madame, although it didn't seem likely that he would ever have invited "that woman" to dinner. She hummed a tune from *The Nutcracker*, the *Waltz of the Flowers*, and continued with her culinary preparations.

In the distance she heard voices on the stairs – two voices, her father's and that of another man. Suddenly she recognized the second voice, let a cracked egg fall into the half-prepared custard, and ran out onto the landing. There, coming up the stairs with her father, was her fiancé! Weeping for joy, she rushed to greet him on the landing. He gathered her up in his arms, while Reggie discreetly disappeared into the kitchen. She buried her face into his shoulder, and he buried his into her hair as he lifted her off the ground. "John, John!" was all she could whisper into his khaki uniform, and "Shirley, Shirley!" was all he could whisper into her hair. Conscious only of each other, they were not aware of Ted creeping out of the living room to join his father in the kitchen, and even then they were unable to string two sensible words together.

Over dinner, the conversation was stinted: the two lovers gazed into each other's eyes in silent communication across the table, while Ted and Reggie kept their eyes fastened on their plates. Embarrassed by the silence, Ted took the plunge: "So where have you been lately, John?" he asked.

John wrenched his gaze away from Shirley. "Oh, all over the place," he replied cagily, "but now and then returning to base in Aberdeen, with the occasional trip down here to London."

Almost apologetically, he explained, "Unfortunately I wasn't needed in Wales, so there was no way I could get in touch with Shirley at all." He smiled at her and paused, wondering what to say next.

Ted took advantage of the pause to ask, "You're a liaison officer, aren't you?" He was hoping for an expansive reply but expected only a brush-off.

However, John answered quite openly. "Yes, that's right," he said, "and my next stop is Washington DC; I'm sorry to say I have to leave tomorrow."

Shirley uttered a little cry and turned pale; Reggie gulped and let his fork drop onto his plate with a clatter.

Ted alone had the presence of mind to continue the conversation, asking, "So how are you travelling? Not in a convoy, I hope?"

The conversation was now well and truly about the War. "In fact there's less of a worry about convoys now, because as you probably know, we bombed twenty-five U-boats out of action in the North Atlantic a couple of months ago!" said John with a triumphant smile. "That was a great victory, another sign that maybe at last the fortunes of the War are beginning to turn in our favour. Goodness knows, though, that sign has taken a long time to come." He shook his head. "Roughly speaking they" – he meant the enemy – "were bombing upwards of six hundred thousand tons of shipping a month and, as I'm sure you know, at the cost of thousands of lives."

Shirley sensed that the conversation was degenerating into another of those long-winded discussions about the War, of which she had heard so many. John directed a quick pensive smile at her, as if reading her thoughts, before addressing Ted again. "But in answer to your question, Ted, no, I'm not travelling in a convoy; I'm lucky enough to be going in a flying boat from Southampton! That should be fun! I wish you could all come with me." He glanced round the assembled company of the father, his son and his daughter. Ted and Shirley caught each other's eye, each willing the other not to mention their mother and her flight to Southampton from America in a flying boat.

"Yes, yes, indeed, we should all like that," said Reggie quietly, though without any show of enthusiasm, "but there's not much hope of doing so," he added.

Ted and Shirley kept quiet: both knew that, quite apart from the flying boat dimension, a trip to Washington DC, unlikely though that was, would inevitably involve meeting their mother again, and that was not something that either of them was keen to do. Indeed they were surprised that their father had embraced the idea at all, not that he had done so very vigorously.

Untypically, Reggie stood up to start clearing plates away; Ted took the hint, picked up the serving dishes and followed him out of the room. They were gone a long time and the noises from the kitchen suggested that they were giving the four dinner plates, the cutlery and the serving dishes, the most vigorous scrubbing they had ever had. Then there came some discussion, which, it transpired afterwards, centred on the parlous state of the egg custard, the top of which was punctuated by bits of eggshell.

In the mean time, John leant across the dining table and took Shirley's hands in his. "Your hands are cold, my darling!" he exclaimed.

"That happens when I have a shock," she said. "I didn't know you were coming home, and now you tell me you're leaving tomorrow! I thought you were with Monty in the desert!"

"I'm sorry about that," he replied. "I was with Monty, but not for long this time. I suppose you might say that trip was for strategic discussions. I've been trying to get in touch with you ever since I came back. That last parting of ours was terrible. I don't want that ever to happen again. Then I was so worried about you when Cardiff was bombed; that was your first stop, wasn't it?"

"Yes. It was supposed to be, but we went to Swansea instead, and after that everything was more or less fine. It was an extensive tour, though, and we are all exhausted now. I was longing for you and me to have time together, but it looks as if that's not going to happen."

She glanced up at him with such a woeful expression that he came to her side of the table and sat with his arm round her shoulders.

"Let's make the most of this evening," he said. "Why don't we tell your father and your brother about our engagement? We could have quite a party before we have to separate."

Shirley brightened up. "I'll fetch my ring!" she declared and bounded out of the room.

When she returned, Ted and Reggie were doubtfully eyeing the egg custard, which they had put down in the centre of the table. "I don't think we are going to be able to eat that; look at all the bits of eggshell in it!" Ted observed.

"I'm sure it'll be fine," said John encouragingly.

"Oh, that's my fault!" Shirley chipped in, addressing John. "I heard you coming up the stairs, and dropped an egg and its shell into the mixture – and I forgot the nutmeg," she said, laughing, "so it's partly your fault for taking me by surprise!"

Reggie served the pudding which resembled scrambled eggs with sharp fragments in it, rather than custard.

"Oh, even worse," Shirley admitted after tasting a spoonful. "I forgot to put the sugar in!"

In the midst of this jollity, John chose his moment to stand up and make the announcement, letting Shirley's father and her brother into the secret of the engagement. It was wholeheartedly received, amid so much rejoicing that Reggie went downstairs and came back brandishing a dusty bottle of champagne which bore an ancient, torn and stained label. "This should be good!" he announced as the cork flew across the room.

In the days after John left for the USA, Shirley's mood swung repeatedly between blissful happiness as she surveyed her emerald ring, and despair, not only at the continuing state of warfare which might bring that blissful happiness to a sudden and tragic end, but also at the niggling concern that John had probably not yet told his own family about the engagement. There had been no time to ask him before he left, and in any case she did not want to spoil the fast-disappearing, precious hours, minutes and seconds left to them. Now it was too late for that, with the result that her imagination began to run riot at the reaction the news might receive from his family, most of all from his mother.

John had promised to ring occasionally from Washington DC, if and when the opportunity presented itself, but the niggling worry had ceased to be niggling, for it had taken such a strong hold over her that she feared not being able to contain herself when she spoke to him. Despite her best efforts to contain it, the question of his parents' reaction to the engagement would inevitably come tumbling out of her mouth and, depending on the answer, might lead to a quarrel over the phone, which would be disastrous. Rightly or wrongly, she told her father and

Ted to say either that she was out or that she was asleep, if a phone call came through from the USA.

Reggie and Ted were not at all happy about conveying this message of half-truths to someone they liked and greatly admired. After a couple of such calls, Ted said so. "What on earth's going on between you and John?" he asked her rather sternly one evening after he had had to deliver another off-putting excuse over the phone. "He's such a nice chap, and so brave. Pa and I don't like the way you are treating him. Why on earth don't you want to talk to him? What's going on with all this dithering? Why don't you just make up your mind and have done with it? I'd give anything to be able to talk to Hélène."

"He's nice and he's brave, but his mother is awful!" she retorted sharply. "I still feel scarred by that visit when I accompanied John to Norhambury, and as long as she is so hostile towards me, I don't think there can be any future for us together, even though we're engaged. You of all people should know what that's like!"

Ted was taken aback: he would never forget the hostility shown him by Hélène's mother, Madame de la Croix, when their teenage relationship blossomed. He therefore modified his tone and spoke in French, as he often did when talking about events that had happened or were happening in France.

"Ah, *voilà*, I see," he said slowly. "I do understand, because as you well know, I have been, probably still am, in the same situation myself. But that doesn't stop me loving Hélène, nor does it stop her loving me. And I know that's true because she sends me coded messages at work almost every day. If I don't hear from her, I'm frantic with worry."

"Well, I'm glad you hear from her – that must mean she's alive and well," said Shirley, modifying her own self-pity at the reminder of the stresses and strains of her brother's love life.

"Yes, it is a relief that her messages do come through fairly regularly," her brother replied, "though if they stop, then I really shall panic, because there's now a horrible man, a Gestapo Nazi, working in Lyon. His name's Barbie, Klaus Barbie: they call him the Butcher of Lyon – and I dread Hélène falling into his hands. He personally tortures Jews and Resistance fighters to death. You may not have heard they captured Jean Moulin, the head of the Resistance, a couple of weeks ago, and Barbie has just killed him." He shuddered and a shiver ran down Shirley's spine.

"As I keep saying, anyone would think you were ten years older than me!" she exclaimed. "You've put everything, including hostile prospective mothers-in-law into perspective, Ted! Let me know when John rings again, will you? I think I've been rather stupid – yet again!"

John did ring again, and Shirley did speak to him. "I'm so sorry!" she said immediately. "I should have come to the phone when you last rang, but I'm still recovering from the tour, which was much more exhausting than I was expecting, and I spend most days asleep before going out on patrol." This much was more or less true, so it was not necessary to tell him that she had previously decided not to talk to him. There were a few more calls from Washington, which she answered without mentioning his mother.

One evening, when he had already been gone for more than two weeks, and Shirley had begun her exercise and practice regime for the autumn repertoire in Madame's studio, John rang with an urgent question. "Are you free tomorrow?" he asked.

"Oh, yes! Tomorrow's Sunday, isn't it? So it's a day-off, not a practising day," she answered.

"Thank goodness!" he declared, at the other end of the crackling line. "Tomorrow I will be arriving in Southampton, and on Monday I have to return to barracks."

"Oh, no! Do you mean in Scotland?" she asked with a sinking heart.

"That's right, but I will be passing through London, and I wondered if we could meet? I'll catch an early train from Southampton, spend the day with you, and then catch a night train to travel north."

"Of course! Yes please! I long to see you. But come and stay here if you can!" she cried, releasing much pent-up anxiety and frustration down the phone line.

"In that case, I'll see if I can postpone my return by an extra day; it should be possible," he said with audible relief in his voice.

"Please do!" she urged him.

After a glorious day spent in London – glorious, not on account of the weather, but on account of the bliss of their reunion – Shirley took John home to stay for the permitted twenty-four extension to his leave. She was sure of a warm welcome for him at the flat, even if that were not yet to be accorded her by his mother in Norhambury. He, for his part, had brought back treasures from the United States for all the family. For Shirley, he had brought the thrill of the latest fashion invention: two pairs of nylon stockings.

For Ted, there were three bars of soap that floated, even in the meagre amount of water in the bath, and for Reggie, a couple of magazines, one on railroads, as they called them in America, and the other on cars, limousines so large and luxurious that they made his eyes pop out of his head.

"That's how it is over there," John explained, "everything's larger than life. You wouldn't believe it – huge cars and huge roads, huge spaces, and huge houses everywhere, not all cramped together as they are here. And the wealth is unbelievable! The people are bigger than we are, too, but that's because the meals are so enormous. They seem to live on steak. And what's more they don't have rationing. They are very friendly, informal and welcoming too." The conversation went on in this vein all evening, with many an expression of amazement at the wonders of the United States of America.

"Why don't you come up to Aberdeen to visit me?" John suggested in a moment of calm when he and Shirley were alone together. "This visit is far too rushed, and I want to see so much more of you."

"I'd love to come, but where would I stay?" she asked.

"That's not a problem; there are a few guest houses, in the parts of the city that haven't been bombed. I'll be sure to find you somewhere you'd like," he promised her.

"All right, that would be marvellous!" she agreed willingly. "I could still take a couple of weeks off before we start the autumn programme, so I could come any time soon, if you'll promise me you won't be dashing off somewhere else just as I arrive."

"I'll do my best," he promised, "but I had better warn you that Aberdeen is in a real mess; the Nazis came back in April, on the 21st to be precise, and blitzed the city, yet again. It seemed they were determined to obliterate it. It's not a pretty sight – in fact it is devastated. You'll find it changed from when you were there before."

"Even that wasn't good, but I'm fairly used to it, being in the ARP and living here," Shirley answered with a shrug, adding, "There's no end to it, is there?"

John left the next day, but not before having a quiet chat with Ted and Reggie in the kitchen. Shirley wondered what exactly it was that they were discussing.

The expectation of seeing her fiancé again very soon softened the blow of their separation, so that after seeing him off, there was a lightness in her step that she had not felt for some time, except when on the stage. It was a source of regret to her that there were still so many things about John that were a mystery to her, particularly concerning his role in the army. Since she had not had the opportunity to ask John himself, she decided to quiz her father, because he was most likely to know – and, of course, Ted if he were at home, which he was that evening.

Her father sighed at the question. Ted laughed. "You mean to say you're engaged to a liaison officer, and you don't know what he does?"

"No, why should I?" replied Shirley indignantly. "I've never met a liaison officer before, and I don't understand why he's always dashing about all over the place. Why did he go to America, for instance, after he'd come back from meeting Monty in the desert?"

Reggie intervened. "Come on, Ted. Your sister is quite right to ask, because a 'liaison officer' is really a cover for a much more serious appointment, so don't poke fun at her. As I understand it," he went on, choosing his words carefully, "a liaison officer is a military intelligence officer, and his job is to collect information, sift it for its accuracy and then use it to advise on strategy, and assist commanders in the field in the way they carry out tactical operations."

At this wordy and technical explanation, Shirley burst out in alarm, "Do you mean John's a spy?"

"No, not exactly, but he will be analysing information brought in by spies, which can be very inaccurate, and he will be testing it against other sources."

"What sort of information?" she wanted to know. "Oh, about the enemies' capabilities and weaknesses in their defences. So the intelligence officer will find out, for instance, if there's a build-up of enemy fuel or armaments, because those can indicate tank or army deployments, and he will pass this information on to the policymakers. Your John will have had specialized training, and they only choose the most intelligent and level-headed people for that."

"Is that why he went to America?" Shirley persisted.

"Yes, I imagine so. Rumour has it that there must be something big in the pipeline, so he doubtless went to talk to the American military." Reggie's information was in full flood. "And what's more, that's why he leaves his base often and comes to London to the War Office – even perhaps to Number Ten Downing Street as well, I shouldn't wonder."

Reggie paused to consider, while his offspring digested in silence what he had already said. He then resumed his discourse. "He's a brave chap, your John, Shirley, and I bet that's why he was seconded to Montgomery out in the desert in North Africa. Who knows where he will go next?" No sooner were his words out of his mouth than he regretted them, for Shirley's expression quickly changed from a glow of pleasure and pride to one of anxious dismay. He hastened to add, "Of one thing we can be sure: your John is a hero whose efforts will win the War for us!" Her father's attempts to allay her fears were unsuccessful.

That night, she turned her engagement ring from right to left and left to right on her finger, watching the small diamonds, on either side of the larger stone, sparkle in the lamplight while the emerald glowed a deep, rich, velvety green. Whatever happened, she must commit fully to the relationship, she realized, and perhaps that meant she should marry John as soon as possible. Then so many of the obstacles to their being together would be removed. Maybe she could live with him as his wife in the lodgings where he was billeted, and would be recognized as his next-of-kin in all circumstances.

"But what about the ballet?" a voice in her head intervened. How could she desert the ballet and the company that she had formed and for which she had worked so hard? The ballet was her lifeblood – without it she would be a nonentity. What would happen to Aurora without her? Cynthia wouldn't be able to run it on her own. The whole system, the whole organization, depended on her being at the centre of it. Not only on the practical level, but also on moral grounds, she had a duty to stay with Aurora as long as needed.

The performances brought joy and magic to the dull lives of the forces in their barracks, their bases and their garrisons, even if, as she suspected, some members of the audience came only to see the girls in their scanty costumes. That didn't matter. What did matter was that touring was her contribution to the War effort and she had to see it through. Whether in her heart of hearts she liked it or not, that was her duty.

Still, that need not stop her visiting John in Aberdeen and relishing the opportunity of being close to him, whenever possible. She would ask Cynthia and Madame to take over the rehearsals together for a week, or even two, and would leave for Scotland at the weekend.

34

On arrival in Aberdeen, Shirley was appalled to find the city in a worse state of ruin than when Aurora had performed there. Then she had been told that it had suffered more bombing than anywhere else except London. That was no longer the case: Aberdeen had now been bombed *more* than London. However, the sight of John waiting for her at the station, looking fit and handsome, distracted her from the chaos all around. He drove her in a staff car to her lodgings, introduced her to the landlady, Mrs McCrae, and then took her out to dinner in one of the few remaining restaurants in the city, far removed from the bomb sites.

"This being Sunday..." he began to say as they sat together at dinner. "This being Sunday," he repeated with a twinkle in his eye, "I wondered if you would like to get married next weekend?"

The knife and fork she was about to use to cut into the mouth-watering fish and chips on her plate, fell from Shirley's hands. "You *are* joking, aren't you?" she replied, her mouth wide open in astonishment. She quickly closed it into a winning smile. "If you're serious, of course I would, the sooner the better! But I've only just arrived, and I don't have any special wedding clothes or shoes with me, and it would be nice to have Pa and Ted here and... and..."

Before his sudden suggestion of the wedding came up, she had been on the point of telling him about Alan and the baby, for on the journey she had decided that honesty was the best policy, and that once and for all, she should be quite open with him about the tragedy in her past. How could he not be sympathetic? The prospect of marriage in less than a week's time threw her into confusion, and words failed her.

"Don't you worry about any of that," her fiancé reassured her, referring to the practicalities of the wedding, and unaware of her brief abstraction. She realized that she was missing what he was saying, which was, "It can all be arranged in a flash, and I'll buy you whatever you want. Though, as far as I'm concerned, I have to say you look fine as you are." Fashion clearly was not his strong point.

"And what about your parents?" she asked anxiously, unsure that this was really such a good idea. "They don't even know we're engaged – think what a shock it'll be for them to find out we're married!"

"Look, my love, we're grown-ups," he said, smiling, "we don't have to run our lives to please anyone else, though it would be nice if my parents could be happy about our wedding, like your…" He was about to say "father and brother", but stopped himself in time, deciding to leave that for later.

"Anyhow, I did write to tell my parents about our engagement and to invite them to come, so now they know. And if you want to invite some of your ballet friends, we could throw a party."

"How can we do that?" she asked.

"What do you mean 'how?'" he replied. "Obviously these things take some organizing, but we have five days to do all that. Five days is a long time in the army!"

"All right, Let's go ahead, then, if you're sure there won't be any problems!" Shirley agreed, relaxing into the discussion and lavishing an even more ecstatic smile on her fiancé. "I can see I shall have to learn to trust that you can organize a wedding in five days."

"That's not difficult," he said with amazing assurance. "I started on it as soon as I arrived here from London, so most of the arrangements are already in place! And don't worry about your father and brother. I have to admit I told them what I had in mind the morning before I left."

By this stage Shirley had placed her knife and fork neatly on the edge of her plate, for plainly, eating that unaccustomed treat of delectable, battered cod and chips, and digesting all of John's plans at one and the same time were incompatible, so she abandoned her meal in favour of closer concentration on every word he uttered, in case either *she* missed something important, or in case *he* had forgotten something important.

"I say, you are a dark horse, aren't you?" she said with a grin, looking him straight in the eye. "So you had all this in mind, without telling me! I'm glad, though, that you thought to tell Pa and Ted." She took a moment to reflect. "What about the church, and what about my clothes, and flowers, and where will the reception take place?" she asked, showering him with questions.

"Anybody would think you had done this before if you can arrange it all so quickly!" she teased him, raising her eyebrows quizzically.

"No, rest assured, I certainly have not – no chance of that!" he said firmly, looking down at his plate. He ate a forkful of chips hastily, and then glanced up at her. His face was rather flushed as he went on, "The truth is I'm so excited that I want to marry you as soon as I can. Don't you feel like that too?"

"Yes, of course I do, but I do want it to be right. And oh, there's dear Eileen who's been like a grandmother to me, and her husband, Cousin Archie, who works in the shop with Pa. I'm afraid I have to invite Madame Belinskaya, my ballet mistress. She's an amazing character, but she would never forgive me if I didn't invite her."

She was about to produce a torrent of more names when John reached across the table and took her hand, saying, "Calm down, my darling, it's all under control. You see, I have a staff to help me. There's a secretary and her assistant – they will deal with invitations and accommodation and take you shopping for whatever else you might want, lipstick and powder or whatever you girls put on your faces, and a hairdresser to make you look unrecognizable, and a florist – that's all taken care of. I've booked a church and a reception, so all you need to do is sit back and enjoy it and be ready for the car that will pick you up next Saturday morning."

"Wait a minute, though," she wailed, "I don't have my ration book with me; I left it in London, because I never thought that I would be buying clothes here."

"I'm sure we'll manage somehow. Why don't we send a telegram to your father asking him to send it? It will be with us in a day or two," came his unfazed response.

John had an answer for everything until she asked, "Will it matter that I was born a Catholic?" That was the one question that left him flummoxed, and her wondering why on earth she had posed it. It had never been her intention.

No longer quite so sure about all his arrangements, his face fell, as he said, "Ah, well, I didn't know about that. I'm Church of England, and I don't know what the protocol is for marrying a Catholic, or the other way round for that matter."

Shirley was surprised at his hesitancy. "I don't think it will matter," said she, wishing more than ever that she had not confessed to being a Catholic, but endeavouring to sound positive. "I haven't been to a Catholic church for ages, but as far as I know the services are not very different from the Church of England's, except that they are all in Latin. I went to a Catholic church sometimes with my mother, but didn't really understand what was going on. I think I must have been christened in a Catholic church, but does it really matter? My mother is a Catholic, but she left us, so perhaps it's not relevant."

She pushed her plate aside, no longer fancying the battered cod, and placed her elbow on the table and, with her chin in her cupped hand, sighed. "I wish I knew what my parents did in the Great War," she said, "and how they managed to marry, because Pa's certainly not a Catholic. I'm not sure what he is – Non-Conformist, or something like that."

Having said all this, but carefully avoiding all mention of France, she then remembered that the problem was not so relevant in that country because the civil ceremony took place separately from the religious one.

"We can't ask them, so I think I had better find a Catholic priest and ask him," John was saying, his earlier confidence having swiftly evaporated. "I believe there's one who comes to the base. Let's hope it's not a problem."

A gloomy silence fell between them, until after some deliberation, Shirley, spurred into action by thoughts of French procedures, perked up and announced, "It's just occurred to me! If all else fails we could get married in the Registry Office. How would you feel about that?"

"That's fine by me," he answered, perking up. "It would've been nice to have a church wedding – my mother would have liked that – but the Registry Office will save us a lot of bother. Anyway, don't let it spoil things. Let's have it in the Registry Office, followed by a small reception, for as many people as can come!"

The ration-book arrived in record time, enabling the bride-to-be to browse the few available dresses in a department store, which showed dismal signs of bomb damage in its battered façade, and in the barricades around a whole wing that seemed to be tottering on the point of collapse. On the other side of the main building, on a plot where evidently a bomb had fallen, the debris had been cleared away and the crater filled to allow for a hastily erected prefabricated structure, which served as the dress department.

Since she was not now looking for a white wedding dress, Shirley did not need the help of her future husband's staff. All things considered, she was happier not to be wearing white. Instead, she found a pretty, close-fitting two-piece suit in a peachy pink linen, matching shoes and a small white hat with a veil, all of which showed off her slim figure and blonde curls to advantage. The fit of the suit, she reckoned, would dispel any suggestion that she might already be pregnant. There were plenty of clothing rations in her book, since she had not bought clothes for years, or even worn her best clothes, and that was the result of rationing, and also because all her attention had been focused on her ballet costumes.

Buying new clothes reminded her of dear Miss Patience's wedding to Dr Ellison near Brighton. For that, Shirley was certain that she had worn that lovely, green outfit her mother had bought for her in Paris before the War. She laughed to herself at the memory of her crazy friend, Violet, dashing late for the train in London. Violet had looked such a frightful mess that she and Cynthia had to brush her hair on the train and take her shopping in Brighton before the wedding to buy the cheapest clothes available. Shirley's thoughts then wandered to the wedding itself in that little village in Sussex – what was it called? There in the street she saw a man who must have been Alan's father, because he resembled her lost love so closely. Wrongly she had supposed that Alan might be with him too. Oh, how that sudden recollection brought back memories of those long years of searching for him, that wonderful man, the Spitfire pilot, her first fiancé!

The shock of that unexpected memory was so acute that absentmindedly she made her way to a tearoom where she sat down, distracted by the sudden re-emergence of recollections, which so recently she had tried to repress. She was glad to be alone. Perhaps this would be her last opportunity to commune with Alan and remember their passionate love for each other, the love that had known fulfilment during those few short days before he was shot down over the Channel and never seen again.

The pain of that memory had not diminished; it was still searing. She abandoned her tea, paid the bill and, carrying her collection of shopping bags, went for a walk along the seashore. There, more ghoulish remnants of bombing raids, visible on the beach and on the promenade, disturbed her reflections. She stopped occasionally to look out over the sea, deceptively calm, blue and clear in the summer sun, the same cruel sea into which further south, Alan had disappeared in July 1940.

She walked on until there were no more memories, but could not bring herself to retrace her steps, for she felt herself once again to be caught in a limbo between Alan and John: turning round would mean turning her back on Alan – and that she suddenly did not feel ready to do, not yet. It was right to give him all her attention for the last time while John was otherwise engaged. He would not be free, he had said, until eight, and it was now only six. After all it was not as if she were having to choose between Alan and John.

Alan was no more whilst John was alive and healthy, his strength renewed after the horror of the North Africa campaign: that is, he was strong and healthy when last she had seen him only a couple of hours previously. Supposing some terrible fate had befallen him since then? You could never tell in this War. She panicked and told herself yet again that she must reconcile herself to Alan as a memory from the past, while John was the future, her future.

Thus resolved, she headed for her guesthouse. There she found her fiancé, soon to be her husband, waiting for her on the doorstep. "Shirley!" he cried out. "Where have you been? I finished early, so I came to fetch you. There's a party tonight and I wondered if you'd like to come and meet some of my friends."

Jolted into the present, she simply replied, "That's nice. I went for a walk for a breath of fresh air after doing my shopping – so here I am!"

They embraced on the doorstep. John was full of news. He had cancelled the church and booked the Registry Office for the following Saturday morning; he had rung the reception venue to tell them that the wedding would be a modest luncheon affair; and he had been in touch with a handful of friends to invite them to come, and so on, seemingly *ad infinitum*.

Shirley hardly registered all the items on his list of arrangements and limited herself to nodding at each one and saying, "Good, that sounds good."

"Aren't you pleased?" he asked anxiously as his list drew to a close.

"Yes, yes, of course I am!" she said, trying to sound appreciative. "I would like to put these parcels down, though. I've been carrying them a long way!"

"Oh, I'm sorry!" he said. "Here let me carry them for you." He reached out to take them from her.

"No, don't worry. I can carry them up to my room, and then I think I'll put my feet up for a little while," she replied. "I'll feel fresher for the evening if I can have a little rest now. I'll see you later!" She kissed him on the mouth and went inside.

The party that evening proved to be somewhat exhausting. John enthusiastically introduced her to a stream of his friends, who apparently worked with him. "Here's Roger," he said, introducing an older man. "He's a colonel. And this is Paul – he's a major. This is Richard – he's a ship's captain. Here's Tom – he's a sergeant…" And so the list went on, endlessly. Shirley shook hands with each one of them. They all smiled and said how nice it was to meet her, and what a fine fellow John was, until every one of them was accounted for. It was, she supposed, like a roll call, and it left her weary.

Was this the society she was going to be moving in? she wondered, hoping to meet some women – wives or girlfriends perhaps. Maybe even some of them had seen the Aurora performances, but women there were none – not at this party anyhow.

The day of the wedding dawned bright, clear and warm. With some regret that the marriage was not to be a church affair with all the traditional splash of excitement, colour and show, Shirley wondered whether it really was worth dressing up. She doubted that her father and Ted would have been able to get away from the shop, and considered it highly improbable that Eileen would be with them.

What's more, neither Madame nor Cynthia and Pete would be free to make the journey to Aberdeen, and in any case the cost would be prohibitive for them. Those of John's friends she had met were a nice enough bunch of chaps, though not exactly her friends, and she had little to say to them. This of all days, her wedding day, was when she needed her own friends around her most of all.

With a hint of despondency, she cast her eye over her linen suit hanging on a hook in the bedroom door. It was pretty, but ordinary by comparison with her ballet costumes. She took it down and put it on, regretting that it was so ordinary. Nevertheless, she comforted herself, it was better than most of the clothes money could buy in wartime. She had decided not to go to a hairdresser that morning because, as John had said, she knew she would come away looking unrecognizable and, since she was not going to dress up in a gown and veil with all the trimmings, it seemed rather unnecessary. Anyhow, with her hat perched on top of her curls, she decided that her outfit would suffice.

A tap on the door interrupted her musings. There on the threshold stood Eileen.

Shirley flung her arms round the elderly lady and, in tears of joy, exclaimed, "Eileen! I never expected you would come! I'm so pleased to see you! I was feeling rather low, here all by myself."

Eileen hugged her, saying, "Shirley dear! I've said it before: you are the closest I have ever had to a granddaughter. I couldn't let you get married without being here for you, especially as your mother is so far away! Sit down; I'll have to put your hat on again. It's all skew-whiff, but your hair needs tidying up first: you can't go downstairs like that."

Shirley sat while Eileen busied herself with a brush, comb and hairpins. "Now that's better," Eileen declared, then glanced at her watch. "I think your car will have arrived by now, and your future husband will be waiting for you at the Registry Office, so down we go!"

Thereafter the day's proceedings improved immeasurably as far as Shirley was concerned and exceeded her expectations. The guest-house staff and Mrs McCrae, the proprietor, greeted her with a cheer when she came down to the stairs to the lobby. When they opened the main door for her, the sight of the crowd of familiar faces waiting outside was overwhelming. First and foremost, her father and Ted, dressed in their pre-War best suits, enveloped her in big bear hugs, which, she was afraid, would send her hat awry again. There, extremely prominent, was Madame Belinskaya, looking as if she had just stepped off the stage, her greying-black hair scraped back into a bun on the top of her head. Plastered in rather lurid make-up, she was wearing the most extravagant outfit of flowing purple silk.

"*Ma chérie!*" she proclaimed for all to hear. "Thees ees thee moss bootifool ballet I 'ave evair been to!"

Secretly amused, Shirley suspected that Madame's gown had been made from the rest of the purple silk in Eileen's attic. She hoped Eileen had not been called in to make it for her. Behind Madame and scarcely visible stood Cynthia and Pete.

"Shirl!" exclaimed Cynthia. "We had to come – we couldn't leave you to do this all on your own!"

With Cynthia there stood a group of Aurora dancers – Maria and Pedro, Andrei and even Doris. "I thought you were supposed to be rehearsing in London," Shirley said in the sternest of tones, but then broke into laughter, exclaiming, "I'm so glad to see you all!"

The group dispersed into the fleet of cars sent by John, and set off for the Registry Office. "My poppet," said her father, who sat beside her in the first car of the convoy, "I won't say this is a surprise, because you surely know that John told us about it in London, but I am very pleased that you are marrying that fine young officer. I have no doubt he will be a good husband to you." He gazed out of the window before sounding a note of caution. "Make the most of your happiness, because I don't have to tell you, this War is ruining lots of lives, and it's not finished yet."

"Yes, Pa, I do know that – you don't have to tell me," answered Shirley soberly. "And there's just one thing, Pa: please don't ever mention Alan and my miscarriage to John, and tell Ted too, will you?"

"Of course," Reggie promised. "Don't worry your head about that!"

Thanks to John's immaculate organization, everything went according to plan; indeed it exceeded expectations. John, in full regalia, stood at the door of the Registry Office with another officer on one side of him and a tall, young woman with long, dark brown hair, on the other.

"Shirley, darling, you look wonderful," John exclaimed on opening the car door. "Good morning, Mr Marlow," he said to Reggie. "I hope it hasn't been too much of a challenge for you to leave your business?"

"No, no, my cousin Archie is looking after that, so that Ted and I could manage to get away," Reggie replied. He then introduced Eileen, saying, "This is Eileen, Archie's wife. She's like a mother or grandmother to Shirley."

Given how relatively small the gathering was, the introductions seemed to go on interminably. Shirley and her father had to make the acquaintance of John's best man, an army friend called Arthur, who had not been at the party, and also of the young woman whom Shirley had noticed on her arrival. She seemed familiar, though Shirley was having difficulty placing her.

"Shirley," said John finally, "I don't think you met my sister, Evelyn, when you came to Norhambury."

Shirley searched Evelyn's face for signs of a hostile reaction, like the one John's mother had given her, but Evelyn's expression showed not the least sign of hostility. Indeed, she gave Shirley a welcoming smile and, instead of shaking hands with her, stepped forward to hug her. "Shirley, you will be my sister!" she exclaimed.

Shirley was moved, and did not have an answer to that warm reception, except to smile in return and squeeze Evelyn's hand. She whispered, "Thanks for coming. See you later."

On the whole the ceremony was conducted with the military efficiency to be expected of a garrison city, once Reggie, with his daughter on his arm, had succeeded in negotiating his bulk through the filing cabinets of the Registry Office and the scattered chairs provided for elderly guests.

The more youthful of the guests had to stand for the duration, which was long enough only for the bride and groom to answer the questions appropriately, declare their intent of being man and wife and sign the register, witnessed by the best man and by Evelyn.

The Registrar, clearly more interested in processing as many couples as he could that Saturday morning, dispensed with niceties and hurried the wedding party off to make way for the next couple. Their joy unsullied, John and Shirley emerged arm in arm into sunshine and the sound of bagpipes. The sight of a guard of honour in Highland dress on either side of the path, holding up drawn swords in an archway above the heads of the newly-married couple, drew exclamations of amazement from the wedding party, and then smiles, laughter and cheers, confetti and congratulations burst out all around.

Reggie and Eileen were the first to receive the guests at the reception. Shirley's guests, especially Madame, wanted to talk for much longer than John's, although the former were fewer in number. Indeed it appeared that the whole garrison had turned out in support of John. Shirley was on edge, fearing lest one of her party, most notably Madame, might prove to be a liability and bring up information about her that she definitely did not want aired on that occasion. She need not have worried: Madame was charm and dignity itself, as if she were on stage playing the part of a gracious queen in a ballet.

The only slight cause for anxiety occurred when she wagged a finger at John, ordering him not to interfere with Shirley's career as a dancer, because if he did, he would have her to answer to. He laughed off the command and said, "Of course not, Madame. I should be far too afraid of you to do any such thing!" At this Madame moved on and went to talk to the dancers who, like her, had come so far north to be with Shirley.

There followed a lavish banquet, consisting of smoked salmon with asparagus, quail with green beans and lemon posset with honeycomb wafers, delicacies that had been unavailable in London for as long as Shirley could remember. It made her wonder how John was going to pay for all this, and if she should offer to help out. Her attention, however, was divided between the food on her plate and conversation with her immediate neighbour, John's sister, Evelyn.

Sensing Evelyn's shyness, Shirley took the lead, for, after all, Evelyn had not been party to her mother's hostility, although she had witnessed it.

"It's so good of you to travel such a long way to come to our wedding!" Shirley began enthusiastically.

"Yes, well," Evelyn replied gently, "it was too far for Mother and Father, but I wanted to come. The journey was long, but not so bad in the Flying Scotsman from London, quite good fun really, and very fast. And I love the scenery up here; I'm going walking tomorrow and that will be a treat."

This, Shirley considered, was a good start. "Oh, I haven't seen much scenery yet," she confessed. "The last time I came here I was working – ballet, you know – and there wasn't a minute to spare for sightseeing. In fact I really wasn't expecting to get married here so soon. I imagined we would get married when the War was over, but your brother sprang the idea on me when I arrived last weekend to stay for only a couple of days, so my Pa had to send my clothing coupons, and I've had to shop for clothes, shoes and everything else to be ready for today! And what's more I didn't even know that my Pa and my brother, let alone my aunt and my friends, would be here!"

Evelyn was clearly startled at this. "Is that true?" she asked. "We – that is, mother, father and I – we thought this had been planned for ages!"

"No, not at all," said Shirley, somewhat complacent at having truth on her side. "We were engaged, but I had hoped John would have told your parents about that. Anyhow I'm glad he did spring it on me, because now he's my husband, come what may, and that's one certainty, whatever else happens in this horrible War. He's such a lovely man!"

Evelyn nodded in agreement. "But may I ask," she enquired tentatively, as if embarrassed at having to ask this question, which perhaps she had been told to ask by a certain person who was absent. "Didn't you think of having the wedding in a church? I'd have liked to play the organ for you." Shirley was surprised and then, caught off-guard, said something that she later regretted. "Yes, it would have been more traditional, but the problem was that, like my mother, I'm a Catholic, a lapsed Catholic, and it would have taken too long to apply for all the necessary dispensations. But I would have been so pleased if you could have played for us!"

"I see," said Evelyn pensively, and said no more, at which Shirley feared that the mention of her Catholic background had not been such a good idea.

At that moment, the piper, who was also acting as the Master of Ceremonies, called for silence and announced that the speeches were about to begin, so what had become an uncomfortably awkward conversation drew to a close. Too preoccupied by Evelyn's hesitant reaction, Shirley scarcely paid any attention to the speeches except when John proposed a toast to his "beautiful bride". She fervently hoped that she had not further tarnished her reputation in the Platt household, but defiantly told herself there was nothing wrong with being a Catholic and she shouldn't have to apologize for that.

Everyone around her was laughing while she sat in solemn contemplation. She forced herself to listen to the best man's speech which, delivered in broad Scots, was unintelligible. He seemed to be telling his audience what a great and courageous chap John was, and how proud she should be to have him as her husband. She forced a smile and gave a gracious nod in his direction.

Glasses were being filled for more toasts when again the Master of Ceremonies called for quiet before introducing a speech, as he said, from the bride's father. At first Shirley could not think who this father could be, never imagining that it might possibly be her very own pa! She was astounded to see him getting to his feet, let alone making a speech! The last time he had done that was when he had addressed the ARP patrol after the blitzing of their neighbourhood, but giving a speech at his daughter's wedding was bound to be different.

But speak Reggie did, and his speech was charming and encouraging. He told the military guests not of Shirley's French Catholic background, nor of her dual nationality, nor of Alan, but talked briefly and movingly of her constant courage in the Air Raid Precautions team in some of the worst and most terrifying blitzing London had ever seen. He listed some of her major achievements, particularly her rescue of little Albert and his grandmother from a collapsing house. He also talked of her prowess as a ballet dancer and her determination to entertain the troops by touring to RAF, naval and army bases with her ballet company – and, as if that were not enough, he praised her care, her housekeeping and her cooking for him and her brother, Ted, injured in action in France. Here he gestured to Ted to make sure that everyone present could see Ted's sleeve tucked into the pocket of his jacket.

Finally he said how glad he was that two such dedicated people should have found each other, and he had no doubt that their marriage would be a happy one, whereupon he invited the wedding guests to raise their glasses to the bride and groom, which they all did with cheers and cries of "To John and Shirley!"

That evening the dewy-eyed couple reminisced about the day, over yet another luxurious meal in a first-class hotel up in the Highlands, where to Shirley's relief, there were no signs of bombing. Ecstatically happy, neither of them wanted the day, their special day, to end.

"Let's make every day like this for ever, shall we?" John suggested, and Shirley readily agreed, adding the proviso: "If this horrible War lets us..."

Although younger than John, all her experiences had made her more cautious than him.

"I think the tide's turning; it won't go on for much longer," he reassured her, but she had heard that too many times for too long to be convinced.

"We'll have to take each day as it comes," she said sagely.

"Of course, but don't let's spoil tonight by worrying about what might happen next." He took her by the hand and led her upstairs to their honeymoon suite.

When she woke the next morning, she reached out across the wide double bed for her husband's arm, but on his side of the bed, the sheets were cold: he was not there. She was alone in the bed! Horrified, she sat up, her heart beating rapidly. Where was he? Had there been a bombing raid in the night? His clothes had gone, and so had he. Had he deserted her already? She jumped out of bed, dressed hurriedly, pulled a comb through her hair, and then ran downstairs.

She pushed open the heavy glass door into the breakfast room, and there he was seated at a table for two, reading a sheet of paper and eating a kipper! She was furious.

"John, John, what are you doing here?" she demanded angrily, already breaking the previous evening's vows to maintain their wedding day happiness for ever.

He looked up in surprise. "Shirley, darling," he cried, "I came down because you were in such a peaceful and deep sleep, I didn't want to disturb you—"

Still furious, she interrupted him. "But this is our honeymoon – you are supposed to stay with me and make the most of our time together before I have to leave!"

"I know that, and that's what I wanted to do more than anything, so please sit down and let me explain." There was a pleading but also a commanding note in his voice which she instantly obeyed.

He embarked on his explanation with a sigh. "A telegram was brought up to our room at six o'clock this morning. You didn't hear the knock on the door because you were in such a sound sleep. I'm afraid it wasn't good news, so I had to get up, dress and come down to ring HQ from the reception desk. The fact is I have to go back to base as soon as possible."

His face had turned grey and glum; there was no doubting the truth of what he had said, nor of his disappointment. "I thought you might like to stay here; it's a lovely day and you could go for a walk, have lunch, and I could send a car to pick you up later on to take you to the train."

He spoke with such sadness that Shirley's heart melted. She reached out to put her hand on his. "If there's time for me to have a cup of tea and a piece of toast, I'll shove everything into my suitcase and come with you. I'm so sorry."

Tears plopped onto her empty plate. "I'm more than sorry," he said. "This is not what I intended for us, and if it weren't so serious, I would leave it to someone else, but I can't do that. Please try to understand."

"Can't you tell me what's happened?" she asked softly.

"I will, but outside before the car comes, where there won't be anyone else listening, though only after you've had a proper breakfast, so let's order that now."

All the wedding clothes were thrown willy-nilly into Shirley's suitcase in the rush to leave the beautiful hotel with its glorious views over the mountains.

"We'll come back one day and have another honeymoon!" John promised while they waited for the car. Then he said, "What I am going to tell you is top secret, so please don't on any account talk about it to anyone – not to your father, nor to Ted, nor anyone else."

"I won't," she replied, anxious to gain his trust.

"I have to return to HQ, because this is about an ongoing operation I have been leading for quite some time. It is extremely difficult and has had a few successes and many failures, and I'm afraid this is one of the failures. It's deeply distressing, all the more so because the chaps involved are friends of mine."

Shirley listened with bated breath.

"In Aberdeen we have with us a team of Norwegian resistance fighters. They are extremely courageous and ready to undertake anything to save their country from Nazism. Have you heard of Quisling?" John asked.

"Yes, I think I've heard Pa mention him – he's some sort of traitor, isn't he?" she queried.

"That's right. He's a dictator in league with the Nazis, so the Norwegians are in the grip of the Germans, although there are many in the Resistance."

"Yes, yes, I do know that. Pa has told me all about it. He knows everything that's going on," she assured him.

John picked up the thread of his explanation. "On Thursday, a group of our Norwegians set out by boat overnight for Norway, intending to blow up a very important German installation on the coast, but word has just come back that they were all captured and shot as soon as they reached land. I have to try to find out exactly what happened, and if any of them survived and can be rescued."

His jaw was set into a determined rigidity. "It looks as if we have an informer in our midst," he announced grimly.

"You had better get going fast, then," said Shirley in a state of shock.

She hated the Nazis so strongly that any organization working against them had her full support, even if that meant the end of her honeymoon. The staff car arrived. They sat in the back kissing passionately, all the way to Aberdeen.

John had instructed the driver to head for the mainline station in Aberdeen, but as they approached it, Shirley gently tapped him on the sleeve. "I've been thinking," she said, "you obviously have to go back to base to try and sort out this catastrophe, but I don't have to go back to London. I don't know why I arranged to do so, not yet at any rate.

She gave him a winning smile, and, as if she were repeating her wedding vows all over again, said, "You are my husband, so you take priority over everything else, even the dancing – that can wait. I'll ring Pa and then I'll ring Cynthia, and I'll tell them I'll be away a few days longer. I'll stay on at Mrs McCrae's and ask her for a double room. She's very kind, and I don't think she's busy at present, so you can come and stay with me whenever you manage to escape. We'll be able spend the rest of our honeymoon here in Aberdeen!"

"Do you really mean that?" he asked.

"Of course I do!" she replied, overcome with emotion.

35

Aurora's performances went on as planned, despite Shirley's absence in the first week. Cynthia was not at all upset on receiving a telegram from the bride announcing the prolonged honeymoon.

"That doesn't surprise me at all, Shirl," she said on phoning Shirley at her lodgings. "Pete and I didn't think a weekend would be enough for you and John; in fact he agreed with me. 'Cyn,' he said, 'I bet they stay longer than two days. We'll make sure when our time comes, we go away for a fortnight!'"

Shirley was put out at this, but resisted the compulsion to tell Cynthia the true, unromantic reason for the lengthened honeymoon. As for the ballet, there were several members of the cast who were well enough trained to take on principal roles, and many of them were glad of the opportunity, not only because of the chance to be in the limelight, but also on account of the extra money it would bring in.

Nor was Mrs McCrae surprised at Shirley's request for a change of room and her lengthened stay, for she was well versed in the surprises and changes of plan that life in the army, air force and navy regularly sprang on newlywed couples. She treated this young couple with kindness itself, bringing them early morning tea, and insisting on providing copious breakfasts of kippers or bloaters.

One morning, when John had wolfed down his breakfast and dashed out with scarcely more than an apologetic "See you later, darling!" Mrs McCrae, who had been clearing tables in the room, came over to where Shirley was sitting forlornly, wondering how she was going to fill her day, and sat down opposite her.

"Och ay, ma wee lassie, I've seen this so often in this toun," she began. "Your husband, he's a fine young man, and he'll be back, but you must learn to be patient with him. It's a hard life up here, that it is. If it's not the wind and the weather, the rain and the snow, it's the sea. And as if that's not enough, it's also that evil enemy out there, hidden under the sea, waiting to murder our seamen and occupy us, just like they've taken hold of Norway over the water…" She gestured out to the sea, today stormy and turbulent, and patted Shirley on the arm before returning to her tasks.

Minutes later, she reappeared. "If you might be looking for something to do, why don't you come and help me in the shelter this morning?" she suggested.

The shelter was a refuge for stranded seamen, fishermen and merchant crews rescued by lifeboats when their ships had either been wrecked, gone down in storms or been attacked by enemy fire and torpedoes from U-boats. Most of them were Scandinavians, and had taken up semi-permanent residence in the shelter, although a few came from other parts of Britain – England, Wales and Northern Ireland – and were waiting for transport to take them home. The voluntary helpers reminded Shirley of the ladies of Newport who had given her and her company accommodation and food overnight in their church hall, when the train had come to a standstill. The difference was that this organization was much larger and took in far more refugees. And *refugees* was the appropriate term to describe many of them. While they were relieved to be away from the persecution being meted out to their compatriots at home in Norway and Denmark, they were also anxious for news of their families. They were hollow-eyed and clearly frustrated by idleness. Shirley wondered if John had ever recruited some of his Resistance fighters from among this sad bunch of exiles.

She was surprised when Mrs McCrae handed her an apron and asked her to start peeling potatoes and carrots. Shirley frowned. If these were to be served to the inmates, who were sitting idly with nothing to do, she thought it ridiculous that they were not being set to work to do the peeling and chopping themselves. Not slow in coming forward, she said as much to her landlady. "Why don't these people help out? They don't have anything else to do!"

"Och, wee lassie, we can't give them knives – they might start attacking us or fighting among themselves," came the startling reply.

Shirley looked around the hall and saw the weary and unhappy faces, but failed to see anyone who appeared in the slightest bit aggressive. "I don't see anyone here who's likely to turn a knife on us," she countered. "Why don't we select two or three to start with and see how that goes?"

Mrs McCrae was doubtful, but agreed to allow just two men to peel and chop vegetables. "Don't blame me if they attack you," she said as she went off to some other task.

Shirley walked among the ranks of dejected men sitting on the floor. "Hello!" she called out good-naturedly. "My name's Shirley. Anyone here speak English?" A host of hands went up. From among those prospective volunteers, she selected two middle-aged men who happened to speak good English.

"Of course we want to help these kind ladies who are looking after us," Jorgen, the older of the two men, grey-haired and evidently a captain, explained, "but we don't understand the way they speak. It's not like the English we have learnt, so communication is difficult. If we could understand them, we would then be able to translate for our crews, and they would willingly help!"

Shirley nodded with a smile: it was simply a matter of interpretation, and, for her, of acting as a go-between. All she had to do was interpret Mrs McCrae's strong Scottish accent – which it had to be said was not always very easy to follow – for the Norwegian captains so that they could translate what was required into their own language for their men.

Potatoes and carrots, and also cooking apples for dessert, were quickly peeled, and also a faulty gas burner on the stove and a leaking tap were mended, sausages were grilled, and lunch served to some fifty men by the handful who had eagerly been doing the work. The group decided amongst themselves that they would take turns, and effectively prepare and cook their own meals, and wash up afterwards, all day and every day. Now operating in only a supervisory role, Mrs McCrae gave Shirley grudging praise: "Time will tell whether this scheme of yours will really work," she said. But by the end of the day, when so much more than peeling carrots and potatoes had been accomplished, Shirley felt that she had done well, without so much as a complaint, let alone a knife attack from the inmates of the shelter.

That evening she told John of her success; he was impressed and suggested that the shelter project should be expanded to give the men more exercise. "Not only could they peel and chop potatoes and carrots," he proposed, "but they could dig them up as well in the outlying fields, although supervision would be necessary in case there were informers among their number…"

"True, but give me a chance! I've only just started on this project and I'm only here for a week. I'm not a Land Girl, so arranging potato and carrot harvesting is not in my line," she replied.

Nevertheless, her organizational skills were put to greater use, as she began to investigate the possibility of finding agricultural work for the shipwrecked sailors. As yet, transport and supervision seemed to be the main obstacles to adventures out in the countryside, and her few remaining days in the shelter were certainly not going to suffice for putting such a scheme into practice. In the event, she found that arranging and supervising the work of the land was not so very different from the skills needed for organizing a ballet troupe. Consequently she had more to tell her husband at the end of each day.

Conversely, she was disappointed that, although he seemed worn down with anxiety, he did not confide in her at all. In fact he told her little about his work. Because of the blanket of secrecy, she dare not ask him about his day at work, let alone enquire for news about the disastrous attempt to send Resistance fighters to Norway, which had put paid to their honeymoon.

It came as a shock a couple of mornings later, when, after Mrs McCrae had gone out to buy bread, John appeared in the doorway of the shelter carrying a sack of potatoes. He put a finger to his lips. "Here you are, miss," he said for all to hear, "Just sign for the potatoes you ordered, will you please?"

As she bent over to sign a scrap of paper, he whispered in her ear, "Don't let on that you know me, but show me the two Norwegian captains, will you?"

She quickly cottoned on.

"Thanks for the potatoes," she said loudly, "but you've forgotten the carrots!"

John was taken aback, not expecting this reaction from his wife. "Oh, I'm so sorry," he said, "I'll fetch some." He turned to leave.

"Wait a minute!" she commanded in stentorian tones. "I'll send someone to help you."

She scanned the inmates, now busy cleaning the shelter or washing their own clothes. "Captain Jorgen!" she called out. "Will you please help the greengrocer bring in more vegetables?" Jorgen willingly complied.

At dinner that evening, John squeezed her hand across the table. "You were amazing – so clever, so subtle!" he said in hushed tones. "I've been trying to find ways of meeting someone like Captain Jorgen. That's why I came into the shelter. I wish all my contacts were like you! Why don't you come and work for me here?"

"Thanks for the compliment, my darling," she replied, "but much as I would love to help you out, I have my work to do, as you know, and I must leave on Friday."

"Well, then, we should make the most of the time left to us, if not by day, then by night," he answered with a mischievous and thoroughly beguiling smile.

With sorrowful reluctance Shirley left her John on the Friday, taking the Flying Scotsman from Edinburgh. "I'll be in London before long! And I'll phone you every day!" were his last words to her.

The journey, though swift, gave her time to reflect on how lucky she was to have found her heart's desire at last – or rather that, by a happy chance, her heart's desire had come into her life and married her. He was handsome, kind, considerate and hard-working. He also possessed a subtle sense of humour which appealed to her. She regretted that he had not yet seen her dancing, but that was because the War always intervened just when it might have been possible. He had expressed his admiration of her intelligence and quick-wittedness, but more than ever, she wanted him to see her on the stage, for then he would not be left in any doubt as to how important her career as a ballerina was for her.

The constant speed of the train lulled her into a doze, from which she woke as it pulled into King's Cross. Yet again there was a special dinner, prepared by Reggie and Ted with Eileen's help, to welcome her home. "I say, that was a lightning wedding, wasn't it?" Ted was teasing her, yet she was irritated at the implication of his remark.

"It was 'lightning', as you say, only because we wanted to get married as soon as possible, *not* for any other reason," she retorted.

Then she laughed, because clearly there was no malice in her brother's observation, though she realized that other people, who had not been at the wedding or seen how tight-fitting her costume was, might well attribute other reasons to the speed with which the marriage had been arranged. What's more, she had to admit, had Alan lived and had they married, then there would have been good reason for a hastily arranged wedding.

John rang that evening to check that Shirley was safely home. "I have a meeting in London in a week's time," he said, "and then I can have the weekend off. I wondered if you'd be prepared to come and meet my parents again – properly, I mean. I'll write to them to make sure it goes well this time, and no one embarrasses you. What do you think? Perhaps we might stay in a hotel near Liverpool Street on the Friday and catch the first train on Saturday morning?"

Shirley was tired from her journey, and although she wanted to be with John for ever, she was already mentally slipping back into dance mode. In any case, Saturdays were performance days, and she was fairly sure that the next Saturday was scheduled to be her first appearance on stage since the summer break.

"I'll check the diary tomorrow," she said, "in case there's a performance next Saturday. And I'll let you know."

In any case, there still remained the other problem, the problem of his mother. Evelyn had been delightful at the wedding until the question of Catholicism came up, though why anyone should reject her on account of that, Shirley could not fathom. She was a Christian of sorts and always tried to do her best, especially in her dedication to the War effort. What did it matter if she were a Baptist or a Congregationalist or a Methodist – or a Catholic? They all worshipped the same God as the Church of England, and believed more or less in the same religion. She could only hope that she might be able to win his mother round if she trod carefully and did not put her foot in it when next they met.

On replacing the receiver at the end of John's call, she wrote and posted a note to Cynthia straight away. This proved to be not such a good idea, for Cynthia rang, as usual, from a call box, to hear every detail of the honeymoon, which strained Shirley's powers of imagination: she was not going to tell Cynthia that John was working on secret operations, and that meanwhile she had been helping out in a shelter for distressed seamen. Only when Cynthia was finally satisfied with descriptions of the beauties of the Highlands and was amazed at the luxury of the hotel, was she content to answer Shirley's questions about engagements in the forthcoming week, especially on the following Saturday.

"I know you were down on the list to dance on Saturday, Shirl, but we weren't quite sure when you would be coming back, so Maria is taking the leads for the time being; she was incredibly good this past week and is looking forward to dancing the principal roles next week, on Tuesday, Thursday and Saturday. She really enjoys the Sugar Plum Fairy. I'll dance Odette – I know I can manage that now, and Doris is happy as Odile in *Swan Lake*, so don't worry – but do let me have the name of your hotel. Pete and I would like to go to Scotland for our honeymoon, and we could stay in that hotel in the Highlands."

"OK, thanks, Cynnie, glad to know all is in hand. I'll be in touch," said Shirley and banged the receiver down.

That telephone call had really put her out of sorts: not only were Cynthia and Maria taking over her roles, but she would also be sacrificing her return to the stage, even though that stage was at an RAF base, in exchange for a visit to Norhambury. She sensed that another visit to Norhambury was highly unlikely to go well and would undoubtedly leave her feeling miserable, whereas dancing in *The Nutcracker* or *Swan Lake* to rapturous applause, would have given her morale a huge boost. Evidently there were no two ways about it; she would have to accompany her husband to Norhambury. She was glad not to be expecting a call from John again that evening, because she was not in the frame of mind to talk to him, nor was she better reconciled to meeting his mother. Were he to ring now, she might be tempted to tell him exactly how she felt, and that would be unpardonably hard on him.

In fact the next day's practice and rehearsal in Madame's studio only served to increase her frustration, so in the evening she stormed out of the flat on her ARP round, having asked her father to tell John that she would speak to him later in the week. Only when out alone in the night air of late summer, did she begin to relax and view the situation more calmly. Of one thing she was certain: marriage meant compromise, and that was not at all easy for her to accept.

By the end of the week, after days of concentrated practice and rehearsal under Madame's eagle eye, she succeeded in putting a brave face on the situation on the Friday evening, and flung herself into her husband's arms when they met at the hotel he had booked for them. After that long embrace, he said, "Can you forgive me for dragging you away from your ballet? I know you were looking forward to being back on the stage, and here you are with me!"

At that unexpected apology, her irritation dissolved, and she was sure that there was nowhere else that she wanted to be. "I wouldn't miss this opportunity to be with you for anything in the world!" she declared.

Although they arrived in Norhambury by mid-morning on the Saturday, they did not take the bus directly to Beech Grove. "I want you to see my beautiful city first," John said, "and the best way to do that is on foot, particularly because we don't have much luggage." He was carrying a small rucksack, and Shirley had packed the minimum into a small sling bag, which she flung over her shoulder.

"The only caution is," he said seriously, "don't tell my parents we've spent the day in the city!"

"Ah, yes, I understand," she replied, thinking that it would never have been necessary to tell even a white lie to either of her parents.

John proudly showed her the treasures of his city, its castle, its cathedral and its multitude of small churches. They sat at lunch at a window table in a department store overlooking the market with its colourful awnings flapping in the slight breeze.

"This afternoon we'll go to the Regency Rooms for tea – you'll love that! I've told my parents we'll arrive in time for high tea. That's what we have in the early evening, you see, not a cooked meal."

"That's fine by me," she answered. "This plate of fish and chips is very filling, so I won't need to eat for the rest of the day."

He smiled. "I thought you'd like it; the sea is only twenty-five or so miles away, so the fish is very fresh. It would be good to go there sometime, though I don't think we'll have time for it this weekend. And anyhow, the War means that the coast is out of bounds."

They strolled arm in arm through the market stalls up the slope to the Regency Rooms, where the iridescent, crystal chandeliers thrilled Shirley. Like many a small child, she gasped in delight at all the colours of the spectrum glistening in the balls of light suspended from the ceiling in each room, and was reluctant to leave.

"I'll have to drag you away," said John, "but I think we had better be on our way. Mother and Father sit down to high tea at six o'clock, so we mustn't be late."

He looked at his watch. "Hmm, I'm afraid we're going to have to run!"

"No problem," Shirley declared. "Just show me the way! I'll beat you to it!" She easily outran John, but had to wait for directions from him at each street corner.

"My goodness, you are fit!" he exclaimed.

"Well, I have to be!" she said. "You're forgetting, I'm a dancer!"

"There's so much about you I still have to learn," he observed, shaking his head.

The wait at the bus stop was long and tedious. John kept glancing anxiously at his watch while Shirley clung to his right arm. "We must have just missed a bus," he remarked.

"Never mind – if it's only a cold supper, surely they'll wait for us," she said, trying to calm his anxiety.

When the bus arrived, he did not climb the stairs to the top deck as was his habit, but sat as close as possible to the open platform. Shirley sensed that he would probably have spent the journey standing *on* the platform, had he been alone.

"I'm enjoying this bus ride; I can see things like those funny little lanes I didn't see last time," she said. Then, nestling up to him, she enquired, "What's the matter? Why are you so anxious?"

"Oh, it's because I don't like being late and we are already twenty minutes overdue," he replied.

Before the bus had drawn to a halt in Beech Grove, he had stood up, saying, "Here we are – let's jump off!" And scarcely had the bus stopped than he did jump off, almost dragging Shirley with him.

"Hold on! I may be a dancer, but my partners don't pull me across the stage like this!" she grumbled. "You'll break my legs!"

He ran across the road and opened the front gate of one of the houses, which Shirley recognized from the last time. A chill ran down her spine as she followed him slowly along the driveway. He ran ahead, but instead of going straight to the back door, where the way was partially blocked by a motorbike and side-car, he rang the bell at the front – perhaps, she happily surmised, to make their entry as a couple more formal.

John's father, wiping his mouth on a napkin, opened the door. For one who previously had appeared so genial, he appeared quite agitated. "Come along in, you two," he said. "We have just finished eating, so come and have your supper quickly!"

He ushered them into the dining room, where John's mother was pouring out two cups of tea from a pot that had, to judge by the colour of the dark liquid, been brewing for some time. She stopped what she was doing to embrace her son and bestow an unsmiling nod on Shirley.

"So, hello, Mrs Platt junior," she said without any hint of warmth. Still looking at Shirley as if their late arrival was her fault, she announced, "You will have to eat in a hurry, because we were expecting you at six o'clock and it's now..." – she glanced at the clock on the mantelpiece – "it's now a quarter to seven, and you'll have to leave in five minutes to catch the bus into the city. We're going on the bike."

Shirley had already sat down and was alternately eating a ham sandwich with a slice of tomato and a lettuce leaf, and sipping the undrinkable tea.

"Why, where are we going?" John asked between mouthfuls of sandwich and salad.

"Oh, John, have you forgotten?" said his mother. "Evelyn's taking the solo role in the concert this evening in the City Hall! She's playing the Mozart piano concerto Number Twenty-One with the Norhambury Symphony Orchestra. I'm sure I told you about it!"

"Wonderful!" exclaimed Shirley. "But if you will excuse me, I've finished eating, and I'd like to make a quick visit to the bathroom before we go out. Thank you for the supper!"

"The bathroom's at the top of the stairs," John muttered as she left him to deal with his mother. She mounted the stairs two at a time and did not bother to stand in front of the mirror arranging her hair or powdering her nose, but came down again in less than two minutes, straightening her clothing as she went.

From the hall she could hear two voices in the dining room, John's and his mother's. "I'm sure I told you about the concert!" his mother was declaring defiantly. "I expect you've been too busy messing about with that flibbertigibbet wife of yours!"

John came storming out of the dining room and nearly collided with Shirley. "Grab your bag and coat and run out to the bus. Try to hold it up for me, will you?" he pleaded as he climbed the stairs to the bathroom.

Shirley waited anxiously but he reached the garden gate just as the bus arrived. She suddenly developed a limp in her left leg, which meant that the conductor had to help her onto the bus and John jumped on behind her. "Are you all right?" he asked anxiously. "Yes, yes, don't worry! it's something that happens from time to time," she explained briefly in the hearing of the bus conductor. "It's the remnant of an illness I had a long time ago. It doesn't happen very often, only when I'm stressed."

Still helping her, the conductor settled her into a seat, and John sat down beside her.

"That's worrying!" he said. "What happened?"

"I'll tell you later," she replied. "It's nothing to worry about any more." Indeed there was nothing to worry about, because she had deliberately assumed the limp to delay the departure of the bus.

At that moment, the roar of a motorbike overtaking the bus distracted them. "That's good – Mother and Father will arrive in time; the only problem is that Mother forgot to give me our tickets. Never mind, I expect we can buy two on the door!"

They got off the bus at the stop where they had boarded it less than an hour previously; Shirley duly let the conductor help her off, and walked with a limp until the bus was out of sight; then she broke into a run. By the time they reached the city hall, retracing their steps from earlier in the day, there was only a handful of tickets left at the box office, and those were for seats in the gallery, from where the sightlines were not very good.

"That doesn't matter," Shirley reassured John. "We've come to listen to the music, not to perform on the stage, and that will suit me for a change!"

He was peering over the balcony searching for his parents. Naturally enough they were sitting in the front row, but to his dismay he saw that sitting next to them were a couple of friends from church. Clearly no seats had been reserved for him and Shirley. He did not mention this to her. In any case there was no chance of doing so, because the concert was about to begin.

Shirley was bemused by the performance, which opened up for her a dimension, that of orchestral music, of which she had little more than a passing appreciation. This omission was for the simple reason that she had been immersed in ballet music for nearly all her life, and had never attended an orchestral concert. She picked up the rhythms easily, and as this was a popular concert, the melodies were lyrical and accessible. The opening piece, Fingal's Cave, she found entrancing, evoking the ebb and flow of the tide as waves washed against and over the rocks on some Scottish island.

Then, as the orchestra regrouped and the grand piano was pushed into the centre of the stage, a buzz went up from the audience. John and Shirley waited in silent anticipation for the pianist to appear. To judge by the applause as Evelyn, tall and slim, wearing a full-length, royal blue dress, came onto the stage, she was already revered in her home city. Smiling, she bowed to the audience before settling herself at the piano. She then glanced up at the conductor, who brought his baton down, and the orchestra began to play.

Shirley was carried away by Mozart's music: it could only be described as divine and Evelyn's playing as heavenly. Her fingers danced over the keyboard in the first movement. In the second, the pace slowed into a melody of such heart-rending beauty that it brought a lump to Shirley's throat. Momentarily memories of Alan playing Ted's piano came to mind in a disturbingly upsetting way. Never had she imagined that music alone, without ballet or song, was capable of evoking such powerful feelings: it was wordless, its only expression coming from the orchestra and the solo performer at the piano. The emotion of it was overwhelming – she did not think she could bear it. She reached out to hold John's hand and squeezed it to tell him that Evelyn's performance was affecting her deeply.

At the interval, pushing his way through the crowds with Shirley trailing behind him, John went in search of his parents. They were surrounded by well-wishers, all complimenting them on their daughter's playing. He beckoned to his father, who cleared spaces for him and for Shirley. Mr Platt was beaming from ear to ear. "Wasn't she marvellous?" he asked rhetorically.

Shirley saw this as her opportunity, not to flatter or ingratiate herself, but simply to assert herself a little in the family circle by complimenting her father-in-law on his amazing daughter. "Evelyn was magnificent! I've never heard anything like her playing!" she said. "It brought tears to my eyes!"

Mr Platt nodded modestly. "We are very proud of her. She certainly has talent!"

He caught his wife's arm. "Here are John and Shirley," he said, pointing to them.

Shirley repeated her admiration of Evelyn, hoping to win her mother-in-law over. The latter gave a faint smile. "I'm glad you liked her performance," she said. "She has worked hard and now she's reaping the benefits." Then, rather caustically, she added, "I gather you've met her, but I'm sure you didn't realize how special she is."

Shirley took a moment to digest this reaction before replying, "You're right, Mrs Platt, I have met her, and I thought that she was lovely, but I certainly hadn't a clue about her piano playing." She was inclined to say "And I'm sure you haven't a clue about my performances as a prima ballerina", but of course she did not. Instead she added, "And I'm so glad we arrived in time to come to her concert! I am so happy to have Evelyn as my sister-in-law." She was also tempted to say, "Such a pity you didn't tell John about the concert. Had we known we would have arrived sooner," but of course she did not do that either.

The second half of the concert consisted of Beethoven's Seventh Symphony, which did not capture Shirley's interest in the same way as the Mozart piano concerto, until that is, the *scherzo*, the penultimate movement, when her feet started tapping in time to the whirling *tarantella* rhythms. At the end of the concert, she and John did not try to find his parents in the crush of concert-goers leaving the hall, but set out on foot to the bus stop.

Halfway there, Shirley stopped short and said, "John, we've forgotten Evelyn! How will she be getting home? We should have taken her in a taxi!"

"She'll be fine. Don't worry about her. She'll probably be there long before us. She'll be sent home in a specially commissioned taxi, and my parents have the motorbike, so they'll be there first." The newly-weds arrived to find the family plus a young man well settled in, and toasting Evelyn's success with a glass of home-made elderberry wine. Shirley and John joined in the toast with pleasure, after which she hoped that perhaps glasses might be raised to congratulate them on their marriage, but a toast to them there was none – whether by accident or design, she was not sure. She and John spent that night sleeping in single beds in the back bedroom. The only double bed was in the front room, and that was occupied by his parents.

The household was up early on the Sunday because church was on the agenda. "Do you mind coming to a Church of England service?" John asked his wife. "Mother goes every Sunday and likes me to go with her when I'm home."

"No, of course not," said Shirley. "I don't mind where I go. I'd be happy to come with you." She hastened to dress and smarten up while John went down to breakfast.

As she descended the stairs, she heard his voice in the kitchen, saying, "Look, Mother, Shirley doesn't mind which church she goes to, and she said quite clearly that she would like to come with us!"

"I don't care what *she* would like; it all depends on what the *vicar* thinks about it," came the reply.

"The vicar doesn't have to be told," John declared, in exasperation. "If she wants to come you should encourage her!"

Shirley appeared in the kitchen. "Good morning, Mrs Platt!" she said brightly.

"There's toast and marmalade there for you on the side, if you want it," John's mother said by way of a terse greeting, and went to put her coat on.

"She'll get used to it," John said quietly, nodding in his mother's direction, while Shirley ate her breakfast and drank a cup of cold, bitter tea.

Although his mother had gone out by the time Shirley had put her coat on, she and John, walking briskly, soon caught her up on the way to the medieval village church on the city boundary. Evelyn was already there, turning pages for the organist, the young man from the previous evening's party. She looked round and nodded to her family as they took their seats, facing the organ in the front pew of the side aisle. John sat between his mother and Shirley, who cosied up to him and whispered, "What a pretty church! It's so light and airy, and look at all those lovely flowers!"

She loved the simplicity of the place: its tall, chalky-white pillars, the dark, wooden pulpit only yards away, and the sunlight shining through the stained-glass windows. If she and John were to have some sort of church ceremony, perhaps it could be here. It would be perfect. It smelled of old beams and damp stone, and resonated first with the sound of the organ, and then, when the service began, with the clear voices of the choirboys singing the hymn as they processed up the nave. The service was easy to follow because it was in English, though strangely there was no celebration of the Eucharist. She asked John why not. He shrugged and said softly, "It's Matins, and we don't have Communion at Matins."

Halfway through the service, a white-haired clergyman climbed with some difficulty up into the pulpit. "He's the vicar," John said *sotto voce*. "He'll be there for hours."

By the time he had finished his rambling set of ideas on some abstruse passage of the Old Testament, Shirley had begun to doubt that he was the sort of clergyman who would look kindly on an Anglo-Catholic marriage, nor would he probably ever contemplate some sort of blessing in church, so she would have to discard that idea.

However, more prayers and a rousing hymn brought the service to a close. The organist then brought his hands down on the organ in resounding chords which seemed to say, "Thank goodness, that's over for another week!" Shirley stood up to leave, before noticing that John's mother had sat down again and was listening to the organ voluntary, so she resumed her seat.

At the end of the voluntary, Evelyn and the organist came to join the family group as they emerged from the front pew. While the young man shook hands with her parents, Evelyn greeted Shirley with a warm hug, saying, "Thank you for coming this morning, as well as last night! You met Charles, didn't you? But I don't think you were properly introduced.

I'm afraid I was too tired." She tapped the organist on the shoulder. "Charles," she said, "this is Shirley, John's wife. As you know, they were married in Scotland two weeks ago yesterday!"

"I'm sorry we didn't meet properly last night," he said, shaking Shirley's hand in a firm grasp. "There was too much excitement, wasn't there? But I'm pleased to meet you now! I'm Charles Stannard. Congratulations on your wedding! Evelyn tells me it was beautiful!"

Shirley beamed at this unexpected compliment. His and Evelyn's behaviour made up somewhat for Mrs Platt's cool reception, which was still as chilly as it had been on their arrival. Evelyn, John and Shirley left to join Mrs Platt, and Charles went off to have lunch with his mother.

"What a lovely church!" Shirley remarked on the way back to the house, hoping that her mother-in-law would respond in kind.

"It's just an old English church, much like any other," the latter retorted drily. "But we do like it, and we try to keep it in good shape."

"It looks in very good shape," Shirley commented, "so airy and fresh – and I loved the windows. The sun coming through them made such pretty patterns on the pillars."

Perhaps that was not the right thing to have said; perhaps she should have remarked how interesting the sermon was or something of that nature to please her mother-in-law. Instead of agreeing with her, Mrs Platt, who was walking between the couple, ignored her daughter-in-law and turned to her son.

"I think Father will need your help, John," she said. "There's a problem with the air-raid shelter, and I don't think he can manage it on his own."

"Of course – I'll do it before we leave this afternoon. There's no hurry, is there?" said John.

In fact his father needed help as soon as they came in through the gate, labouring as he was under heavy sheets of corrugated iron. "There's a leak in the roof and I need to replace those faulty corrugated sheets with these new ones," he explained.

"I'll look for some of my old clothes in the wardrobe and be with you in a moment," John replied. He hurried into the house, leaving his wife with his mother.

"We'll make the coffee while they're at work," said the latter. Shirley sensed that the moment of truth had come.

Mrs Platt senior put the kettle on, then lifted down the Camp coffee bottle from the kitchen cupboard. She poured a spoonful of the brown liquid into each of four cups, took milk out of the larder and then, although the kettle was beginning to whistle, she sat down at the kitchen table and beckoned Shirley to do the same.

"Are you expecting?" she asked outright.

"No, I am *not*!" Shirley said emphatically, defiant at this impertinence, and thankful that this opening put her in the right.

"Well, why then did you get married so hastily, and up in Aberdeen too? That's a really difficult journey for us." She sounded angry, and Shirley realized that no excuse would satisfy this mother-in-law, so she told her the truth.

"The problem is, you see, that this War is dragging on and on all over the world, and is becoming more and more dangerous, and John has to go to all sorts of horrible places, so when he suggested we should get married straight away in Aberdeen – well, as soon as we could arrange it – I agreed with him that that was the best solution. Of course I said yes. That meant I, as his wife" (she emphasized this last word) "would be able to stay with him and visit him, and it would be much easier for us to keep in touch."

"Yes, that's as may be," said Mrs Platt dismissively, "but why not in a church? Why in a Registry Office?"

"We weren't able to arrange a church wedding in time."

"Oh, and why was that?" John's mother persisted.

Shirley began to speak. "It was complicated, because—"

"Because you're a Catholic?" Mrs Platt spat the words out, but Shirley stood her ground.

"Yes, I'm afraid so, but I *am* a Christian, so I don't see why that matters! I love John and he loves me! I would have gone over to the Church of England, but there wasn't time for that, so it had to be the Registry Office."

The time had come to put this hostile woman in her place. Her reply was adamant, giving her a breathing space in which to think up more good reasons. Finally she said with a hint of a stammer, "The truth is, Mrs Platt, John and I love each other so much we couldn't bear to be parted!"

"Hmph!" was all Mrs Platt said.

Shirley was becoming heated, and wished John would come in from the garden to rescue her. The kettle was now whistling furiously and had to be taken off the stove. John and his father had heard it from outside and appeared in the doorway.

"A good morning's work so far, thank you, ole boy; we'll finish it by lunchtime," Mr Platt was saying.

John noticed the unhappy look on Shirley's face. "All well, darling?" he asked, putting his arm round her as she sat on the stool.

"Oh, I'm all right," she muttered unconvincingly, shrugging her shoulders as she did so.

After that dismal weekend in Norhambury, it was with relief that Shirley returned to the ballet studio. If John's family, particularly his mother, were not going to welcome her as their daughter-in-law, then she would continue with her own career, and put as much distance between her and that family as possible. Nonetheless, she did not understand Mrs Platt's open hostility and was very hurt by it. When she observed her mother-in-law conversing with her friends after the church service, Mrs Platt had appeared relaxed, warm and friendly, and was busy lending a helping hand to some doddery, ancient ladies, so why could she not behave in the same way to her – not that she was doddery or needed a helping hand?

She and John were married and therefore, in her view, the fact of her being a Catholic had become increasingly immaterial. She herself was not bothered by it, never had been, and nor was he. What's more, it was so unfair because it was he, not she, who had suggested a quick, spontaneous wedding: that was a truth which his mother staunchly preferred to ignore, instead implying that she, Shirley, must be pregnant and had forced John into marriage.

John's suggestion of a quick wedding had certainly taken Shirley herself by surprise, since that was not at all what she had expected from her weekend visit to Aberdeen, yet everything had worked out well. It had been simpler but much more romantic than a normal wedding, without all the planning, the hassle of guest lists and present lists, not to mention having to choose hymns and clothes, and book an elaborate, expensive reception.

To her surprise and joy, the important people, the people that mattered most in her life, Ted and her father, Eileen and Madame, Cynthia and Pete, and several of her friends from Aurora, had come to the wedding. Archie had stayed in London to keep the business going, which was fair enough, but it was a shame that John's parents had not made the effort. Nevertheless, that was their choice, and the less she dwelt on that, the better.

Surprisingly, Evelyn *had* come, doubtless taking time away from her rehearsals and practice for that wonderful concert. It had been such a pleasure to get to know her.

Probably she had fallen silent at the wedding on hearing of the inter-denominational situation, because she was already anticipating her mother's reaction, and was concerned about its effect on the couple. The most important part of it all was that she, Shirley, was John's wife, so whatever happened to him in the course of his duties, she would be the first to hear about it, and, in the event of his being injured, she would have the authority to decide how to handle the situation.

Although she was determined to put Mrs Platt senior's unfriendliness out of her mind, it continued to distress her, since she foresaw that it could have a bad effect on her marriage. If she were to tell John that she did not want to accompany him to Norhambury in future, how would he react? What would he say? Would he be hurt? The last thing she wanted to do was to upset her husband: she loved him too much for that, and there was no doubt that he loved her. It was, put simply, that he was a man and would not be able to understand this, the trickiest and the most unfortunate of relationships.

This thought brought her mother's relationship with Pa's mother, Granny Marlow, a pest if ever there was one, to mind, so perhaps there was nothing new in her difficulties with John's mother. One easy solution presented itself for the time being: she would put herself down for all of Aurora's performances on Saturdays. Then there would be no question about going on weekend visits to Norhambury. After all, John had had to rush off from their honeymoon to see to a catastrophe in Aberdeen, as that was his job, so if she had to be present in the London area on Saturdays to carry out her contribution to the War effort, there would be no valid grounds for arguments or complaints. She was not as yet able to foresee what his attitude might be, given that she had known him for only such a short time. With any luck he would understand that her work meant as much to her as his did to him, and take it in his stride. Anyhow, as she saw it, he was still in her debt over the honeymoon fiasco.

The question did not arise: John was so busy sorting out the crises in the Norwegian Resistance and seeking out the informer, that there was no chance of his coming to London, let alone continuing his journey from there to Norhambury. They talked regularly over the phone, usually on Sunday evenings, lamenting their separation and commiserating with each other over the burdens that work placed upon each of them. His occupied him not only all day, but all night as well, it seemed, because he was responsible for ascertaining the best times and places for the fighters to land safely on Norwegian shores.

When that went wrong, as it had on the weekend of the wedding, he was weighed down with guilt, feelings of inadequacy and remorse. Shirley deemed it undiplomatic to stress how much she enjoyed her work. Instead, she told him how tired she was, since not only was the life of a prima ballerina physically exhausting, but as the leader of the ballet troupe she was often mentally tired as well. Neither was there any need to tell him that her love for the ballet almost rivalled her love for him.

As well as his phone calls, they wrote to each other in spare moments, which for both of them were infrequent. The messages were brief and consisted of a postcard about once a week. His showed Aberdeen in better days with the setting sun shining on a golden sea, or views of the heather-covered Highlands. Hers were less artistic, showing sepia pictures of Buckingham Palace, the Thames, Westminster Abbey or the Tower of London, which in her opinion would be a good place to lock Hitler up before beheading him when finally he was caught.

The postcards were always sent in envelopes which bore the letters SWLK – "sealed with a loving kiss" – amusing and tangible reminders of their love. They pined for each other, but it was tacitly agreed that, unless she gave up the ballet and went to live in Aberdeen, which he never asked of her, the present arrangement was the only practical one. In any case, he hinted that he might not be in Aberdeen much longer. She for her part had a slight inkling of what this might mean, and was disturbed by it.

The inkling, in all probability, signified that John might again be posted away from Aberdeen, where he was reasonably safe, dealing with Norwegian problems on the western side of the North Sea. Just as earlier in the year when he had been seconded to Montgomery's forces in North Africa, it seemed that Aberdeen was a holding station where he could perform important work before being sent to some more critical zone of warfare. She feared he might be sent back into an active war scenario, most certainly Italy, where, according to her father, Sicily was the present target of the Allied forces in the summer of 1943.

She preferred not to hear about that campaign, but it was unavoidable, because Ted had tacked up a huge map of the island of Sicily above the fireplace, and was tracking the Allied movements with a red pen. In addition, her father and her brother listened to every item of news broadcast by the BBC. Even if she were not present at the time, perhaps out on patrol still making sure that no chinks of light appeared through curtains on her rounds, they would tell her every detail of what they had heard as soon as the patrol was over.

The Allied forces had captured Palermo, the capital of Sicily, in July while she was away in Scotland, and by the middle of August had captured Messina, the last defence of the Axis powers in Sicily, opposite the toe of Italy. The next target was the mainland, where Rome, Turin and Milan had already undergone massive Allied bombing offensives. This, she reckoned, was where John was heading eventually, probably to help coordinate forces and strategies in the advance northwards, battling German strongholds on the way.

From the kitchen, she overheard Ted discussing the strategies with their father, whose view was that this was most likely to be the focus of the Allied effort. If Italy were captured and the Germans driven out, a vast area of the Mediterranean would come under Allied control, but there was a long way to go before that happened. The prospects looked grim for anyone joining that battleground.

John rang one evening later in August to say that he was on the point of leaving Aberdeen on the new assignment, without saying where he was going. She asked him straight out, "Are you off to Italy?" but he did not reply to that. Instead, sounding hurried, he promised he would be back before Christmas. He told Shirley that he loved her and asked her to keep on sending postcards to the forces' mail address, then the line went blank.

Noticing her downcast face, Ted asked, "John's off on his travels again, is he?"

"I'm afraid so," she replied.

Ted's reaction was not sympathetic. "Lucky him!" he declared, "How I wish I could join the troops and give the Italians a good bashing! Then, through them we'll be able to get at the Nazis and finish them off! It will be the beginning of the end! Ha, ha!"

Shirley was not in the mood to be facetious. "Maybe you're right," she retorted, "but think of all the casualties there'll be before this comes to an end, and I don't want John to be one of them! As you've probably guessed, I'm convinced he's been seconded to the Italian campaign!"

"Hm," said Ted, more soberly, "much as I'd like to be with them, they've a lot of work to do to push the Germans out. You know, don't you, that Mussolini met Hitler in the north of the country, and then was deposed, but he's still around, released by the Germans, and is helping the enemy out? That was while you were away on your tour."

She nodded wearily. "Oh yes, I know that!" said she. "I wasn't totally out of touch with the news, you know."

Ted, ignoring his sister, carried on, "There's some anti-Fascist chap, Badoglio – or something like that, I forget his name – in charge now in Rome, but they still have to get rid of the Germans and, oh boy, they are going to have to keep fighting!"

He blew his cheeks out, just like his father often did. Depressed by her brother's review of the Italian situation, and rather than listen to more news, Shirley withdrew to her room where she did her ballet practice in preparation for the following day in the studio.

There Madame watched with eagle eye as Shirley rehearsed some of the sequences from *Swan Lake*, in particular the *Adagio* danced by Odette and Prince Siegfried. Partnered by Andrei, she did not have to assume Odette's personality, or convey her emotions, for she *was* Odette and Odette's emotions were her own.

"My dear," said Madame to Shirley at the end of the rehearsal, "I have never seen you dance like that, not since..." Here she stopped abruptly in full flow. Shirley guessed that she had been on the point of saying, "not since your fiancé died in the Battle of Britain."

Hastily trying to make good her faux pas, Madame went on, "You express emotion in every step. You have always been a good dancer, but now you have truly absorbed Odette's character, as well as her role in the ballet!"

This was music to Shirley's ears, because of late she had begun to wonder whether her performances had become a little tired and jaded. She did not resent Madame's unspoken reference to Alan, but that allusion had brought home to her once again how her life had changed since the heartbreaking events of 1940.

Marriage to John had undoubtedly given a new impetus to her creativity, and at the same time, his unpredictably dangerous situation had produced an edgy anxiety in her moods, which had transferred itself into the dance. The fear was forever inescapable, and frequently came to the front of her mind, that she might, for the second time, lose her real-life, beloved partner.

In modern life, the enemy was not a fairy tale evil witch or baron, but the War itself. These unprecedented elements in her performance appeared only where they were essential, that is in the tragic roles, in *Giselle*, *La Sylphide* and *Swan Lake*. In light-hearted roles, like those in *Coppélia*, she revelled in the comedy, which allowed her all-too-rare glimpses of fun and happiness.

As August progressed, news from the Mediterranean came through more often and in more detail. The capture of Messina had enabled the Allies to bombard the mainland and establish a foothold in southern Italy, before beginning to move north in a line across the country. Nonetheless, Italy's eventual surrender in early September did not bring about the end of the campaign. On the contrary, the entrenched Germans not only fought for their lives, but inflicted appalling atrocities on the population, contaminating water supplies, destroying food reserves, and making off with as many works of art as they could carry.

As usual Reggie, not to be distracted from the Nine O'clock News, whooped for joy at every advance the Allies made, and groaned when there were setbacks, as for example around Naples, where the Nazis were murdering thousands of civilians and deporting captive soldiers to labour camps in Germany. Not until the end of September did the city fall, and that was weeks after the Italian surrender and declaration of war on Germany.

Shirley needed to know about the reports, conveyed with irrepressible delight by her father, but could not bear to listen to them. Although she did not let her guard down, she lived in fear in case the worst happened to her husband. The strain would have been unbearable, had it not been for the ballet.

Reggie's interest was not limited to Italy: he also listened eagerly to the encouraging news from Russia where the Soviet Army had won back Kursk in a massive tank offensive. By swiftly launching lightning attacks, it was moving west into Ukraine. Good news came also from Yugoslavia, where the Resistance was capturing the coastline, aided by Italian resistance fighters. Nevertheless Reggie, too, harboured a deep concern for the son-in-law whom he respected and admired. That concern was magnified by anxiety about his daughter's well-being, should John not return from the Italian campaign.

So fearful for both of them was he, that at night he sometimes felt the terrors of shell shock taking hold of him again. Then he would stumble out to the kitchen and reach up to the top shelf of the cupboard for the pot containing a new prescription of his medication. There were plenty of pills which, he was sure, would see him through any crisis without the rest of the household ever being aware: both of his offspring had too much to worry about without having to take care of their poor, old father.

It was always a moment of immeasurable relief for Shirley when brief letters and the occasional postcard from John came through, but on account of censorship, those messages conveyed little of significance. She had no idea where he was. Whether he was in Naples, or Rome, or Milan, or Turin, she had no way of finding out. The only worthwhile aspect of these limited communications was that, as long as they kept arriving, they told a lovelorn Shirley that John was still alive and loved her passionately. She tried to reciprocate in her letters, though she found it hard to tell him anything of major significance or interest, except that she loved him, missed him terribly and was so glad that they had married before he left. To write about the ballet would appear frivolous, and because he knew so little about it, it would not make much sense to him.

Shirley had one companion in adversity: a few weeks after John's departure, Pete was told to prepare for being sent abroad in the near future. Poor Cynthia, normally so calm and collected, was beside herself. "He doesn't know where he's going, and I worry where he might be sent. Supposing it's the Far East with all those Japs?" she moaned. "They say they're worse, even more cruel, than the Nazis. I wish we had married, but there wasn't time, because he was never home for long enough!"

Shirley comforted her as best she was able, saying, "Pete's very resourceful; he'll keep himself and his troops safe."

Her attempts at reassurance rang false, since her own experience was about to be repeated so closely in Cynthia's, and she herself lived on the edge of despair.

Again and again, she was saved from total despair by the ballet. Had it not been for her dancing, she might not have bothered to get up in the morning. Nevertheless, once out of bed, she disciplined herself to put a brave face on it, taking on board whatever challenges the day put in her way, and this is what she encouraged Cynthia to do.

"Look, Cynnie," she said gently, "Pete and John will come back from this campaign as heroes. Neither of us are encouraging our menfolk by moping and telling them how miserable we are. We have to carry on with our lives as best we can and make light of our worries and our sadness.

They know that we are supporting the War effort here, and they want to be told that we love them and will be waiting for them to come home. Anyhow, when is he leaving?"

"He doesn't know yet," Cynthia cried. "It might not be until next year, but he has been told to be ready!"

"Ah, I see – I thought you meant he was leaving straight away!" said Shirley through pursed lips. "In that case, Cynnie, don't start worrying now – leave that until he really has gone." She went back into the studio and applied herself to rigorous *barre* exercises.

It did not help that Cynthia lived at home with her mother. She, a talented seamstress who had made many of Aurora's most complicated costumes, was quite out of her depth in helping her daughter through the perceived crisis, because she had not overcome the agony of losing her own husband at the very end of the First World War. At that time, a full six months before Cynthia was born, everyone believed that War to be nearly over.

Being of a nervous disposition, yet susceptible to the daily reports in the newspapers to which she was addicted, Cynthia's mother read every report from the War zones and then repeated what she had read to her daughter. Even the news of an Allied victory would plunge the mother into gloom. "They may have broken through," she would say, "but I wonder how many casualties our boys have suffered in the process." Or, shaking her head gloomily, "That must have been such a big battle – there will have been many deaths."

Cynthia tried hard not to react, but would retreat into her bedroom, where she would spend a sleepless night panicking at her mother's interpretations of the state of affairs. Fortunately for Aurora, Cynthia succeeded in summoning up sufficient self-discipline to prevent her private life from ruining her performances. In this she took a leaf out of Shirley's book by using her depth of emotion to enhance her roles, rather than scuppering them, and found that concentrating on her work took her mind off her personal problems.

Madame was pleased with her and complimented her often. "Zeenzeea, your interpretations 'ave become vairy conveenzeeng. You 'ave shown true feeleeng in your dance."

Cynthia nodded politely before going to the cloakroom, where Shirley would find her in floods of tears. She always tried to comfort her friend with words that, eventually after frequent repetition, began to sound hollow.

"Cynnie," she would say, putting her arm round her friend's shoulders. "You have done so well! But remember, we're not the only ones in Aurora who are suffering in some way; almost everyone in our troop has someone dear to them involved in this War. It's up to us to keep dancing to show Hitler that he can't defeat us!"

"You're right, Shirl," Cynthia whimpered, wiping her eyes. "I'm being rather silly, I know. And I know it's hard for everyone. Sometimes when someone like Madame says something nice to me, I think how sad it will be when Pete's gone, and I won't be able to tell him!"

Shirley was becoming rather tired of these outbursts and had resorted to saying, "Well, Pete's still here and you can tell him later, so let's get back to the rehearsal, shall we?"

Pete's posting was cancelled just before Christmas. Shirley endeavoured to show how glad she was for her friend.

37

Although it was normal for the troops to be given leave on Christmas Day and New Year's Day, this relaxation, for obvious reasons, did not apply during campaigns, so Shirley held out little or no hope of seeing her husband over the festive period. Ted took down the map of Sicily from the living-room wall, and in its place pinned up a map of Italy, explaining that the Italian campaign was in full swing. With his father he also discussed news that Shirley did not want to hear. The truth was that the campaign was already taking a massive toll on Allied as well as Axis forces. It would come to be recognized as the most costly campaign of the War in terms of casualties. In Britain, food shortages were becoming extreme, so nowhere could the anticipation of Christmas 1943 be described as particularly joyful.

Even Eileen's brother's stocks, normally such a reliable source of treats, were low: all he could spare for Christmas Day were a few eggs and a rather skinny chicken, which nevertheless, Eileen and Archie insisted on sharing with Reggie and his family.

"It's a shame your Madame went off to her friends in the country," Eileen said. "I would have liked to invite her, but although she would have been welcome here, I suppose it would be even more difficult to make this chicken go round, considering how small it is. But thank goodness you are all here! It wouldn't be Christmas if we had to sit here eating all on our own."

She carefully carved the breast meat of the chicken into thin slices to make it go round, and added a small amount of leg meat to each plate. Then she scooped out the stuffing of breadcrumbs with dried herbs from her garden, and distributed that to the guests. "A pity the butcher wouldn't let me have any sausage meat," she brooded. "It would have made the chicken go further. If you ask me, he was keeping it for his own family."

"Can't blame him for that, I suppose," said Archie, but nobody, least of all Ted, agreed with him.

"Well, we do have plenty of carrots and parsnips," Eileen said brightly. "Archie dug them up in November and we've kept them in the garage, so you can't have more wholesome veg than that! Do help yourselves to the apple sauce. We've managed to keep a few apples in the shed as well." Her guests eagerly helped themselves to the apple sauce and duly expressed their appreciation of the carrots and parsnips, which tasted sweet and delicious, aided by a good glass of Châteauneuf-du-Pape, brought back to England in better days by Reggie.

The conversation turned to the War, as did conversations at dinner tables all over the land. Shirley shut her ears to it, and helped Eileen clear the plates after the first course, while Ted maintained an awkward silence, his mouth firmly shut. Archie and Reggie, as was their wont, kept up a running commentary on the events of the past few days and weeks, although their stomachs had a tendency to rumble loudly, interrupting their talk.

"We're getting the better of them on their home territory, aren't we?" Archie remarked, posing a question to which the answer had to be "yes" from his audience.

"You're right there, Archie," Reggie replied. "How many of their cities have we bombed now?"

"Well, let's see," said Archie, as he began to count up the toll to date of German cities that had fallen victim to RAF night-time bombing raids. He was slowly counting up the tally of British successes, but his calculations were becoming more complicated when the Allied cities themselves were enemy targets.

"We bombed Berlin in August 1940 – but that was because they had bombed Norhambury on 9th July that year."

"You're jumping ahead, Archie," Reggie butted in. "What about our bombing of Cologne in May 1940? That was long before Berlin."

"Well then," said Archie, "maybe the bombing of Norhambury was in revenge for Cologne. Anyhow, you only have to go to Norhambury to see for yourselves how dreadful that was! And the Luftwaffe battered that fine city really badly again last year in the Baedeker raids. Don't you realize, though, we haven't even mentioned the Battle of Britain? That seems a long time ago now."

"Yes, but you're losing the point, Archie," Reggie said, and reminded his cousin that they were supposed to be talking about RAF and American successes in bombing Germany.

"Oh dear, I'm getting confused," said Archie. "You take over, Reggie – your memory's better than mine."

Reggie stroked his chin – even he had difficulty remembering the next one. "Ah," he exclaimed, "now I remember – the next success for us was Münster in July '41. Then I think it was Lübeck in March this year. Oh, and also a huge raid, the second on Cologne, last year, and Bremen later in the year."

He racked his brains and blew out his cheeks. "Of course we bombed Berlin again in March this year, and Hamburg non-stop for those eleven days in the summer. And this past autumn there's been Hanover – and the third raid on Berlin. I think that's about it up to now – that's to say, that's all I remember."

Here Ted, who had not stirred since the conversation began, chipped in, drily observing, "What about Augsburg in April '41?"

"Yes, of course, I was forgetting that one," Reggie confessed. "Bless me, I thought I had them all memorized, but there are so many more than when we last counted them up. You're right, Ted, that's not surprising – your memory's better than mine."

"Anyhow," said Ted, "however many there are, it's too many on both sides, though the Nazis started it in October '39, and it's still going on, and will for a long time yet."

The timely interruption of Eileen's appearance with the pudding put a stop to this morbid discussion. "I can't say it's exactly my best Christmas pudding," she said apologetically, "it's more of a sponge with currants and some apples in it, and a bit of holly on top, but I hope it's better than nothing. I darkened it with gravy browning – you wouldn't know it, would you? They say you don't taste it at all! Shirley is bringing the mock cream to go with it."

She turned to Shirley, who stood behind her. "There you are, dear, put it down beside the pudding, would you?"

Shirley carefully placed the mock cream on the table, and silently resumed her seat. From the kitchen she had heard the conversation in the dining room and had shivered at the mention of the Battle of Britain.

"Oh, come on, Archie!" Eileen scolded her husband. "Aren't you going to light a few candles? They would liven up the place!"

Archie found three candles in the sideboard, kept for blackouts. "I suppose we could use these," he said doubtfully, "but what happens when the lights go out again?"

Eileen was crestfallen. Despite her efforts to make something out of practically nothing, this Christmas was becoming the most miserable ever.

Reggie intervened, calming her disappointment. "Don't worry about that, Eileen!" he said, coming to the rescue. "I'm sure there are plenty of candles in the shop. I'll let you have some!"

Although Eileen cheered up, it was now Shirley's turn to feel wretched. The totting up of the bombing raids on Germany by the RAF and the Americans, which had been quite audible in the kitchen, had dampened her resolve to bring an air of jollity and sparkle to the rest of the festivities by starting a singsong of 'We Wish You a Merry Christmas'. She had heard that the casualties in those German cities had been enormous, although most people considered that just revenge for the havoc, destruction and death that the Nazi raids had wreaked all over Great Britain. She had seen the results of bombing for herself all over the land, most recently in Norhambury, in Wales and in Scotland, as well as in London. She had no illusions about the effects of it on the populations of those places, because she well knew what it was like to be caught up in one of those raids. Coventry, where she and her baby had been among the victims, would be inscribed on her heart for ever.

Part of her, the part that had lost a fiancé and a baby to the War, considered the raids on Germany well and truly justified, but another part could not help but imagine all those families with innocent babies and little children, caught up with no chance of escape from the horror of the explosions, the collapsing buildings, the raging fireballs, and the red pillars of fire reaching up to the sky, such as she had seen all too often when out on patrol. These were the inevitable and deliberate consequences of raids wherever they happened. She tried her hardest to enter into the spirit of the Christmas dinner, but, like Ted sitting silently on the other side of the table, did not succeed.

Ted was not making any effort at all to participate in the somewhat forced attempt at Christmas jollity, and seemed preoccupied; she wondered why. Perhaps there had been bad news about Hélène. She would ask him what was troubling him as soon as there was an opportunity.

After dinner, which ended in the late afternoon with a small cup of real coffee, which had been Madame's Christmas present to the gathering, Reggie and Archie decided that they would go to the pub for a drink as soon as it opened. Meanwhile, they settled into the armchairs in the lounge and soon nodded off. Eileen said she would like to go to the pub too after her nap, and asked Ted and Shirley if they would join in, but Ted stood up briskly, saying, "Thank you very much, Auntie Eileen, for a truly delicious Christmas dinner. I think I ought to be on my way now." He did not specify why he ought to be on his way, but he caught his sister's eye; it was clear to her from that glance that he wanted to talk to her, so she also stood up.

"Let me help with the washing-up, Eileen," she said, "and then I'll go to keep Ted company. I think I need a nap too; I'm so full!" She had cleared the dishes before Eileen was able to stop her, then hastily ran cold water into the sink in the kitchen and started to do the washing-up. Eileen protested, but Shirley assured her that she would leave the drying-up and tidying all the plates, utensils and cutlery away to her.

It was a chilly evening when Shirley stepped outside and set out for home. She wrapped her coat around her and ran most of the way, keen to find out why Ted had been so quiet at dinner. The food that Eileen had so painstakingly managed to prepare was not the best Christmas dinner ever, but it had been enjoyable, and, with all the vegetables, sufficient considering the straitened circumstances: indeed the gravy browning had not lent any unusual flavour to the pudding, but had given it a rich dark brown colour.

Normally, since he had become used to English cooking again, Ted would rise to the occasion and enter into conversations, peppering his comments with witty observations and jokes when provided with a good meal, and a glass of wine. Certainly the one they had just eaten did not, in present circumstances, fall so very far short of the standards of an acceptable Christmas dinner, so it was puzzling that he had been so sombre and uncommunicative. Even Reggie's bottle of special French Burgundy had failed to lend a touch of *je ne sais quoi* to the occasion and liven him up.

Shirley was ashamed that she herself had not made any effort to bring more joy to the gathering, and felt very sorry for Eileen, who certainly did not deserve the miserable reception her cooking had encountered. If only her father and Archie hadn't chosen to talk non-stop about the War and the bombing of Germany with some references to the bombing nearer home by the Luftwaffe. If only her darling, absent John had been with them, then she might have felt more inclined to laugh and chatter about nothing in particular, in the hope of raising the spirits of those around her.

She slipped silently into the private entrance and climbed the stairs. From the landing, she heard Ted talking into the phone – in French. Clearly he was sitting in the dark in the living room. "*D'accord,*" ("right") Ted was saying. "*Je comprends; ne t'inquiète pas; je serai très prudent. Merci, au revoir!*" ("I understand; don't worry; I will be very careful. Thank you, goodbye!") She tiptoed downstairs, and noisily bounded up again. Only then did her brother realize that she was back.

"Hello, Ted!" she called out. "Are you there somewhere?

"Yes, I'm here in the dark," he answered. "I'll draw the curtains, then I'll put the light on."

Shirley went into the living room and sat down in their father's sagging armchair.

"Dear Eileen, how hard she tried to give us a good dinner, didn't she?" she observed. Ted merely nodded in agreement. "Shirl," he said, "you're on patrol tonight, aren't you?"

"Yes, I'm afraid so. I wish they'd given us at least tonight off. It's not as if there's anything happening at the moment."

She shrugged with her hands apart, fingers spread wide in that very French gesture so natural to her. "It's been quiet for a long time now, yet we still have to go out scolding people for letting a chink of light peep through their curtains, and rescuing old ladies who've fallen off the pavement because they can't see where they're going. Honestly, it's true, isn't it, we've nearly won the War, and Hitler's running out of ideas."

For a moment she felt quite jubilant, but then, glancing at the map on the wall, she was reminded that victory was still a long way off. "Well, perhaps not yet," she added soberly. "There's still Italy to be dealt with." With bowed head, she gave a despondent sigh.

"Hm," said Ted. "It's not at all as simple as that, but I'm coming out with you tonight."

"That's kind, but you don't have to. You already do my weekends when we're away performing, as well as your own nights on duty," she protested.

"No, it's all right – I need to talk to you and that's the only time we can have a quiet chat together," he replied.

"I hope Hélène is safe – is she?" was the immediate reaction that sprang into Shirley's mind.

"I hope so too," her brother said. "As far as I can tell, she seems to be as safe as possible, although that's not saying much."

A ring at the doorbell interrupted their talk, causing them to frown at each other in puzzlement. "That's strange," said Ted. "We're not expecting anyone, are we? Pa won't be back from the pub yet. He'll only just have gone. Anyhow, he keeps his keys in his pocket all the time."

"I'll see who it is," Shirley replied, already on her way to the landing.

From upstairs, Ted heard the squeals of joy from below when his sister opened the front door; the squeals gave way to silence and then to steps ascending the staircase. "Ted! Ted! Look who's here! It's John!" Shirley called from the staircase.

Travel-weary and even thinner than he had been after the North Africa campaign, John greeted Ted like a long-lost friend.

"Hello there, brother-in-law! Long time, no see!" he declared, shaking hands vigorously with Ted, but keeping one arm firmly around Shirley's waist.

Ted responded with equal enthusiasm, giving the impression that here at last was someone with whom he could have a worthwhile conversation, although for fear of being in the way, he discreetly edged towards the landing.

"I'd better be off on patrol," he said as he went, "and leave you two to catch up with each other for a bit. I'll start by going down the road and round the corner past Archie's and do that neighbourhood, but if you want to join me, I'll hover outside the front door for five minutes in about three-quarters of an hour before setting off in the other direction. No need to hurry, though, and if you don't want to turn out again, I'll carry on without you."

The newly-weds were indeed grateful to have the flat to themselves after the months of separation. There were plenty of questions to be asked and answered, but those could wait for later, or even until the following day. To be together was the best Christmas present either of them could have wished for, and to feel the other fit, reasonably well and passionate in a long-awaited embrace, was the fulfilment of months of longing. Shirley would happily have nestled down with her head in John's shoulder for the night, but he glanced at his watch. "Ah, my love," he said, "your brother will be waiting at the door in ten minutes' time, I think we ought to go and keep him company."

"Must we?" Shirley groaned. "I'm happy here. I've never been so happy! I suppose I must come, though, because apparently there's something that Ted wants to talk about. He's been very morose all day. When he's like that, he won't say what it is until we're well away from other people, so it must be something serious."

John, with obvious reluctance, offered to stay behind if his presence was going to be an embarrassment to Ted, but Shirley insisted on his accompanying them on the patrol. "I'm not going to let you out of my sight," she said adamantly, "so we'll go together, whatever Ted has to say about it."

John did not take much persuading. "Fine," he said. "However confidential it turns out to be, that's all in a day's work for me, and even better because it's work I shall be doing with you! I hope Ted won't mind!" he said, unexpectedly lively after his long journey from a major theatre of this most dreadful of wars.

Shirley had always regarded the patrol as a duty, sometimes a rather wearisome duty, so John's readiness boosted her morale, although she wished that Ted could be left to carry out the patrol on his own. The reunion with her husband had been so brief, after such a long time apart, neither of them wanted its magic to end. But if Ted was, of necessity, to be a party to that magic, that was how it had to be.

Ted, as good as his word, was waiting for them outside the shop and needed no prompting to say quietly to John,

"I'm glad to have you with us, John. What I have been wanting to say to Shirl is highly confidential, but I know that you can be trusted if you hear it too. Maybe you can use it in some way best known to yourself. So let's set out, shall we?"

There were many chinks of light peeping through curtains that Christmas evening. Some curtains were so open that it was possible to see candles flickering on Christmas trees indoors. Shirley was unwilling to call out warnings of fines or worse to the inhabitants, as many of those people had become friends over the years and shared the general feeling of discontent, frustration and weariness at all the unending perils, privations and sadness of the War as it blighted their lives, and ruined all their plans for the future. Indeed many of them had lost friends and close family members, either in Britain or abroad, so there was not much that they didn't know about the dangers of warfare.

"Come on, Shirl, do your duty!" Ted urged her. "Tell these idiots to close their curtains. You can't allow them to be blasé about the dangers, not just to themselves but to the whole neighbourhood, and, who knows, maybe people further afield! I'll do it for you if you feel uncomfortable about it!"

"No, Ted," she retorted sharply. "Don't do that! Poor things, they've had enough of this War, and I can understand that; I have too! So let them enjoy their Christmas without harassing them!"

"I can see it's time to let you into a secret," said Ted, in exasperation. "We'll leave these stupid fools and go where we can talk in private. Come on, let's go to the recreation ground. There's a bench where we can sit down. I reckon I can find my way there in the dark."

38

Stumbling over tree roots, guided by the faint light from their tiny torches, the three of them found the bench and sat down on it in the pitch darkness. Shirley would have preferred to carry on walking arm in arm with John to keep warm. This was not to be, because Ted had other plans, so instead she snuggled up to her husband and listened.

Her brother was insisting on the three of them staying out of earshot of any night-time eavesdroppers.

"Pay attention carefully to what I have to tell you, and on no account repeat it to anyone else, not even Pa!" he warned them in a whisper, though maintaining that stern tone he reserved for those occasions when he really meant what he said: it implied that he was not prepared to brook any frivolity.

He would normally have been speaking in French in such confidential circumstances, but out of deference to John, and his reluctance to be drawn into any discussion of his dual nationality, he murmured quietly in English, "I was glad I'd come home early after the Christmas dinner, because I had a call: the phone was ringing as I put the key in the lock. I was half expecting it," he said. "Fortunately the caller hung on. I won't say who he was, but I recognized the voice; it was someone I had known in northern France. He put himself at risk by ringing me, which is why we must be so cautious how we use this information. The fact is that the Germans are bringing their planes to airfields on the French coast and are planning to attack us again – another Blitz, probably."

There was a stunned silence while John and Shirley absorbed her brother's news. "Here, do you mean?" she whispered at last, in shocked disbelief.

"Yes, I do mean here, and quite soon. Apparently Hitler is furious that the RAF have been so successful in their bombing campaign over German cities, and he knows the end will soon be coming into sight, so he wants us to pay the price for his defeat!"

He stopped talking. Shirley sat trembling with the shock until she found her tongue, and asked what on earth could be done.

"Not much immediately, without terrifying the whole population, particularly of London, but at the very least we can make sure they still go on obeying orders," Ted replied. "I'm sure this information has probably already filtered through higher up the chain," he continued, "so they'll be prepared, but I think we should be stricter, possibly coming out more regularly, that is twice or three times at night, until people get used to observing the regulations again."

His listeners kept so quiet, he felt he had to offer them some consolation, though that was minimal. "I'll come out with you, Shirl, and shout at the offenders until they do as they're told. They're not likely to argue with me!" he declared with some satisfaction: his voice was known to strike the fear of God into even the most determined of culprits, and inevitably he was well known everywhere locally on account of the loss of his left arm.

He was generally regarded as being out of the War, and simply a seriously wounded victim who could no longer play any part in the conflict. The advantage of his suffering meant that no casual observer would have suspected him of having any knowledge, let alone secret knowledge, of what was happening. As a result, he no longer had to keep his identity secret, although he was forever extremely careful about what he revealed about himself and his work, which was top secret and still ongoing, making him an easy target for spies.

Shirley had come to her senses and was considering her own part in preparing the neighbourhood for an eventual attack, but John, having maintained an eloquent silence during the exchange between brother and sister, spoke first.

"Can you tell me what to expect? Do you know when this is going to happen and where it's coming from?" he whispered.

"Nobody knows," Ted replied, "but, as I have said, what we do know is that they are bringing what aircraft they have left to the coast stretching north from Normandy to the Pas-de-Calais, just across the Channel in other words, and further north into Belgium, maybe even Holland."

With a hint of despair in his voice, he went on, "I gathered from my colleague that action is likely to begin quite soon, but perhaps not until the New Year, because they still have a lot of preparation to do, shifting aircraft around and bringing them to the front line. That means we'll have time to get this area in order before then. As you are aware, that will only happen if everyone does as they're told. What my friend did say, though, is that to save fuel, they are using horses to pull the planes onto the runways!"

"Gracious! They must be desperate!" Shirley exclaimed almost joyfully, but then quietened down quickly for fear of upsetting her brother. More seriously she picked up the thread of the conversation. "Here we go again!" said she, "I can scarcely bear the thought of it. But did your friend say what sort of aircraft they still have?"

"Fighters and bombers, mostly," he answered.

"The heavy brigade again, in other words," she observed.

"That's right, so if there are lots of them – and that we don't know yet – we'll have our work cut out keeping people safe."

John kept silent: clearly he was storing up all Ted's information.

Having made those ominous pronouncements, Ted stood up and set off along the path to the road. John and Shirley followed him.

Loudly enough only for Ted and John to hear, she promised, "Tomorrow – if, that is, we are spared tonight – I'll check the siren and make sure that wretched little box for the key in the church porch is in good working order. It's always getting jammed up with rust, in spite of all the endless repairs Pa has given it. It was a real nuisance last time and wouldn't open just when it was most needed. I've been tussling with it ever since the Blitz began in 1940! I'll have to ask Pa to help again."

"Good idea," answered Ted, certain that his father could fix anything.

John suggested letting the alarm off a few times, so that people would realize there might be a good reason for it, rather than thinking it went off by accident. "We could even tell them, if they ask, that we're doing it to make sure it's in good working order." He went on, "That's about as much as we can say, and if they're bright enough to put two and two together, they'll see that we're doing it for a reason. If they ask more questions, we'll tell them it's our job to keep the borough safe. They can't argue with that."

Ted and Shirley were both grateful for this eminently practical and decisive contribution to the task in hand. "Though I don't think we should do that tonight: it wouldn't be fair – it's still Christmas, after all," said she.

The next morning, Boxing Day, Shirley, Ted and John were up and out before six, heading for the church porch. "As I suspected," Shirley blurted out with annoyance as she pulled at the door of the siren key box. "Look, John, this box is no better than it ever was. I would have thought that the repairs after the vandals had attacked it would have solved that problem!"

He gave the door a good tug and it eased under his strength. "It certainly needs more attention," he said. Ted offered to run home and ask their father to come and have a look at it, while she and John checked the siren.

"They won't like this!" Shirley declared at the prospect of rousing the whole neighbourhood so early in the morning while it was still dark.

Ted ran off to fetch their father while, by torchlight, John and Shirley hurried up the narrow staircase to the top of the tower and, with their fingers in their ears, let the siren off, not once but twice.

"You are naughty! You're really enjoying this, aren't you?" John laughed as he pulled his wife towards him and hugged her. The same people who had left their curtains open the night before came running out of their houses into the black, early hours, still in their nightclothes, shouting and screaming, "What's going on?" On each occasion Shirley switched the siren off, and the wail died away.

A crowd had gathered outside the church by the time Ted reappeared. They pounced on him. "Hey, why's the siren going off? It's gone off twice. What's that all about?"

"Oh," he said with a complete lack of concern, "it's just my sister – she's testing it."

"But why?" they all chorused. "We haven't had a raid for ages – why now?"

Shirley and John appeared at the bottom of the staircase, rather embarrassed by the commotion they had caused, although in the dark their red faces were not visible to the protesting neighbours.

"It's orders," she explained. "We have to make sure the siren is in good working order at all times, day and night, in case of trouble."

"Why now?" somebody called out.

John simply shrugged. "You never know, do you?"

Ted added, "It's a long time since it had a proper going-over, and we're still at War, remember?"

As the disconsolate assembly dispersed and day began to dawn, a tall figure loomed out of the departing crowd. It was Madame, wrapped in an entirely unsuitable, green silk dressing gown. "What eez 'appeneeng?" she asked, her teeth chattering with cold, but when she saw Shirley and Ted, she yawned and reverted to her preferred language, French, which, of course Shirley and Ted had no problem in understanding. "I was afraid there was a bombing raid coming! But I am so tired. I only just arrived back from my holiday. I must go home to bed!"

"Yes, good idea, Madame. There's no raid – not at the moment. We're just testing the alarm," Ted reassured her, "but wh—" (he was about to say "when", but changed that at the last minute to "if") "if the alarm goes off for real, you'll have to be quicker than that getting out of your house, and wear something warmer next time!" She took no notice of him, and, turning on her heel, she hurried home.

"I say," remarked John, "you two do speak good French!"

"Oh, I have to with Madame," said Shirley.

As they set out for home, the three of them, Ted, John and Shirley, noticed a large figure trying to make himself scarce by hiding behind a tree. Ted dug his sister in the ribs and sniggered, for that figure was none other than their father, who had come to mend the box, but was taking refuge from Madame.

When she was out of sight, Reggie emerged sheepishly from his hiding place, carrying his torch and a tool kit. "That woman's gone, has she?" he asked, peering into the darkness. "Archie heard the siren," he continued, once he was satisfied that Madame was not in the vicinity, "and he came running round, so he's manning the shop, although there aren't any papers today. Still, one never knows when people will come in, asking for candles or cigarettes. So I've come as quickly as I could. Where's this lock?"

He took the lock to pieces, cleaned and oiled it, before restoring it to its position in the porch. "That should work for a bit," he declared. "The trouble is, the same as in the Blitz, it gets very damp against that old stone wall and then it jams again, and those vandals didn't help. Now, what else is there for us to do?"

The four of them then went to check the public air-raid shelter and discovered another lock that needed Reggie's attention. "This is strictly another of the Council's responsibilities, but we'll be blamed if it's impossible to open that door," he muttered, "I'll fix it temporarily and then ring them when we get back to the shop, except I won't be able to do that today, because it's Boxing Day, so I'd better do the job properly now."

By mid-morning all four were of the opinion that they had done a whole day's work, touring the area, and rectifying, or noting, faults in and omissions from their schedule of air-raid safety measures. When at last they were satisfied that the district was as safe as could be in the circumstances, they went home.

Then it was that Reggie started plying Shirley with questions. "Why are you so busily going round our area? And why drag poor John with you? Poor chap, he needs a rest after all he must have been through in Italy. Is there something happening I don't know about?"

John jumped in with a quick reply. "Oh, Mr Marlow, don't worry about me; it's all in a day's work, and I'm glad to be here. Whatever we have to do here, it's so much better than Italy!"

"Just trying to be on the safe side, Pa," Ted added airily and went to wash his hands.

Shirley, who was searching for food in the cupboards for lunch, was no more communicative. "Ah, good! Here's a tin of sausages in baked beans!" she finally remarked with satisfaction. "We'll have that for lunch with some potatoes! Sorry, Pa, lunch is a bit late, and we've worked up quite an appetite since six o'clock this morning. I'll have something on the table in a jiffy."

That Boxing Day afternoon, Shirley and John went out for a walk. "There's not really anywhere much to go round here," she said regretfully, "not many green spaces or hills with lovely views, only street after street of houses, many of them bombed, but not many people about."

"Don't you worry about that!" he said, "I don't care about the view – all I care about is being with you!"

They ambled aimlessly through smart residential areas of bomb-damaged, red-brick Edwardian houses, and less salubrious areas of ruined, drab, grey streets.

While they were walking on through one of the desolate areas, John said he had a question for Shirley, and he hoped it was not impertinent.

"I'm listening," said Shirley, anticipating what was to come.

"How is it your brother speaks French like a native? And you too?" he asked, adding, "I know of course that you speak French with your ballet teacher, but you are so fluent! I'm amazed!"

Shirley had a more persuasive, ready-prepared answer to hand than that she spoke French with Madame. She did not want to relate their family history: it was too complicated and too tragic. Instead, she simply told her husband an easier version of the truth.

"Pa used to take us on holiday to France sometimes, because he liked to revisit his old haunts from the Great War, so we learnt a bit of French, and we had very good teachers in our schools, native French people, refugees from across the Channel mostly. Ted speaks the language better than me because has a French girlfriend," she explained hurriedly. "He went to work for the Resistance hoping to find her, and, as you already know, that's how he lost his arm. It was in an ambush. Better not talk to him about that; he's very sensitive and frustrated at not being able to go back to France. Of course, he still has contacts there, and that's how he finds out what's happening on the other side, as he has just done. And you know, he works for the SOE."

It all came out in one breath, rather incoherently, but it was the truth, although not the whole truth, that Shirley told her husband. She hoped that her version of the truth was enough to satisfy John's curiosity. "Yes, he's told me a little about it himself. He's a true hero!" was John's comment.

"Now," said Shirley, rapidly but quietly changing the subject. "What I want to know is how you managed to come on leave. You haven't told me yet."

"Well," he said, taking a deep breath, "there's still such a lot to do in Italy. It's been a hard battle on all fronts. We've had some successes and captured some of their key positions, but they're putting up a very stiff resistance. Can you believe it, the enemy's even taken over a virtually inaccessible monastery and made that into a fortress! Monte Cassino, it's called. Goodness knows how the monks are coping with that!" He paused and then appeared to be talking to himself: "All was going well until they rescued Mussolini and took him up north to help them direct operations from there."

Finally, he began to answer her question by telling her that he had returned to England with Monty's entourage, not on leave, but for a meeting to discuss the conduct of the Italian campaign. He looked her straight in the eye, as if to prepare her for what was to come.

"I'm sorry to say, the meeting is tomorrow, Sunday, and I have to be there because all the top brass will be attending, including General Dwight Eisenhower, the commander of the American Forces in Europe: they are fighting with us. Ike, as they call him, has just become Supreme

Commander of Allied Forces. I rather dread how Monty will react to that! Ike is well liked and has the reputation of reducing friction between people, while, as I may have told you, Monty is pretty direct and, let's say, very sure of his own opinions."

Shirley was learning to keep quiet. Sensing his sadness and frustration, she held his arm tightly, wondering what to say to cheer him up. "It sounds appalling," she began. "I've heard about it from Pa – but try to forget that for today, and let's enjoy being together! Come on! Let's go home and ring up a hotel somewhere near your meeting place – I suppose that's in Whitehall, is it?" He nodded while she carried on talking. "We'll book ourselves in for a night, and then when your meeting's over, we'll be together for that one night. That's better than nothing, isn't it?"

"That would be wonderful, and I want to book it straight away!" he replied with a smile. "But I have to warn you, these meetings sometimes go on all night. So it might not be the sort of stay we were hoping for."

"That doesn't worry me – I'll be awake waiting for you when you come in!"

"But what about your ARP duties?" he asked.

"Ted can take care of those," she replied without a second thought. "Anyhow, if you remember, he said that his contact was giving him advance warning, and that we have time to prepare, so it's unlikely there'll be a raid just yet."

"Right-o, if you think so," said John uneasily. As a military man it was not in his nature to change plans simply to suit himself.

He spoke with such seriousness that Shirley was discouraged from revealing with even the slightest trace of dismay at the prospect of spending the whole of the next day alone in Whitehall, except for the exasperated sigh which escaped her lips.

Calmly she asked, "So when will you be going back to Italy?"

That, evidently, was a foregone conclusion.

"On Monday, probably, I'm afraid," he answered, his voice faltering.

"Come on, then," she cried, trying to sound buoyant, "the sooner we find a hotel, the better!"

They hurried home, but their plan to book a hotel near Whitehall was frustrated when Reggie came bounding out of the sitting room onto the landing as they came up the stairs. He was hardly able to contain his joy.

"Have you heard the news?" he asked, obviously expecting that they had not, and impatient to be the bearer of it.

"No, what news can that be?" Shirley enquired, irritated at having to delay making the phone call.

"Well, it mightn't mean anything to you, miss, but it will to John!" her father replied. "I've just heard that the, um, battleship Schumhurst, if that's how you say it, has been sunk!"

"Ah! Good news indeed!" exclaimed John, while Shirley stood by, wondering what on earth they were talking about. "Yes," John went on, "the Scharnhorst is the one remaining pride of the German navy! Their largest remaining battleship! Do you know where it was sunk, Reggie?"

"Off the coast of northern Norway, I think they said," said Reggie.

"That's even better!" John declared. "With the Scharnhorst gone, there'll be less danger to convoys in the Atlantic, both those going to the United States and those heading for Russia. And what's more, with the Bismarck gone as well and the Tirpitz damaged, we'll be able to send our larger ships to other areas!"

"It's time for a little celebration!" Reggie said, clapping his hands as he went off to look for a bottle of beer.

"It's good news for the Norwegians too!" John remarked to Shirley. "It will make life a lot easier for their Resistance fighters."

Shirley had given up all hope of finding a hotel that evening when Ted came in. He too had to be regaled with the news and share in a celebratory bottle or two of beer. She did not like beer, so was repairing to the kitchen to make herself a cup of tea when she remembered the other phone in the shop. Downstairs, out of the way of the men and their discussions, she thumbed through the central London directory until she found a hotel near Whitehall, rang the number and booked a room for herself and her husband for the next day and night.

It was well after midnight on the Sunday, after a long day's discussions, when John found his way to the hotel. As good as her word, Shirley was still awake when he arrived.

When she asked him how the meeting had gone, he answered, "Better than I expected. Eisenhower is very moderate but purposeful, so Monty is having to concede to him, which is no bad thing. I've never seen him so subdued!" he laughed. "Even better than that, there's something I have to tell you! Three guesses?"

"I don't know," she replied. "How could I? I've no idea what goes on in those meetings."

"I'll tell you, then," he conceded. "The return to Italy has been put off for another day so that everything that's been decided here can be put into place!"

"You're pulling my leg, aren't you?" she retorted, not sure whether she could believe her ears, or whether there was some truth in what he had related.

"No, really, I'm serious. I don't have to leave until Tuesday afternoon, so I'll be here tomorrow night as well!"

They hugged and kissed, but he pulled away. "And there's something else," he said with a grin. "The others are all going off for a posh lunch somewhere tomorrow to celebrate the end – hopefully successful – of the meeting, but I don't have to go with them, so I'll be free to come back here! And I bet they'll take ages over lunch, so even if I'm not at my desk until four-thirty, or even later, they won't ever find out!"

The following afternoon, Shirley waited impatiently in the hotel from midday until half-past two for John to appear.

"Let's have lunch here, shall we? I'm hungry!" he said, those being the first words he addressed to his wife as he walked through the door. This greeting was not met with any show of pleasure, sounding, as it did, like Ted's greetings, asking for food or tea as soon as she came home after a day's work in the shop, or a rehearsal, or housekeeping for her father and brother.

"I think you ought to give me a hug and tell my why you're so late!" she countered, aggrieved.

"Yes, of course, sorry about that – but let's order lunch first, and then I'll tell you!" he said, undeterred and cheerful. He scanned the hotel menu and then picked up the phone.

"Two steaks with roast potatoes and salad, and then, let's see, two zabagliones and two glasses of Saint-Émilion, please!" he ordered. Shirley gazed at him open-mouthed as he put the phone down.

"Won't that be very expensive?" she asked. "And it'll use up all my rations!"

"Don't worry. It doesn't matter. No rations needed," he replied nonchalantly. "It's official business, and I've told them you are with me. It's all being paid for by Whitehall, including the hotel. What's more, the meeting is over – well, more or less… and it's all bureaucratic and so on from now. That means I don't have to go back to work today after all. We'll have the rest of this afternoon, and tonight together!"

Shirley clapped her hands and exclaimed, "Oh, what bliss!"

He smiled. "Anyhow, I want to celebrate your birthday and Valentine's Day, because I don't expect I'll be back in February," he said, his expression becoming morose all of a sudden, far too much for her liking, resembling Alan's reaction on contemplating the inevitable dangers of his duties in the RAF.

"Oh, that's a pity! It would have been lovely to have you here for our first Valentine's, but I suppose in that case, we'll just have to make the most of the time we do have!" she said, trying hard, though not very successfully, to sound optimistic. Then she enquired, "What time do you have to leave tomorrow?"

"We're leaving at three in the afternoon," he replied. "But there are still a few things to finish off in the office, so I'll have to leave a bit earlier – but now I come to think of it, not until about one, which means that we won't need to get up early! Let's have lunch now and go for a walk. There's something I want to talk to you about." Lunch was so deliciously filling that after it they had to retire for a rest to recover before setting out on their walk.

There was still light in the sky, although at ground level all was dark when they left the hotel for their walk, arm in arm, along the Embankment. On the road, noise came at them from the traffic and from the boats on the river, while only the tiny torches prevented pedestrians from bumping into each other or accidentally stepping off the kerb. What's more, only shielded headlamps stopped the slow-moving vehicles from crashing into each other, or mounting the kerb and running down the pedestrians.

Shirley was glad to be clutching John's arm, because he was clearly gifted with an unerring sense of direction, and seemed to possess the night vision of a cat. He did not have to concentrate on where he was going, unlike Shirley, who, despite her ARP training, and perhaps because of her experience in Coventry, checked every step she took.

"Sorry I'm so slow," she apologized. "I once had a nasty fall during the Blitz in the dark, so I've become rather cautious!"

"Oh, poor darling, I wish I'd been there to pick you up!" he commiserated. "There's no hurry – we'll take our time, and if you can listen while we walk, I'll tell you what I've been thinking."

"If I cling to you, I'll be all right, so carry on. I'm all ears," said Shirley, without voicing the thought that had come into her mind, which was that it was just as well that he hadn't been there on that fateful night, 14th November 1940, in Coventry. He didn't need to know any more details about that episode than that she had had a fall, and he did not ask for any, which was a relief, because she feared that those tragic details might have spelt the end of their marriage, had he found out about them.

"This is all because of some news I've been given today," John began. "It seems I may be back in London sooner than I was expecting. Well, that depends on how things develop in Italy, though it seems they want me to be involved in the planning of the next big operation. Everybody, including Hitler, seems to know what is going to happen, but of course, I'm not allowed to talk about it. Anyhow, it means I shall be based in London when the Italian business is over and done with!"

Shirley almost swooned for joy. "I'm thrilled!" she whispered with her eyes closed, imagining a secure peacetime future with her Prince Charming, this man she loved, who had come into her life and rescued her from sadness and heartache. His arm was steadying her even now.

While she had been dreaming, he had been talking. "What do you think of that?" he asked, rousing her from her reverie.

"Oh, sorry! I was dreaming and thinking how wonderful it will be to have you home with me!"

He laughed. "Yes, do you know something? *I* believe it will be rather good too!" He turned towards her and kissed her on the forehead. "But," he said, taking up his thread again after a considerable interruption which irritated many a passer-by, standing, as they were, in the middle of the pavement, "but we'll need to have our own house. We can't go on living with your father and Ted now that we're married. It's not fair on them, and anyhow we need our privacy."

"What can we do, then?" she enquired.

"First we need to ask ourselves where we want to live; secondly how much we, that is I, can afford, and thirdly what sort of house we'd like to have," he said, appearing to have worked it all out.

"So you're thinking of a house, not a flat, are you?" she asked.

"I don't think I'd be very good at having people upstairs and downstairs as well as on both sides, so I would prefer a house," he said quite firmly.

"And where would that be?"

"That rather depends on you," he said. "I don't want to take you away from your father and Ted, so if you want to live south of the river, that might be possible, but I would prefer to live on the north bank, and by that I mean somewhere round here, because I'll be on call and will need to be able to get to Whitehall quickly." He gestured to the War Office on the other side of the road. "Mind you, if that's not possible, the Northern Line would bring me right down to the Embankment."

"Yes, I understand. But how are we going to do this, buy a house I mean, with you away in Italy?"

"I wondered," he said cautiously, "if you might have time to look at some houses while I'm away. I know you'd make a good choice."

They continued this conversation far into the night, so it was providential that John did not, after all, have to leave early the next morning.

39

All was quiet over the next few days in South Cross after John's departure for Italy. To the depths of her body and soul, Shirley missed, longed for and grieved for her beloved husband, beset by that recurring fear that once more in her life she had said goodbye to her other half, never to see him again. Gradually it dawned on her that the task that John had set her, house-hunting for the two of them, was in itself a positive token of his determination to return. This token she clung to with all her heart, determined to fulfil his wishes.

Although he had desperately regretted parting from his wife, he had shown only slight anxiety for the future by comparison with Alan's deep sense of foreboding. Instead, John had taken a pragmatic approach and concentrated on practicalities, telling Shirley how to go about house-hunting, what to look for in the properties she would be visiting – for example, signs of damp – and how to deal with estate agents. Also, he had told her how much he could afford, although she was determined to contribute her share. All of which set her to work, at first calculating how much she would be able to put in from her earnings and from the partial repayment of her loan to Aurora, and not forgetting a contribution from her inheritance. All in all, she decided that she could afford to search out a property that would fulfil every one of their needs. Next, ever practical and decisively positive, she developed a strategy.

She deliberately was not going to tell her father and brother about the plans, but would wait until she had actually found a suitable property. There was no need to upset them unnecessarily. Meanwhile, she pored over maps of North London, advertisements in newspapers and maps of the Underground, until she managed to pinpoint an area from where John would be able to travel speedily into central London on the Northern Line, and where house prices were roughly compatible with their budget. It was easy enough to borrow newspapers and maps from the shop in pursuit of her research, and return them later.

Until she had settled on a possible property in a reasonable area with good connections, she decided, there was no point in traipsing round North London in the hope of finding what she visualized as a *pied-à-terre*. To her frustration, none of the houses she saw advertised in any way resembled her idea of a *pied-à-terre*. They were mostly grey Victorian or Edwardian properties, back to back in terraces with small yards at the rear. Nonetheless, she kept an open mind. By no means could any of them be described as spacious, but, with two modest bedrooms and a box room which, although very small, might serve as a third bedroom, one of those would be large enough for the two of them, until they were able to afford something bigger and more attractive. Even if she found something that met her requirements, she would still base herself in South Cross in John's absence, and thus would continue to dance in Madame's studio.

On the Friday of that week, New Year's Eve, Reggie took a call in the middle of supper. He was not best pleased to have his meal interrupted. "What is it now?" he grumbled. "I bet it's one of the paper boys saying he can't do the round tomorrow morning."

As soon as he picked up the phone and heard the voice at the other end, his mood changed as he listened patiently. "Yes, yes, we know the War's not over yet, and we do know what to do; everything is in order and the population is getting used to returning to full blackout again," he told the caller, who must then have asked how it was that he seemed to have everything ready-prepared, not to mention the siren going off frequently in the middle of the night, because there had been complaints about that.

"Oh, well," Reggie replied, "we mustn't take any risks, and it seemed to me that people were becoming rather careless, particularly over Christmas, leaving their curtains open, for example, so I thought it time to bring them to heel." He said this assertively without mentioning Ted or Shirley's involvement. This explanation appeared to satisfy the person at the other end of the line, who then promptly called off, but not without first issuing the warning that blitzing was still a real possibility.

"Well done, you two!" Reggie said in praise of his family. "Now I know what you were up to, testing the siren and shouting out to the residents to close their curtains. You knew, didn't you, that we're in for another blitzing?"

Neither Shirley nor Ted said anything, until the latter replied innocently, "How could we have known, Pa?"

Reggie snorted. "I think you do know, Ted. Can't you tell me?"

"Well, they did say it's imminent," Ted admitted without saying who
"they" were, "that is, within the next week, so I reckon we should go
out every evening, from now on, all three of us, and get the district used
to our more rigorous patrols."

He looked for approval from his father and sister. She was about to
speak when Ted remembered another aspect he had overlooked. "I'm
sure Pa and I will be able to manage, Shirl, if you have to be away dancing," he added.

"Thanks," she replied, "I hope we'll still be needed at those RAF
bases, but it looks very unlikely to me." She shrugged her shoulders,
hands spread wide in her customary Gallic expression of uncertainty.

Reggie fell silent and lit his pipe before settling down to listen as
usual to the War Report, while Shirley and Ted did the washing-up in
the kitchen. They abandoned their task when their father called out
urgently after the chimes of Big Ben.

"Quick, come and listen to this!" he exclaimed as they came into the
room. "Hitler's got the wind up! Oh bother," he said as his son and
daughter came to sit down, "that's just over. He was wittering on about
all his efforts for the German people, and declaring that Germany would
never be defeated by force of arms nor by time, and blaming the Jewish
and international conspiracy for causing the War."

Reggie gave out a sarcastic laugh on hearing this, but Shirl gestured
to him to be quiet. "Ssh, there's more, Pa!"

The newscaster was now introducing the speech that the Deputy Prime
Minister, Clement Attlee, had given to mark the New Year.

"The hour of reckoning has come for the Nazis," he was saying, "but
we do know that in 1944 the War will blaze up into greater intensity like
never before, and we must be prepared to face heavier casualties. 1944
may be the victory year: it will only be so if we continue to put forward
our utmost efforts and allow nothing to divert us from our main purpose.
The War has brought us heavy reverses. It will make heavy demands on
all the Germans."

"Aha," remarked Ted, "so word *has* reached the powers that be, and
they really do know something's afoot. Maybe John had something to
do with that! Come on, let's leave the washing-up and go out on patrol."

As he was struggling into his uniform, the phone rang again. "Hey, are they on the way already?" he exclaimed, hopping across the room half dressed, to pick up the receiver.

"Yes, we'll be there straight away!" he assured the operator, and slammed the phone down. He became suddenly decisive and energetic in a way that his father and sister had not seen since the loss of his left arm. One might have been forgiven for thinking that he was even enjoying the prospect of a raid. In fact it was more likely that, given his own unfortunate circumstances, he was glad to be in action again, confronting the enemy with renewed determination and vigour.

"Come on, let's be off; it's time to switch the siren on!" he called to Shirley and his father, both of whom appeared, fully kitted out for a night out patrolling the area.

They were standing at the top of the stairs when the phone rang yet again. Shirley ran to it, listened, and simply replied, "Thanks," before putting the phone down. "False alarm!" she said. "But we still ought to go out on patrol."

All was calm in the cold night air. Ted, naturally rather deflated, suggested setting the siren off anyhow, as a practice run to put the residents on their toes, but Reggie vetoed that idea. "It seems to me," said he, "you and your sister put the neighbourhood on high alert after Christmas. Sufficient unto the day is the evil thereof. People have been coming into the shop all week asking if there's going to be an air raid. I said I didn't know and simply told them what I told that chap on the phone, that is, the War's not over yet and we have to make sure all is in good order." There was little need to shout out orders to the residents that night. Curtains were tightly closed with not a chink of light to be seen.

On New Year's Day barrage balloons appeared in the sky to the south and distant ack-ack guns fired a few shots, either as a warning to inhabitants or as part of a test practice. By now everyone was on tenterhooks, and although they all had their curtains dutifully closed by mid-afternoon when the sun receded over the horizon, the skies were quiet. An air of nervous anticipation pervaded the streets, as if the residents were well aware of what they should expect.

Nevertheless, it was not until the following night, the 2nd of January, that their fears began to materialize. The siren wailed and the distant ack-ack guns fired into the night at the advancing enemy aircraft.

Sheltering in Archie's porch, Ted listened. "Mm," he said, "I can hear Messerschmitts and Junkers – quite a collection they've got there. They've brought the whole lot with them to ward off the RAF." He turned to look at the southern sky, which was streaked with the reddish-gold light of fires blazing.

"Let's hope those fires are caused by burning German aircraft and not houses on the ground," he observed darkly.

The rumble of engines drew closer until a whole flight of bombers, heading north-east, flew over within only a mile or two from where they stood.

"Your Madame's safe, is she?" Reggie enquired of Shirley.

"She's in Archie's shelter," she reassured him, grinning inwardly at his asking after the safety of "that woman".

Unscathed by the first visitation from the Luftwaffe, there followed a day's grace in which people everywhere wisely waited in long queues for provisions, checked their Anderson shelters and warned their elderly relatives and friends to be prepared for the next raid, which indeed happened on the night of the 4th of January, killing adults and children in rural Surrey.

"Why Surrey?" people were querying in disbelief. The general reaction was one of defiance, though tinged with despair. "I can't believe this is happening again," one of Reggie's customers who had lost a son in the RAF moaned.

"I know how you feel," said another, an elderly pensioner. "It's been going on for such a long time. I thought when my Jeff died in the Great War, that would be the end for me, but still it goes on and I'm still here. It just doesn't make sense, except once I heard a preacher say that our souls are immortal; I have to hang on to that or life wouldn't be worth living." She cast her eyes to the floor, shaking her head in sorrow and wiping back the tears she was endeavouring to hide.

"Well, come and visit me, my dear," the first speaker said in a gentle burst of spontaneity. "I'm all on my own. My niece gave a me a lovely cookbook for Christmas. It's by that person who works for the government, Marguerite something-or-other. We could make ourselves a cake or some buns, and then have a cup of tea."

A close friendship, unlikely to be struck up so quickly in peacetime, but not untypical of wartime, thus developed between the two bereaved ladies.

Shirley observed this unfurling companionship, glad that at least some benefit for two old people was coming out of this War. She wished some benefit might be forthcoming for herself soon as well. John had left merely a week ago and her feelings were still raw with the sorrow of that bitter parting after his lamentably short leave. Despite embarking on the house-hunting enterprise, she had during that time longed for his return and missed him every moment of the day and night, so much so that an outside observer might have thought that she was in mourning. She wrote to him daily, trusting that the forces' mail was actually delivered to its destination; she wished he would phone so that she might tell him about her research, although the more she found out about hardships of the Italian campaign, the more unlikely a phone call from him seemed, and the more anxious she grew, the while trying to hide her feelings from Ted and her father.

The intense, night-time patrols were a distraction from her worries, since, when on patrol, she had to concentrate on the matter in hand, turning on the siren, directing the population to the shelters, checking that everyone was accounted for, and suchlike matters. Then, after the all-clear, she tended the wounded and waited for the ambulances, while trying to clear paths through the rubble and glass. Finally back home, she was so tired she flopped into bed and went straight off to sleep.

To her surprise, she woke reasonably refreshed and ready for another long day, helping when needed in the family business, scanning the advertisements for houses, shopping for scarce provisions, and cooking, before setting out again on patrol in the evening. Naturally, any spare moment was spent practising and rehearsing in Madame's studio, but without much prospect of ever performing on the stage again. Yet, whatever the future held, she was thankful more than ever for that ephemeral, unreal world which still absorbed, reflected and calmed the dissonances in her own real world.

By mid-January it became obvious that the hitherto sporadic German attacks were intended as a repeat of the 1940 Blitz, when much of London had been reduced to burning rubble. People were killed when more than two hundred aircraft filled the skies over and around the city on the night of the 21st of January, but only fifteen of them actually attacked the capital in that raid. Shirley, Ted and Reggie watched from a distance, fearing the worst, but perplexed that, when it came to it, the flames and explosions over London were minimal by comparison with the horrific scenes that Shirley and Reggie had witnessed in the early days of the War.

This, however, was not the only German attack that night: the sirens went off again and woke sleepers in the early hours when another wave of bombers approached. Once more, the damage and the casualties were far fewer than expected, the most notable German success being the partial bombing of the Palace of Westminster.

A couple of days later, Maud, Aurora's secretary, who was still working from a spare room in Eileen and Archie's house, asked to have a word with Shirley. Maud, not given to small talk, came straight to the point.

"I'm sorry to have to tell you, Shirley, that the performances in RAF bases have all been cancelled, one after the other. The airmen have to go into action against the German bombers and against the Messerschmitts every evening and all night. They've promised to let me know when they can start again, and then, they promise, they will ask you to put on the programmes that you would have been dancing now."

Shirley was stunned. "Couldn't we go earlier in the day?" she stammered. "There are some bases where we have already performed in the afternoon to allow for night-time operations."

"No, I'm afraid not," said Maud. "I asked that, but the answer was 'no' from every base. Not at present, anyhow," she said, in a belated attempt to sweeten the pill.

Although she had suspected that this particular blow might be coming, Shirley stumbled home, repeatedly thinking, "No more ballet! No more ballet!" As she put her key in the door, her train of thought had moved on to wondering if it was worth the effort of practising every day. Next she asked herself what would happen to Aurora. She could not live without the dance, even if eventually she had to travel from a new home in north London to South Cross to be able to do it.

She tiptoed upstairs, hoping no one was at home. To her relief, Ted was still out at work and her father was in the shop. Glad to be alone, she shut herself in her room and sat down on her bed, flattened, drained of all energy, hardly able to assemble any worthwhile thoughts. She was about to lie down when she heard the phone ringing in the living room. She debated whether to answer it, and then, realizing it might be a daytime air-raid warning, she hurried to pick up the receiver.

Before she did so, she heard her father down in the shop, shouting into the receiver, "No, sorry, old chap, she's gone to bed. I'll tell her…"

Here Shirley screamed, "No, I'm here, upstairs – who is it?" She rushed into the living room and grabbed the phone. Reggie put his receiver down, hastily tiptoed into the kitchen and closed the door.

"It's me, John! Are you safe from this new blitzing, my darling?" a faint voice asked from hundreds of miles away.

"John! John! We're all right, so far, but my love, where are you?" She cried, her hand trembling so badly she nearly dropped the handpiece.

"I'm still in Italy. Yes, I'm fine," he answered.

"Good! Are you coming home? My performances have been cancelled, so I'm free for you whenever you come home!" she called out.

The line went dead before John could reply, but just those few words with him, though inconclusive, were enough to make Shirley ecstatic. He was safe and he sounded well. Obviously, he wouldn't be coming home yet because, of course, he had only just gone back to Italy. How silly of her to waste time asking that question! Nonetheless, since all Aurora's forthcoming performances had been definitively cancelled, it was true that she would be free to live with him whenever he did return, and to go wherever he wanted to go, except perhaps to Norhambury. She felt the relief tingling throughout her body. Longing for her beloved was so much better than mourning him.

That evening, dressed in uniform, ready for their patrol, Shirley and Reggie sat at the dining table poring over the Aurora accounts. "It looks to me as if there's enough money in the kitty to tide Aurora over, for the foreseeable future," Reggie declared, drawing on his pipe between phrases. "We'll pay everyone a retainer, perhaps eight pounds a month, and suggest they look for other work to keep the wolf from the door, until we have a clearer idea of how things are going to develop."

His daughter nodded, impressed at her father's sanguine assessment of the situation. He continued talking in the same vein. "It depends how bad these raids are and how often. Maybe this is Hitler's last gasp. From what I read in the papers, he's furious with his staff for being inefficient, but they haven't much choice because they've lost so many planes and so many airmen. Would you believe it, they're having to put recruits who've scarcely any idea how to fly in the cockpit?"

Shirley shuddered at the image of young airmen of whatever nationality, doomed to die on their first sortie.

The phone rang; this time it was an urgent instruction to turn on the siren.

Telling the company about the cancellation of all their engagements was not a task that Shirley anticipated with any pleasure. Before doing so, she took Cynthia into her confidence and was surprised to find that her second in command was even more down to earth and philosophical than usual.

"We've had a very good run thanks to you and your father, Shirl," Cynthia observed, "and you've been generous with the pay, but frankly I'm not surprised our performances have been cancelled, though it would have been nice if at least some of them had been spared the chop. And don't worry about the company: they are all realistic about what's happening, so they'll understand if Aurora has to fold. It *was* set up to entertain the troops, wasn't it? And now it looks as if those troops will be leaving their barracks soon, including my Pete."

She sniffed and wiped her nose. "Everyone knows that something big is going to happen before long, so engagements being cancelled, as they are at the moment, is probably one of the first steps in that direction." Shirley nodded, encouraged that her announcement might meet with more understanding than she had feared.

"Well, Pa says there's enough money in the company to pay people for the time being," she said, "but I'm not sure how long that will last."

"Don't worry about it," came Cynthia's confident appraisal. "I have something to tell you," Cynthia added, colouring slightly, "but I haven't been able to find the right moment, so I'll tell you now. You see, Pete and I have decided to get married at Easter, although, of course, we've been wanting to do just that for a long time now, since before there was all that talk of sending him away at Christmas," said she, wincing at the memory of that earlier crisis. "Once we're man and wife, I'll be recognized as his next of kin, and it will be easier for us to be in touch wherever he has to go. Thank goodness he wasn't sent away before Christmas!"

This was an aspect Shirley and John and had considered when arranging their own wedding, without actually divulging their reasoning.

Shirley now reckoned Cynthia's approach to be rather optimistic, for marriage to John had not made it any easier for her to be in touch with him, though rather than pour cold water on her friend's plans, she said, "I'm pleased for you, Cynnie, really I am. Getting married is the right course for you two, but how will the others react to the end of Aurora, do you think?"

"As I said, don't worry," Cynnie replied, "The colonials are all intending to join up with their own forces as soon as possible. Maria and Pedro have decided not to return to Franco's Spain, but are planning to leave for South America as soon as it's really safe enough to cross the Atlantic. I don't know about Doris; she did once say she was thinking of training to become a vet, but I'm not sure if that still applies. I'll find out. Anyhow, I believe the only two who don't have other firm plans are Andrei and Dmitri. Maybe Madame could fix Dmitri up somewhere, do you think?"

"I've no idea," said Shirley. "Let's give it a little while and see if anything turns up for them – or perhaps for us."

When Shirley, who with a lump in her throat, told Madame that Aurora was probably going to close because of the lack of engagements, Madame's reaction was pragmatic. Unemotional and forthright, she said, "You must ask yourself, *ma chérie*, whether you want this horrible War to go on for ever so that you can continue to dance, or whether you would prefer it to come to an end – when we will be safe from Hitler, but the opportunities for a touring ballet company will cease, because entertainment for the troops will no longer be needed."

Although she realized that Madame's reaction to the news was well considered and appropriate, Shirley allowed herself to quibble slightly, saying, "I know, Madame, there's no choice for us. Of course we want the War to end, but we still want to dance! The ballet is our life!"

"Yes, I see that, my dear, but we cannot change fate," came Madame's rejoinder. "I suggest you keep up your practice and learn new repertoires, and maybe new opportunities will appear one day – then you will be prepared for them. Don't forget, I will always be glad to have you as a teacher in my ballet school, because you are so talented." She paused and eyed her pupil like a wise old owl. "But surely you want to be free to live with your husband when he comes home?" she asked.

"Of course I do!" Shirley exclaimed, and turned away on adding, "But who knows when that will be?"

By now the whole company was aware that Aurora's days were numbered, if not already over. When Shirley and her father called a meeting to outline the situation, not only to the dancers but also to Maud, the invaluable secretary, they were met not with the resentment they had anticipated, but with acceptance tinged with sadness. Nevertheless, Reggie still went ahead with his promise that Aurora would give a temporary retainer to those people who could not find work, but Shirley noticed that the amount he was proposing was rather less, at only six pounds a month, than the eight pounds he had originally told her.

"Why did you do that?" she asked him after the meeting.

"They were all, or nearly all, saying they had prospective employment, some of them going to be understudies at Sadler's Wells, for instance, and others going off to dance in musicals, so I thought we might save a bit of money," he explained. "After all, you put a lot of your own money into the company, and... I hesitate to say it, but although you repaid most of mine, there's still some owing to me."

"I see," Shirley said, pouting. While she was grateful to her father for considering her interests, she had not expected him to be quite so mercenary as far as the rest of the company was concerned, although she did understand his reasoning.

She was immensely grateful to all – the dancers, the music operators, the scenery builders, the stage-hands, Jack the driver and, especially, the dressmakers. There had not been much that could be called rioting in the ranks, except perhaps for the sporadic problems with Doris, the occasional protest from the others and that insurrection at the beginning of the Welsh tour, for regularly everyone had given of his or her best and had been a pleasure to work with.

Now that her cherished dream seemed to be coming to an end, she dreaded parting from them, almost as much as she dreaded losing her role as the principal ballerina of her own ballet company. As yet, she had not fully come to terms with the drastic change in Aurora's fortunes, and clung to the delusion that the cancellations were only a temporary blip, and that performances would resume, once this nasty return to the Blitz was over. In the mean time she had wanted to make absolutely sure that no one suffered financially as a result of the closure of the company.

It occurred to her that there were members of the group who were more likely to suffer than others, and one of those, the most important, was her best friend and co-founder, who supported her mother from her earnings. "I don't think Cynnie has anything in view yet," she burst out accusingly, determined to make sure that her father did not forget her partner in the enterprise, even if he were reducing the compensation for the others.

"I thought you told me she was getting married quite soon," her father replied, balking at this perceived rebuke.

"Yes, she is hoping to at Easter, but who knows if that will happen, and don't forget, Pa, how helpful she has been in running the show, as well as dancing in it! And what's more, you've overlooked how hard her mother worked, making all sorts of wonderful costumes for us, with only the minimum pay we practically had to force on her. She's not well off. She only has her widow's pension from the Great War. Eileen couldn't have done all that dressmaking on her own."

"Oh, all right, then," Reggie conceded, irritated that his calculations would have to be revised, "What do you suggest we offer Cynthia?"

"I think she should have the full eight pounds a month," Shirley declared. "And by the way, what about Maud? She's been amazing, just the sort of efficient secretary we needed. I wish we'd known about her sooner."

"I'd already thought about her," Reggie replied. "She's going to work for me doing orders and accounts out in the stockroom."

Despite her sensible advice to Shirley, Madame, when it came to addressing the gathering at the final tea party, gave lengthy and expressive laments in Russian, French and English, with a smattering of Italian, telling of her sorrow that Aurora was probably soon going to close down. She had given so much of herself to the company and become so close to its dancers that the thought of not seeing them, training them and encouraging them every day was understandably unbearable.

"You are oll my cheeldren," she wept; then she announced, by means of Shirley's translation of her French, that she was racking her brains to find ways of keeping the company active and would continue to do so until she came up with a solution for those dancers, including Shirley and Cynthia, and other members of the troupe, who had not yet found other employment.

Madame was certain of being able to find work for Dmitri eventually, and if not immediately, probably soon in the recording business, which was expanding fast. Perhaps, she surmised, after the ultimate performance of Aurora, Andrei might be able to join him there. With any luck, the skills of the two of them together would enable them to set up a company under their own label.

To the others, she announced that the likely end of Aurora's reign as one of the most successful wartime touring ballet companies did not come as a great surprise in the circumstances. Nevertheless, she was determined to keep the company together as long as possible, in a simplified form, so that even if the takings were considerably reduced, the soloists – Cynthia, Andrei and Shirley – and some of the *corps de ballet* might have at least the opportunity to dance. She suggested that those of them still available and not employed elsewhere should rehearse seriously, as if there were a performance in the offing. She herself would get to work, looking out for a suitable uncomplicated ballet that would not be too demanding on anyone.

Shirley had nothing else she wanted to do, so as Cynthia and Andrei had no other employment in view, they would be able to rehearse regularly, which was some consolation. Therefore, with the three of them as soloists and a handful of *corps de ballet* dancers, a modest show might be feasible, should an engagement be forthcoming. What's more, Dmitri was still available to deal with the music, since Madame had not been able to find work for him during the short space of time she had been searching.

Nevertheless, the question of transporting and erecting scenery was more difficult to sort out and proved too much to organize, especially since Jack had found work in a West End theatre. A solution was found in neutral backdrops, which meant bringing out and smartening up the old painted sheets that could be used in any future ballets, if and when they were to occur. Doris offered to clean, repair and repaint the sheets, while reluctantly Reggie promised the loan of his beloved Lanchester – driving it himself – in the highly unlikely event of an engagement appearing out of the blue.

Madame's eventual discovery of the perfect ballet, balm to the three leading dancers, took the form of a hitherto-little-known Petipa ballet, set to music by Glazunov. The ballet told the story of Raymonda, a bright, innocent young girl who is betrothed in an arranged match to a handsome white knight away in the Crusades. However, the Saracen chief who has been besieging the city where she lives bursts in and prostrates himself at her feet, offering peace and wealth in return for her hand.

Raymonda is torn between the two proposals, but when the White Knight appears in a dream, she falls for him. The Saracen chieftain, determined to make her his own, comes to kidnap her. He is thwarted by the White Knight, who makes a dramatic entry in person on his return from the Crusades, and beats his rival in a duel. Unsurprisingly the ballet concludes with a lavish wedding.

Cynthia, Andrei and Shirley were kept entertained and busy, learning and practising excerpts from *Raymonda*, without much hope of performing it, but then a handful of other former Aurora dancers reappeared on the scene, among them Pedro and Maria, whose return to South America had been postponed. They all realized that the likelihood of opportunities to perform the ballet, or at least excerpts from it, on bases or in theatres was slim, yet with Shirley and Cynthia they were thrilled that their dancing careers, even with only small parts in the proposed ballet, were not completely over.

They all were silently aware that despite this one remaining chance, the day was inevitably close when the era of Aurora would be gone for good: the irony was not lost on any of them that the eventual end of the horrendous evil of the War would bring with it the end of a remarkable period of professional success. That would be the time, Shirley promised herself, when she really would have to look for a new beginning, a new venture to see her through for the rest of her working life, though first of all, before that could happen, she would have to find a house for herself and John.

Raymonda was performed to a rapt audience – on the floor of the new church hall where the stage was not yet ready for dancing safely. The scenery was perfect, thanks to Doris's efforts, with Reggie and a couple of local boys changing the backdrops as required. Archie ran the box office from a garden table in the entrance, and Dmitri dealt with the music. The vicar summoned a team of parishioners to set out chairs and sell interval drinks, which amounted only to orange squash. The performance was a sell-out, and generally regarded as a success, the more so because it took place in the direst of circumstances. Happily, there were no air raids that evening: the volunteer who manned the phone dozed off at his post.

For Shirley, Cynthia, Andrei and the handful of other dancers, that performance marked the decisive finale of an era, and definitely was Aurora's swansong. Shirley wondered how she would survive, without her darling John, and without her cherished Aurora, the two great mainstays that had kept her sane throughout the traumatic years of the War.

The end of Aurora by no means marked the end of the Second World War.

THE END

TO BE CONTINUED IN BOOK FOUR
OF THE IMMORTAL SOUL QUARTET:
Time's Ever-Rolling Stream

Acknowledgements

I am hugely grateful to Alex Gallenzi of Alma Books, who agreed to take on the publication of *The Fiery Pillars of War*, to Laura Shanahan for her acute professional judgement and editorial skills, to Maisie Michaelson-Friend for proof-reading the text, and to Elisabetta Minervini, who has consulted me at every stage about the presentation of my books and opportunities for promotions.

I owe Andrew Ade-Kunle an immense debt of gratitude: he is a wizard who is ready to drop everything and rush to put an ailing or even a defunct computer to rights in no time at all. Without his help, this book would have disappeared without trace.

Thanks are due to the many friends who have encouraged me in my writing, are always interested in my progress and wanting to know more.

My heartfelt gratitude goes to Simon Fielding for sharing his compendious knowledge of military matters with me, even to the extent of searching out my father's changing military situations in the Second World War. Also, to Jean-Pierre and Beatrice Degand for answering my questions about the War in France.

I hope my family are aware how grateful I am to them for their understanding over the periods when I have been shut away and out of touch of the real world, in the interests of finishing this book.

Above all, I am immensely grateful to my husband Jonathan for his patience when I have interrupted him with pleas to sort out the numerous computer problems which beset me every day, and which after many years I am still too technologically incompetent to correct myself.